CUL-
DE-
SAC

BY
NICK PERILLI

MONTAG

First Montag Press E-Book and Paperback Original Edition October 2022

Montag Press ISBN: 978-1-957010-17-5
Design © 2022 Amit Dey

Montag Press Team:

Editor: Charlie Franco
Author Photo: Britny Perilli
Managing Director: Charlie Franco
Cover Illustrator: Nodjadong Boonprasert
Cover Design: Rick Febre

A Montag Press Book
www.montagpress.com
Montag Press
777 Morton Street, Unit B
San Francisco CA 94129 USA

Montag Press, the burning book with the hatchet cover, the skewed word mark and the portrayal of the long-suffering fireman mascot are trademarks of Montag Press.

Printed & Digitally Originated in the United States of America
10 9 8 7 6 5 4 3 2 1

To Robert Sr. and Maureen Perilli
Sorry

PRAISE FOR *CUL-DE-SAC*

"A beautifully-realized portrait of adolescence in paralysis, Nick Perilli's first novel is luminous, surreal, hilariously bizarre, and strikingly original. From the start, we are thrust into a mind-bending adventure through suburban purgatory—a supernatural realm where one›s salvation or damnation rests in a teenager's hands—and the suspense never lets up from there. *Cul-de-sac* is part absurdist coming-of-age, part phantasmogorical thriller, and it may be the most unforgettable book you read this year."

—Jonathan Koven,
author of *Palm Lines* and *Below Torrential Hill*

"All roads lead to the Oughtside, and if you are not terrified you should be. *Cul-de-sac* opens readers' eyes to the red, dead world that awaits us all in the next life. In the Oughtside, all life is as fragile as a cracking porcelain mask, and judgment awaits around every dark turn. Perilli's *Cul-de-sac* is a page turner that asks the reader to reconsider everything we know about life and death. Are you ready for judgement?"

— Ed Bonilla, author of *5 Clones*

ACKNOWLEDGMENTS

Thank you to my partner Britny, who has had to deal with this story and me for quite a while. Your unflinching editorial eye has helped shape this book into something of which I can be proud. To my blurbers Stephanie Feldman, Jonathan Koven, and my Montag Press mates Ed Bonilla and Ron Dakron. Your blurbs bolstered my opinion of my book at a critical time. To Paul Elwork, who helped shape this thing in its infancy over two years. To the beautiful shadows behind the publishing scenes, in the form of my editor Charlie Franco, cover artist Nadjadong, Rick Febre, and the design team at Montag Press.

A clacking thank you to these creative skeletons with skin: Nick Mehalick, Christina Rosso-Schneider, Maggi McGettigan, Kailey Tedesco, Mike Salgado, Chad Frame, Lauren Shelton, Josh Isard, Amanda Joachim, Natasha Dunne, Kaylynn Schuetzner, Alex Schneider, Joe Soler, Brenna Dinon, Dwight Evan Young, Daniel DiFranco, Nick Gregorio, Outrider Connor Feeney, Alyssa Feeney, Kevin Travers, Jeremy Tenenbaum, Joey Edsall, Zach Woodard, Maddie Anthes, Chad Towarnicki and exactly 7,000 other people who got me here.

Who else? My brother and sister, Robert Perilli and Christine Perilli. The characters that are obviously you aren't exactly you. The magazines that have kept my short writing in circulation: Milk Candy Review, SORTES, and XRAY to name a few. The many animals that ensconce my home.

And to my daughter Merlyn. You were only just born as I'm writing these words, but I imagine you are older as you're reading them. I love you with all my spooky heart, Meryl. This book is mostly about my parents dying when I was younger. I hope I didn't go and die on you yet. But if I did, I'm a ghost inhabiting the nearest skeleton.

THE ILLUSTRATED
MAP ON THE FIRST FEW PAGES

Derek spent most of his last day watching TV in his room with his cat. He alternated between sitting upright in his bed and sitting in the chair by his bedroom's one window. When the strain of watching television for twelve hours straight caused him to get a migraine, he watched his neighbors instead. The practice eased the auras in his vision and calmed the aphasia swirling his thoughts.

100 HABRE CIRCLE. Across the street, Mrs. Bell stood outside her door, pacing on the porch and whispering under her breath. She carried an empty box. There was no doubt in Derek's mind that she had left Mr. Bell again, as she did at least once every year. She would go back inside. They might even forgive each other. Then, the cycle would begin anew. *The same thing*, Derek thought, *year after year. Buildup, fight, break, reconciliation, repeat.*

"Stale," Derek said to the cat sleeping on his bed. "I wish they would change things up, Antigone."

Antigone slept.

102 HABRE CIRCLE. Next door to the Bells, the entire Mont family funneled in and out of their maroon colonial, busy with

school, work, and activity after activity. Derek's old friend Ryan Mont sometimes stole glances of him in his bedroom window as he left for his runs, but he didn't this time. His face was sunken, and his eyes were dark. Some blood crusted under his nose.

Derek watched him the day before, too, carrying skeleton Halloween decorations on his back and talking to himself in the street. This wasn't like Ryan, who was always the most composed of the neighborhood kids.

"He's losing it, huh?" Derek laughed.

Antigone slept.

104 HABRE CIRCLE. The abandoned yellow colonial stood dark. Garter snakes moved through the long grass, searching for a spot to bask on this gray day. Derek daydreamed people in the dirty, broken-out windows sometimes. Ghosts, too, or a murder that he needed to solve from the confines of his room. Something moved on the front porch—something that was actually there. Derek's eyes widened. He leaned closer to his window to get a better look at what turned out to be a mother possum lumbering across the porch wood.

106 HABRE CIRCLE. Davies Tuch sat on the porch of his midcentury colonial, sleeping through the hours in his wicker rocking chair. The wrinkles carved into his face softened between his labored breath. At an exact moment between inhalation and exhalation, he became a young man, blond and fit with decades yet to live, before he hurtled forward through his grueling years.

Derek half-expected to see the man slumped over dead in his chair every day he looked towards Davies's house. Today, he kept breathing. A light drip of red began streaming from his nose as Derek watched. The man quickly wiped it away. Derek worried about tomorrow.

107 HABRE CIRCLE. Green light poured from the open garage of Dr. Kellyn Hodges's modern home. In her make-shift office of hoarded technology, she tinkered away on a machine hissing steam out into the soft bend of the street. As if she could feel Derek's stare from across the circle, she rushed out onto her driveway to look around. Blood gushed from her nose, dripping from her chin onto the asphalt. She wiped it with the sleeve of her white lab coat before retreating into the garage and shutting the door behind her.

Derek pulled back from the window. He leaned into the darkness of his room, questioning Antigone about what he had just seen. He rubbed the migraine in his eyes.

Antigone slept.

105 HABRE CIRCLE. Nothing much at all was happening at the only brick colonial on the street. A kid named Robert sat on the lawn, staring straight back at Derek. Here too, red ran down from the boy's nose when they saw each other. The wind picked up outside, and pressure built with it behind Derek's eyes.

"Okay," he said, wincing. "What is with these people today." He grabbed a handful of day-old microwave popcorn from a bag at his feet and ate it.

103 HABRE CIRCLE. Mira Peretz and her mother unpacked moving boxes in her room, though Derek couldn't see this. He didn't know her name. He barely remembered any of his neighbors' names; he had never spoken to some of them throughout his nearly two decades of growing up in Habre Circle. *That's right*, he thought. *Who even are they?* Derek's migraine flared;

his vision spotted. Antigone chattered; she joined him at the window.

"Maybe we're all lost today," Derek said, scratching the cat's white head. "How about you?"

Antigone hissed; she left him alone at the window.

101 HABRE CIRCLE. Downstairs, Derek's brother and sister sat down to a dinner for three. They called for their brother, knowing he filled up on three bags of microwave popcorn just so that he wouldn't have to speak to them tonight. They ate in silence, not realizing until after their meal that they had finally chosen to sit in the chairs of their deceased parents.

Later, on the other side of Derek's bedroom door, his sister yelled that he needed to get a job if he wasn't enrolling in any more classes at Hill Community College. She told him they all agreed to keep the house in the family, so all of them had to help cover the bills they weren't meant to inherit.

Derek's nose bled. It meant nothing to him. An anxiety attack, maybe. In two of the three other bedrooms in the house, Derek's brother and sister reddened their white pillows.

It did mean something was coming, dripping into the cracks and people of Habre Circle, anticipating the necessary and sudden shift from this side to the other.

Derek never went to bed anymore. He sat at his window or on his twin mattress until his eyes closed on their own. He held his pillow tight against his chest and breathed long and slow, just like a video online told him to when the anxiety gripped him. Another migraine crept into his head on the back of his daily one, different than his others, more distant, more thorough.

The TV flickered through the frames of his life and his neighbors' until Habre Circle shattered, until the red sky hung above it, the impossible surrounded it, and shadows teemed beneath it.

BOY

A boy ripped himself out of sleep again. For two minutes, he lay in his twin bed stuck between full consciousness and uneasy rest, paralyzed by an unseen hand pushing down on his chest. Sometimes, like this time, it felt like the hand wanted to crush through him but held back just enough not to crack his sternum.

The boy still wore his jeans and button-down gray shirt from the day before. The clock sitting on the edge of the electronic piano next to his bed read 12:00, blinking in bright red digits floating in the dark. It wasn't until the fourth 12:00 that he caught on. He sat up, rubbing the sleep from his eyes, and did his best to slick back the mop his hair became whenever he slept. He didn't hear the muted din of a television set, the cry of a hungry cat, or the voices of his older brother and sister preparing for work as he was accustomed to in the morning hours. They usually woke him up, only for him to say that he was already awake, then sleep until the late afternoon.

He reached for the pull-string on the adjustable reading lamp attached to his wall. It had been there since he shared the room with his brother, bunk beds and all. As he ran his right arm up the wall, his finger caught on the thin bottom edge of a poster hung by tacks beside him and tore through an inch and a half of it. Panic welled up through his stomach, and he pulled his hand back. The poster was a mint original of the first *Pogbots* movie poster. That tear demoted it to GREAT condition.

The boy thought for a few seconds, shutting his eyelids hard and opening them quickly to wake himself up. Light peeked in from the spaces in his window's blinds. He swung his legs over the side of his bed and stepped over the faint outlines of a TV remote, two worn controllers, and one purring cat, who leaped to the windowsill, where the feline sat, eager to breathe in the rush of the outside world.

The boy pulled the blinds up, revealing his entire cul-de-sac colored red by a new sky. Every house on the street remained visible, but everything outside it—the entire neighborhood and beyond—was gone. In the rest of the world's stead was, in a bending succession of locales: a dense forest, a vast ocean, a gorge, and several other places where children are taught not to go. His cat cared little about the difference and began her window ritual after the boy slid the window up in a curious sort of frenzy. The cat sniffed the outside air, rubbed her body against the screen, and laid down to enjoy the empty breeze. The boy scrunched his nose up to the stinging cross-stitch wiring and inhaled as well. The air was dry, certainly, but other than that it was not much different than normal. He sensed a hint of machinery, though—the hint of the oil and heat that ran the haunted houses on Jersey boardwalks.

An aggressive, rasping cough from outside the door to his room grabbed the boy's attention from the new view. He reached for his splintered wooden sword, resting at the foot of his bed as it had been since third grade. His uncle had made it for him when he had dressed up as a teenage mutant ninja turtle for Halloween all those years back. He had no formal training with it or in any type of combat, but the boy figured he had watched enough anime over the years to mimic some devastating attacks against this intruder if they meant him harm—if they meant to do anything other than cough in the dark.

Flipping the hallway light switch squirreled more light away from the world. Only the red from the skies through the bathroom window brightened the second-floor corridor enough for the boy to see the vague, familiar shapes of his home. He held his cut of wood out in front of him, as far down the carpeted stairs as his arm could stretch. He swung it slowly, side to side. At the bottom of the stairs, two neon blue eyes opened and met the boy's shrinking pupils. The eyes cast the stairs in enough light for him to make out a vague figure sitting, as if wounded, as if dying, on the beige carpeted landing.

This figure's body was a shapeless mass of rippling human shadow on which the boy could not quite focus.

"Are you alright?" the boy asked before rattling off a litany of further questions to it, including the predictable fare of where his family had gone—though he realized now he hadn't checked on them himself—what had happened to his circle, or if the thing was some kind of ghost.

"The very last of what I am," it said in a bare whisper, "is a ghost. Come along with me, won't you?"

The figure stood up like it had stiff muscles woven beneath its shadow. In doing so, it let out protracted and wheezing breaths, then proceeded towards the front door with flowing legs. Its hands blended with the dark, barely red air, so it looked like the figure may have opened the door with willpower alone.

That would have been impressive, but once the red poured in through the door, the boy could see the figure's basic humanoid hands with five fingers each, simply covered and dripping with some sort of obsidian shadow. It beckoned him outside with one of its digits and an impatient voice.

"Come, come on."

Holding hard to the frame of the front door, the boy called upstairs for his family.

"Ray. Cameron."

Then, he called out the door for anyone at all, shouting the names of those neighbors he could still remember after those of his family.

"Um, Ryan. Mr. Mont. Mr. and Mrs. Bell." *Who else?* He couldn't recall.

His family cat fiddled down the steps, then away from the boy and into the kitchen. She crunched at a bowl of dry food, gently lapped a helping of water, then crunched more food. The boy felt a loyal party member should be on this new journey with him. He crouched to the foyer's linoleum floor. "Antigone," he said in a soft voice. "Come on. Pspspspsps."

Antigone paused in the half-shadows long enough so that he knew she heard him.

"Pspspspsps!" the boy continued.

The cat shunned his call with a curt turn into the dark and a flick of her tail. She threw up, then disappeared into the shadows of his home.

The boy grunted. He turned and joined the figure, whose beatific eyes blinked once.

Outside, the red had no apparent point of origin—no exploded sun, moon, or meteor. It was as if the night sky had just turned overnight into this deep, sick color. Street lamps stood unlit and split open, wires and electric guts hanging out of their trunks. The trees and plants slumped, stripped of their final autumn leaves. The three cars in the boy's driveway, and all the others in the rest of the circle he could make out from his front yard, sat on flattened tires, rusted over. Window glass lay in jagged pieces across neighbors' lawns and cracked asphalt.

The houses had become decrepit with age and now appeared abandoned, haunted by the tattered curtain specters, moving with what little wind the circle now enjoyed. Though the boy's house remained untouched. It stood tall, as the white aluminum-sided edifice shone like a beacon amidst all the decay, save for the lawn, which was unkempt and overgrown as always. The boy, his sister and brother, had all agreed that lawns are easier to maintain when they are a chore, when there is an allowance on the tip of the last cut blade of grass.

The surrounding environment, slipping softly through all the backyards, had turned into an ocean in the night—vast and impossible—improbable, at least, the sound of the waves easing through the houses.

The boy trailed the figure out into the street.

"102, 103, 104, 105?" the figure mumbled under its considerable breath. "102. A couple lived there alone. Together."

"I know," the boy said, standing on a manhole cover between his home and another. "You sound unsure."

The figure's mumbling faded, like the descending volume of a television he wasn't meant to hear.

They crossed over to a blue house. A couple lived there alone, both aged 30-something. Together. They argued outside the thin bubble of privacy that came standard with every home in the neighborhood, giving everyone the chance to gossip about them, the boy's mother and father included. Meanwhile, his parents fought inside, in the deepest and most secluded room of the house, like all decent people did.

The boy was fond of the wife. She had befriended his parents when he was little and sometimes even babysat him when work pulled them away. She smelled like rosewater and artificial lemon. She allowed him to lay across her cool legs on warm nights just like his mom.

During the business week, the husband worked during the day and came home late in the evening. On weekends, he worked on his yard. When the boy would play with some friend next door to the couple, the husband would curse and seethe at them when either of them walked or rode a bike near his measured lawn or when they threw a ball of any shape or size near his immaculate hydrangeas, all hanging their dead blooms now. Quickly it became a dare and a test of courage for the neighborhood kids to ride a bike up and down his driveway, even when the home was vacant during the weekdays.

The children spread rumors as far as they could about the couple—that the husband drank a lot and that the wife had episodes. That they killed a drifter in California before moving east; this last one was the boy's.

The figure and the boy stepped up onto the porch of that couple's home, the screen door lying in shambles. Blue paint peeled off the split woodwork in curls. Shards of glass were strewn all about, so he was careful. The figure did not take any caution. No light was visible inside.

The figure stood in front of the doorway and peered down at the nervous boy, a deep, hacking voice escaping its formless lips, its words full and throaty, now peppered with coughs.

"Judgment," it said. "Your innocence has brought you fortune. A career! Congratulations. But for these neighbors— these woeful neighbors."

"Is this like a reward or something?" the boy tried to interrupt, but the figure continued.

"You should see what you may or may not deem as crimes—sins of these basic lives—one after the other, dwelling after dwelling, and you will choose their fate."

It held up a fist.

"Damnation?"

Then an open palm.

"Salvation?"

Wind poured through the street on cue, loose debris— asphalt and shards of his neighborhood—running with it. The figure leaned closer to the boy's face.

"Do you accept the position?"

The boy had one pressing question.

"Wait, is this Hell?" he asked in a tired and disappointed voice.

The figure shrugged.

"Oh, it is, isn't it?" he sighed.

"No. There is here and there—not an above or below," the figure said, agitated with the boy. "Beliefs like those will neither save the people of this here circle nor will they condemn them—you will."

The boy was about to protest with maybe a furrowed brow or a couple clenched fists, but it would only have been as a courtesy to his parents and his elementary school teachers—to their correct interpretations of right and wrong. In truth, his stomach was near aflutter, and a smile crawled across his lips. Something different just happened in his circle of doppelganger architecture and well-kept gardens. He decided to lean into it. His mind raced with the possibilities of reward and recognition, of the power and responsibility that he would have to contend with in this, his brand-new career. His brand new narrative.

"You shouldn't feel the need to lie to me," the figure said, "I am not a judge—only a guide."

The boy nodded. "I accept," he let the smile out. "Who wouldn't?"

"Several people."

"No one," he said. "I can save them all?"

"You can do whatever you please," the figure said, anticipating the thought. "Morality is not a concern to the process just now."

The cream-colored front door on the blue home hung open, clinging to a single hinge. The figure moved through the doorway and receded into the darkened house.

"Oh, husband. Judgment comes for you—," it said, as its voice and vivid eyes melded into the shadow.

"Who?" returned a man.

The boy put his right foot forward, stepping over the threshold into the home—then he dropped straight through the floor. He heard whispering, static voices all around him as he fell. They sounded foreign at first, but soon became recognizable as *his* family, friends, and colleagues. Fuzzy images of memories that were not his own flickered in the dark, letterboxed format. They looked to be through the eyes of a stranger, then an acquaintance, then the boy. Eight years of university and law school, three years of junior partner, eight years of marriage, eleven months of an affair. *All of it,* he thought, *was a bit much for any real person.* The images only worsened—not in content but frequency and brightness. His eyes leaked tears, a dull pressure building in his skull.

He landed hard on a rough couch in a living room, lit by the dancing light of an old television set—wood trim, knobs, dials, and rabbit ears—perched on the floor. There was one door in and out—an old office door with a bubbled glass window and words assembled neatly on the outside. It took him a few seconds to decipher the reversed letters: *HUSBAND AND WIFE.*

The couch was the kind not meant for sitting on. The boy knew it was the husband's—luxurious and decorated with brass beads. It smelled like antiquity. He rubbed his eyes and licked his lips. They felt off—close to his own, but maybe a centimeter or so too far to the left and the right. His whole body felt like this.

The television set showed the interior of the couple's house—the foyer that the boy just entered a minute ago. Outside, a sunlit day brightened the hall in glorious Technicolor. Even if they were outdated versions of the colors, it did much for the boy's eyes to see half-vibrant greens and yellows again, just beyond the glass of the kitchen's sizable pane windows. He searched for the remote but couldn't find one. He reached for the knobs on the set, but his depth perception had diminished, and he couldn't reach them. He dizzied himself trying. He was stuck tuned to the foyer, with its gaudy chandelier and a thin table up against the hallway wall.

A title faded onto the screen in bold, flourishing font—*Husband & Wife*—accompanied by the swell of strings, percussion, and piano. Credits followed, but under each one—from executive producer to writer—Husband or Wife had sole credit.

The broadcast was lit and staged like a soap opera, made on both a tight budget and schedule.

"This is the worst season of our marriage," said a woman seated on the couch cushion next to the boy.

He was unsure if she had already been there since he fell into the room. She must have been. The TV set's soft glow only gave his weary eyes an outline of her thin frame. But he knew the voice.

"Mrs. Bell?" the boy asked. *That was their name*, he thought. *The Bells, of course.*

Mrs. Bell's voice was only a shade of what he remembered from her babysitting days. He asked, "Would you happen to have a mirror?" His voice sounded as off as his body felt.

"But final seasons are always rough, are they not?"

The boy nodded. He couldn't agree more. "I like to say it's either the best or worst season of any show. There's so much to do—so much closure. Endings are tough for audiences and creators alike—especially if they didn't know that things were ending."

"Well, I knew," Mrs. Bell said, the faint shadow of her body leaning back. She crossed her legs. "The first five seasons, man: fantastic. Everything—learning to live together, traveling, sex—was fresh and exciting. It was exactly the brand-new jolt our relationship needed. Season six, we stumbled. We weren't asking the right questions. We were trying to do more of the same when we needed to evolve. We tried to get back on track in season seven, but he added a new character without telling me. And season eight, well, here's the finale now. The unexpected series finale. It had such prestige potential, too. All of it squandered."

The boy hated watching any episode of a television or film series without knowing the full continuity.

The camera panned over to the white door onscreen after the credits. It lingered on that shot to build suspense, the sound of white noise and film filling the air. The door was shoved open. It bounced closed off the foyer's closet door behind it, then was pushed again. Husband—in his suit and his greased work hair—barreled through it. His face tightened and crunched upward in a scowl. It hurt. He had a bruise across his jaw. He could move a few of his teeth with his tongue. He did that until his gums bled and his mouth tasted like metal.

The boy licked his gums. They were raw. They tasted like metal.

After slamming his briefcase down on the console table up against the hallway wall, he continued into the kitchen and picked up the corded phone from its place on the marble countertops. His fingers stabbed a number into it. After ten rings, a steady, robotic voice informed him that the number he dialed was no longer in service. He chucked the phone at the auburn-painted kitchen cabinets. It shattered over the dirty dishes in the sink. He sat down at the ornately carved oaken dining table in the middle of the room and rested his head against his clenched hands.

The boy identified with him—not as a character, but as an extension of himself connected deeply by the glow and thick sheet of warm glass on the television screen. *He shouldn't*, he thought. *He should remain objective.* While watching, only the slightest tinge of self-awareness separated the boy from Husband at times. Most of the boy seethed right alongside the man he watched. The boy called the wife all the things he knew she hated to be called, then he threw the phone. He wallowed with Husband as the man trembled with a sweaty mix of rage, shame, and regret.

"Do you feel him?" Mrs. Bell said, leaning in closer to the boy. Close enough that he should have felt her breath on his neck. "I've been told these image-transmission contraptions here will do that to you. That they will influence you. But I have found it's not that difficult to fight."

By way of onscreen flashback—the tasteful variety, with no bright lights or noise—Husband's memories returned to his wife leaving earlier in the morning. He never dared to let it probe all that deep into the conflict that made her run. He touched it, then backed away. Touched it, then backed away. The boy only gleaned that there was an argument that escalated, featuring one stray comment made by Husband's father years back when Husband was young and listened to his parents' evening fights from the top of the stairs:

"I only did it because I love you," his father had said at the time. He unclenched his fist, then Husband's mother tackled him to the ground and rained her fists on him. In the morning, his blood was still on the carpet. The stain was never fully cleared.

They fought each other with their fists until they just couldn't do it anymore. They unraveled from there, with their son watching from the top of the stairs.

A key slid into the front door, interrupting Husband's slip into the past. He stood from his chair, wiped some moisture from his eyes, and sprinted to the door, opening it before whoever was on the other side could. And there, before Husband, stood Wife. A lone violin played as the screen faded to black.

"Aw," Mrs. Bell said. "Damn commercials."

The boy approached watching television as he did movies: in silence and darkness. Ideally, talking was reserved for during advertisements only. That was the time for any discussion of the program so far. It was a practice he tried to force on anyone watching with him and he thought about broaching the subject with Mrs. Bell just to get them on the same page.

A commercial faded in. Husband and Wife faced the camera, side by side at their kitchen table, each with a lit cigarette in their mouth. They both read from cue cards.

"Hey, honey," Husband said, "how about instead of fighting tonight we just reach for a couple of smooth Dart Frog brand cigarettes?"

Wife cracked a wooden smile. "Sure, babe," she said. "One Dart Frog brand cigarette could calm the nerves of a bull elephant, and I love the way it makes my skin glow."

The *Dart Frog Cigarette* logo overlaid on the screen as an announcer suggested bliss was just a puff away.

"I miss my skin," Mrs. Bell said.

"You don't have skin?" the boy asked, trying to look away from the TV to Mrs. Bell but failing. He pulled a neck muscle trying.

"No skin," Mrs. Bell said. "No porcelain, either."

The TV fritzed, fuzzed, and switched to another channel. The screen paned over woods of some kind. It showed wilderness with a blue moon hanging above it.

The shape of a person stumbled through the trees, trying to think, trying to grasp, trying to find, and trying to remember. She was bone, covered in clay, a thick living shadow that was once genuine porcelain skin until the wolves chipped it away. Until the wolves pulled it from her for their shells. It hurt when they did, and it didn't seem quite right for her to hurt anymore after all that she'd been through.

Others roamed clumsily out there too, trying to find someplace, the name of which was whispered to them in the dark before they lumbered their way out of a mill and into these trees: *The Oughtside*.

Mrs. Bell threw the remote at the TV and it switched back to *Husband & Wife*.

"Ugh," Mrs. Bell said. "Slipped into a shitty prequel. Please, please, William," she grasped her thin head in the dark and curled forward. "Let's just stay focused."

Husband's blank face filled the screen. His lips curved into a slight, doleful smile.

"You weren't supposed to be here," Wife said, off-screen.

Mrs. Bell shouted at the screen. "That means 'don't go in,' idiot. She's so pigheaded."

The buffeting wind outside kept whipping Wife's dark blonde hair across her face. She used the arm not holding a large empty cardboard box to fix it every few seconds. Images of Husband's hand pushing it behind her ear years before this in the backseat of his mother's Cutlass Ciera flashed across the screen. So did a brief instance of the two of them trading blows.

"I couldn't work today," he said. "We need to talk." The smile had faded.

"We're past talking."

Wife started up the stairs to pack.

Mrs. Bell cracked her neck—the sound was loud and hollow—and stretched her arms.

"This idiot."

Husband squeezed his lips together. He was ready to clash—to fall back into their relationship's favored rut. But as his wife ascended the stairs, the camera focused on her stomach. She was not showing yet but took care in how she stepped.

"No," the boy said. "Really?" He couldn't take his eyes off the screen.

"What's wrong with you?" Husband asked as he grabbed her by the arm.

"You," she said.

Husband—eyes wide, sweat dripping down the back of his neck—released her arm, and Wife moved quickly up the stairs. The room shifted around the boy and Mrs. Bell. Thoughts and solutions to this fight swarmed from the speakers in magnificent surround sound.

"He's going to kill her," the boy said.

"You're ruining the twist," Mrs. Bell said.

"Oh, come on. It's not a twist at all."

"It was for me."

Husband went to retrieve a gun and the camera followed. The boy would have let the camera stay at the bottom of the stairs, focusing on the sounds of Wife packing and Husband getting his weapon instead, even cranking both up in post-production if necessary. But he understood the directing choice to stay with the man, even if it was a bit narrow and obvious. That was the kind of show they were producing.

Oh look, the boy thought, *he's getting the revolver. Oh look, he's angry and can barely load it. Oh look, he's taking a shot of whiskey.*

The man winced and rubbed his temples.

Mrs. Bell had lit the Dart Frog Brand cigarette in her mouth. The smoldering end revealed her face, barely there across the front of her skull. Patches of skin and muscle were missing. It wasn't exactly a gory sight, though. She looked more like a high-end family adventure movie prop. Or a Halloween decoration that only the truly devoted could afford.

"Get out, get out, you doomed girl," Mrs. Bell said, exhaling smoke through her bones.

"Why do you keep blaming yourself?" the boy asked, unable to look away from her exposed skull.

"Like you don't hate who you used to be?" Mrs. Bell huffed. "The murdered live on in the minds of their killers, kid. I have to binge this series every time it ends."

Husband climbed the stairs like a raging, dying beast. His nose poured buckets of blood. At his bedroom door, he took a beat and a breath, then sauntered in like it was season three, episode five. He wiped his nose and leaned up against the doorframe, keeping the revolver tucked behind him in the back of his belt.

Wife didn't look at him, but she knew he was there. She folded her clothes in a rhythmic, assured way—as if she were just going for a weekend trip with some friends. The violin returned pitched higher to elevate viewer heart rates.

"You're pregnant," Husband said.

"Well it's not yours."

"Bullshit."

She feigned disinterest in Husband's presence. "Maybe your long nights just got a little too long for me, huh?"

Mrs. Bell howled with laughter, startling the boy. She shook her skull and waved his attention away from her and back to the screen.

Husband lifted the gun.

Mrs. Bell giggled to a close. "I think," she said, "I wanted to see how far I could push him here——" She stared at the screen as she said it. "How far off I was when I chose you."

A nervous convulsion welled in the boy's stomach, like he had to throw up. His trigger finger moved with Husband's twice. Two shots rang out into the living room as if he fired right beside them. Wife collapsed on the floor, her blood dripping out onto the carpet from the two red holes in her chest. Husband watched as her stomach rose and fell for the final few times, never looking at her face. The boundaries of the television pulled back.

"I wasn't expecting this, to be honest," Mrs. Bell said. "I thought I'd get more than enough be rid of you, William, but not this."

"Wait," the boy said, leaning back and reaching for reality. "When was this? I would have remembered a murder across the street, wouldn't I?"

"Years ago," Mrs. Bell said gently. "Maybe hours. There's definitely a distance."

Husband scooped Wife into his arms and struggled to carry her down to the basement. He laid her on the stained pink carpet that covered part of the cement floor. He set up a folding chair in the corner and waited there until evening, surveying the body for all those hours.

"Actus reus," Husband said to his wife. "Mens rea. Second degree. Crime of passion?"

A voice crept down the stairs, followed by the light drag of steps on the wood. "Life in prison, though."

The boy recognized it; Husband didn't. He looked up from Mrs. Bell to see a silhouette standing over her now—a shadow.

"Killer of wife, killer of son—Judgment comes for you," it said. "Remain in this world, and you will surely pay for your crimes. Enter mine, and you may yet have a chance." It moved through Wife, encroaching upon Husband.

"It wasn't mine," Husband replied, his voice wavering. He felt his legs buckle and fell hard to the cement floor next to the body.

"False," it said, placing a wet, dark hand on his head.

"It wasn't—"

Freeze frame. Cut to black.

Executive producer: Husband.

In loving memory of Wife.

Mrs. Bell put her hand on the boy's shoulder, her palm and fingers sheer bone—a skeletal hand from her living room grave.

"Alright, I think you can go now," she said. "I'd like to be alone." She stood up and turned off the TV set, her bones knocking together as she moved.

The boy didn't get up after she shut off the set. His eyes felt dry—burnt, even—from the broadcast. He shifted in his seat, finding his way to the edge of it. There, he managed to pour himself out of the sofa, down onto the area rug. His knees hit the ground first. Then, like a broken catapult, he slammed his face into the rough carpet. He shut his eyes. The air felt like thin needles in his pores—not painful, but pressured.

"Hold on a moment," the boy said, his stomach churning again. "I—" he started to doze off against his wishes. Fear rose in the lane between his ribcage as if he were falling asleep while driving.

"No," Mrs. Bell said. "I have things to do too, you know. I have to rewind and start it over." There was a slight sob in her voice. "Season one, episode one."

"I'll watch too," the boy said, drifting away. "From the beginning this time. The full continuity."

The boy felt his body lift from the floor, slowly, at a measured pace.

"No, Judgment," the figure said. "You have seen enough."

○   ○   ○

The red pressed hard against the boy's eyelids, so he opened them. The fog, the weight, and some of the disorientation lifted. He rose to his hands—to his knees where he heaved and vomited on the aged oak floor.

What did he eat last? Popcorn? That's right.

"Mrs. Bell, am I okay?" he said, his eyes shut tight until felt the room stop spinning.

But he was back in the red, in the house across the street from his own. Both Mrs. Bell and the living room had gone. He hunched in the Bells' foyer, only a foot from where the corridor had swallowed him. It was as if he had just walked inside and vomited. He checked the floor at the entrance, finding a seam cut between the boards in a measured square: a trap door for the stage.

"All part of the adjudication process, of course," the figure said.

It stood in the kitchen down the hall, beside a broken and silent William Bell sitting on a chair with his head between his knees. He fit right in with the wrecked expensive appliances and fixtures in the room. The oak table split in two. Other than what little light emanated from the figure's eyes and the bulging red pushing in through the tattered drapes, the space was dark.

"I think," the boy said, letting some excitement out with his voice. He swallowed. "I thought I teleported." He stood and looked at his hands—flexing his fingers.

"Well, you didn't," the figure said, drifting over to the boy's side. It sounded eager to get on with the next part.

Husband sprang from the chair, closing in, it seemed, for an assault on one of them or an escape attempt. An unruly, splintered section of his hardwood floors caught his foot and tripped him, landing him at the boy's feet.

"Look at this," the figure said. "Salvation or damnation?"

"Judgment," Husband said. "It wasn't mine." His voice shook. "That would be one step too dramatic, right? Don't you think? A bit too far so early on?"

The boy watched him for a few seconds, his breathing growing heavier; his fists clenched. He had a tight, violent look on his face. He knew what he knew; the boy did too.

"Damnation," the boy said.

The answer was obvious. *A killer should be damned*, the boy thought. *That's how this works. That's how all of this works.*

The floors beneath Husband shook, then burst open and swallowed him whole. No screams—no cries. It happened half as quickly as the bullets left his gun. A hole into the deep of this new world sat in Mr. Bell's place. The boy walked to the edge and peered down. Through the basement. Through the dark. He heard the distant sounds of machinery, whirring away. At the edge, he felt the call to jump in but the sound grew to be too much for him to bear so he stepped back.

"William Bell," the figure said. "Damned!" It backed away, towards the front door. "That turned out well. Concise. Good work, Judgment. Keep this up and we'll do just fine."

The boy stood still for a moment, his eyes wide and mouth parted. He put one hand on his forehead and let out a long sigh. He turned his head to the figure.

"I don't know," he said. "This feels like pure, unadulterated madness, right?" He rubbed the budding migraine in his temples. He wasn't completely sure of what 'unadulterated' meant, but he tended to use the largest words he could find when flustered. In response, the figure turned around and left out the front door.

The boy found his wooden sword in the foyer, placed—with considerable care, it appeared—in the umbrella stand by the front door. He grabbed it before following the figure back out into the red.

○   ○   ○

Mrs. Bell's corpse stuck in the boy's eyes. Some moments he could feel her arm twisting in his palms or the warmth of her body dwindling against his chest. He had seen violence like this in films and television, games and art. But here, he could smell them, hear them better and feel them on his skin. The influence, as Mrs. Bell had put it, of the exaggerated, sensory story down there remained with him.

As he left the blue home, returning to the dim, red street, a name stopped him. Her first name—light and wistful—glid its way out of his mouth.

"Anna," he said. "That was it. Her name."

It had been missing from the couch and the viewing room. Unspoken.

He directed the words at the figure as he said them. Even so, he didn't expect a response.

"Side effects will linger," the figure said, moving forward. "But you did her justice. Didn't you, Judgment?"

"These aren't side effects," the boy said. "I know every inch of her, figure—I know every inch of them. Even the wedding day is there in the back of my head. She's taking a piece and smearing cake across his face. Then he does it to her." The boy felt Mrs. Bell around him, like he could turn and find her sitting on her porch or in the windowless, rusted-out coupe in the driveway.

The figure was consistent. It said in a dismissive droll, "Well you'll need to get over them if you want to be effective in this career."

The boy did have a talent for stuffing away the hard thoughts and memories. And maybe he *had* gotten Mrs. Bell some skeletal justice.

The figure moved in silence as if on sidewalk rails, leading the way to the next house. It seemed to the boy that only the collapse of the universe would stop this process—if that. The blue home snapped and let out a metal cry before its sides came together to form a dusty, jagged heap. He scurried from the noise, running up closer to the figure. It was a strange sight to him; a house, much like his, collapsing in on itself.

ERRAND

The boy once knew the maroon colonial next door to the Bells and diagonal from his own house quite well. He had spent the summer days of his grade school years there, basking in the glow of sixteen, thirty-two, and sixty-four-bit gameplay in the basement, and the flashing cartoons in the living room. Much of his childhood took place on the carpets of the home where his best friend Ryan lived with his family.

He stopped on the sidewalk in front. Siding and shattered glass littered the yard where he had played so many games of tag: classic, TV, freeze. He tried to see inside—to see someone in the darkened doorway. It could be his friend in there. He had a family, sure, but it could be *him* that needed to be judged.

"Judgment," the figure said, moving up the driveway, watching the boy as it did. "Are you losing your nerve?"

"No," the boy said. "Just reminiscing."

"Don't be too long."

He wouldn't be—just a few thoughts.

The cul-de-sac forced them together. It always stood as its own small community where the opportunities for play between the children were dictated by the families' distance to one another. Confined to that area, options were limited for anyone. Parents didn't choose the neighbors they interacted with—just as the children didn't choose their friends,. Kid would lie about their first meeting, but only because they didn't know the exact details. They'd fabricate a better story—meeting in the ravines of childhood, wild and unhinged—than the one they actually had.

"We both moved into the neighborhood on the same day," one would say to his nosy aunts and grandmother.

Two years apart, in truth.

"Same minute," the other would add.

Two years and forty minutes apart, in truth.

Ryan became a doorway to other relationships. Neighborhood kids had sought Ryan out based on some reputation—that he was amazing at sports or amazing at video games, or just an amazing buddy to hang around with and talk about life. These same kids who would want to spend time with his friend ended up being with the boy too, so it was fine. Really, it was fine. The neighborhood children eventually became a roving mass of snickers, language, and loud noises, with kids joining and leaving as the movements of their families permitted.

Yet as the two of them rose in height and age, their interests diverged onto different paths. The boy's hobbies lingered on video games, on trading cards, on *Pogbots*—things that his peers rapidly outgrew. The boy liked to keep himself wrapped in his shroud of budding nostalgia while his friend and his friend's friends cut through theirs with tools of increasingly intense sport and pubescent ambitions. In time, Ryan and the boy's interactions devolved into a simple wave on the street and a kind greeting.

"Why don't you pal around with that kid, Ryan, anymore?" the boy's dad had asked whenever he found his son sitting in front of the television alone. That was years ago—almost five.

"He doesn't like what I like," the boy had said. "He's always running after this and that now—they all are—"

"Typical things," his dad said in response. "College isn't too far off. That's where I did most of my wising up. Just buckle down on your studies."

"Buckle down on your studies," ended many of their conversations.

A red wind blew a piece of trash across the boy's sight line. It was one of the free county newspapers that people picked up off their driveway to put directly into the garbage bins.

The boy had known Ryan and the rest of the Mont clan for almost all of his life. The family ran door-to-door charitable drives every few months, collecting things like socks in the spring, canned goods in the fall, and blankets and jackets in the winter. They were the kind of family that everyone hated under their breaths because they pretended to be better—not richer but better. Thinking back, the boy half-hoped that the mother, sister, or father had done something terrible—that behind closed doors, the rest of the Mont family was rotten to the core. Mostly, though, the boy just didn't want to deal with his old friend Ryan today.

The figure stood on the Mont porch, lifeless, with its eyes fixed on some invisible point, waiting for the boy to make his way over. From the sidewalk, the boy took note of this and waved his hands at the figure, trying to see what kind of response he could get. The boy danced smoothly toward it, his hands and hips swinging to an inner beat. The figure stayed still, watching. By the time the boy reached the porch, he had lost interest in looking like a fool. He stared into the creature's abyssal skin and decided instead to stab it with his wooden sword. It stuck in the figure, who had no reaction, but the boy couldn't remove the shaped piece of wood. It belonged to the figure, now—an impaled accessory.

"Can I have that back?" the boy asked, stepping up onto the porch. He pulled on the hilt. The figure lingered for a brief, awkward moment, glancing down from the sword in its stomach to the boy, and then moved on into the dark maroon home. It turned like a slowing top just before vanishing.

"Oh, child—oh, Ryan Mont—Judgment comes for you."

"Figures," returned Ryan, deep in the house. " I'm still here, hoping you're a nightmare."

"I am what I am."

There were noises in the kitchen.

"Who is that in the doorway?"

The boy didn't move. He hoarded together every memory he could of his friend—fond, dramatic—and parsed through them frame by frame. The time they found a one-eyed squirrel featured heavily. In their hilarity, they promised each other to make it an eye patch, but never delivered and never saw it again. They jumped on the oversized trampoline in Ryan's backyard, higher and higher until the boy landed weakly, twisting his ankle, ruining all the fun. Mrs. Bell was there, doing mundane things in the backyard next door—gardening, sipping sparkling water, living—her bones peeking out from under her tight, porcelain skin. The boy's trigger finger flinched a couple of times. He shook her away.

He stepped backward with one leg, keeping his eyes sharp and fixed on the doorway. He turned his torso and prepared to run across Ryan's curled, dried lawn. *Just go to the next house,* he thought. *This shouldn't be so damn linear anyway. Open world is more popular.*

"It's just me," he clucked nervously.

The boy knew what he had seen of the figure so far—slow, impervious, spooky, and his guide. It appeared to have a set way of doing its job and would not stray from it. The boy convinced himself that it would remain inside until he entered. He licked his lips, took a breath, then sprinted. He only made it one and a half steps before he heard the voice of the figure from behind.

"Stop!" it roared, but not with complete conviction—more like a caged lion going through the motions of lionhood for tourist scraps at the safari park.

The boy swiveled around to see the figure's glowing blue eyes emerging from the doorway. It moved with an immeasurable speed towards him. Before he could hope of reacting, the figure's hands wrapped around his neck, squeezing him like a turning vise. The figure's grip and pure terror set upon the boy from the neck up—not wanting to die overtook not wanting to judge Ryan Mont. *Really, who gives a fuck about Ryan Mont?*

The boy screamed and struggled, trying and failing to pry the figure's hands from his throat as they lifted him off the porch mid-run. The figure leered upward at the boy in its clutches and repeated in a hushed voice, "You must, Judgment. You accepted, so you must. We cannot back down from what we owe. From our responsibilities."

The boy didn't feel any pain as the figure crushed his neck bone. It was simple pressure, followed by a loose release—no pain, minimal death. His eyes rolled back, shut, and the rest of him went limp for only a second or two.

The figure then let go of him and turned back into the maroon colonial.

"Now hurry, Judgment."

The boy opened his eyes, his face pressed to cement. He shot up and grabbed at his neck. His spine was no longer split. In a matter of seconds, the boy's throat had pulled itself back together. It had healed, save for a set of bruised indentations from the figure's fingers. They remained for a moment more and then popped back out to smooth skin.

The boy understood, and with no hesitation, followed the figure back inside. He breathed heavily as he stepped over the threshold, and then fell hard into the house's hollowed corridor. Its trap door. Plummeting was easier this time. The images flickering—assaulting him—in the dark. They were, at first, somewhat familiar. He remembered Ryan speaking of his summer vacations at the beach, his disdain for chocolate, and how his dog could grab his father a beer from the fridge when instructed to do so. Recollections like these slid through the filter of boy's mind, connecting the inklings of this relationship. His head splintered. He recalled instances of his own life and Ryan's simultaneously. For moments in the corridor, he became unsure of whether he was himself or a friend of himself.

"Me, I'm me," he said.

"Who is me?" he replied.

When memories unknown to the boy began to screen, the corridor became harder to handle. These new memories bored their way into his skull. At some point, the pain and the confusion that characterized the entire drop into William's room returned. He found that he couldn't just conjure his own memories or Ryan's. The fall quickly became a blinding hurt followed by strobing images. Had the boy been able to see his bleeding nose and ears in this corridor, he would not have been surprised, not in the least.

Ryan's mother, father, sister, dog—half-known persons of sudden import to the boy lit the rest of the corridor in quick repetition until the floor rose to meet his face, a single humming fluorescent tube swaying above him.

Some shopgirl dressed in a polo shirt and black slacks—standard big box store uniform—helped him to his feet. He didn't recognize her at first—new and old faces overlaid themselves on hers, the light adjusting some of her features as well.

"Mom?" he said. "Cameron? No—"

"Yikes," the girl said. "It's Mira. Are you ready to move? Those things are meant to prime you for the devices. I know they can be a bit intense."

He knew her. Where from? She turned a bit and he recognized her brown hair, pulled back into a loose ponytail.

The boy's spine snapped to attention—his knees, too.

"Ryan killed you?"

She had lived right next to the boy, a newcomer to the circle. Her family bought the mauve colonial next door. He watched her when she jogged by his house, but not quite in that sort of way.

They never interacted before. He saw her with Ryan once—outside his house, talking to each other, smiling, and touching each other lightly. He thought he saw them, at least. Right now—down there—his head was muddled and fractured. So, he left it alone.

"What?" Mira said. "No, I'm just working a double shift today." The words came out not as the boy expected—they were as lively as they would be any other workday at an actual retail store. She brushed dust off the boy's arm. He flinched in response.

Thoughts formed easier as the boy's distance in time from the corridor grew. His features didn't feel as displaced as they did in William; his nose sat only a centimeter too far to the left and felt lighter. His lips drooped—they were fuller than they should be. But he could stand and probably even crawl around if he had to.

"Double shift?" he asked.

"Yeah, this thing here—then you'll be over later." She curled her fingers, brought her hands to her cheeks, and flared her face to mimic some horrendous beast. She feigned a roar.

"To judge." She laughed a solid laugh. Her green eyes gleamed in the fluorescent light. "The shadow told me earlier. You know the guy."

"'The Shadow,'" he said, "is a 30s radio show and pulp comic character. I've been calling it 'The Figure.' If you don't mind, I think that should be the accepted moniker. Everyone on the same page, you know."

Mira shrugged. The figure's official title wasn't important to her, the boy supposed, and he spoke again as if he had never said that dumb thing he just did.

"So, what did you do? Why are you down here?"

Mira gestured for him to follow her—another light popped on when she moved out of the first. Another lit her way after that, and so on. The boy dropped to his hands and knees and shuffled after her. It was the only movement he could muster. She called back an answer to him, two lights away.

"I'd rather not say right now, what I did," she said. "Later, okay?"

"Okay," the boy said. "You don't seem too upset about it."

"The apocalypse is the apocalypse. I figure we just have to go along with whatever deities were right, no? Isn't that what you're doing?"

The boy pondered over his words before answering, then said, "No, I think I'm making genuine choices."

Mira stopped at the edge of her current light and turned around. "And I'm not?"

He stopped just before bumping into her shins. "You just said that you weren't."

"I could've said no. The figure might have strung me up and manipulated me into taking you through this then, but I'd be defiant whenever I got the chance. That'd still be a no. I'd still have some control."

Instead, she chose yes. An easier path. The easiest.

Maybe, the boy thought. He had given up control on the porch—first, on the Bell's, and then again on Ryan's. He sat back and clapped his hands free of their dust coating. Next, he rubbed the powder from his black denim-clad knees. Some of it had gotten too deep into the material to be brushed away by hand, so he left it.

"Then why didn't you say no?" he asked. "Did it threaten you?"

Mira played with a badge on her shirt. The light speared across it with the flick of her fingers. It was tarnished and scratched gold, it didn't bear her name—instead, it just read *Girl*.

"Not in words, but our families are missing. That suggests some ransom policy, right?"

The boy nodded and feigned some concern. Whatever his brother's and sister's predicament was, it didn't plague his thoughts like Mira's parents' must have plagued hers. Even though he knew it should have.

Mira continued on her path and the boy followed. He didn't bring up the pressing point that—in his opinion—the red was not as something as tired as the apocalypse. It was more than that.

"What deity do you think was right?" he did ask.

"Oh," she said. "I'm taking a Classics Mythology course. Give that shadow a boat and an oar and it would remind me of the ferryman. Maybe this is the final screening for which level of Hades we're heading into, yeah?"

The boy's mother had an interest in the Classics; she named Antigone after—after who, he couldn't say, but she was someone. A character. This subject might have been a good way to continue the conversation.

"Who is the God of judgment?" the boy asked. A speck of asbestos dust floated to the back of his throat—he hacked it out.

"Hell, if I know," Mira said. "We were only two months in before this red." She looked uneasy. "And I failed the first test."

"Did you study?"

Mira shrugged. "Doesn't matter," she said. She flicked her name tag. "Not a student anymore. I have a job, now. I'm a member of the Oughtside Workforce, just like you. Executive Assistant to a shadow."

"Did we even apply for these jobs?" he asked with loose, weak lips.

"I think we did—with the culmination of our lives, I guess," Mira said. She brightened, then pressed her hands together. "Again, though, it. Does. Not. Matter. You dwell too much on things." She looked around, then stared into sequential parts of the surrounding dark. "Things could be much worse, and they very much will be if we don't get moving."

Another light and another. Mira led the boy through twenty of them, twenty humming circles of brain-deadening fluorescent light. It occurred to the boy that he hadn't even bothered to look outside the path Mira was leading him down—he had been so focused on staying as upright and straight as his marshmallowing limbs would allow. He paused under the eighteenth light. A muted and fuzzy gray met his gaze on either side. The outlines of toppled store shelving— like islands on a clouded horizon—sat in heaps.

Closer and within reach, small rectangular shapes littered the floor. The boy put his chest to the concrete and stretched his hands across the mingling shadows. His fingers curled around some textured plastic and he managed to scoop up a coverless VHS copy of *Husband and Wife: Season 3*. He reached for another—a Betamax copy of *Boy Who Would Be Judgment: Season 9*. Then one more—a VHS of *Thieves: The Final Season*.

The boy sighed and spoke under his breath. "Am I the only one in Betamax?"

He reached out for more tapes to prove or disprove his haunting theory, but a gaunt hand snatched his wrist and pulled at him before he could grab any more. It clamped with force equal to the figure's, but felt colder, like winter's ice clinging to the boy's skin. It pulled his torso from out of the fluorescent light and into the gray. The boy's eyes adjusted to the murk, showing him an old electronics superstore, shattered like his circle. The dust and half-hung signs had taken time to cake and fall. Wires hung from the asbestos ceiling and a stark twilight beam cut across it from the only small window in the cathedral-sized store.

A crowd of shadows gathered from behind and underneath the fallen shelves like rats, taking time from perusing the store's limited selection to see what the commotion was. Expressionless, their smooth faces eased into the boy's sight. They wore the smatterings of fine and glossy porcelain castings of people, fully clothed and painted with precision. The porcelain might have covered their entire forms at one point in the past, but now it was cracked and all the shadows had sections missing. Left where a ceramic arm or leg might have been, a foggy appendage, like that of the figure's, poured out. Care had been taken to protect their faces, as none of the shadows lacked more than a chin or a forehead from the neck up. Some of them walked with their uncovered hands to their cheeks, holding their faces still.

"I got one," said the shadow holding the boy's wrist in an empowered voice. "Selling one adjudicator for ninety pieces of porcelain! Eighty-five to whoever helps me with the kill."

Its needle fingers dug into the boy, who screamed more in surprise than in pain. He struggled to stay inside the light. *Fatigue doesn't exist in the full red up above*, the boy thought. He missed it gravely. He put his focus on the shadow—it had only a dwindling porcelain face, revealing one shadowy eye. It was not a piercing blue, but a washing turquoise—brighter than the boy's, but still kind of human. With all the exertion it had to put out to hold him, all the shifting and adjustment with each struggle, more of its porcelain fell—ceramic raindrops to the floor, some becoming dust when they hit.

The boy felt Mira's hands wrap around his ankles; she gave two fierce tugs. The gathering crowd closed in with careful steps, scraping their porcelain feet on the ground. One more tug and the shadow holding the boy tried to account for its loss of grip by choking up on his arm and digging its digits in farther. Blood bubbled from the boy's triceps. Ribbons of his skin and shirt stayed with the shadow when Mira pulled him back on the path. She laid down beside him, out of breath.

"I guess I didn't tell you not to leave the path," she said. "It's my first day." She turned over on her side. "What did you see out there?"

"Shadows," the boy said. "And these tapes." He applied as much pressure as he could to the red trenches in his right arm. There had been no pain out in the red—now a dull helping of it swirled in his arm's sweat. Still, the wound healed quickly enough. The skin filled in minutes, rather than seconds. But it healed.

Mira sat up and looked over each tape the boy had taken from the toppled shelves.

"Is there a VCR around here?" He lowered his voice. "Or a Betamax player?"

"Not on the path, no." She lobbed each cassette overhand back outside the light. The boy heard them break when they hit the floor. He tried to stop her from throwing more but couldn't see straight enough and collapsed at her feet when he tried to stand.

"You're an ass," he said in a bruised whimper.

Mira faced the boy again with a stern face, saying, "Don't you give a shit?"

"About what?" He shut his eyes.

"Your family, my family—Ryan's? Well, his is the only other one I know around here, but the others too." She thought hard. "Oh, and the Bells. That's one of them."

The boy smiled slightly at the mention of the Bells. "I know you're curious about this Oughtside too," he said. "Hades. Deities. It's an adventure. It's an exploration."

Mira grabbed one of the boy's sleeves and tore it off in three ripping snaps. She handled him as if he was a child she had to help get ready for school. She wrapped his arm and the boy became an unwitting ragdoll through it all. Taking his free arm in her hands, Mira stood and dragged him through the next set of lights.

"Not curious enough," Mira said. "Our families should be our only concern. There's nothing we can do for them but this." This sounded practiced. "I'm trying to help you here, asshole. Be a better Judgment so we can all get out of this."

She sounded like his sister at that moment—critical, like she knew what's best.

"Mister Bell put a couple of holes in the missus," he said, over-enunciating. "Who knows what awful thing you've done, Mira?"

Mira let go of his arm and sighed. "Yeah, who knows? I could be a serial killer. So, stop fucking around or I'll make a lamp out of your skin."

She continued along the path. The boy had to crawl after her for one last light—slower and tortoise-like.

The last light buzzed and flickered. It cast down onto a silver, body-shaped machine as tall and wide as two average men. Hoses, wires, and steam poured out of it in equal measure as Mira approached and pressed two buttons on its console. She kicked it twice, then turned a few knobs, adjusting the measurements of the outline machine to better fit the boy. Haggard and dusty signs salted the floor just in front of it:

Step Inside and Enter Ryan, Friend of Judgment.
Be him. 10pi/hour. GRF: Get Ryan Fever.
Full Sensory Experience! 99% Accuracy!
Studio audience!

Faded cartoon renditions of Ryan surrounded the machine on tall wooden boards, depicting him skateboarding, swimming, reading, eating, sleeping, arguing with his parents, arguing with his dog. He looked so cool, wearing a James Dean jacket he never owned and Kid Chameleon shades.

"Do they play this? The porcelain shadows?" the boy said, leaning against the machine—the steel had an iced kiss for the back of his neck.

"Not anymore," Mira said. "During training, our shadow said it costs too much for most users these days—so they leave it alone. It was once popular—almost as popular as the real thing."

The boy adjusted his blood-soaked bandage. "It seems everyone knows Ryan," he said. "And me, I'm on a Betamax that no one can watch."

Mira sighed. "Nobody cares, 'Judgment'", she said, helping the boy to his feet. "I know you, too, you know. You're the sad guy in the window checking me out every day."

They boy stepped in and laid back against the cushioned outline of a body—it was comfortable enough. During her adjustments, Mira had estimated his specifications well. It was snug enough that he could have fallen asleep if given enough time. The girl fixed his arms and legs into their appropriate sections. She reached up and lowered a metal helmet onto his head. He pulled his face and neck away from her chest as she did this. She then turned a larger knob on the console that released his appendages to his sides and allowed him to move freely again. The bolted frame held him in place, but only in his outline. He could perform the motions of running, jumping, kneeling, and so on. *Like an advanced hamster wheel*, he thought.

Mira pulled a piece of paper from her jeans pocket and started to read from it, giving tired motions with her hands. "Oughtside Amusements Presents: Ryan's Days. Experience the new craze. To begin, hand your ten pieces to the attendant, who will then strap you in. Next, they will insert the tether into any porcelain free section of your body. Then, off you go— enjoy the ride."

"I don't have ten pieces of—pieces of what, exactly?" the boy said, starting to run in place.

"Porcelain, but the shadow put it on free play for you," Mira said. She dropped the paper to the floor and unspooled a long, bundled wire from the front of the console. It had a nasty metal, pointed end the length of an index finger and the width of a thin wrist.

"Free play?" burdened voices wailed from outside the lights. "Since when?" Cracking porcelain faces appeared in a circle around them.

"Now, these porcelain people are freewheeling when it comes to, like, where exactly their consciousness is," Mira said. "You can plug it into anywhere on their exposed bodies. The shadow gunk." She stopped and breathed in. "But for us—well—I need to shove this into your brain. Through your eye."

Her face squirmed. The boy's encased body did too.

"Which eye?"

"You pick."

"The left one. Should I take my contact out?"

"I would."

"Oh, I didn't even put them in today." He let out a weak chuckle.

The red must have helped his vision, too. *What a thing, that red.*

"Awesome," Mira said.

She hauled back with the wire, aiming and cautioning the boy to keep his eyes open—both knew that he wouldn't. As she jammed the wire into his one eye, he wondered if a little of her enjoyed this.

Suddenly, applause—the distinct clapping that announced the arrival of a sitcom's favorite son—sputtered out over the machine's speakers.

Starting from the boy's left eye, the store peeled away into black. A sunlit park and clouds faded in as a replacement. The outline machine disappeared—its tether, too. Mira stood in front of him, fading out.

"See you later," she said. Then a flock of pigeons flew through her stomach, dissipating her image.

His feet ached, his heart raced, his brow sweated. He checked his pulse against his watch. He took a refreshing swig from the straw hanging over his shoulder leading to the thin camel pouch of water strapped near his back. He exhaled with a marked breath.

"Me, I'm me," he said.

"Who's me?" Ryan asked.

"What did *you* do?" he said. Ryan said.

FRIEND

Ryan had a footrace on his mind. Not one in particular but one not far off. He could feel it in the ground through his worn white sneakers and in the breezy air as well. There was never a footrace too far away from him—not in this field, not since he was younger. Any excuse to run, he would take. Any argument with the neighborhood kids that needed settling, he would challenge them to a run. Anywhere he needed to go, he would use his feet, springing over bushes and through secret back ways to destinations miles away while the neighborhood kids struggled to follow on their bikes and skateboards.

"Race you to the—," his sentences would start. He reveled in the victory—the neighborhood kids trained in vain attempts to beat him, and he loved it. When they lost, they called him names. But the names, try as they might, couldn't catch him either.

The park sat five miles from the circle—he ran there that day as he did every other. Another early-morning jogger on the distant path down the hill caught his eye. She wore knee-length black micro-fiber shorts, sneakers, and a light blue tank top. She had her hair back in a brown ponytail. *Those are quick legs*, Ryan thought. He stretched his solid calves and his torso, then he sprinted down the grass, heading for her—a brave new challenger—like a speeding train.

He hit the dirt path two leaps ahead of the jogger and ran in place until she passed him. She paid him no mind, the upbeat drums playing from her cushioned headphones fading in then out of his ears alongside the hints of her lavender body oil and sweat in the air.

"Race you to the end of the trail," Ryan called out, coming up on her right with a toothy grin.

"I'm sorry?" she said, removing the headphones. The sun hit her in the eyes when she turned to see him. She put her hand up like a visor.

"I'll race you to the end of the trail," Ryan urged, slowing next to her. "Through the pine trees and over Moon Creek—we'll stop at the quarry. Then we can get some ice cream."

They split to the grass, around an elderly woman that was being walked on the path by two leashed Great Danes.

"Don't you recognize me?" the girl said.

"I don't. Should I?" He scanned her sun-bleached face, though he would have already recognized her by the muscle tone in her legs had he known her—not a nose, mouth, or eyes. Her brown hair seemed familiar.

She tutted. Her feet scuffled the dirt in a fit of motion.

"Go," she said.

Not only did Ryan always have a footrace on the mind, but he always had a starting pistol to his ears, cocked and at the ready with a hair-trigger. It pulled as soon as the air shifted around his challenger—just before she took off. He was right with her on the path, their speeds matched at its fork.

Ryan took the lead with ease. The girl took it back.

The wind rushing by their ears sounded like the canned laughter of a studio audience.

They traded first place through the wet, sweet air of the pine trees, crunching conifer cones and twigs beneath their paced feet. Bird calls and bike bells filled their ears. The wooden bridge over Moon Creek, where—per the park's flyer—*Lunar light first met Earth*, was barely a passing babble or series of creaking thuds over their frantic steps and gorging pulses. And then, the finish line rose into view. Pine trees separated like theatre curtains to reveal the stone quarry—the impossible pit that Ryan and the neighborhood kids used to pore over. Its jagged walls hadn't changed much. Ryan could still carve faces in the rock without much straining of the eyes.

Ryan and the girl trampled over the long-fallen chain link fence and stopped a handful of steps from the quarry's edge, both winded.

"Who won?" the girl asked, in blithe spirits. She spat on a bundle of dead pine needles, then coughed, hunched over—her hands on her knees.

"It was a tie," Ryan said, depressed at the very idea but certain that was the case. "Just a tie." He stood at the quarry's edge and looked in. Something moving in the wind at the bottom—dancing across the exploded rock—took his eyes for a ride. *A person*, he thought. It moved like one, certainly. Then it moved like a trash bag. Like what it was, of course. *Nothing more*, Ryan thought.

"What's wrong with that?" the girl said in a gentle huff. "You've found an equal. We'll just have to run together again now. Good for you."

"Nothing's wrong, really," Ryan said in a quiet voice. "I've never tied, though. Lost, sometimes. Won, most times. Never tied."

She socked him in the arm, grabbing his attention from his internal studies of tying in a footrace and the bag at the bottom of a quarry. Or a person at the bottom of a quarry.

On the wind, again, an audience laughed with him.

"Then we should know each other," the girl said. "I'm Mira."

"Ryan," he said.

Ryan took another drink from his camel pack. When he finished, Mira lurched up on her toes and took one too. She put her hands on his shoulders like they were grade-school kids during their first slow song, wisps of her hair tickling Ryan's face.

"Thanks," she said, removing her hands and backing off. "Abandoned quarry, huh?" Almost in response, a falling pile of slate rock echoed from the hole. Mira crept closer to the edge than Ryan. "Anyone ever fall in?"

Ryan and the neighborhood kids used to dare each other to climb down into the pit to retrieve dynamite boxes or blasting caps—things they thought must be down there for them to find and keep. They hoped they might be able to explore a lost cave too.

"We weren't brave enough," Ryan said. He beamed with the memory. "We dared and were dared right back, then just threw rocks down into the rocks. No coming-of-age adventures."

"That's God damn adorable," Mira said. She picked a small rock up from one of the patches of grass and tossed it in. It echoed down the man-made canyon like a series of finger clicks from below. It landed by the pile of trash. A gaunt hand reached out from under the white plastic and snatched it under.

"Listen," Ryan said. "Listen! Could we do ice cream next time?"

"Were you serious about that?" Mira asked. She took Ryan's hand and checked the time on his watch. She pretended to be disappointed. "Okay, I have to get home anyway." She hit him again—this time in the chest. "See you when," she said, trotting off back to the pine path.

Ryan pored over the trash—it breathed, a set of breastbones expanding and palpable underneath.

Her number, Ryan thought.

"Your number," he said, turning back to the pines as he spoke. She was too far gone—just a light blue dot moving in the trees. Ryan returned his eyes to the plastic trash in the quarry. Was he brave enough now? Not even close. But he edged closer to where the land fell away and he squatted down, looking for ledges that could prove to be decent hands and footholds. Then he lost his footing for a millisecond and his stomach climbed up into his throat. He scrambled back to the path. Ran the long way home.

Habre Circle was silent when Ryan returned. Late morning was like that. Every individual at work or school, save for the few stragglers who kept abnormal hours or had nothing much to do. One of the old neighborhood kids that lived in the white house diagonal from his own—his brother worked and his sister, too, but what did this other sibling do all day? Sit inside and waste away. *He probably has Pogformers posters on his walls and dusty consoles on the same shelves just like he used to*, Ryan used to think when he paid him any mind.

Ryan had no idea how to talk to him anymore, so he never tried. He felt his eyes on him, though. Always watching from his dark window above the garage.

A dog—not his dog—barked somewhere in the neighborhood. It echoed over the houses as Ryan rounded the curb into the circle. He slowed to a jog as he passed the Bell's house, its hydrangea's blooms were browning and would soon be grounded with the leaves. In a wheelbarrow by the garage, Mr. Bell had marigolds waiting in the wings to take over. After them, he would have poinsettias sitting there, ready to plant. The Bells always had color in their yard—color befitting the missus over the mister. And yet it was the latter, and only the latter, who tended to the gardens in a sort of methodical concentration. Each pull of a weed and each mulching of an edged flower bed was achieved with his stern consternation.

Ryan's mother did the gardening at his house. On weekends when Mr. Bell planted, she stayed in and did household chores. Most people did, unable to compete. No one envied Mrs. Mont.

A Nina Movers truck sat in the mauve colonial's driveway across the street from Ryan's house. Hired men in forest green t-shirts went about their work in quiet, industrial motions. A couple—younger than Ryan's parents—stood out of the way on their new porch sipping coffee. They each gave him a cheerful wave. He returned the gesture, looking their bodies over as he did. They didn't run.

"Missile," Ryan said, a gentle tide of dog smell and last night's taco dinner washing over him as he entered the house. A deep brown Labrador poked her head out from around the foyer hall's corner. Cautious, then beaming with bright eyes and a smiling, wide-open jaw at Ryan's return. She bounded down the hall to meet him and they exchanged nuzzles and pats. He let her out into the backyard after, and she rejoiced in the grass. Mr. Bell's six-foot wooden fence that grandstanded over the neighborhood's four-footers had become her enemy in the past few months. She scratched at it every chance she could. Ryan's parents had to replace each panel the dog damaged— one a month, usually. His father knew woodworking, so the family chose to see this as a small price to abate the neighbor.

Upstairs, Ryan washed off his run in the shower. The quarry's trash bag rustled with quick snaps and bends in his thoughts. He went about his day from there—to his Econ course at Hill Community College, an evening run around the campus, back home for a pleasant and caloric dinner with the family, some light lifting in the basement, and to sleep.

That quarry trash moved in such an odd way, Ryan thought as his eyes surrendered to the weight of the day. *Such an odd way.* It called to him as he slept.

The next morning, Ryan didn't look for Mira at the park—only that bag of trash. He ran from the park gates, which opened to him stretching at seven, all the way to the quarry. The whole path blurred by in earthy colors. He could rent some climbing equipment from the gym if the bag was still there—maybe enlist his sister to help him down.

Ryan stopped at the tipped edge of the pit, sucking down half the water from his camel pack in two long motions of his lips. His heartbeat drowned out all other noise from the area. The trash was gone. Taken? If so, Ryan figured, it must have just been trash. Whether by township worker hands or the gale wind that frequented the neighborhood as of late, it must have been light enough to carry. No person could get out of the quarry without some help.

It was just some trash, moving like a walking torso, in the quarry wind. He laughed. The studio audience did too.

He started back home, walking the first few jelly-legged steps to catch his breath. Mira was waiting for him on the Moon Creek Bridge—she leaned over the side a little, her elbows on the wooden rail. Her right leg supported her, while her left one tapped the boards in off-beats. She stared at the creek water until Ryan approached.

"Hey," she said. "You flew right by me on the path."

"What are you looking at?" Ryan asked, taking the spot next to her. He leaned over the rail with her and saw it just beneath them—that bulking quarry trash splayed on a large rock, creating ripples in the flow of the creek. He could climb down, and he did immediately—to the banks and deeper. Water filled his running shoes.

"Garbage, I guess," Mira called. Watching. "Some people just don't give a shit."

The trash was not a bag. A rough, non-porous tarp with tattered and aged edges covered something—it didn't contain it. He took the material in both his hands and yanked it off, losing his footing on a rock as he did. Mira let out an audible gasp as the tarp now draped over Ryan.

Ryan moved his hands in a flurry, shuffling the tarp off his head to see a Halloween dummy—a decoration—laying on its back and staring him in the eyes. A skeleton with life-like glass eyeballs and patches of faux latex skin hanging all over it. Ryan smiled, then tightened his lips. This decoration was familiar to him—the legs, especially. Long and fit for running. The eyes, too—the facial structure, even. A neighbor of his.

"Mrs. Bell," he whispered. His nose dripped blood, so he wiped it away.

"What is it?" Mira asked, seven feet above; she started down the slope around the bridge, careful with her steps. She laughed when she saw the bones. "Free decoration." She raised her arms in triumph. "You lucked out. That's one of those expensive ones."

Ryan hauled it out of the creek. It was heavier than it looked and well-constructed. It stayed together, despite the rickety sound it made as he dragged it onto the grass. His right thumb grazed the skin on the collarbone when he set it down—much too warm to the touch.

"So," Mira said. "Ice cream?"

Ryan placed his hand on Mrs. Bell's forehead—still too warm. Maybe it was filled with a bug's nest, he thought. No, that wouldn't make it warm. Or it had some exploded batteries in it—would that generate heat? He turned it over to look for any sign of electronic function.

"This looks like my next-door neighbor," he said. He inspected the dummy closer. The features were carved with close precision to mimic Mrs. Bell's. He knew her face. She used to babysit him when parental functions pulled his parents away for a night.

"One hundred or one hundred four?" Mira said.

"One hundred. The blue one. The Bells," Ryan said, picking at the finish on Mrs. Bell's face. He then looked over his shoulder at the girl and asked her, "Are you stalking me?"

She smirked, "Get over yourself. I just moved into one hundred three. You haven't seen me around the circle? I figured this was a whole coy thing we were doing."

Ryan shrugged. "I usually keep to myself unless you run. You run, so we met." He moved his index finger around in a circular motion the shape of the cul-de-sac. "That's how it goes for me."

Mira hesitated like she was waiting for a punch line. "In my considerable experience, no one keeps to themselves when there's a new neighbor. They look out windows and find excuses to come over."

"Has anyone done that yet?"

Mira shook her head. She brushed a mosquito off her arm and it flew over to feast on Ryan's neck.

"People don't do that anymore," Ryan said. He lifted the Mrs. Bell decoration and shook it. It jiggled and dripped as he would expect of a wet decoration. "Maybe when everyone was younger—I remember having block parties and cookouts with the whole neighborhood, but that ended when the youngest in the families grew up."

"That's so sad," Mira said. "I bet someone will come over—someone next door, I bet. The one hundred one people or maybe the one hundred fivers."

Ryan wrung the wet parts of his shirt out over the grass. He held the Mrs. Bell decoration over his shoulders and started back toward the park. "Nope," he said, "and we tend to call the houses by color around here. So, one hundred is the white one, one hundred five is the brick one."

Mira put her hands up, her palms facing Ryan, and pretended to act apologetic for an offending remark. "Sorry to go against your secret circle society bylaws, bud."

Ryan didn't know why he would say that. "It's just we're the only circle in the neighborhood with all different colored colonials. Isn't that interesting?" He paused to adjust his left shoe without dropping the Mrs. Bell decoration. "That used to be neat to me." Ryan clenched with resolve. "No, it's *still* neat to me."

The diversity of Habre Circle's house colors used to be a point of pride—something the adults just joked about loving in public, but anyone could tell they truly loved in private. After all, what development doesn't have a repetition of color in its cul-de-sacs? Ryan knew it was silly, but he could see the logic of it—the embracing of whatever differences the people could muster out of their near homogenous homes.

He'd been there too long. In that circle.

Mira and Ryan walked home together. The Mrs. Bell decoration on Ryan's back got them some odd looks from the cyclists and power walkers. Ryan talked with Mira about himself, mostly: his family, his history, and what he studied at school which was business management. Mira deflected most of the questions he directed at her, instead she made snide remarks and poked fun at him. He didn't call her on it. She told him her major, though: hospitality management. Neither of them talked about their programs with much enthusiasm. They made concrete plans for ice cream on Friday, two o'clock at the Main Freeze.

Ryan didn't walk straight to his house. He stopped in front of the Bell's where only Mrs. Bell's car sat in the driveway. He and Mira stood at the end of the driveway, with Mira facing the middle of the street.

"I'm going to ask her about this," Ryan said, rocking his head back to the decoration.

Mira laughed. "I'm telling you it looks nothing like a person—not her, or anyone. Look at those eyes. They're inhuman." She poked the decoration twice in the right eye. Her face fell into a look of unease. She looked above and behind the decoration, now. Ryan turned to see.

A mopped head of brown hair in the top right window of the corner white colonial disappeared, reappeared, and then disappeared faster.

On the wind, came a laugh track. Louder than ever.

"That's the guy," Mira said, grinning. "He looks at me every day when I go running. He's so obvious."

"Oh," Ryan said, looking back at the Bell's house. "He's harmless. Just one of the neighborhood kids."

"Is he all right? Is he—your weirdo? Your Bates."

Ryan took a second. He could lie for him if he wanted. "Nah," he said. "His parents are dead."

"Great," Mira said. "Now I feel bad." But that feeling must have been fleeting. "Were they—killed?"

Ryan raised an eyebrow and said, "Stop doing that."

She waited for an answer.

"No," Ryan said. "He might have loved that—but no. His dad to cancer four years ago. His mom to a heart attack last year. Just unfortunate and normal afflictions. Early, but normal."

"Serious," Mira said.

"It happens," Ryan said.

"Didn't happen to us, though."

"Why would it?"

Ryan had woken to the sirens coming for the boy's mother in mid-May. Everyone in the circle peeked out from their houses and some of them even came together in the street to talk about what might have happened. Ryan had watched the EMTs wheel the body out.

When the kid's father had died, Ryan walked over and tried to console his friend, with mixed results. He couldn't make the trip across the road when his mother passed. They just didn't have that kind of relationship anymore. He went to the funeral, but he just shook the hands of the boy and his siblings in the same soft way.

Mira stopped staring at the window and brought her eyes back to Ryan.

"Is he staring again?" she said stepping slowly away from Ryan and making her way towards her house.

"I assume he always is."

Mira stared into Ryan's eyes as she moved across the street. She smiled.

"We're cancelling him out," she said. "It's just you and me and your freaky garbage decoration, confirming our date for ice cream on Friday."

And it felt that way to Ryan, until Mira made it home, a bubble of blood in each of their nostrils.

Ryan knocked twice on the Bells' door with his hand. He remembered they never liked people using their decorative doorknocker. He heard Mrs. Bell's voice from behind it, muffled and shouting over the phone.

"I have to go," she said, lowering her volume.

She unlocked the front door and swung it open before Ryan could walk away. Mrs. Bell, wearing a sweatshirt, jeans, and a fair amount of makeup, grumbled when she saw him. Boxes packed in haste and a suitcase sat in a small heap on the landing of the stairs just inside. A woman's belongings filled the boxes. She caught him staring.

"Yeah, yeah," Mrs. Bell said, "the whole neighborhood's been waiting for this." She paused to sigh. "What is it, Ryan?"

She called him by name. An old sound.

She noticed the decoration on his back and narrowed her left eye.

"Is this yours?" Ryan asked, hunching over a little to give her a better view of the uncanny decoration version of her.

Mrs. Bell sighed, "What?" She put her index finger and thumb up to where the bridge of her nose and her brow met. She squeezed it. She didn't inspect the decoration much, just took a glance at it before she must have realized what the conversation was about. If it had looked as much like her as it did to Ryan, she would have said something. She would have been frightened of it—unsettled, at least. She gave Ryan a curt "No," before shutting the door. The knocker rattled. Inside, Mrs. Bell started yelling into the phone again.

Ryan grimaced. When he was younger, his mother used to make him go around the neighborhood and collect canned goods from the neighbors, many of whom felt forced to give after all those pamphlets in their mailboxes. He hated that unwelcome look he got on their doorsteps—like he was a nuisance.

He crossed the merging lawns to his house and unloaded the decoration on the wooden chair sitting unused on his porch. His dad opened the door just before he reached it. They caught each other by surprise.

"Goddammit, Paul," Ryan said in a husky voice. "Always running late."

"Dear me," Paul Mont said. "It won't happen again, Mr. Mont."

"It better not."

Laugh track.

Paul hustled to his truck and tossed his lunch and jacket through the open driver's side window. Then, he caught the eye of the new decoration on the porch and slumped his shoulders.

"You didn't buy this garbage, did you?" he asked. "That stuff is expensive kitsch, Ryan. Your mother and I do hay bales, stalks, and carved gourds for a reason."

Easy, tepid laughter.

"Relax," Ryan said. "I found it in the creek."

Paul walked away from his truck and to the Mrs. Bell decoration, stepping over the blooming marigolds in their bed. He touched the figure—picked at its skin and bones—but Ryan could tell his dad didn't see the same resemblance that he did. A patch of hard dirt fell off when Paul brushed the side of its head. This revealed a smooth veneer as tan as Mrs. Bell's skin.

"This is excellent craftsmanship," Paul said. "Old, too. Look at this chip—it's porcelain. It probably used to cover the thing." He looked at Ryan with pride. "Damn good find, son." He wanted to take it apart, no doubt.

"Does it feel warm to you?" Ryan asked.

"You look nervous." Paul shook his head. "Porcelain doesn't feel as cool to the touch as metals. You were just feeling your own elevated body temperature or something."

"Yeah," Ryan said. "Never mind."

Paul looked at his watch and cursed as he jogged back to his work truck to leave. He praised Ryan again through the driver's side window before backing out of the driveway.

The smell of rain hung in the air, but the clouds didn't open yet.

Ryan went inside, showered, did some Econ homework, went to class, came home—his usual Thursday.

On returning home from work that evening, Paul Mont lingered on the porch before coming inside. Ryan, his mother, and his sister watched him from the kitchen table through the front storm door that they left open for him every night. Under the porch lights—moths circling—Paul tested the mobility of the decoration with care. The range of motion in the neck, hands, arms, and legs. He stood back as if to take in the majesty of the *David*, let out a small sigh, and came to dinner.

"That *is* something out there, Ry," Paul said, sitting down across from his son and scooping some mashed potatoes onto his plate. "No craftsmen or manufacturer's mark that I can see—and work like that? No artist could resist leaving one. I don't care who the hell you are." He looked to his left and then his right, at his wife and daughter. They stifled laughs. "What?"

Ryan knew. None of them had seen Paul like this in some time—not since the gazebo project in June of the previous year. He needed projects—ongoing things to work on—like Ryan needed to run. Ryan's mother had often made that comparison.

Paul scarfed down a dollop of potatoes, small white pieces of them getting caught in his mustache. He pointed his fork at Ryan, chewing. "You should bring it inside. It'll be raining overnight."

"In your room or the garage, Ry," Mrs. Mont said, sighing. "Nowhere that ugly thing will scare the crap out of anyone but you."

"My car is in the garage," Ryan's sister complained, getting a fake and dramatic chill. "In your room, please."

"Then tomorrow," Paul said, "we'll call around, and maybe get Davies to come down and give us dates and a number." He said the next part louder and with emphasis. "Damn good find, son!"

Paul always thought Davies knew about antiquities because the man was antiquity himself, living two houses up from them. Ryan knew his dad pitied him more than anything.

Ryan ate some of his steak and more of his potatoes—his peas, too. "I have a date tomorrow," he said when he sensed the dinner topic shifting to everyone's day.

"Another girlfriend?" his sister asked. She said it every time.

"Don't bring her home after the last one," Paul said.

Mrs. Mont agreed with her husband. "This isn't a dormitory."

"The new girl across the street," Ryan said, scratching his eyebrow. "Mira. She's pretty cool."

Mrs. Mont put her silverware down on her plate and looked at her son with a sharp glare. "Ryan, no. We have to live across from them for who knows how long and you're going to cause drama."

"That's how the Hatfields and McCoys started," whispered Paul to his daughter. He elbowed her arm, knocking her fork out of her hand, prong-heavy with a piece of sinewy prime rib, onto the linoleum floor. Missile's collar heralded her entry into the kitchen from the living room and back out.

"Laugh track," Ryan's sister said. "No nudging." She retrieved a new fork from the kitchen.

"I don't cause drama," Ryan said.

"Sure," his mother said.

Ryan rolled his eyes. "It's fine. I'm not the drama kind, Mom, and she isn't either."

"Everyone is the drama kind," a dry Paul offered. "Even the pope is the drama kind."

Uproarious canned laughter. Paul was a hit.

Ryan stood up from the table. "Guys, can you just pretend I'm an adult making adult decisions with other adults from now on? I know it'll be hard for you, but it would be spectacular for me. I don't cause drama. I don't cause anything because I don't *do* anything."

He could threaten to move out again. *No Mont ever went far from home,* he thought. His grandmothers, aunts, uncles, and cousins all lived within fifteen miles of Habre Circle. Except for Cousin Dennis, who they didn't talk about. But he could threaten to transfer to an out-of-state university again, even though he didn't have the grades or the money. And every time he made that idle threat, it had less of an impact on his parents. He held it back that night. He excused himself from the table, retrieved Mrs. Bell—staring straight at him through the front door out there on the porch—and went upstairs, the decoration's legs dragging up the steps behind him.

"Was that one of those adult decisions?" he caught from his sister before shutting his bedroom door. "I just want to know to prepare." His family enjoyed an outburst of cheers and laughter to end the night. A fork clanged on the floor, and the sound of Missile's collar followed, jingling into the kitchen and back to the living room.

"Dad," Ryan's sister said. "I really do hate you. You even embarrass me when there's no one around whose opinion I even care about."

"Alright, Janie," Paul said. "Fuck."

Laugh track, fading into soft whimpers and cries.

Ryan shut his bedroom door. He put Mrs. Bell down on his desk chair and faced her away from his bed. Rain started against his windows.

O   O   O

"The murdered live on in the minds of their killers," the Mrs. Bell decoration said at three in the morning. It woke Ryan in a cold sweat. He had one of those dreams that auto-erased upon waking. He sat up in his bed, breathing like he had pushed himself to his limit during a run; he was almost certain of where the voice came from, but he had to make sure.

"Do you remember me saying that?" she asked—her voice pitched exactly to Mrs. Bell's, only haggard and a little hollow. "I guess it was right."

An angle of light from the streetlamp outside his window and the shadows of raindrop trails on the window covered her body in the office chair. She turned around to face Ryan.

He started a sentence, but his throat was drowsy with sleep. He cleared it. "I didn't kill you, Mrs. Bell," he coughed. "You're right next door."

She glanced at the clock on his night table. "No, I'm gone by now—silly me, though, I'll come back." She clicked her jaw, unhinged it, then fixed it. "But shut up, Ryan. I'm talking to what's-his-name."

Ryan looked around his room. No one else was there.

Mrs. Bell stood, her joints cracking and her movement clumsy. Her face was in the light now, the space on her forehead where Paul had cleaned her with his finger shone brightly. She leaned over the side of the queen-size bed and took a close look into Ryan's eyes.

"Well la-di-da," she said. "You're jammed right in there. Can you believe he gets a state-of-the-art machine and Bill just had a couch and a TV? I stayed there much longer than I should have. I'll own that, but damn." She sat on the edge of the bed and grabbed Ryan's hand—that warmth again, like skin on skin. "Okay, Ryan, just do what you were going to do anyway. You don't want to lose it, right? Go out with that girl, she seems nice—just don't murder her or anything, and I think you'll be good. You were always a decent kid."

"Is this a dream?" Ryan asked, mostly aware that it wasn't. Regardless, it felt like the thing to say now. Just to clarify things.

Mrs. Bell released his hand and moved back over to the office chair. The shape of her bare skull nodded. "Good, go with that." She turned to his desk and started leafing through his textbooks and notebooks as if bored in a waiting room.

"Then, could you just be a decoration again?"

Mrs. Bell shut his sociology text with some force and reclined as much as she could; the chair squeaked. "Pretend again? Would that help now? I gave you the day, but I can't stay still that long. I was too still in life, you know."

Ryan threw his quilt over her. She pulled it off.

This is schizophrenia, he thought—*the quarry, the trash*. One of his aunts was bipolar, or so his mother said, but she was the only person with any hint of mental disease in the family. It had to start somewhere, though, and it would be with him. What could he do? He would need to hide it. He didn't want to be one of those people with everyone's eyes on him at all times, waiting for the medication to wear off—waiting for him to snap. Certainly, though, someone in history had success in hiding the voices—the hallucinations—and was able to lead a normal life with their own Mrs. Bell in their ear.

"I'll just," Ryan started. "I'll just sleep downstairs tonight." With cautious motions, he picked his pillow up off the bed and the blanket off the floor. "If I brought someone in here, would—"

"They see me?" Mrs. Bell finished. "As a decoration, yes. But not doing this." She made jazz fingers with her hands.

Ryan took a moment to think by his bedroom door, pillow and blanket in hand. He shrugged and broke into a quick nod. "Yeah."

The living room couch was comfortable enough, though Missile never cared for sleeping companions. She watched him with miserable eyes as he failed to nod off through most of the night.

o   o   o

Ryan woke after a couple of scattered hours of listless rest to daylight and Paul in his work clothes, standing over him on the couch with a thermos of slow roast coffee, the bitter smell filling the house.

"You could have just put it in a closet if you didn't want it in your room, Ry." Paul grinned.

Ryan sat up. "I was watching TV—*The Shadow* was on."

"Oh, cool. I miss 90s Alec Baldwin."

"No, the really old one." *Why push the lie?* Ryan thought. The TV was off, and Ryan stayed awake most of the night watching the stairs.

Paul accepted it and moved on. "Hey, do you mind if I take a look at the thing later without you? If you're not back from your date? Davies can only come down at five for an hour. I think he's becoming even more of a hermit, the poor man."

Ryan said, "Just be careful." He never knew his father to be anything else.

"Yeah, okay, you too," Paul said, looking kind of offended. He left out the front door.

Ryan didn't want to run today. On a normal day, he would be up already and out running as early as his dad was leaving. Today, he put his head back on the armrest of the couch and didn't wake up again until noon, when his sister and mother were leaving for school and work. They had woken him up, and he muttered to them about an illness. His mother left the Robitussin on the coffee table.

He would have to go upstairs at some point before class—that was his first thought. Missile sat outside the sliding glass door across the room, ready to come in. Mrs. Mont must have let her out before she left. Ryan's sluggish body whined as he went over and slid the tracked door open. Missile frenzied inside with gentle huffs and shook the rain from her coat, drops landing on Ryan's legs. The dog went straight to her food. Outside, one of Mr. Bell's fence panels hung apart from the rest, nearly destroyed.

Ryan listened for noises in the empty house—nothing. He took the stairs up one at a time, not a joyous two as he had been doing since he was ten years old. His bedroom door was open. Inside, he found the skeletal Mrs. Bell with the old binoculars from his closet held to her eyes, hunched and looking out the far right of his window, at the non-decorative, non-skeletal Mrs. Bell's driveway. He tried to ignore her as he retrieved a fresh change of clothes, his nice shoes, keys, and all other necessities, so he wouldn't need to come back in after his shower.

"I wonder if he thought about it today at work," Mrs. Bell said. "Putting those bullets in. It might have looked like a snap decision to you, but that's a thought you have more than once before the act. Fucker."

"Mrs. Bell," Ryan said. "Please—just stop talking to me." *Next*, he thought, *she'll be telling me to do things—to hurt small animals*. He didn't leave the room. He looked her over.

"Do you think it was the red? This place? Those encroaching shadows beneath us?" she asked. "I remember it hung in the air for a whole week and I had this nagging pressure on my temples and behind my eyes." Her hand reached up and massaged her left temple, which still had some faux skin on it. "I bet *you* feel it, Ryan. I bet everyone in the circle did."

He did now that she said something about it—a pressure welling in his skull.

She turned away from the window. "That's it—the Oughtside slipping right on in. Boundaries collapsing. Judgment coming for Habre Circle. Tragedy before it."

Ryan indulged his break from reality with a question. "Is that where you're from?"

"No," Mrs. Bell said, incredulous. She scowled. "I'm just dead—and bored!" She laid down on Ryan's bed as she said it. One of her eyes slid closed, and then the other, like an old doll with a slow ocular mechanism.

This is not how to seem normal, Ryan thought as he backed out of the room. *Do not engage. Do not indulge.*

The shower did his head some good.

Little effort went into getting ready for his date.

○   ○   ○

The Main Freeze had a family atmosphere, filled with yelling children, sticky tables, and pink, white, and blue all over the walls in painted swirls. It didn't fit Ryan's new, sour face, the headache growing on his drive over. That feeling of his eyes being pushed forward from his head now consumed much of his usual spirit. Mira was already there. She sat at a high table for two and looked over a menu that listed ice cream and its most usual flavors—special sundaes as well. She waved Ryan over when he entered the door, signaled by hanging bells. She put the effort into her appearance that Ryan didn't. A flattering light autumn sweater and a gray skirt—her hair out of a ponytail and down to her shoulders.

"Late to a first date," she said, following him to his seat with her eyes. "Does not bode well for our lovestruck future together."

Ryan—his face blank—pointed to the ice cream cone clock on the wall beside her. The hour hand reached its purple two, and the minute hand had yet to leave the sprinkled twelve.

Mira gave him an exasperated look. "Lighten up, dude. You look like you've seen someone with skinny legs flailing down the street with poor running form."

Sparse laugh track. From the back of the shop, where they store the ice cream.

"Nothing like that," Ryan said. "Just—do you have a headache? One of those pressure ones?" He took Mira's hand—she let him, though the look on her face suggested it was unexpected—and guided it to his left temple. "Feel that vein pulsing. That's not normal for me."

"What, are you worried about a stroke or something?" Mira smiled. "People get headaches all the time."

"But do you have one?" Ryan knew his eyes must have looked a little wild. *Again, that's not how you hide the disease.*

"Sure," Mira said. "A small one, maybe." The kids in the shop screamed louder as a clown came out of the kitchen with a giant birthday ice cream cake and a grating harmonica hooked around his neck. They all started singing off-key. Mira watched them.

"It's probably going to rain tonight," she continued. "The barometric pressure is just shifting and it's affecting you. That's all."

"Maybe," he said.

Mira ushered Ryan up and out of the shop. Main Street—with its slow passing traffic—wasn't much quieter, but the rumble of engines hit Ryan's ears softer than Eye Scream the Ice Cream Clown's performance.

"Let's call this," Mira said. "Till you're feeling well."

"No," Ryan said. The sunlight poked him in the eyes. "I just need to go for a run. We can continue on the trail."

Mira adjusted her slim purse strap over her shoulder. "I already ran today, and dates should be an escape from our daily lives, right?"

Escape from running, Ryan thought. *An odd idea. You escape to running. With running.* Mira looked at a job posting in the window for ice cream shop clerk.

"Do you need a job in town?" he asked. "My dad—"

Her laugh cut him off. "No," she said. "I actually have some bullshit to take care of today anyway. Work stuff."

"Oh," Ryan said, rubbing his temples again.

"Yeah."

They parted on the street after Ryan didn't ask her about where she worked and neither of them tried to make second plans for the near future. Ryan forced himself to run for a couple of hours to the quarry and back again, arriving home just as the evening sun colored the sky an orange red, a streak of uncanny crimson bleeding from the horizon.

The light of Paul Mont's open garage poured onto the twilight asphalt of Habre Circle. Inside, Ryan's dad and Davies Tuch—the resident elder of Habre Circle who used to give candy to the neighborhood children—stood with their hands on their hips, discussing something. Paul's work light was set up beside them and pointed down at the cement floor. Ryan approached, catching their attention halfway up the driveway.

"How are you, Ryan," Davies said, in the gruff near monotone he always had. His white beard needed trimming.

"Coming down with something," Ryan said. "You?" The run hadn't helped. He stepped closer to them to see what they were staring at. Mrs. Bell lay on the cement like a patient in a surgical theatre. She wasn't moving. He bent down to her face.

"Same here, I think," Davies groaned. "But I'm always hurting these days—years."

"Headache?" Mrs. Bell said, her eyelids lifting. Ryan only blinked and grimaced. *That is how you hide the disease*, he thought.

Davies went on, "This is something, kid. Porcelain mask on parts of the face—I can't even date the material. Not Shang, Han, Sui, or any Dynasty—not European. No history fits—not modern, either." He rubbed his chin. "I can't believe this was just lying there in that damned creek." He took a moment as if to process the idea again. "And all that junk on the skeleton? That's calcified plaster, like a ceramic mold around its bones— might even be human framing under there. Your pop and I are going to call the university on Monday. They can clean the dirt and really get in there" He clapped his hands once. "Maybe get some cash."

"If it's alright with you," piped Paul, giving Davies a sideways glance. "This is your find, Ry." His son didn't respond, so Paul said his name again, which snapped the drained boy out of his staring contest with Mrs. Bell.

"That's fine," Ryan said. "That's all right."

"Bad date?" Davies said, leaning up against the garage's dividing cement pole. With his meaty hand, he scratched his belly peeking out form beneath his olive drab t-shirt.

"Bad date."

Mrs. Bell added, "But you didn't kill her, did you?"

Ryan scrunched his face and shook his head, in some disbelief that she would think that about him. "I'll talk to you tomorrow," he said to the three people in the room. "I'm tired." He walked inside after giving them a kind goodnight.

"It'll be out here in the morning," Paul said in a sweet way. "Talk then."

He passed his sister and mother in the living room, watching the world news. He wished them well, patted Missile on the head, and went straight to bed. He collapsed into sleep, fully clothed.

Ryan slept almost all the way through Saturday, citing a stomach virus; he showered twice, took ibuprofen every three hours. His dad brought him soup and Mrs. Bell didn't make an appearance until early Sunday morning. He woke to his door creaking open at four in the morning, and in she walked. He watched her shape rattle up to the side of his bed. She prodded him twice with her bony fingers. He wasn't surprised by her presence—he had expected it, like that of a much younger sister always bothering him as his own used to do.

"That girl is out on her porch," she said.

Ryan got up, made an aggravated sound, and peered out his window. And there was Mira, sitting across the street on her porch and looking up at the moon, which had turned harvest and bloody for the week.

"Yeah," he said, "I'll just go over there so she'll know I was creeping up here by the window with my skeleton neighbor." He tried to pull away from the window, but Mrs. Bell, with much more strength than a full person, positioned herself behind him and held him. He struggled.

"You've become shit with people, haven't you?" Mrs. Bell said, disappointed. "You go on thinking about how what's-his-name over there is always in his room, playing his games and watching the neighbors, but what do you do? Run, go to class, and barely pass that class—not much more than him. Your parents tell me—," she caught herself, a loosely forlorn expression on her face. "They told me—living me—that you find someone at school to fool around with once in a while? No shame, but that's kind of just elevated masturbation, isn't it? Don't you crave connection?"

Ryan looked over at the neighborhood kid in the white colonial's bedroom window. His light was still on, in keeping with his normal hours.

The ceramic skeleton let Ryan go. He sighed. Without a word, he went outside and crossed the street. Habre Circle stood silent—the entire neighborhood, too. At four in the morning, he should have been hearing the lumber yard less than a mile away putting deliveries together, or the train by the park arriving with a cutting whistle. Each house he could see—all the way around—stood dark in its lot. The wind had picked up and started ripping at the trees; the Bell's wind chimes fell from their holder and landed with a jumbled crash on the ground—the living Mrs. Bell's car was back, but not in her driveway. She parked it by the curb, instead. Ryan's headache lessened with each gust of wind.

Mira waved him over. She wore pajamas and her hair back—they matched in their efforts to look presentable this time. She had a distinctive sad look on her face.

"What's wrong?" Ryan said, but the wind took the sound from the air. Mira pointed to her ears and shook her head. She gestured for him to follow her inside.

Ryan had never been inside the mauve colonial—it was just like his if the walls were bare. Moving boxes and bubble wrap sat in every room. Mira led him to the living room. They took a seat on the couch. A cat hissed behind it and bolted.

"Ismene is like that," Mira said. "Every time I bring a man in from the street."

I should chuckle this time, Ryan thought, so he did. A little too much, which made the next few seconds awkward until Mira spoke.

"I don't want to be here," she said, letting the line linger before saying more. "I should be living with some friends on campus, doing work-study or some boring thing. Shouldn't I? Shouldn't you?"

Ryan nodded. "Maybe." Unhelpful. "I'd love to leave, but my dog's here—and I live rent-free. There's the park for running, and—well, that's about it. But can't you just go?"

"No," Mira said. "We moved here because of me. It would be shitty to abandon them here." And that was all she wanted to say tonight. They closed the distance between each other. Equally.

Mrs. Bell would be disappointed in us, Ryan thought. He did a quick scan of the room as Mira kissed his neck just to make sure she hadn't followed him over and broken in before leaning into the scenario, and Mira, more. Their hands roamed. They inhaled each other. His t-shirt came off—both of their shorts, too. She mounted him. A tree branch fell in the backyard, removing both of them from the moment and making Ryan yelp. They sat up, breathing in the dark, then grinned at each other. Mira put her shorts back on over her lime green underwear and went over to the back door. She gave Ryan a thumbs-up.

"Ryan," she said. "Check out the sky."

The mauve home had a small and rather ugly skylight in the living room, so all he had to do was look up. The sky had taken on the color of the harvest moon.

"The red," Ryan said. "The Oughtside?" There was no disease to hide.

A quiet followed, save for a gentle laugh track humming from the speakers of the unplugged flatscreen wrapped in bubble wrap on the floor.

"Ryan Mont," said the darkest corner of the room. "Judgment comes for you." The figure took some shape when it opened its eyes and cast a blue glow over the room. Ryan chucked a throw pillow towards it, but he missed.

Mira heard and saw the thing too. She threw open the back door and fled outside. Ryan hurried after, calling for her to wait for him. She didn't. The circle was no longer quiet— hurricane winds ripped at the houses, peeling siding off and blasting their windows into pieces. Most of the twenty-year-old rooted trees stood up to the pressure, but the wind took all their leaves. An ocean surrounded the circle, then a forest, a cliff, and a quarry—it changed with each step Ryan took.

Imposing landscapes swallowed the neighborhood beyond Habre Circle. Ryan screamed; tears poured from his eyes.

The figure caught Ryan just as he stopped to scan for Mira in the backyard of the neighborhood kid in the white colonial. It broke one of his legs, and then the other.

"Stay in your world and you will never walk again," it said, "Enter the red and you will heal."

Ryan writhed in the grass, calling for the skeletal Mrs. Bell, pondering at his bedroom window. Calling for Mira, running faster and farther than he ever could. Calling for Paul Mont, asleep in his bed. "I don't want to go anywhere with you!"

"Yes," the figure said, bending down. It moved close enough for Ryan to view two pupils deep beneath the blue—they were human. "That's actually right on script," it continued. "Ideally, though, we would still be in your house right now and it would be ten minutes ago. I would have said that there, to keep it dramatic, just as you people like. But death and judgment are all improvisation today, Ryan Mont!"

An obsidian laugh track poured from the figure's unseen mouth. It placed its hand over Ryan's eyes.

ACQUAINTANCE

A nd removed the outline machine's bloody plug from the boy's. He had become numb to the pain—to any sensation at all. The figure unlatched and unbuckled him. The boy slumped forward out of the machine, his face hitting the concrete of the Oughtside store again.

"Where's Mira?" he asked when his throat started working again as he had a small seizure on the floor.

"She has other responsibilities to attend to," the figure said. "This guiding is a two-person job."

The boy could accept that. He had more pressing questions, anyway. "Did Mrs. Bell travel through time?"

"In a way, I suppose she did." The figure had to think. "She was a side effect of the machine, yes, a bit of red bleed between the sides." It breathed out. "But Ryan Mont's crime would have been the same even if he hadn't found her, right?" It sounded unsure of things now.

"Do you have any idea what you're doing?" the boy spasmed. "This whole operation—"

"Enough of one, Judgment. Come now. You will just about die down here. You need to be in the red."

The figure gathered the boy's shirt collar in his hands and dragged him out of the fluorescent lights. No other shadow bothered them. The boy heard and watched them in the store, perusing the video aisles and asking each other if a video was any good or if they could spare a few pieces for a rental, but that was all. One shadow did get close, so the figure kicked it away. The figure took him through a door labeled BACKROOM—back into the light show corridor playing Ryan's memories on repeat. Standing upright, the figure walked up the walls, dangling the boy it. When it approached the top, it hurled him up through a gaping hole in the floor of Ryan's house with such force that he smashed against the foyer ceiling and landed hard on the linoleum.

The full red immediately salved the boy. It filled in his eye with more eye, healed his arm, and replaced his skin. He stood, stretched, and cracked his knuckles.

"I actually fell through a floor this time?" the boy said, looking back over it.

"Both times," the figure's voice oozed from below the boy. "Mira was able to patch it up before you were done next door. Two-person job." The figured hummed. "Maybe three."

"Well this is shoddy," the boy said, bummed. "Like a low-rent haunted house."

"I know, right?" Ryan said. He sat in his blue boxer briefs on his peeling kitchen floor, throwing Missile's old tennis ball into the air and catching it. And again. He met eyes with the neighborhood kid from the white colonial. "You'd expect the afterlife to have this kind of stuff together."

"Judgment," the figure said, climbing up out of the hole and taking its place at the boy's side. "Salvation or damnation?"

The boy stood there and watched Ryan, shirtless and covered in dust and grime.

"What's that pissy look for?" Ryan asked, catching the tennis ball. "Save me."

The boy picked up a wood panel from the floor that looked to be from a drawer. He threw it at Ryan. It struck him in the head, bouncing off his skull a couple of feet back towards the boy. The hollow sounds of the board echoed through the home. Ryan reacted as he would back in their reality—a place with pain and death. He dropped the ball and clutched his skull. Blood trickled down his fingers, stopped, turned around, and went back up and into his body.

The boy pointed at Ryan and forced a stern look. "I am not just a neighborhood kid to you, Ryan Mont."

"You were right, Shadow," Ryan said to the figure. "He's going to be petty."

The boy sneered. "Stop calling it the shadow. It's a figure. An outline."

"But look at him," Ryan said, "The Shadow knows what evil lurks in the hearts of men."

The name fit, now that the boy was looking at the figure with it in mind. But the name had been taken decades ago and was unoriginal to him. He couldn't have that, nor could he let Ryan have that certain satisfaction over him.

The boy said to the figure, "You don't know what lurks in the hearts of man, do you?"

The figure lifted its dark arm to where a chin should be, and said, "I can make well-educated guesses." Ryan and the boy both waited for it to continue, but that must have been all it had to say on the matter. It went back to staring and waiting a second later.

"Well, there we go," Ryan said. He stood and stretched his arms over his head and yawned as if waking up from a nap.

"No," the boy said. "He's the figure. It's my call."

Ryan mimicked the boy, "It's my call."

He was always like this with the boy—above him, thinking he knew better. Being Ryan helped knock away some cobwebs around their relationship in the boy's head. He was just this neighborhood kid to him. Never anything more. And he always put ketchup on his potato chips.

The boy dimmed; he put one finger up. "Damn—" he started. The figure breathed out. Ryan rushed the boy and tackled him to the ground.

"What is wrong with you?" Ryan asked, holding the boy's body down. He placed his hand over the boy's mouth. "You'll damn me just for—what—hanging out with a girl you saw once from a window? Calling you a neighborhood kid? Those aren't *sins*, asshole."

The boy bit Ryan's hand, like he used to when they tussled together on the lawn, and the boy had feared he was going to lose the match. The other neighborhood kids would surround them in a tight circle, cheering and laughing.

"No biting," Ryan said. "Biter Boy." He looked back to the figure, laughing a little. "That's what we used to call him—the whole neighborhood."

The figure shrugged—it moved where its shoulders might be in some direction, at least.

"Okay," it said.

"Damn—" the squirming boy said again with a ticklish smile.

Ryan put his hand back, and the boy bit down again. Ryan didn't take it away this time. A calm, knowing look ran over his face. In the red, he could keep his hand there for as long he liked. The boy could keep his jaw clenched and tense, his teeth burrowed in bitter, bloody skin, for just as long. They had reached a stalemate—somewhere they had never been before. Then the figure drifted over to the two boys and lifted Ryan by his head, palming his skull. Ryan scrambled in the air and then went docile like a cat being held by the scruff of its neck.

"We usually have an eternity to do this part," the figure said. "Hence the red and removal of pain, death, fatigue—but wouldn't you both rather get on with it?" He sounded urgent like he had someplace else to be. "Judgment has made his decision already."

Specks of Ryan's blood floated off of the boy's teeth and tongue as if in zero-gravity. The droplets traveled from his lips through the air and back into Ryan's dangling hand before its gashes closed up.

The boy sat up. He put one more "Damn—" out there just to see Ryan's face tighten.

"I am not just a neighborhood kid or a 'Biter Boy,' Ryan Mont," he said, standing now and getting up close to his friend. "What am I, figure?"

"You?" the figure said. "Judgment, of course. Arbiter of sinners' fates and all that."

"But," Ryan said, "I didn't do anything wrong. I didn't sin. Mrs. Bell was murdered by Mr. Bell—right, Shadow? That's a crime. What did I do? Nothing. Not for my entire life."

"A transgression against Judgment counts in the Oughtside."

"Oh, this is some bullshit," Ryan said, scrambling in the figure's grip. "You both suck." Still, he hung his head lower. It may have just been the figure getting a better grip on his skull.

The boy tapped the tip of his foot against the floor. With little inflection, he said, "Salvation." Then he chuckled like a trickster.

The figure dropped Ryan, who landed on his knees. He rose to his feet, a mixture of relief and rage on his face.

"I don't make the rules," the figure said, heading past the two of them toward the door.

The boy had expected a dazzling show, perhaps a ray of light that might burst through the ceiling to lift Ryan out of the red. Instead, the maroon house whimpered like the blue one before it fell. The stairwell banister a young Ryan used as a slide fell first. It cracked into a heap of cheap wood. The upstairs tub fell through the kitchen ceiling next, almost landing on Ryan, who didn't flinch. The boy did flinch.

"Do you want to be crushed?" the boy asked. He ran his hand over his bruised neck. "You can still die for a second, you know. It's not fun. It feels like an abyss."

"We're already dead, Biter," Ryan said. "You heard the shadow: 'Death and judgment is all improvisation today.'"

That sentence did sit in the boy's ears as a strange line from the figure. "Maybe I just saved you from real death. True death."

"Did you now? Do you know that for sure?" Ryan looked weak—vulnerable. A flash of hope scrawled across his eyes.

The boy stammered, "Sure—no." He turned to the figure, who was breathing heavy on the porch. "Figure?"

"When Judgment's work is done, you will be free to go," it said.

"Go? Where to?" Ryan choked on the drywall dust that hung in the air.

"Anywhere you so desire, Ryan Mont. Most of the saved choose to return to their old world, the memories of the Oughtside removed. Others stay, joining their loved ones in the lower levels of the Oughtside or the wilderness around it." The figure paused like it was deciding whether or not to continue. "Co-workers of mine told me a story, once, of a saved man and woman who wanted to go live on the moon."

"And?" Ryan and the boy asked in unison.

"They live on the moon."

The boy nodded, assured in his decisions today and satisfied. "Well, you're welcome, Ryan." He joined the figure, stepping over the hole leading down to the Oughtside store. "Watch your step."

Ryan grabbed his running shoes from the living room before walking out of his home along with the boy and the figure.

Outside, the clouds above them swirled and moved in spherical patterns. The figure looked up and studied the sky, its frame moving slightly in the wind. The boy stared up at its eyes, trying to find the pupils Ryan had spotted behind the encompassing blue. No luck.

"Are we okay?" the boy said to the figure.

"For now," it replied. "Come along, we have talked enough." The yellow house next door beckoned. The figure took his standard route over: along the sidewalk, up the driveway, and onto the porch.

Ryan sat on his porch chair and slipped his white and black striped running shoes on over his bare feet. His house fell into a heap of wood, dust and memories behind him. Somehow the porch roof stayed intact—it formed a sort of gazebo, mirroring the one Paul Mont never finished in the backyard. Neither he nor the boy ran from the noise of the house tumbling down. Ryan turned his attention to the circle, taking it all in. He settled his gaze on Mira's house, across the street.

"Where's Mira?" he asked. "My family?"

"Well Mira's around," the boy said. "I'll be judging her later." His family was most likely around as well.

Ryan affected a stern tone and rubbed his eyes. "Don't pull this shit with anyone else. Tricking them into thinking you're going to damn them—it's cruel. These are people, not just 'sinners.'"

The boy mocked him. "Because you care so much about her." He tapped a finger against his temple. "I was there, Ryan, you two had a moment, sure, but it wasn't like—"

"It's not about that," Ryan said, a sleight bewildered look painted on his face. "I just said these are people."

"I know," the boy said. "I was kidding." He wasn't—not exactly. "I know how to do my job."

Ryan glared, his mouth open. "You just got this job."

The boy walked to Paul's rusted truck and peered inside. He punched through the cracked glass window, something he always wanted to do. He pulled his fist back, mangled and bleeding. He then held it up to the sky and watched it ease back into form, a warm pleasure sliding through his bones.

"Hey," he called back to Ryan. "You don't think this is all some kind of mental break for you, right?" The boy took a playful, bobbing fighting stance like an idle character waiting for input in some video game. "If you're going to join my party, I'd like to know what I'm dealing with. Are you a wild card?"

Ryan sat back in his rough-cushioned porch chair, sticking his legs out and crossing his arms. He shut his eyes. "No." An all-encompassing *No*. A nervous waver ended the word.

He'll adjust, the boy thought. Like him. Like Mira.

NEIGHBORHOOD KIDS

No one lived in the mustard yellow house anymore. The boy couldn't even remember who lived there before—a dark spot in his knowledge of Habre Circle. But the figure didn't care; it readied itself to enter the mess of a home. The boy picked up the ancient *FOR SALE* sign in the grass that the red winds had toppled over. He held it above his head, right in the figure and Ryan's lines of sight.

"Ryan," he called. "No one lives here, right?"

Ryan, still sitting on his porch, opened his eyes for the length of this audible sentence: "Not that I know of."

He's not tired, the boy thought. *No one is tired in the red. He just wants to shut his eyes until it's over.* The boy chucked the sale sign into the street, the jagged and broken metal frame slitting his hands' skin. The wounds tied themselves back up in two instants as the sign thundered on the potholed asphalt.

The yellow house began as the others did when the boy took his place on the porch. The figure did his light, graceful backward move into the dark and said, "My wayward souls, Judgment comes for you."

Three voices answered, confused and distant in the bowels of the home, "Who? Is that? Judgment?"

The boy recognized them in some far-off corner of his mind, but he couldn't quite conjure faces to place with the sound of their voices. He stepped inside, prepared for the fall this time, but it didn't come. Whole, creaking wooden floors met his forward feet. Kerosene met the hair in his nostrils in the foyer, the red diminishing as he entered into the home. A human frame, holding some large apparatus, stood in the kitchen by the basement door.

"Figure?" he said, squinting. He banged his knee on a stray table. He touched a wall, wet with the smell in the air, to keep his balance.

"No," Mira said. "It went downstairs. Here, take this." She held out a video camera—the kind news camera operators used. He obliged.

"Mira!" The boy said, remembering the feel of her bare skin against Ryan's for a stray, invigorating moment. "How are you?"

She sighed, breathing like she was about to jump into a frigid lake. "This is going to be rough for both of us."

"Who am I judging?"

"Some old friends of yours, I gather." She reached for the camera and flicked a switch on it. The spotlight attached to its top burst on, casting the shadows of Mira and an assortment of orange gas canisters on the wallpaper-peeling walls. Matches littered the floor.

Mira wore a smart, light violet suit, sensible flats, and her brown hair up in a bun. She had a microphone in her hand—it looked more like a reporter's costume than the actual attire of a reporter. The boy tucked his shirt in and pushed his tangled hair back with one hand to appear professional.

The camera shared some similarities with the outline machine: same material, same color, same industrial and pragmatic design. Typical of the Oughtside, the boy guessed. He ran his fingers over a label that read *Oughtside Amusements: Neighborhood Vids.* A cartoon of a rotund porcelain face—a mascot fattened by delights—sat next to the label, smiling with dead but not unhappy eyes.

"Start rolling," Mira said, opening the basement door. The squeal of fire engine sirens oscillated up the stairs—stairs that warped and went on for far longer than any basement stairs should. Heated, eye-stinging air followed the sounds.

The boy pressed the record button; the camera sputtered on like a generator. He held it up next to his face and pulled it back against his shoulder. "Is it supposed to get so hot?"

"Yes. Ready?" Mira said.

"I think I have this right," the boy said as he adjusted the eyepiece without looking into it yet. "Ready."

"You know, I'm surprised you didn't damn Ryan." This statement robbed some of the drive from the moment.

"I guess I do give a shit."

"I wouldn't go that far." Mira stepped just inside the basement door, flattened her hair and adjusted herself. "Okay, on me in three, two, one."

"I've been pointing this at you since I hit record," the boy said.

Mira huffed. "It seemed like the thing to say." She took on an authoritative tone and glowered as she brought the microphone to her mouth. "Test, test. Mira Peretz, reporting for the Shadow—"

"Figure," the boy said.

"Just hold it up to your eye so you can see the shot. The camera doesn't speak."

He pressed the eyepiece against his right eye while closing his left. White framing border, translucent red blinking light. The shot seemed perfect. Smoke billowed from the basement behind Mira, lending it all an apt sinister feel.

"Let's go," Mira said.

They started down, although it did become harder to discern whether they were descending or ascending after a few minutes. The steps began as a wooden, basement stairway on a typical incline. Then they became an elegant spiral toward the sirens. Then, a sort of rollercoaster track complete with loops. The walls, once drywall and spackle marks, diminished as they went—into insulation, into wood, into twilight skies, into an evening one far too clear, far too rife with stars and cosmic color to be his world's.

The camera didn't—wouldn't—leave the boy's eye. It stuck itself to him by its eyepiece about halfway down.

"Mira," he said. "Did you know about this?" When she turned her head to him, he shook his head, no hands on the camera.

She smiled. "I did."

"You really don't like me, do you?"

She didn't answer. She didn't need to.

The stairs ended on the paved outlet of Mill Street, a street two lanes and two roads away from Habre Circle. Three houses—Victorian style—burned in the moist night air.

Onlookers stood in groups, not talking much but pointing at the crumbling and roaring homes.

"Eye on me," Mira said, walking towards the fire and its fighters. "Judgment, I'm standing here on Mill Street, where—as you can see—a three-home fire has broken out. As of right now, not much is known about where or how it began, but tomorrow investigators will find evidence of—"

"I remember this," the boy said. "It was arson. Three of the neighborhood kids' homes went up one night—what were their names?" Only their voices came to him—their younger voices, from when he knew them. "Two of them had pets die in there—the other's mom had lung problems for the rest of her shortened life."

Mira dropped her mic to her side. Her face tightened. "Yes, I was just going to say that."

A firefighter in full gear rushing toward the fires knocked past the boy, sending him to the ground. The camera hit first, a small crack jutting across the lens. Mira helped him up.

"Sorry," the firefighter said, giggling.

The firefighter joined the brigade, where they all started chatting and laughing instead of doing their jobs. But the hoses didn't stop—they continued pumping, gushing out large streams of water. They moved around in wild sweeping motions with no direction from anyone on hand.

A skeletal woman moved about in the boy's head. Mrs. Bell strolled across his camera viewfinder, transparent then physical then non-existent.

"Mrs. Bell?" he shouted, his head heavy with the recording equipment.

The brigade went back to pretending. "You just had to touch him, didn't you?" the boy caught one saying.

"I'm over here," Mrs. Bell said, standing over among the onlookers, who continued pointing at the fires. She waved to the boy and Mira. "Hi. Hey, Mira."

"Hey," Mira said. "You left your room."

"I left my room!" Mrs. Bell beamed. "I'm having the adventures I deserve."

"Good for you."

The boy surveyed the onlookers. Their faces caught too much light—more of it than even Mrs. Bell's dusty bones. Their skin shined. It was slick and smooth like what it was: porcelain. These were complete human shells, made with painstaking detail and housing shadows like those in the Oughtside store—more figures. They stopped pointing at the fires and backed away as a group when he stepped close enough to see the cracks in their ceramic skin.

"I feel so alive," one said, frightened of the boy.

"Well worth every piece," said another, flustered and in awe.

Another put its thumb into its ceramic eye, cracking a piece inward then fishing it out. A genuine human pupil and sclera lay behind the porcelain, if only for a few seconds. Like a time-lapse of a browning apple, a yellow glow took it over. The porcelain person tossed its eye to the boy, who caught it.

"For you, Judgment. Buy yourself something nice!"

He held it up in the firelight. The inset pupil wiggled and an eyelid slid down to cover it.

"I'm winking," the porcelain person said.

Mrs. Bell offered a hushed line. "Don't waste yourself like that."

"Get away from us, barebones," one of the onlookers said. "How did you even get in here?"

"I hitched a ride with my good friend Judgment."

Gasps broke out among the porcelain crowd as Mrs. Bell sauntered her lanky self over to the boy and put her arm around him. He was still inspecting the eye, which had stopped moving on its previous owner's whims.

"It's a show," he said to Mira. "A production?"

Mira nodded her head, her one hand on her slanted hip and the other tapping the microphone against her leg. "Not very convincing, is it? I said the same thing to the shadow, but here we are."

The boy flipped the porcelain eye like a coin. "And they paid with their skin to be a part of it." He looked to Mrs. Bell, who winced.

"Apparently," she said, "we're supposed to get porcelain shells when we die—to keep some semblance of our humanity or something. But I guess the universe doesn't care about the murdered. I just woke up, right there in William's locked room, all covered in shadow skin. It evaporated into the air until I was bone." She did a quick spin like she was showing off an outfit. "Then you showed up, Judgment, and I could leave."

"She was murdered," said one onlooker to another. "Makes sense—no class." They snickered.

"Oh, get fucked," Mrs. Bell said. She picked up an orange safety cone by her side and chucked it at the insulter. The rubber cone broke the porcelain person's shoulder on impact, and the others bent down to steal the pieces of it that fell to the ground for themselves. "And what were you, then?"

The insulter stood, wisps of shadow leeching into the air from its shoulder. In a haughty, affected way, it said, "Suicide." It then looked around on the floor for its porcelain. Carefully.

"See," Mrs. Bell said, calm again. "I hear they give people who kill themselves extra bits of porcelain." Her voice rose. "The Oughtside seems to think that they're on the frivolous side with their spending, you know. Economy stimulation." She took a beat. "But death is death, in my limited experience. Doesn't matter how you get there."

The insulter prodded the other onlookers, requesting its pieces back. Each of them played dumb, suggesting the porcelain may have bounced into a drain, the closest one being thirty feet away. Mrs. Bell grinned watching them. She went on about how they would never physically fight one another, because of the terrible fear they had of breaking their own shells.

The boy pressed the porcelain eye against Mrs. Bell's cracking, glassy pupil when she turned back to him. It fell to the ground when he let go of it. He watched the perked onlookers as he knelt to retrieve it.

"Nothing to stick to or hold in anymore," Mrs. Bell said, frowning.

"Sorry."

"Great," Mira said. "Can we continue, please? We should be six years ahead by now."

A question had been bouncing around in the boy's head since William's room. "If it's a production, Mira, how do we know this is even accurate?"

The onlookers became a rabble. "It better be accurate, damn it. I gave my left hand for this. If it's not, I'm going to riot." Others—even the fire brigade—screamed into the faux night fire at the mere thought of inaccuracy.

Mira shushed the boy, her eyes showing some fear. "It's accurate."

"The shows, the film, the outline machines," Mrs. Bell said, "are all they have to remember. Slices of human life, so we can still pretend. It's the backbone of the Oughtside's continued function. While the productions might be lacking in value, critics praise the stories' accuracy all the time."

The boy pocketed the porcelain eye, turned to Mira, and set the shot right.

"You should give that back," she said.

He gave Mira a thumbs up. "Maybe later."

He didn't even feel the weight of the camera anymore.

○   ○   ○

Mrs. Bell tagged along, offering pointers like a segment producer. It seemed to the boy that she didn't have much else to do. Mira didn't mind. She continued acting in her role as a reporter, going on about forensics and findings in the rubble in her preferred cadence. Kerosene was used as an accelerant in one, gasoline in the other two.

Three porcelain children sat on the curb in front of the row of fraudulently burning Victorian homes, dressed in the neighborhood kids' old clothes. The two boys wore matching striped baseball uniforms and the girl a frayed brown windbreaker and jeans. The clothes roused their names from the boy's memory: Malcolm, Fran, and Lynn.

They spoke, all despondent and weepy.

"Malcolm, we killed Lacey," Lynn said. "You said you were going to get her out."

"I tried," Malcolm said. "Fran, we killed Digger. I thought you tied him up in the backyard."

"I tried," Fran said. "Lynn, was your mom inside? Weren't you going to—"

"I tried," Lynn parroted.

They each—aged eleven to thirteen—cried on the curb. They had burns all up their arms and across their chests. Given the severity of their burns compared to those of their parents and siblings, some investigation was done into them being involved. The similarities in their wounds, too, was factored in. But nothing came of it—Mira spoke of court documents indicating that a payment was made from fathers to lawyers to judges. This was the purview of the owners of Victorian homes. The people in them could afford that kind of thing. They were the wealthiest in the neighborhood, even outpacing Mr. Bell by a wide margin.

William Bell's colonial stood closest to the Victorian line. Every day as he dressed for work, William watched their pointed roofs peer down on all the colonial tops of Habre.

Lynn said, "Do you really care, though, Malcolm? I think I should feel much worse than I do."

Malcolm wiped the tears from his cheeks, the porcelain child actor's hand scraping as it moved across his face. "I wasn't going to say anything, but no—I think I've grieved all I'm going to. Lacey bit me two days ago, you know. Fran?"

"I was just pretending to cry," Fran said

The fires made the neighborhood kids popular, the boy remembered. They took on the roles of the loners, their hearts hardened by their conjoined dark past and eventual proclivity for smoking. While Ryan had that natural pull, the draw of the firebrand kids was artificial—forced and kept alive by their wild action rather than mere effortless existence like Ryan's.

The boy passed the homes and the fires went out. The porcelain firefighters removed their gear as onlookers jogged past the boy and company, ready for their next roles. The three children stayed on the faux Mill Street, on the curb under a streetlight. Malcolm picked a prop book of matches up off the street-swept asphalt in front of him. He handed one match each to Lynn and Fran.

o   o   o

An infinitely long crevice marked a scene and setting shift to the city—downtown—twenty miles from Habre and six years after the fires. Tall, brown, and brick buildings blocked the night sky, the manholes spewing noir mist. *The real city is, in truth, rather quaint in comparison*, thought the boy, but he did enjoy this aesthetic. Three new, svelte, and older porcelain neighborhood kid players ran into the filthiest and tallest of the buildings, one that went on for miles above. Their wardrobes had darkened. The other porcelain people became the un-homed and the dog-walkers, with one donning the costume of a saxophone player with no saxophone but instead a portable Oughtside brand radio playing smooth jazz next to him.

"Judgment," Mira said, "I'm standing now in front of one of the neighborhood kids' college apartments. More on this story—right now."

They stepped inside the building—not into a lobby, just straight into the grimy apartment where Malcolm's parents paid his rent. When they spoke, the neighborhood kids now finished each other's sentences, sitting on a splitting leather couch among prop take-out cartons and pizza boxes.

Malcolm began, "I am so tired of this damn specter hanging over us." He had a check for rent in his hands, signed by his dad: *Dr. Baum, PhD.*

Fran continued, "It's always going to be there, forcing us to be on Mill Street, at holidays and reunions—"

Lynn finished, "Begging for this money."

Malcolm lit a match and Fran took the check from his hands, putting it into a blackened medium-sized saucepot on the coffee table. Lynn dripped some kerosene into the pot from a plastic jug. Malcolm dropped the match onto the check, and it went up in a flash of fire. The fire spread from there—theatrically controlled—around the borders and crown molding of the apartment. Up the walls, until they burned into ashes. One wall's absence revealed a long corridor of other rooms in other houses.

Lynn began, specks of soot sticking to her face, "So we burn Mill."

Malcolm continued, "Of course, we burn Mill."

Fran finished, "And everywhere in between?"

"And everywhere in between. Then ourselves."

"What is this, pyromania?" whispered the boy to Mrs. Bell. "This can't be right." *There would have been signs of pyromania,* thought the boy. Maybe not for him, but Ryan would have seen them. He would have done something. These were his friends, on occasion.

"Why not?" Mrs. Bell said. "I remember these kids too, always breaking William's flowerpots and setting firecrackers off down at the quarry every night. In December, of all months. Seems like a natural trajectory to me."

The neighborhood kids grabbed their simple supplies—matches and kerosene—before sprinting into the corridor, dousing and setting each room on fire as they tore through. Lynn, in a sort of flammable pirouette, spread the kerosene around the walls and floor. Fran picked a match from the messenger bag slung over his shoulder and handed it off to Malcolm, who lit it with the gusto of a symphony composer and let it fall to the saturated floor. Their process was pragmatic and efficient—right at home in the Oughtside—but also elegant, like a lick of flame on the wick of a candle.

Mira raced after them through the houses, shouting out street names and numbers. "Two hundred Gray's Lane, one ninety Fjord Avenue, six hundred Bryan's Way, ten Mound Street," and so on. Each home lay somewhere in between the city and Mill Street. Mrs. Bell and the boy kept up through the extreme heat of the theatre fires.

Porcelain people sat in some of the homes, screaming in numerous ways as the neighborhood kids barreled through—like a child, an adult, a cat, or even a dog. One wore a goldfish costume and screamed with its head in a bowl of water. The boy appreciated the dedication of that bit player.

Mrs. Bell said, "Run behind them but a bit to their side. It'll make it all the more cinematic."

The boy tried it out and it worked. The angle did inject more adrenaline into the scene.

Again, like the basement stairs of this yellow home, the hall warped—sometimes it headed straight on, sometimes down, and sometimes up. He kept his eye on Mira as she sped, gritty and hardened in her role, through the smoldering homes.

He fell into his role as the camera, watching her.

Red-blue police sirens and then a squad car driving perpendicular to the hall and the running neighborhood kids arrived by the time they hit one ninety Fjord Avenue. Two porcelain officers in uniform shouted at the neighborhood kids to halt, stop, and turn themselves in.

Mira said, "Judgment, in the ongoing pursuit of the neighborhood kids who are wanted for a rash of arson, the police have hit a wall." As she said the last bit, the squad car slammed into a stage wall, falling well behind the neighborhood kids, its sirens fading. "The police chief, in an impassioned speech, cautions everyone in the city to be vigilant against these 'monsters.' We take you now to that press conference."

They came to a room and the floor was asphalt again. A porcelain crowd milled around, looking for a better position, each holding a fake microphone. The neighborhood kids kept their heads down as they weaved through the shuffle.

"I don't remember a rash of fires in the area," the boy said, trying to keep track of Mira in the commotion.

Mira said, having to shout over the conferring people, "Judgment, the way Ryan talks, it seems like you cut yourself off from community news in the last year."

She wasn't wrong. He turned to Mrs. Bell for some confirmation.

"I think I read something," Mrs. Bell said. She shook her head. "I don't know, I had my own shit to deal with."

"Judgment," Mira said. "Eye on the podium." A porcelain police chief stood at a wooden lectern. Shadow wisps seeped out of the collar and cuffs of his clothing. The crowd fell silent and held up their microphones to catch the man's voice.

"We," the chief said, "are doing our best to catch these—what do I say?" He flipped through the script placed in front of him beforehand. He chuckled. "Ah right, monsters!"

Porcelain reporters started shouting questions. A chorus of, "Release their names," rose above their voices.

"Nope," the chief said. The actor placed an undue pause here. The boy coughed before the chief continued. "Witnesses have heard loud laughter and 'whooping' from inside each of the twelve burnt homes, which I believe suggests that these monsters—oh wait, 'murderers' this time—have a deep and feral need for chaos." The police chief actor appeared satisfied and assured by his own performance.

The crowd fell silent, separating to form an ordered path for the neighborhood kids and their three pursuers to ease through, leaving a trail of kerosene behind them.

"Judgment," Mira said, the lone reporter in their path. "Did you hear them laughing? I didn't."

The neighborhood kids sprinted toward the next room, a quaint home on Fjord Street, and set it ablaze. However, contrary to existing reports, they didn't laugh or rage in the interest of chaos, each of them at a calm medium as they set their fires—pragmatic, efficient, and dedicated. As the boy followed, he became entranced by their small dance of fuel and ignition, fuel and ignition.

Fjord Street led to Mikkelsen which led to Habre which led to a wall in the yellow home's basement bearing a well-realized mural of the red sky. There, the neighborhood kids stopped, as did Mira, the boy, and Mrs. Bell, all the sets crumbling behind them.

The lights turned low, and the boy's camera spotlight took precedence over any other source of light. It cast long shadows on the walls. One additional shadow—substantial and three-dimensional—decorated the mural, moving when no one else moved.

"Trapped, children of the flame," it said, opening its blue eyes, "What luck, for you to have found your way here this morning, as the boundaries topple around us. I offer you this: continue your heated ways in your world and you will surely burn. Enter mine and you may yet live."

They answered without hesitation. "I think we're good right now," they said in unison. "Yeah, burning was always the endgame," they each agreed. Lynn started by covering the room in kerosene. Fran rummaged through the match bag, taking his time to find the perfect one. Malcolm stretched his fingers and cracked his knuckles.

Still, the figure reached out from the wall, scooping them into its dark.

"Offer may have been the wrong word," it said.

The porcelain neighborhood kids turned to the boy, waved, and bowed low, their production coming to a close. The boy—struggling to catch his breath—gave them a long round of applause. He then directed it at Mira, who rolled her eyes. Mrs. Bell clapped her bone hands together a few times as well. They sounded like dead sticks.

Mira took the boy by the arm and pulled him into the path of the figure. She messed with the camera, hitting buttons and opening latches.

"I did well, right?" he asked.

"Sure you did," Mira said. "Welp, see you later."

He thought her opinion of him might have changed while they were running through the fires—while he was her camera. But she said the words in the same way she had before, like they were just another part of her job. Mrs. Bell put her hand on his shoulder.

"So, damnation?" she asked.

"I'm not so sure," he said.

The camera released and fell into Mira's arms. "All set."

The porcelain people—all the players—gathered around her, each asking with deep, wounded concern when the video will be uploaded and available for them to add to their respective reels. "Calm down, calm down," she said. "Editing and touch-ups first. You all know the drill."

Mrs. Bell looked on with a light smile on her skull. "Watching themselves do something human," she said. "Heightened, eccentric, but human and with humans. That must be a trip."

"I got shots of you in there too, Anna." The boy's trigger finger twitched. He pulled that one onlooker's porcelain eye from his pocket and offered it to her.

"Those are porcelain concerns," Mrs. Bell said, turning the piece away. "I don't share them. You should give it back."

The boy nodded, slipping it back into his pocket. He wanted to keep it, of course. It was given to him, not stolen. "I didn't steal this, Anna," he said.

"You might as well have," she replied.

Still, the boy kept it.

The crowd dispersed after Mira took down all their information. She had been glancing at Mrs. Bell throughout the production. "Then what are your concerns, Mrs. Bell?" she asked.

Mrs. Bell had to think about that. "I seem to be more capable here than I was in life," she replied as her eyes lit up. "That's something to consider. Judgment is a concern. William, too. Also, I think I traveled through time, which is something I was never concerned with before but now I can't stop thinking about it."

"Side effects," Mira said.

"Well William's gone," the boy said, smiling. "Damned." He clenched his fist tightly as he finished the word. "Strike him right off your list of concerns."

Anna Bell shook her skull. "Still, he's here." She touched her chest, picking a piece of calcified plaster from it and crushing it to dust. "He lingers." She then directed the boy's attention back to the yellow home's mural. "Don't worry about it, though. You're needed."

The figure had its dark hand through the piece, waiting for the boy to grasp it.

"Judgment," it said, wiggling its fingers. The boy reached over.

O   O   O

The figure pulled the boy through the mural, bursting through the bricks into the basement of the yellow home proper back in Habre. The neighborhood kids sat in a circle on the cement, playing cards with an old, singed deck.

"Hey, there," Malcolm said, folding his hand.

"Judgment," said the figure. "Salvation or damnation?" It started reassembling the brick wall, using freshly mixed concrete in a wheelbarrow by the stairs. He finished quickly.

The boy joined the neighborhood kids on the floor, the sparse red through a small window healing his aching calves and calming his rapid heartbeat. The kids had left a spot open for him in their game.

"Five-card draw," Lynn said, dealing the boy into the game. He didn't know how to play or what formed houses and flushes. He would have to stick with of-a-kinds and—when he felt he had something more—just act confident and reveal his cards, hoping the neighborhood kids' reactions would take care of the rest.

"Aces wild," Fran said. He nodded.

"So, Biter," Malcolm said. "Damnation or salvation?"

Damnation, but separation, the boy thought. That was the way to handle it. He picked up his cards. They were slick with kerosene, of course.

"A little bit of both," he said. He removed two cards from his hand and took two from the deck. His hand: queen, nine, seven, four—all of clubs—and an ace of diamonds. They could all be the same suit if he wanted. *These cards must form some kind of straight or something*, he thought.

Fran, Malcolm, and Lynn smiled at the boy.

Lynn spoke, her eyes down on her cards, "We should have hung out more before this red, Biter. Ryan's an ass now, but you—we like you."

The figure, standing at the bottom of the basement stairs said, "You will decide, Judgment. Will it take long?" It looked up the stairs, its body language impatient. *First unsure, now impatient*, thought the boy.

"We'll play a hand for it," the boy said.

The neighborhood kids grew giddy at the idea.

He continued, "Whoever beats my hand gets salvation, and for the rest, damnation."

Fran shook his head and placed his cards face down. "I fold."

Malcolm winced, tossing his cards away. "I fold."

Lynn scratched the back of her neck. "I fold. Well, that's it." She laughed. "Plunged into the fiery depths, I guess. Here's the pot." She reached over for the bag of matches, resting up against the wall, and put it in the middle of their small square. "Good job."

They all wanted damnation—of course they did.

"Figure?" the boy asked, "are the 'depths' even fiery?"

"Sure. Sometimes," it said, leaning on the basement railing.

Not the answer the boy wanted the neighborhood kids to hear.

"Oh, and by the way," Malcolm said. "We really do like you, Biter. Could you guys imagine if we all hung out in life? Biter, you would have been the best of all of us combined."

Lynn said, clenching her fist in front of her scrunched face, "You have real, operatic tragedy in your life, none of this forced, 'oh, poor us, our parents and privilege' bullshit that we had to find for ourselves." They looked at him now in an almost provocative way, the basement shadows hiding half of each of their faces.

The boy exclaimed, blushing a little, "Play then! Losers saved. Winners damned. Let's do this for real."

The neighborhood kids, with some excitement, snatched up their slick cards from the floor. They discarded what they didn't need, took some from the deck, and played their hands in less than a minute. Lynn revealed hers first: two pairs. Malcolm next: four kings, jack high. Fran last: a straight flush. He beat Lynn. Malcolm and Fran win—right? He hummed as he looked towards the figure for help.

"I suppose someone should have taught you to play poker," it said, offering nothing else.

"What?" the boy said, forcing a laugh. "I know how to play poker, figure." He put his cards down, faces up, and judged the skin around the neighborhood kids' eyes. Malcolm's and Fran's loosened. Lynn's tightened.

The neighborhood kids stood and embraced, their eyes wet with the only tears they'd shed since those first fires on Mill Street. Their goodbyes were quick but more genuine and human than many interactions the boy had experienced or seen in the past few years. They held each other—really held each other. Lynn's arms curled around both of her friends, her head in between theirs. They nuzzled each other and even cooed like children in the arms of their parents. No words or speechifying like the boy had expected—the way he would have done it if it were him in this scene. He cleared his throat of a lump.

"Aren't you going to try and sway me?" the boy asked. "Into damning you all?"

"No," Fran said, collecting himself. "We respect your position, Biter, the way ours should have been respected out of the red—and the way I hope you respect ours. We're not going to gum up your critical work with our sentimental guff."

Lynn stepped away from Malcolm and Fran. She crossed her thin arms and put an open hand to her mouth, waiting.

This is judgment, thought the boy. *It should be tough, both to pass and to watch*. "Figure," he said, "Malcolm Baum and Francis Brown: damnation. Lynn Mear: salvation."

Fran—just before the floor took him—pulled a match from his black jean pocket. He tossed it to Malcolm, who—just before another hole in the floor swallowed him—wrapped a slip of striking paper around the match's handle and tossed the combination to Lynn. She caught and separated them, ready to strike the match.

The figure spoke, heading upstairs. "Malcolm Baum and Francis Brown: damned. Lynn Mear: saved." Now at the top of the steps, it called down. "Let's go, Judgment."

Kerosene saturated the walls, ceiling, and floor of the basement, the fuel glistening in the red rays coming in from the window across the room. The smell of kerosene had been in the boy's nostrils since the hallway scene. His senses had adjusted; fuel everywhere had become the norm to them now. It was olfactory blindness.

"Where can I go?" Lynn said.

The boy approached Lynn, holding out his hand to her. "Anywhere you want, Lynn. Everywhere you want."

Her eyes caught the light, wet and showing some surprise. "How about where they went?"

The boy made a long, unspecific vocal sound. "Figure?" He walked to the bottom of the stairs. The figure leaned up against the door frame and sighed, disappointed. "What do you think, Judgment?"

"Well, no," the boy said with a pained expression, turning back to Lynn. "But—to the moon. That'd be fun, right? Floating around the moon?"

"If they're burning, so am I. If not down there, then here in the red."

Burning isn't salvation. He approached Lynn and grabbed her wrist—the one attached to the hand holding the match. Lynn jerked the wrist towards herself, pulling the boy into her embrace. She had more physical strength than he realized and smelled even more like kerosene than the air around them. Her sweat, her perfume, she was drenched in it.

"Biter," she said. "Let's see if the four of us really could have been friends." She used her free hand to press the match to the striking paper and struck, the scratching and small fizzle of the match hitting the boy's ears first, followed by a muted hum, his ears engulfed in a sudden flame.

It began at the match's head, catching the kerosene scent on Lynn's fingers, and running up her arms. It then split onto the boy once it reached Lynn's elbows and consumed both him and her together. He panicked, his skin wet with sweat then the oils of melting sking. Lynn hugged him tightly, their clothes burning into each other, the fire spreading to the floor, the walls, the ceiling, and the rest of the yellow house. The water heater exploded as did the gas stove upstairs.

The boy looked at his hand, still wrapped around Lynn's wrist. Some of the skin on the back fell away into the flames—some finger bones, like Mrs. Bell's, fully visible now. He wiggled his fingers and the bones moved like pistons. His vision went and his heartbeat slowed. But the red did its work, putting back the skin and muscle that the fire kept on burning away.

The figure stayed at the top of the stairs, the fire steering clear of its body. It waited for the boy until the floor caved in and dropped it back into the basement. It grumbled over the noisy, flaring house.

"Judgment," it said, "you must get better at this."

The boy tried to pull away from Lynn, but they were fused together now. He couldn't find where he ended and she began. She appeared content, her eyes shut, a smile on her face.

The figure tore them apart and threw the burning boy's body over its shoulder like a sack of potatoes. Lynn fell backward into a bed of flames. The figure scaled the cement wall by the fallen staircase with ease and slipped out through the doorway. It stood in the middle of the kitchen where the stove spewed flames at its face, rippling its shadow flesh. The foyer hallway had collapsed, so it went out the back door, moving at its lackadaisical pace. The glass on the floors cracked slightly under its airy weight.

Outside, the red hit the boy better and his melted body started to recover. The figure carried him around to the front of the yellow house and dropped him off on the lawn. There he lay as a sort of charred puddle on the ground, contracting back into himself. Laying there, unable to move, his one fear was that his hair might not grow back. It did, though it happened last.

"Figure," he said to the thing when his lips and tongue worked again. "We should get her."

"She's been saved," it said, looking back at the yellow house. "She'll be fine in there—happy, even."

The home billowed smoke into the red sky from each of its windows. Something else exploded inside—the furnace, maybe—and then it all collapsed into a fiery heap of black wood and melted vinyl siding. A swath of sparks burst from the pile, high into the air. The boy had forgotten the circle still had some power; it looked like 8-bit fireworks to his foggy eyes. He could almost hear the chiptune victory fanfare.

"You okay?" Ryan asked, muffled as the boy's ears finalized. "You looked like bad cheese."

ESCAPE

The soft sound of his voice comforted the boy. It was somewhat distant though, coming from across the street—from
Mira's lawn. The boy managed to stand. Some dead grass had
healed into the skin on his body. He plucked a blade from his
stomach but left the rest—there were too many other blades to
pull and he didn't mind them so much. They looked like war
tattoos—like he'd been through something real.

"What are you doing over there?" the boy asked.

Ryan took a glance at the figure, who stared him down.
"Just taking a look around. Believe it or not, I saw a raccoon."

"Stay out of the houses, Ryan Mont," the figure said.

"I wasn't—"

"You're saved. Be saved. Wait."

The boy fell over, then stood back up.

The figure drifted over to Ryan and stood just-too-close.
The boy only noticed now that his wood sword wasn't stuck
in the figure's chest anymore. *It must have burnt up*, he thought.
The sword had been his true prized possession, though he only
just realized that. If only he had taken care of it. *Uncle Fred
would be so disappointed.*

The figure looked down at Ryan's running shoes. "Are you going for a run? Out here? Into the absolute unknown?" his voice playful as he gestured down the street towards the edge of the circle, where reality warped into imposing places. "I have no exposition about it, no warnings for you. You'll see what it is—all those fabled places you can't go. Far outside even the Oughtside. And you won't come back."

That was some exposition, thought the boy. He followed the figure's gesture with his eyes through the woods, cliffs, crags, the deepest oceans—strange nature unbound.

"I was just curious," Ryan said. "About the houses. I don't think she's in there anyway."

"Mira Peretz?" the figure said. "No, she wouldn't be. She's on the clock."

Ryan looked at the boy, who almost fell over again. His muscles had recovered enough for him to catch himself.

"Yeah," the boy said. "Remember? I told you she was working with the figure—you seemed cool with it."

"You didn't tell me," Ryan said.

"I must have."

"You didn't," the figure said.

"Well, it's no big deal," the boy said, disappointed in the figure. "It's just a job."

"All of this is a big deal. Take it seriously. Was she, like, in on our deaths or something?"

"Fuck your 'take it seriously'" the boy said, picking a small rock up off the ground and chucking it at Ryan. It hit him in the bare stomach. Ryan brushed away the dirt mark it left. "I am taking it seriously." He pointed back at the remains of the yellow house. "Fran, Malcolm, and Lynn were in there, you know—your good friends?"

Ryan blinked his eyes and squirmed. He crossed his arms. "They weren't my friends—not anymore at least. You don't know me."

The boy went on, "They were burning houses, killing people—animals! And they wanted to be damned, so I had to do this whole clever reversal thing with—"

"Lynn Mear did light herself on fire, Judgment," said the figure, making an urgent point.

"Could you just go away?" the boy sighed.

"I was about to."

The figure took another look at Ryan's shoes, then drifted off toward the next house, the run-down farmhouse secluded by a dozen towering trees on the property. Developers had built Habre around it. Developers had built Habre—the entire neighborhood, even—around the man who had owned all the land and still lived there: Davies Tuch.

Ryan crossed the street. As he stepped closer, the boy gazed into Ryan's flustered and frightened eyes. He sweated. He sweated under the red sky. Ryan waited until the figure moved out of human earshot. He stepped up close to the boy, almost like they were still young and Ryan had a secret to share.

He said it quietly, his voice shaking. "I'm having trouble with all of this. I'm having a lot of trouble with this. I see shadows out there in the trees." He had tears in his eyes. Ryan was ready to rabbit, anxious and fidgeting in his running shoes.

"Do you want company while I'm away?" the boy asked as he reached out and touched Ryan's shoulder the way Ryan had when the boy's father died. He took it back after a few seconds the way Ryan did, too. They didn't touch like that. "We can dig Lynn out of the rubble so you can hang, though I think she'll just light herself on fire again. Antigone is here—she might bite you. Maybe Mrs. Bell can come up." At the mention of Mrs. Bell, Ryan flinched, but then he put on an accepting and relieved face as if his nerves suddenly calmed.

"Mrs. Bell?" he asked. "Okay."

"Are you sure?" the boy said.

"Yes." He looked down the circle and then down the street towards the edge of it. "She always has interesting things to say."

The boy walked off to discuss it with the figure after telling Ryan to wait where he was. In the middle of Habre Circle, there was a manhole. A manhole not worth mentioning, save for the fact that Mrs. Bell popped her head up out of it before the boy reached the figure.

"You needed me?" she asked. With ease, she pushed aside the cover that all the neighborhood kids had tried to pull up when they were young, their spaghetti arms failing them.

"You *are* in my head, aren't you?" the boy asked, trotting over to her. He offered her his hand. She took it and he pulled her up. The red hit her bones and tiny fleeting wisps of shadow swung from them, but nothing else. No healing.

"Oh," she laughed. "Let's not get into what sordid things I'm rifling through. In there, out here. I'm deeply everywhere, I guess. Or maybe I'm just following you."

In a rush of black between them, the figure appeared. It shoved the boy to the ground. "Be better, Judgment!" It pointed down the street, to Ryan fleeing into the wilderness outside of the circle. The outside was woods when he went in, deep and dark and fabled. He didn't come back out right away like the boy had hoped he might.

He stood up and called after Ryan, shouting as loud as he could.

"Oh well," the figure said. "If the saved don't want to be saved, there is nothing we can do. Back to work, everyone." It clapped twice. "Your friends should listen better."

Mrs. Bell asked, "Should I leave now, or—?"

The boy saw this as a clear a chance as any for true heroism. Deciding William, Ryan, and the neighborhood kids' fates had been a murkier process than he wanted. Which he should have expected, considering the trend of his life and the genre of this ordeal. But this—heading into a forest to save a friend who was only wearing running shoes and shorts? Nothing murky there.

"We go after him, right?" he said. He started moving like a video game character waiting for input again. "Three-person party, going headlong into the wilderness. An adventure."

"I don't have much else to do," Mrs. Bell said. She seemed excited.

"I do," said the figure, lamenting. "We do, Judgment. This is supposed to be a concise process."

The boy shook his head. "Two against one, figure. Break my neck all you want, but this is happening."

The figure's eyes brightened on Mrs. Bell. A small piece of her jaw fell to the pavement. She picked it up and put it back. It fell again. She picked it up and put it back. It stayed this time. Its eyes brightened on the boy rocking back and forth, his tattered, burnt clothing sticking to his skin. He hummed the *Final Fantasy VII* battle theme under his breath.

"An assembly of bone who could shatter at any moment. And Judgment, terrible Judgment. There is no red out there— not even traces of it like in the Oughtside's lower levels. When you're cut, you bleed. And when you bleed—"

"You put a bandage on the cut until it stops," the boy said.

"Maybe," the figure said. "I've never been back. And I don't remember it well. The dead are reborn—reimagined—there. Plucked by guiding shadows like me for judgment, if needed. Or left to find their own way back into the Oughtside."

"Were you plucked from here?" Mrs. Bell asked. "I don't remember any of it at all."

"You were, Anna Bell. I was not so fortunate."

The three of them moved together down the street. The boy broke away to grab a charred baluster off Ryan's lawn. He felt that he needed it for protection from things. *What things?* The figure didn't say. Damned things, the boy imagined. Damned things that belong in the deepest woods. Mrs. Bell stepped away from the group to pick up the Habre Circle street sign that had been ripped out of the ground during the circle's transition to the red. A much sturdier weapon than the boy's, but likely too heavy for him. She had that ceramic skeleton strength. Not as strong as the figure, no doubt, but not as weak as the porcelain people. He started thinking about stats for the two members of his party—dexterity, defense, strength, constitution, luck. Mrs. Bell swung the sign, slowly but with force. She would be their heavy. The boy jabbed the air with his baluster like a fencer or a pirate. He wanted the wooden sword of his childhood back, but still, he would be their agile, wiry distraction. The figure drifted along, doing nothing much at all. It would be their wild card. And lantern, probably.

Arriving at the edge of the circle, the three of them stopped. The boy looked out into the landscape. It shifted from woods to the sea, to the crags, to a desert, to cliffs, and back to woods.

There was no pattern to the change; one terrain could last for less than a second or much longer.

"Time it right," Mrs. Bell said. She held the street sign over her shoulder like one would hold a broad sword.

He didn't. There wasn't much timing to time right. The woods became a sea, where a large, blue moon lit the surface, its light only penetrating the water a fingernail's depth. Then that turned back to woods, then to cliffs—to desert, to crags, and then to woods again. To sea. To woods. He took a step forward here, out of Habre. Back to sea. The boy tried to lean out of it, but momentum carried him down into the water. The salt stung his eyes more than it should have. It took his vision and his weapon. A riptide then took the boy miles out, one step quicker than the wet cold could take his breath away. Shock. He wanted the red back already. He would even settle for the lesser effects—just that muted red taste of the lower Oughtside levels if he could. Something to soothe his mortality in these instances.

Mrs. Bell, the figure, and the circle slipped out of the boy's line of sight as his eyes recovered from the salt. They stood in the corner of his eye, but he could never catch them head on. The asphalt edge shifted, hall of mirroring the ocean.

The boy swam parallel to the edge of the circle when he could see it, as he remembered he should from his ocean swim lessons in grade school, breaking free of the current with minimal effort. Suddenly, a beast burst out of the water, magnificent, scaly, and finned, about two stories tall with dull blue eyes. It wore the face of a whale.

The beast's surfacing sent a petrified boy rolling atop a large wave, back towards where the circle vaguely existed—towards the welcoming arms of the red. The whale beast cried an almost human cry into the night.

"Ish—Ish," it said, swimming into the horizon. "Ishma."

"Judgment," the figure called each time the circle came back into direct sight. "We're here, Judgment." Its voice guided the boy to the edge of the asphalt dock off the red shore. Mrs. Bell—with that ceramic skeleton strength—pulled him up out of the water, back onto the street, and into the sweet, nurturing, and calming red.

"I think that was pretty solid teamwork," Mrs. Bell said. She picked up her street sign from the ground. "It bodes well."

The boy sprawled out on the edge of the circle, seawater draining from his clothes. His lips tasted like salt. Seaweed had woven through his hair.

"Judgment," the figure said, "I will guide us through."

"I can do it," the boy said.

Mrs. Bell shook her head at him. "Two against one, I think."

Dejected, he pouted. Water drained from his mouth as he stood up. "Fine." He looked himself over. His clothes draped off him in tatters, burnt, wet, and bloodied. "Hold on."

He went home.

Antigone slept in his bedroom like she did on any other blue-sky day. The boy fumbled to his closet in the silent, red dark and grabbed a gray shirt much like the one he already had on, though this one still had sleeves and all its buttons. He grabbed pants much like the pair he already had on, though they still had fabric below the knees. Many more of the exact same shirts and pants hung in his closet.

He changed, finding the onlooker's porcelain eye in the ruined pocket of his pants as he did, and slipped it into his new pair. He knew he should give it back.

Before going back out, the boy checked his brother's room, then his sister's. Their beds had been slept in before the Oughtside came. He stayed out of his parent's room. None of them ever talked about taking the master bedroom for their own. None of them ever would. He stopped peeking before he could think about it too much and went downstairs. He grabbed an old chef's knife from the drawer beside the sink. The trash needed to go out, but he left it. It didn't smell, it was just full. The red kept it fresh.

He walked outside—confident.

"Ready, Judgment?" the figure said watching the boy as he rejoined them.

"Don't say anything," Mrs. Bell said. "If you're trying to look good, you'll look much better without saying anything."

The front of boy's shoe stuck in a small pothole on the street. He tripped, losing the knife to the air, and fell forward onto his face, the knife landing in his spine.

"Judgment?" the figure asked.

"I'm alive," the boy said to the ground. "I just can't move anything."

"Anna Bell, would you—?"

"Sure," Mrs. Bell said.

She pulled the knife from the boy's spine and patted him on the back as he healed.

He could feel a certain disappointment in the air.

The figure stepped outside the circle at the perfect time. Not a millisecond too late or soon: the exact, perfect time. It cradled the boy in its arms—the appendages felt distant but human around him. Mrs. Bell rode piggyback with her street sign tucked through her bones.

"That was easy," the figure said, setting the boy down in the tall living grass. The air was cool in the woods. A wind blew through the trees, rustling their tops, too far up to see. *Redwoods*, thought the boy. He put his hand against a tree trunk. Much too warm to the touch. The bark squirmed. *Not redwoods*. He clutched his knife tighter.

In the dark of the forest, the figure had very little in the way of shape—a faint outline of a form when it moved, maybe, if that. Its eyes floated in the vast woods. At times it looked like its body *was* the vast woods. It kept looking to one side then another like a lighthouse.

Mrs. Bell dismounted the figure by clumsily falling off into the damp earth. She pulled the street sign out from between her rib cage sheath.

Around them, things made noises: crickets, toads, night birds, the wind, and more. The boy missed these sounds in the red. The smell of dirt wafted in the air. Specific dirt, though: wet clay.

"Ryan?" the boy said. He said it louder and longer next. His throat hurt. Every part of him either hurt or felt like it had the potential to hurt at any moment. His stomach wrenched and he doubled over.

"Are you okay?" Mrs. Bell asked, coming up next to him. The figure's blue light hid some of her more ceramic features and let her human ones—what little of them she had left— come through.

"I'm tired here—almost thirsty," he said as he licked his dry lips.

"I see him," the figure said. "He's almost to the middle of the forest."

"I didn't know you were looking for him," the boy said. "What's there?"

Behind them, Habre Circle slipped away—out of existence—for the moment.

"A lake with a mill."

"A mill?" Mrs. Bell asked.

"Not a typical mill for either of you, Anna Bell—but a mill, nonetheless."

"Is it old?" the boy asked.

"Old as time," the figure said. "I would guess." It moved forward through the trees, with Mrs. Bell and the boy in file behind it.

"To the old mill on the lake, then," the boy said.

They moved together, hearing the sounds and snarls of the forest, its many eyes pressed on them.

A porcelain wolf sprang from the dark and twisted Mrs. Bell down to the ground by her face. The creature's shell had been constructed from a bunch of haphazard pieces of porcelain people thrown together. The boy could make out three eyes and six noses on its back. The figure turned and kicked the wolf chomping at Mrs. Bell. The wolf's porcelain shell shattered, leaving it as a shadowy canine form. The figure punted it, far above the treetops. It didn't come back down anywhere near them.

"The red," said another crude wolf shape, this one jumping onto the figure's back and biting into it. "Do you know the way to the Oughtside from here?" it asked, its mouth full.

The circle slipped back in behind them, then out again.

"You don't belong in the Oughtside," the figure said, unable to shake the thing off. Judging from the figure's narrow, flickering eyes, the bite hurt.

The boy stabbed at the snarling wolf, but its porcelain shell broke the knife. Half of its blade broke off and flung back at the boy, missing his face by an inch. He didn't think much of it and tried to pull the wolf off with his hands, failing with each tug at its hind legs.

Mrs. Bell snapped to her skeleton feet and shook some broken pieces of herself out of her skull. The wolf spun off the figure and knocked the boy to the ground. Anna Bell took her street sign and swung it in a wide arc—like a bat—at the beast, knocking it back into the dark brush, leaving a trail of porcelain pieces in the grass.

"I should have kept the baluster," the boy said. He picked up his broken knife. "Figure, are you okay?"

"This is an odd sensation," the figure said.

Part of its back had been torn open. Ceramic bones peeked out into the blue wood. The figure tried to mold his shadow to cover it, like a balding man with his hair. Doing so took some shadow from over his spine. He molded that, too, which took some shadow from its neck. It continued to mold its shadow in a sad, almost frantic display. The tear relocated to its arm and then down to the hand, which it held up in front of its face. It moved its dusty bone fingers and made a fist.

"It's not so bad," Mrs. Bell said, leaning on her street sign.

"Not so bad?" the figure asked, shaken. "Do you know what happens when these bones of ours turn to dust? This, Anna Bell, is the beginning of that process for me."

"I don't," Mrs. Bell said.

"Neither do I."

"Well look at me," Mrs. Bell said. "I'm in that process already and living my best life." She stood tall, swinging her sign over her shoulder bones. The figure blended with the dark, save for its eyes and a bright bare spot of bone on its hand.

It sighed, and the wind carried the sound into the woods.

INSTINCT

A porcelain person stood on their path, deeper among the impossible trees. She moved towards them as if learning to walk. They stopped, save for Mrs. Bell.

"Hello?" Mrs. Bell said, meeting the person among the trees. She held her hand out.

"Don't," said the figure. "Don't touch her, Anna Bell. She hasn't cured yet."

The boy walked out to Mrs. Bell to get a better look. From far back and winding all around the trees, a trail of wet and white footprints led to the porcelain person.

"I'm—," the porcelain person said. Her face dripped clay, but the boy recognized it anyway. It was his sister. "I'm—" she said, holding out her dripping hand to the boy.

"Judgment, don't touch her!"

"Cameron?" the boy said. He kept away from her.

Cameron staggered toward the boy. He backed up in a wide circle around Mrs. Bell and the figure with each step that Cameron took forward. She used to chase him in the yard like this, only faster.

"What's she trying to say?" Mrs. Bell asked.

The figure grumbled. "Nothing of import—nor anything of value. Her name. What she's feeling."

The boy urged it to go on. So did Mrs. Bell.

The figure grumbled. "She is stuck with her thoughts—vivid memories—unable to articulate. It's a clearing of the mind and memory, this particular process." It faced the boy, moving its head with him like a gothic carousel. "The body is torn down and made again, but the mind is nurtured—washed clean of damage from age and injury and even memory loss. She is sharp inside. She knows exactly what she wants to—needs to—say to you."

"What do we do with her?" the boy asked.

"Don't you mean for her?" Mrs. Bell replied.

"You know what I meant," he said.

Mrs. Bell smirked. "I do."

"Look at her," said the figure. It set its eyes on Cameron, determined in her futile efforts to reach the boy. "She'll follow us down to the mill, where she belongs. Just don't touch her. You'll ruin her."

They retraced the path Cameron had taken to get there, her dried clay footprints leading the way, the figure lighting it. They walked in formation: Mrs. Bell, the figure, the boy, and Cameron. Farther back, wolves trailed them. The boy could hear them, ready to pick off stragglers. He spotted snakes wrapped around the trees, more interested in eating their own porcelain tails than what the boy and his company were up to. Silhouettes of other people, adorned in fresh, immaculate porcelain, met his gaze in the woods. They lurched behind the trees if any of the figure's blue light touched them. The boy caught glimpses of familiar faces—some that he knew for certain from the neighborhood, others that he had probably known, and still others that were complete strangers but looked at him in an expectant, knowing way.

The people whispered to the group. "Do you know the way to the Oughtside?"

To which the figure pointed back up the path. Before long, the boy and Mrs. Bell started doing the same. Damned things like snakes and other beasts were not allowed in the Oughtside, but newborn porcelain was. *Simple enough*, thought the boy.

Wolves—three, this time—attacked again, but the small group handled them with ease. The figure kicked one, Mrs. Bell crushed one with her sign, and the boy distracted the last one with his broken knife until one of his companions had a chance to dispatch it. They hadn't reached Lynn, Fran, and Malcolm levels of synchronicity, but the boy felt they would. In time. Together.

Cameron muttered and cooed all along the way. Every "I'm" or "You" she said felt ready to continue into another word. Then it didn't. The boy wondered what she had to say to him. He settled on it being something about their dead parents. Everything had become about them for her those last days. Everything might as well have always been about them.

"Cameron," he said. "It's fine."

The wound on the figure's hand grew as they went. Not much, and not quickly, but it was growing—slowly climbing up its arm.

Whenever it seemed to think no one was looking, it checked on the injury, eyeing it with concern.

Rubble from Mill Street littered a large swatch of the path. It started with half-destroyed brick and stone walls—some of Mill's gaudy streetlamps and decorative benches lying broken around the base of the trees. The destruction in Habre looked calculated and even merciful in comparison; everything here— the surrounding neighborhood now dead in the woods—had seen harsh and swift judgment. Trees and brush grew through the brick and stone. Tall grass grew over it like an old ruin.

The boy stopped to pick up a mailbox from the overgrown floor—the Brown family's mailbox. A letter from the local temp agency was inside, addressed to Francis Brown. He'd gotten a job a week before the red—days before the neighborhood kids' final arson spree. The agency said they were happy to have him. The CEO had even written a personal note: *I see a lot of my own mistakes in your history, Francis. I turned it around, and so can you.*

"Fr—" the boy said. A cool and sloppy touch pressed against the back of his neck. He shivered.

Cameron didn't stop pressing her hand against him, even as her entire hand became a mushed stump, her ceramic hand bones bent and stuck in the material. She brought her other hand up like she was going to choke him when he leaped away. Cameron looked down at her stump.

"You," she said, her mouth running with clay.

The boy hurried to correct his mistake. Neither Mrs. Bell nor the figure had stopped with him. He took her stump in his hands and tried to form it back, using methods he'd seen on pottery infomercials early in the morning. He gave her a crude, elementary pot hand and hoped no one would notice. He then wiped his hands on a nearby tree, the bark trembling at his touch. Surely they could fix Cameron's hand at the mill. He pocketed the temp agency letter and caught up with the figure. Cameron followed him.

Mrs. Bell was the first to speak in a good long while. "I don't remember having clarity, figure—ever." She said it like she didn't get what everyone else did for snack time. "None of the others I've met do either."

"That is interesting," said the figure. "You must have been attacked, Anna Bell. A wolf or some damned thing must have gotten you while you were vulnerable and finding your way to the Oughtside. It happens. You are damaged."

"It happens?" the boy asked.

"It does," said the figure. "Damage your sister enough, Judgment, and she won't remember this clarity either. I wonder if it matters, though. She will find her way to the Oughtside and be accosted by amusements and currency, muddying her all the same."

The amusements aren't to blame, thought the boy. *They do it to themselves. They allow the amusements and delights to muddy them.*

The way to the Oughtside struck the boy at that moment as being similar to the path baby turtles take from the beach to the sea. Led by a bright light in the night sky and instinct, perilous and fraught with seagulls.

"Wouldn't you know?" he asked.

The figure faced the boy, the group still moving forward. It glared at his muddy hands before saying anything. "I was singularly focused when I pulled Anna Bell from the woods."

"On what?" Mrs. Bell said.

"My own clarity. What I had to do."

"Which was?" the boy said, impatience rising in his voice.

"Judgment."

They stopped at a clearing on the top of a large hill. It looked out over a lake—an odd lake, one that was long and narrow, more like a river or an inlet. Two towering, slate cliffs flanked it on either side. A brilliant blue ocean moon hung between the cliffs and above the lake. Light brown and thick, the water wasn't water but a body of thin clay.

Mrs. Bell—her face pursed tight—started down the hill first.

Down there, the old mill faced them, sitting on the beach at the edge of the clay lake. It was wider and taller than the boy had expected. A cerulean glow eked out from the cracks and space in the structure. A quaint, spinning water wheel on one side lent a slight pastoral aesthetic to the view. The top came to a point, like a Victorian cathedral. And there sat Ryan, sitting cross-legged on the glassy sands outside the mill. Ryan watched the mill like he used to watch television, focused and attentive. He had stopped running.

The figure drifted down the hill. Near to the bottom, a porcelain stranger stumbled out the mill's front door, and Ryan stood to catch her before she fell into the sand. He shook both of her hands when she offered them in an awkward introduction.

"Excuse me," she said. "Do *you* know the way to the Oughtside?"

"I'll tell you what I told the others," Ryan said, his hand on his chin, "I think it's that way, but please don't take my word for it." He pointed up at the boy, paying little mind to his friend even as their eyes met.

The boy ushered Cameron down the steep hill in a cautious display.

"I'm sure that *is* the way," the porcelain person said. "It feels like it is."

"Yeah, man, just go with your instinct then. Do you need help climbing the hill?"

She'd already walked off.

Mrs. Bell and the figure reached Ryan, who sat back down and ignored them.

"Ryan," Mrs. Bell said, putting her Habre sign in the sand. "How've you been?"

No answer, just a huff. He kept his eyes on the mill door.

Anna Bell sat down next to him, cross-legged. "Don't be pissed at me, kid. This is the guy you want."

"No," the figure said. "I don't care enough about you to be worth your scorn, Ryan Mont." It stood for a moment, looking out over the lake. It then moved over to the clay water and dipped its wounded hand in, but the clay drained right off, none of it sticking to its skeleton. The figure sighed, miffed at its lot in death.

On passing the new porcelain person—her halfway up, the boy and Cameron halfway down—the boy wished her good luck since it seemed to him that he should say something nice as they passed. She replied with a jaded look at Cameron and then some words.

"Do either of you know the way to the Oughtside?"

The boy steadied himself on the incline, watching Cameron. "As he said, it's that way."

"I'm sorry. It never hurts to check."

He didn't need an apology.

Before heading up the hill and into the trees, she said, "She'll never be the same."

Continuing down, the boy wondered if that comment was born from a sense of clarity for the newly porcelain person.

The boy only tripped once on the way down the hill, and even that trip was negligible. He led Cameron like a good brother would, like Ryan might have with his sister. He then left Cameron to follow him at her own slow pace so that he could join Ryan in front of the mill. He wanted to hit him, but some pain had pooled in his feet and his back flared. So, he took the casual approach, like it was no big thing.

"Ry, you ready to come back?" he said.

"Leave me alone, Biter" Ryan said.

The boy sat on the other side of Ryan, sticking his busted knife into the sand. He played with its dense, compacted grains. They stung the small cuts on his palms.

"There's nothing here for you," he said, giving Ryan a quick glance-over. He had no cuts or bruises on his body, only the dirt on his running shoes.

"Because the Oughtside is such a paradise and a glut of opportunity," Ryan said. "At least here, I feel real. Hey, Figure, will any of my family show up?"

The figure shrugged—an actual shrug. Palpable in the light.

"Did you forget the part about the moon? You can live on the moon!" the boy said as he shook Ryan by the shoulder. "And Mira's here—"

Ryan perked up. He looked around for the girl—stopping to view Cameron for a beat—then shook his head. "You said, 'here.'"

"I meant there, but look at that spark of life in you."

He realized he should have brought Mira.

Mrs. Bell chuckled. "You really should have. Jealousy, jealousy." She winked.

The figure, dipping his hand back into the lake and still getting no tangible result, chimed, "Brought Mira? You could have, Judgment. I gathered you knew what you were doing."

"Thanks," the boy said. He lay back on the glassy sand and breathed out, Cameron's face hovering into view. He sighed and rolled to the side to avoid her, then he stood up to continue his sister's game of tag. "Can we put her back now?"

Another porcelain person stumbled out the door. Smoke followed the tall man onto the beach. Ryan rose to meet him as he'd been doing with them for the past few hours.

"Ryan? Is that you?" asked the man—his father Paul Mont. He glistened, pristine in the blue moonlight. His work clothes had been painted on with expert care.

"Dad?" Ryan reached out to hug him, but the casting must have still been hot because he backed off before they ever connected.

"Do you know the way to the Oughtside?" Mr. Mont asked as he looked past the group towards the humming wilderness.

"Fuck the Oughtside," Ryan said. He moved to catch his father's wandering eyes and to question him on the whereabouts of the rest of his family: Mrs. Mont, Missile, his sister.

"I get that, I'm worried too," Mr. Mont urged, "but if you could just tell me real quick."

The figure drifted back over, having given up on the clay lake. "It's instinct and conditioning, Ryan Mont. It trumps clarity in these newborn moments. Just tell him and let him get on to safety. The damned can smell him already."

The boy was so right about the baby turtle comparison. He smiled to himself as he sidestepped Cameron.

Ryan pointed up the hill. "That way, I think."

Mr. Mont expressed banal thanks and trotted off in the clumsy, awkward way these new porcelain people moved while they acclimated to their bodies.

"I'll come with you!" Ryan said.

Mr. Mont waved his son's offer away. "In that, Ryan? No offense, but I think you'll do more harm than good."

Ryan sat back down on the beach, sullen. He rubbed his hands against his hair, letting out a low, perturbed murmur. "I should wait for Missile and them anyway."

"And where will they go?" the figure said.

"All roads lead to the Oughtside, Ryan," Mrs. Bell said, standing. "It's okay to accept that."

The boy, huffing from Cameron's slow, incessant chase, could only muster agreement and no line.

The runner sucked his teeth and pounded the sand.

CLARITY

Cameron needed to get back. At this point, she was unrecognizable to even the boy.

A muddy mess bearing only a passing resemblance to his sister—to a human—standing in front of the group.

"You, D—" she said, bubbles forming out of the waterfall of clay running out of her mouth. "I'm so—"

Her movement slowed. The boy could take a six-step lead in their chase and stand around for a solid minute before having to worry about her catching up. *If this was still her,* he thought, *this loss would be devastating.* She had a driven streak, a fierce winning streak like her mother's—like Ryan's. The Mont boy had an interest in her at one point for it, the boy recalled. Now that she had been remade as clay, he didn't look at her much.

The group hadn't moved while waiting for Ryan to make his mind up. But everyone, it appeared to the boy, needed the rest. And so, he let them take it. The figure sat by the liquid clay's edge. It finally stopped looking at its skeletal fingers after a dozen attempts at covering its bare hand with the clay. Its eyes rippled out over the lake's surface. Ryan played the presenter and usher to more porcelain people—a simple, easy task that didn't require much of him. They asked about the whereabouts of the Oughtside, so he told them. Asked and told. Mrs. Bell practiced hitting things with her street sign, quickly growing adept with it as a weapon. She made strikes and parries against enemies not present.

The scene had a serenity to it. Even the boy and Cameron's chase became more playful—pleasant—as they went and she slowed. He cracked more than a few smiles. Cameron also smiled before her mouth was covered by her wet upper lip and nose. *This is easy*, thought the boy. *All of this—right now—is easy.*

But she had to go back.

When he said so, his three companions looked up at him. They knew it.

"How do we do it?" he asked.

Rising, the figure said, "You can either shove her into the lake, where she'll go back to the bottom of the slush pile, or bring her in yourself, Judgment. Up to you."

The boy took a few steps away from the clay creature that was Cameron and looked her over. Shoving her into the lake would be tricky.

"And cruel, Judgment," Mrs. Bell said. "I'll come with. Ryan, too."

"I'm staying here," Ryan said. "I don't know how many times I have to say it to you people—people and things. Persons and things."

"I'm a person," Mrs. Bell said, hurt.

"No, you're not," Ryan pushed, adamant about it.

"Wow, Ryan," the boy said.

Mrs. Bell shook her head, sheathing her street sign. "You're being an ass."

"Ryan Mont is lashing out," the figure said.

Ryan lay back in the sand and released a long breath before looking up at the boy. "None of you are people."

"I—" Cameron said.

"Maybe you."

He's uninvited to the mill anyway with that attitude, the boy thought. Mrs. Bell agreed.

The figure stayed with the Mont boy. "I'll watch him," it said, sitting beside Ryan, watching the kid pretend to sleep again. No one had bought it on the porch—no one bought it now.

The figure's eyes being so close made Ryan's skin glow blue.

The boy hesitated to enter the mill, its wood door oozing a cerulean glare. "Is there danger in there, figure?" he said.

"Of course," said the figure, like he shouldn't have to say it at all. "There are things."

"What things?" Mrs. Bell asked, but she was already by the door. She had tried to open it already. Locked.

The boy replied for the figure. "Damned things. What else?"

The figure grumbled an agreement. "You don't need me now, do you?"

Mrs. Bell, more enthusiastic than she'd ever been, said, "Not at all."

The boy was less sure. His hands stung. His feet ached.

Someone unbarred the door from inside and a porcelain person fell out. Mrs. Bell smiled and pointed to Ryan when the porcelain person—an old woman from Mill Street—asked her question. The boy did the same and the porcelain person stumbled towards Ryan, her unsure porcelain eyes shaking around in their sad sockets.

Ryan, pretending to sleep, said, "That way." He jutted a pointed thumb back toward the woods.

Mrs. Bell kept the mill door from shutting with her arm. She poked her head inside and waved the boy over. He looked around the area for whatever reason, like he was sneaking into someplace when he had no idea if he was sneaking at all. No one had told him he wasn't allowed.

Mrs. Bell went in, the boy followed her, and Cameron followed him in sloppy lurches. Blue heat hit boy's skin, pulling sweat from his pores.

"Just hurry up," said the figure.

"Shut the door," said an accented woman just inside and beside the group. She was smaller of stature and of limited porcelain—about half a body's worth. Her entire porcelain face had gone missing and what was left was all shadow with shock white eyes and only the slight bone structures still palpable around them. She lazed on an old wooden chair beside a metal table. The table belonged back in the Oughtside; it was constructed like the outline machine and the news camera. The chair belonged out here in the wilderness with the trees.

The boy shut the door, maneuvering around Cameron who had become interested—calmed—by the mill's insides. He could still watch the figure and Ryan through a slim crack between the door and its frame. They sat together in silence on the beach.

"Bar it, too," the woman said. When it was done, she knocked on the metal table; it made a substantial hollow sound that took off up into the mill. Down into it, too. The structure had depths. "Saw you two eying this thing. Fresh delivery from the," she paused then her voice returned as a whisper, "Oughtside."

"You like that construction?" Mrs. Bell said, making a foul face. "There's no character to it."

"Says someone who lived in the Oughtside." Every time she said "Oughtside," she whispered.

"Oughtside." the boy said at a normal level.

"Do you know the way?" said a smattering of porcelain voices above and below.

The woman wrenched her head back and shouted for quiet. She threw the boy a vile look, her white eyes razor slits.

"Some get lost in here," the woman said. "They overshoot it. You're not a very good Adjudicator, are you?"

"Adjudicator?"

"Oh forgive me, modern man." She feigned this apology then said the next word with a folksy drawl. "Judgment."

"I like Adjudicator," Mrs. Bell said. She was one for antiquing.

"I—" Cameron said. Everyone ignored her.

"Can't change my name now," the boy said.

"True," Mrs. Bell said as she touched a wooden, load-bearing pillar to her left. A loud something—a bang—echoed from the depths below the group. Mrs. Bell looked around with curious curves dressing her face. "You're very attached to the title, aren't you? Like—"

William, thought the boy. *Here we go.* "What is it?" he interrupted to stave off her saying it for a moment more.

"William," continued Mrs. Bell. "He was attached to status, you know. To title."

"I'm not like him, Anna," the boy said. He glared at the idea. "You're in here, aren't you? You can see that." His voice was weak and cracked as he pointed to his skull, his mouth dry.

"Almost, but I don't want to look much further. The murdered live on in the minds of their killers."

"I know that. You've said…"

Cameron coughed, "He—?"

The shadow woman pulled some papers from an overflowing cubby in the wall next to her. She shuffled through them, looking up at Cameron with each new piece she thumbed.

Mrs. Bell stepped closer to the boy. "You fell into him. And I wonder—when I look at you and hear you sometimes—if that hasn't affected something. Or maybe it was just your parents, eh?"

Cameron chimed with a gurgle, "They—!"

"I'm me, Anna," the boy said.

Mrs. Bell smiled. "There's more to you, Judgment."

"There's more to everyone," he said sharply. Then he shrugged. "That doesn't mean it's something awful or something to be frightened of, does it?"

"In the Oughtside and beyond," Mrs. Bell said, the upper mill residents echoing her like a church flock, "Who can truly say what things mean anymore?" She and the boy stared at each other until the half-shadow woman made a noise.

"Here it is," she said. She held a paper in her hands. "Cameron—a recent arrival to the lake. Must have been bumped up the line by friends in high places," she chortled. "Or low!" After affixing the paper to the side of Cameron's wet head, she turned to the boy. "She wasn't needed for judgment, not damned, she's not altogether important, and yet she's already clay. I had to wait for months as lone consciousness and bones in that lake. Lucky girl."

She was lucky, the boy thought. *Always*. "That's fitting," he said with a tinge of prissiness.

"Well, I'll get a barrow," the woman said. Before she stepped away, she turned to Mrs. Bell and spoke: "Anna." Then she whipped back around to the boy on her porcelain heels and said, "Judgment." She gave them both a nod. "I'm Pen. We'll be working together today."

"Working," Mrs. Bell said. She had her hand on her street sign, sheathed in her ribs. "Does that mean fighting at all?"

Pen spun back to the ceramic skeleton. "No, why would it? I only need a hand in bringing her back down to the workshop."

The boy snickered by the door. "Now who's changed, Anna?"

She stepped on his words with her reply. "This has always been here, Judgment. Under the surface." She squeezed the sign tighter. Her ceramic fingers scraped against the hollow pole as she did. "Maybe it's this place, but I feel like tussling against more wolves!"

A loud crack echoed from the bowels of the mill.

The boy smiled. Mrs. Bell moved back and forth, eager for adventure.

"Right," Pen said, cutting through the silence. "I'll get the barrow." She disappeared into a utility closet beneath the ascending stairs.

"Hurry up," said the figure through the door. It pressed itself against the wood to peer inside, some of its body wisping through the seams.

The boy gasped.

The figure continued, "You're still standing there when you should be halfway back by now, Judgment."

A cone of soft, rarely blinking blue light funneled through a split towards the top of the door. The boy stood on his toes against the wood to meet the light. The figure's pupil dilated when the boy stretched up into view.

"We're waiting for a barrow for Cameron," he said.

"Don't let bureaucracy hold you back, Judgment. I never do. Push!" The figure's eye moved left and right. "Where is Anna Bell? Tell her the same."

"I heard you," Mrs. Bell said, back by the pillar.

The boy shut his eyes and breathed out through his nose. "She's being weird. How's Ryan?"

The figure drifted to the side, letting the boy see Ryan sitting cross-legged. He took a handful of sand in one hand, then dropped it like an hourglass's into the other. The figure drifted back to the door.

"He's pouting," it said. "He's giving me the silent treatment."

It struck the boy as melancholia rather than pouting.

The figure shook its head. "Never mind Ryan Mont, Judgment. I have him." It pushed off from the door. "Just hurry up."

Pen reappeared from the stairway closet with a turn-of-the-century gardening wheelbarrow, the type with wood handles and an Oughtside style metal body. Its lone, rusted tire squeaked to a stop just in front of Cameron.

Pen coaxed the girl toward the barrow; Mrs. Bell did too. They promised her the completion of her body to get her moving. Progress was slow.

"I—" said Cameron. She kept saying it as she moved their way.

Ryan said something outside—a low warble of a something. The boy turned an ear to the door, a breeze tickling his bottom lobe.

"Unnatural," Ryan said, still playing with the sand.

"What is?" asked the figure, sitting next to him.

"All of this."

"But this is natural, Ryan Mont. This is the way of things. What's natural is unnatural?"

"It's not what I expected."

"None of you expect this to adhere to any of your absolute beliefs, do you? Honestly? A subsection of a species on some backwater planet in a backwater galaxy. What possesses you to think we can have any idea of anything? I cannot remember."

"We?" Ryan asked.

"Sorry," said the figure. "You."

It buried its bare fingers in the sand.

Cameron was half in the barrow by the time the boy pulled away from the door. Pen retrieved a shovel as rusted as the barrow's bin. She scooped the rest of the boy's sister inside while Mrs. Bell held the barrow still.

"Obstinate," Pen said. She put her arm up as if to rub sweat from her brow, then put it back down and looked around to make sure no one saw, though she had to have known both the boy and Mrs. Bell were staring right at her. "Everyone ready?"

"Are there damned things below?" the boy asked.

"Hey! We can handle it," Mrs. Bell said as she pulled her sign from her chest. It hitched on one of her unruly ribs.

"Some get in," Pen said, not concerned. "But we have our own damned security down there—young, too. A spry employee. Have a listen."

A cracking shot—clearer than before—rang up to them.

"Probably just cracked two wolves and a flock of birds of prey with that. He absolutely has it covered."

They moved to the top of the stairs that wound down. Pen gave them a quick layout of the bottom half of the mill. One floor below: *Firing.* Two floors: *Casting.* Three: *Workshop/Molding.* Four: *Basement.* Five: *Sub-Basement.* Six: *Sub-sub-basement.* She stopped there but assured the boy that at least twenty sub-basements existed and even a library below that. They only needed to get to *Molding.*

Mrs. Bell had her sign unsheathed and at the ready as they started their descent. The boy pulled his broken knife from his belt.

Pen didn't use the barrow like a barrow. That wouldn't be practical, considering all the stairs they'd be taking. Instead, she carried it by the handles over her shoulders like a backpack. Cameron didn't mind.

"You should get an elevator or pulley system installed," Mrs. Bell said.

Pen sighed. "Anna, we should get a lot of things installed."

"Not in the budget?" the boy asked as he led the way. There hadn't been much of a discussion about filing order, so it became him, Mrs. Bell, then Pen. Part of the railing snapped off when he touched it. It plummeted toward the outline of a stone floor marked by the shaking reflection of a fire. The boy forgot that he could die or something here. Die more than in the red, at least.

Pen went on for an hour about the lack of any budget at all. For as long as she'd been there, the workers ran the mill. Or the volunteers, rather—those who had wanted to get out of the wilderness and into some structure. Not every damned thing clamored for the Oughtside like the wolves, so they worked the mill.

The boy looked back over his shoulder at Pen, carrying his sister with ease. "Were you damned, then?"

"Of course," Pen said, "and oh did I deserve it. My adjudicator knew me much too well to decide anything else."

Mrs. Bell let Pen pass her on the stairs before continuing. "What did you do in life?"

Pen laughed. "I don't remember—isn't it great? I remember tearing some porcelain people apart in the woods to reassemble what I could of my body, sure, but before my adjudication? I've buried that so far down that I can't even begin to recall it." She tried to recall it right then and there to show them. "Well, there was a lot of blood, I think. An ax, too. But don't you worry about me! Now I'm just a worker."

A porcelain man met them on his way up, running bow-legged and tripping over his new feet. Waves of heat rose from his body and licked the boy's skin when he stood close. He didn't notice the group until he was seven stairs above them. Pen said some aloofness is to be expected.

"Wait!" he said, "I think the Oughtside is this way, porcelain friends!"

"We're not porcelain," the boy said.

"You're close enough! Come this way. Everything is perfect in the Oughtside. Holy mother is everything perfect!" He had the cheeriest smile cast on his portly face. He looked to be crafted with a permanent, positive outlook.

"Who told you that?" Mrs. Bell said.

Pen cut the man off before he could answer. "He told himself. We tell them of its existence, and they take it from there."

"And what if I said it wasn't perfection?" the boy said.

"He can't believe that," Pen said. "Not if he wants to get by the damned out there who have made themselves look like beasts to salvage his precious porcelain from his sad bones."

The porcelain man nodded right along with Pen, speaking when she finished. "Sure, sure, it'll drive me. Absolutely." He wore a painted-on fanny pack around his waist. "So, wait, what are you guys saying?"

"Nothing," Mrs. Bell said.

"Well, are you coming with me?"

Cameron slumped over the side of the barrow. Some of her dripped out over the edge. The boy and Mrs. Bell sheathed their weapons and lifted her back over. They tried to drip what clay they could back onto her head to fill in their handprints. They did their best.

Pen answered politely. "No. We have our friend here. She needs our help first. A mile up and you'll see a door to the woods. *Don't* leave it open."

The man took off in a hurry—in a near gallop, now. He called down a few minutes later. "Wait, do you know the exact way to the Oughtside?"

"No one does!" Pen called right back.

"You can't know that," said the man after a beat. "Someone must!"

○   ○   ○

Francis Brown and Malcolm Baum stood in a blazing pit on the firing floor. They were mere ceramic bone like Mrs. Bell now, but they seemed content enough. They weren't laughing or dancing as the boy imagined them to be as they toiled in retirement in some hell beneath the red. They sat down, back to back. The boy held up his right fist when he saw them, and both Pen and Mrs. Bell stopped. He wasn't sure if that would work.

"When did they show up?" he asked. "The two in the pit."

"Hours ago," Pen said. "Years? They clawed out of the ground as shadows while I was outside digging through street rubble. They begged us for fire instead of porcelain or the Oughtside, so we gave them fire. They've been a lot of help to Umbra down there." She nodded to a massive, burly shadow seated across the room.

They won't want to see me, the boy thought. But they had to cross the floor. The stairs only continued on the other side.

Umbra—with only a welder's mask of porcelain—sat in a chair next to a crank it kept spinning. The crank was attached to a pulley system, its line struggling and whining to pull something substantial up through the hole. In five minutes, a metal casting of a porcelain person rose up into the room.

Umbra kicked a latch into place on the crank, suspending the metal above the floor. It unhooked the casting and hurled it into the pit with Francis and Malcolm. Its landing shook the immediate area. The shadow returned to spinning the crank.

Fran and Malcolm went about sitting the cast up in the flames. Then, they danced like *Silly Symphony* skeletons, but their steps were lacking. It would be obvious to anyone with sight that they were only going through the motions with their dance. A part was missing—a part crushed under the rubble of a smoking yellow house.

"They really wouldn't want to see me," the boy whispered to Mrs. Bell and Pen.

"We see you right now, Biter," Malcolm said.

"You aren't hidden very well," Francis added. "None of you are."

Finishing their half-assed dance, Malcolm said, "I don't think any of you even tried."

Neither Mrs. Bell nor Pen knew they should be hiding. The boy stood and went the last few stairs down onto the firing floor.

Malcolm took his seat again. "We had no idea we could try and get back to the Oughtside."

"It's a futile endeavor," Pen said, walking by the boy over to the other stairs. "Not even the wolves have gotten through. It's not for the damned."

Mrs. Bell stood beside the boy. She greeted the two skeletons. "Francis. Malcolm."

"Anna Bell," Francis said. "Remember when we smashed your mailbox?"

"Anna Bell," Malcolm said. "Remember when we broke William's windows? What a dick he was, right?"

The two looked at their feet. "Lynn would say something similar here. How is she?"

The three skeletons in the room looked to boy. It was one of the stranger sights he'd seen since the Oughtside slipped in.

"Fine enough," he said. "She burned the house down with me inside."

Francis and Malcolm high fived and burst into laughter. "That's our girl!" Malcolm stood up and the two danced in the fire, only much more boisterously this time.

"It was pretty dramatic," he said. He watched them dance for a few minutes at the edge of the pit; he even started clapping to their beat until the Umbra threw another cast into the pit. He yelled, "Well, I'll see you both on the way back up!"

He had that letter for Francis from the temp agency. Mrs. Bell stared straight at its white edge peeking out from the boy's pocket. He caught her looking and shook his head.

He mouthed, "What would be the point?"

Francis and Malcolm waved him off. They pulled apart the first casting and a porcelain woman fell out of it. She writhed on the ground like an un-swaddled newborn. She made it to her elbows, then collapsed. Then she made it to her knees, steadying herself. The porcelain woman shuffled ahead until she felt confident enough to try with her arms again. When she did, she could crawl, through the flames blasting her in the face. She reached the curved, steep edge of the stone pit and scraped her hands against it, trying to climb out. Francis and Malcolm got under her and lifted her up by her feet.

"Thank you," she said. "Strangers." Her eyes didn't appear to work yet. "Where am I going?"

"To the Oughtside, Miss," Umbra said in a booming, pleasant voice.

"Is that paradise?" She could see now. She scraped her way to the bottom steps.

No one said.

"It must be, right?"

No one said.

"It can't be just this."

She made it to her feet.

"Which way?"

The group continued down.

"This way, I think. Right?" She started up, assured in her footing now but still taking glances at the boy, Mrs. Bell, Pen, everyone, waiting desperately for an answer.

O   O   O

The floor below—*Casting*—was a foundry. The boy couldn't stand the molten air for long; it scratched against his eyes until he shut them. Then, it clawed at his lids.

Mrs. Bell described what she was seeing for him. She guided him through the hissing place at ceramic skeleton speeds.

"It's beautiful if you like blue molten metal. I see no shadows. I think the casting is automated. My arm is on fire. It's out now."

"That's interesting," he said. He did hear the continuous whir of mechanisms other than Umbra's pulley system. "Why is the metal blue, Pen?"

Pen had to move through the bubbling place just as fast, otherwise Cameron would harden in the air, and she was more puddle than person-shaped now.

"I don't know. It just is. It's been that way since I've been around. And it's cerulean. Not blue."

Mrs. Bell kept describing. "A molded clay person is standing in the middle of the room, moving like our Cameron. He's curing in the air. A casting is ready for him."

"They get to decide?" the boy said.

"Looks like it," Mrs. Bell said. "He entered the cast. Closed it on himself. The pulley's hooked, and up he goes. It's a proud moment, I think."

Pen—slowing in the heat—said, "They always decide to be cast, Adjudicator. Your sister is either a fool or what she has to say to you is beyond urgent. You've seen what happens when they come out of the cast."

It would be about our parents, thought the boy. *It always is.*

"It'll be about his parents," Mrs. Bell said. "It always is."

They found the stairs.

The workshop was everything the name might suggest: a place where an old-world cobbler or artisan would feel at home. Or an old-world artisan shadow, like the one they found in this workshop. She had less porcelain on her than Umbra, and just a right eye. They met her pulling a new person's bones from the clay reservoir at the far side of her shop. She had a large bag on a stick to do so. She stood on a floor of deep gray-blue stone, the kind from which an old well would be built.

Ancient diagrams of people drawn on parchment—the human forms, clay forms, and porcelain forms—hung over every wall, in plain view of the crafts table covered in clay stains and tools.

"Penumbra," said the shadow in a gray voice. "Who's that?"

"It's Cameron, Antumbra," Pen said. "You didn't know she was gone?" She put the barrow down, pratfalling backward as she did. To the boy, she looked odd without it jutting out over her now cracked shoulders; she'd been wearing it for almost the whole time they'd known each other.

Antumbra took the paper from Cameron's half-melted head. "Right," she said. "Cameron. Guiltless, natural causes. Walked off like a dolt upstairs. And you let her out."

"I didn't let her out. I was upstairs and the door was left open."

"By you."

"By a porcelain person!"

They bickered for a few beats more, then—with blame firmly placed on Umbra—they agreed to put the matter to rest.

Antumbra and Pen dumped Cameron out onto the workbench. Ant went to work on the girl immediately with her chisels and hands. She formed her into a large, vaguely human ball. Peeling away clay at a rapid pace, she pressed it back into necessary places to compile the desired shape and size. She dug into the form and messed around with the bones. She shaped clay organs—vocal cords, too.

"Hold still," Antumbra said several times in a whisper. Cameron writhed.

Pen wandered around the table, picking up any stray living clay and handing it back to Antumbra.

The boy half expected a pottery wheel to be used. He did find one in a corner of the room, collecting dust.

Cameron—with a clear and obvious Cameron shape— took form in about thirty minutes or less. She sat on the table, curled in a ball, her knees to her face and arms around her legs. She stretched her arms out first, in front and to the side, then her legs by standing up. She cleared her throat of clay phlegm. Antumbra helped her down off the table.

The boy almost called for his sister's attention when another cracking shot from whatever security wandered in the basement levels reached up to them. When it hit his and Mrs. Bell's ears, they both took two steps back toward the stairs and readied their respective weapons. The sound was clear, now, without depth, a raging foundry or firing floor in between them and it. It was not a whip or a vague bang. That was a .42 caliber revolver last seen through a TV screen during the most dramatic moments of the long-running series *Husband and Wife*.

"I knew it," Mrs. Bell said. "I must have felt him or something." She started moving back and forth in place, her eyes on the descending stairs across the room.

"You did not," the boy said. "Pen, how long have you had your security?"

"We've always had security," Pen said. "Lots of it in the basements."

"There's a new guy," Ant said, looking over Cameron for flaws. She thumbed over a divot in one of the girl's legs.

"You—," Cameron said. "Judgment." She hopped down off the table. Antumbra let her.

The boy squared his attention on his sister. "Why would *you* call me that?"

"How new is this 'guy?'" Mrs. Bell said.

"Days, weeks, decades, maybe," Pen said. "It blends out here. He's going through his rounds now—he'll be up shortly, though. You can meet him."

"It's him," Mrs. Bell laughed. "I knew it, Judgment. Damn, I knew it. The victim is right here. The killers, too."

She half chuckled and half cried. The way she moved towards the stairs, she couldn't decide if she was going to run to meet him or wait for him up on the molding floor. She bent out over the edge of the stairway and cast her eyes down. The flash of another shot lit her face. He wasn't far now.

Mrs. Bell spoke again, down into the basement. "The murdered, Judgment! Live on in the minds of their killers. That connection—our connection. Bringing. Folks. Together."

He didn't respond.

Cameron met eyes with the boy and walked towards him. She had to force her words out, but they came out clear enough. "I want to say something."

The boy gripped his knife.

His sister continued. "I'm sorry about the dress."

It was about his parents.

On his mother, at her funeral, they put her in floral print when his mom had stopped wearing floral prints years before. The three siblings fought about it. Too throwback, the boy had said. Ray Jr. and Cameron disagreed. They wanted to see her wearing something they remembered from their childhood and old photos. He had fought against this particular brand. The argument soured an otherwise agreeable funeral.

Cameron had more to say. "But with all your bullshit, I don't really think you deserved a say at all, Judgment. I would choke you right now if my hands worked."

"I'm not Judgment to you, Cameron."

"I'm not so sure you've ever been anything else."

He and Cameron stood in silence. Cameron leaned into him, slumping against his chest. He caught her. By accident, he plunged his broken knife into her abdomen, but Cameron didn't mind. She moved and slathered against him, trying to lift her arms. The earth wafted off her into the boy's nose as she did. Cameron gave up.

"I'm hugging you," she said.

"I gathered," the boy said, anxious and squirming. "We don't hug. We're not that kind of family." He'd said that before, to an aunt at his father's funeral who wanted him and his siblings to comfort their mother. His older brother tried, and it was as awkward to watch as it must have been to experience for both people involved.

"We *didn't* hug," Cameron said. "We *do* now, before my casting. Before they layer over this clarity. Do you remember when Mom sat us all down the night after Dad died?"

He remembered, but just before that he remembered the last time he saw his dad conscious, as he often would before falling asleep. His father, cut down and placed in a bed, in a hospital ward by the broken vending machines. *He said something*, thought the boy. *But I don't need to hear it again. What did Mom say a week later, the night after Dad died?*

Cameron went on, melting around him. "She said 'We all have to take care of each other now.' Just like that. We should have listened. You should have listened most of all."

Mom sounded like she read the words from a bad script when she said it. On her left hand, she had the words scribbled in pen—some bullet points to hit that she found online. This whole thing was new for her. They all knew that. She'd handled deceased pets before—the boy's hamster being an especially trying experience—but not someone that slept inches from her for thousands of nights. Her own parents still lived. Her husband's mother lived, too, his father dead long before any of her children were old enough to care. Even some of the great relatives lingered. The boy and his brother had played grown man on the living room couch, their faces tight—stern—as they listened. Cameron sat in a chair across the room, picking at its armrest with her cracked nails. Antigone lay on the floor, playing with a pipe cleaner and making the noises of a joyous cat: garbled chirps and growls. The boy kind of wanted to turn on the TV.

That was the kind of family they were: dinners and discussions in front of the TV.

For their discussions—their fights—it eased the tension in the air for everyone to have a story to watch and somewhere else to look in between shouts. When their mother had caught Cameron with a boy in her room and the door locked, the news at 5 prattled on. When Mom found matches in Ray Jr.'s room, an edited-for-TV version of *Alien* played in the background. *Gunsmoke* repeats when the boy failed two classes in one quarter. *Twilight Zone* repeats after the boy took Ryan's Tamagotchi without telling him and Ryan cried to his parents about it. *Mysteries of the Manic* when the boy took twenty dollars from his dad's wallet without asking. *Poisson de Triumph*—a French fishing drama—when the boy bit someone at school again for some reason or another. He could remember many more.

Cameron looked like a mess again—a melted human lump crushed up against him. She had won the game of tag. He couldn't pull away without her.

"I should have listened?" he said, his voice trailing at the end. "I was too young. You and Ray Jr. were the ones that needed to listen better. You were older—more prepared. The adults."

"No," Cameron said. "You're not as young as you want to be. But if that's what you want to believe. If that's what helps you, Judgment."

They stood in their embrace.

Watching from the craft table, Ant readied her tools again. "All that work," she said. She adjusted her right eye like someone would a monocle. She drifted over and went to work separating them. She cut Cameron off the boy with an ancient putty knife, then scraped what clay she could from his shirt and pants. Some of her remained on him.

Ant guided Cameron back to the table. There, the shadow fixed her face, her torso, and worked her way down to the legs.

"I wonder where Ray Jr. is," Cameron said. She looked around the room. "He's our older brother," she said to Antumbra.

"I know," Antumbra said. "We know everyone that has and will ever exist."

Penumbra stood by the stairs with a pensive Mrs. Bell, looking down into the Mill. "He's fine, I'm sure. Just like you."

"Haven't come across him," Ant said, shaping and smoothing out Cameron's fingers. "Not yet, anyway."

"I'm not fine," Cameron said in the weakest way. Ant finished with her legs. She looked over to the elevator. Her eyes moved up its singed rope to the hole in the workshop ceiling. An orange-red glow peeked over its edges.

"Considering the state of Habre," the boy said. "You are."

Ant took a step back and admired, her one eye leering over the girl. "Some of my finest work. Anything else?"

"Nothing else for me." Cameron looked at the boy when she said it. "I'm ready."

He scowled back at his sister. "Nothing else."

O   O   O

One summer, back when the boy and his siblings were still kids. Back when he wore neon orange shorts and his hair hadn't fully turned from blond to brown, a hot air balloon running low on fuel had to land in the middle of Habre. It was the kind of thing people in the circle talked about for years after it happened—the kind of thing jealous people in the next circle and the third circle hated hearing about because it hadn't happened outside *their* front doors. This was an event—*the* event of the neighborhood. The boy, Ray Jr., and Cameron—Ryan and the neighborhood kids too—only remembered it through faded pictures and a neighborhood legend that quieted with each family that moved away.

Some Wednesday before the Oughtside, the boy had found a Kodak of the day in his mother's closet. Taken at the street outlet of Habre by the boy's dad—a poor photographer any other day—it caught everyone among the vast neighborhood crowd that had poured from their houses. The half-deflated balloon, yellow with red swirls, loomed down in the middle of the circle. The Monts gathered around in their earthy summer attire to watch. The neighborhood kids, on their bikes, clustered right up close to the balloon's burners, the pilot blocking their eager way. Davies Tuch stood by his mailbox, one arm in a sling and a beer in his hand. Mrs. Bell and William—in their mid-20s and new to Habre—nuzzled each other in the middle of the street. Young trees and houses stood in the background. The boy's mom stood in the foreground. As his father would tell it, he was just trying to take a nice picture of her with the balloon over her shoulder. Not the whole of the crowd.

A dog stood in the street. Not Missile, but a taller dog— the tallest dog the boy had ever seen. Over three feet when standing on all fours, at least. The thinnest, too, but the dog looked like a greyhound so that was okay. Now that he thought about it, it may have just been a tall greyhound, but he still called it Falcor. Cameron stood next to it in the picture, petting its back. Ray Jr. knelt in front of it, patting it on the head as he looked at the balloon. The boy lay on the ground next to them, looking straight toward the camera.

On the Friday before the Oughtside, the boy found the picture in an old album under his parents' bed. He brought the Kodak downstairs to his siblings, both in their work clothes and asleep on separate couches, the glowing television's lullaby kissing their faces.

Cameron woke up first to his presence, then Ray Jr. Their mother used to fall asleep on the couch, most nights after her husband died. The siblings thought they'd try it out.

"What is it?" Ray Jr. said, his haggard voice full of sleep. He smoked like his father did. He smelled like Ray Sr. too.

"Look how big this dog was," the boy said. He handed Ray Jr. the picture with the rounded edges.

"Huge," Ray said. "Damn." He handed it to Cameron.

"Huge," Cameron said as she rubbed the sleep from her eyes.

"Whose was it?" the boy asked. Neither of them would know.

"I don't know," they both said.

Leaning back into the couch, Cameron shut her eyes, then opened them to speak. "Probably one of the neighbors. One of the ones that left. I never saw the thing again, did you?"

Both brothers shook their heads. Maybe it was another one of those pieces of knowledge that had died with their dad and then their mom. Like the combination to the old lockbox under their bed, which they had to pry open to get their birth certificates. Or their tax history. Or how to unclog the ice maker, the clogging of which was a rare enough occurrence that it never became an issue between their dad's passing and their mom's. Or their wants, desires, dreams, and such—philosophies to be shared with other adults, not just their children.

But the siblings laughed about the dog and that had been enough. The boy kept it in his pocket from then on and brought it up to his sister and brother several times in the week leading up to the Oughtside.

"You remember how big that dog was?" he'd say like it was their secret—one eyebrow arched. It got old quickly for Ray and Cameron, but it amused the boy enough to still amuse them. A sort of pity or sympathetic amusement, he figured.

He said it again to Cameron before she was cast. He said it after she entered the elevator and before Ant shut it like a sarcophagus and hollered up to Umbra that the process was beginning.

"You see how big this dog was?" the boy said with one eyebrow arched.

He had no idea where the five by seven photo was now. It might have been in his wallet in his previous pair of pants—the ones caked with dust and blood and burn marks. So he pulled the letter he had found in the Brown's mailbox from his pocket and mimed the motions he would make with the photo.

Cameron's eyes softened, her lips curling in an uneasy smile. She was frightened of the process. That was obvious. "That was a tall dog."

And up she went.

He watched until she reached the ceiling, then turned away.

WILLIAM

Mrs. Bell stood ready to ambush William, her fingers thrumming the pole of her weapon. At the end of the pole, a sign reading HABRE CIR.—in bold white letters on an aluminum rectangle—bobbed with her anticipation. Pen stood beside her, her elbows on the railing, watching for the husband.

"What are you going to do?" the boy said, joining them.

"Jump him," Mrs. Bell flared. "Knock him down the stairs. Something."

"You people make things so lively," Penumbra said. She rested her chin on her hands, her elbows on the wood railing. *She's just a child*, the boy thought. He hadn't seen it until now, watching the way she leaned on the railing and mused. She carried herself as older.

"I am a person," Mrs. Bell said. "Thank you, Penumbra."

A shadow moved up the staircase in the scarce, wandering light. William's body had changed. That was clear from his shape. He fired at something behind him with his revolver, then stopped for a moment to make sure whatever it was wasn't anymore. He continued, with a pleasing chuckle.

"I can't wait to see his face," Mrs. Bell said. Lower and sinister, she said, "I can't wait for him to see mine."

The boy spoke. "He has a gun. You have a sign." He put his hand on her arm bone, interlocking his fingers around it—through it. "We should go."

Mrs. Bell shook him off without looking away from William. "Get off, Judgment. You go. I have that ceramic skeleton strength. You think he doesn't deserve what I'm bringing. I bet you sympathize."

"Of course he deserves it," he said. The air bothered his wet eyes. "But he has a gun. Don't go toward a man with a gun who has shot you before."

"He can't hurt me." Mrs. Bell clacked her teeth together, the raw movements of her jawbones visible.

Penumbra turned from the railing and looked at the boy and Anna Bell. "Could you hurt him? Security is tough. That's probably why we made him security."

"He's weak. Fuck him, he's weak. I've got the strength of character."

She wouldn't move. The boy tried to pull her by the ribs this time. She pushed him to the ground and threatened him with HABRE CIR., still watching for William below. She told him to stop—to not try that again. When he did, Mrs. Bell struck him across the chest with the sign. The aluminum rectangle slashed his shirt and skin open. The small wound bled, but he would keep trying. Mrs. Bell called out:

"William!" she said.

The boy stopped, his heart trembling.

Seconds passed.

Mrs. Bell said it again. "William Bell."

Then, came a voice from below them. It didn't sound much like William'anymore. To Mrs. Bell, though, it must have sounded as much like William's as it did on the day she died.

"Anna?" William said. His shape moved up the stairs. He came into the soft blue light. He was largely porcelain now but other than his face none of the pieces were his. Like the wolves outside the mill, it looked like he had collected porcelain from a dozen others to construct himself. Shadow bubbled through the cracks between his haphazard body like the glue on a toddler's macaroni project. In his right arm, he held his revolver. It too was covered in porcelain and black wisps. Save for its muzzle, it looked as attached to him as the rest of his body.

William continued until he stood at an angled seven or so feet from Mrs. Bell, who had adjusted her grip on her sign to one fit for a spear. Habre Cir almost closed the distance between her and William.

The boy stayed down. William hadn't spotted him.

"Anna," the damned husband said, an excited porcelain smile on his face that hadn't been there since his wedding day. He chuckled, "I don't know what to say."

"There isn't much to say." Mrs. Bell nodded.

"This is wild, huh? This death." He blew out his shiny nostrils. "So how have you been?"

"Not just death for you, Bill," Mrs. Bell spat. "Damnation."

"Rub that in." He scratched at the back of his head. Some porcelain fell off and tumbled down the stairs, but he didn't mind.

"You look worse for wear," Mrs. Bell offered.

William looked at his revolver hand and agreed. "I did my best, in the wilderness with the other damned things. Broke the people clamoring for that place, took their shells for my own. Broke the wolves, too, and took their shells for my own. But you know me well, Anna, I need to work and earn. I'm no rogue fit for the wilderness."

The boy also knew William well. His memories dangled there among his thoughts and William was no freelancer—no rogue. You need to be part of a hierarchy to usurp it is what he would have said.

Penumbra threw a line in. "Sometimes we have extra porcelain for the damned volunteers. Not a bad perk. Keeps them sane and dedicated." No one acknowledged that she had said anything. She huffed and started tapping her fingers on the wood rail.

Mrs. Bell inched a step closer to William. She was tense, he was calm.

"I can't believe you killed me," she said.

"Nah?" William said. "I felt like that was the natural conclusion to our marriage. It's this epilogue that I didn't expect." He took two steps closer to Anna. "All the violence had to lead somewhere. Either my death or yours. To be honest, it's almost as much your fault as it is mine." He shrugged.

That stunned Mrs. Bell—the shrug, especially. She spoke in a plain tone. "You *really* just said that, William. Amazing."

He shrugged again. "The whole experience is meaningless. If there's another life—and we're standing in it right now— does it matter who killed who and why? Umbra, Antumbra, Penumbra could have been a trio of Nazis for all you know, and I don't see you pointing signs at them. If the top of our afterlife food chain can be the judging whim of some shit kid, then truly nothing before or after matters. You're holding on to something you don't need anymore."

"We weren't Nazis," said Pen, cross with her employee. "I know that much."

Mrs. Bell stood poised to strike William down, her skeleton feet planted firmly on the floor, wide enough apart for a powerful leap.

The boy didn't appreciate being called, 'some shit,' but he stayed down.

William had more. "That's who I would go after, Anna: Judgment. If the Oughtside wasn't so unreachable for us damned things, I'd tear his title from his bones." He raised his revolver and pointed it at her, then let his arm drop back to his side. He twisted his free hand out and shook his head.

The boy started crawling across the clay crusted floor toward Ant and her craft table. She had already plucked another person out of the muck to rebuild.

"Forget Judgment." Mrs. Bell gritted her teeth. Offended. Beyond offended. "You killed me, William. I've been stuck with your thoughts—in your thoughts."

"It doesn't matter, hon."

"Nothing matters more."

Mrs. Bell jabbed William with the sign, knocking him down three steps, loose porcelain crumbs falling off his body after each impact. He regained his footing. She antagonized him with further jabs—stripping him of more porcelain with every strike—but William didn't move against her.

"Get your pound of porcelain, Anna," he said. "Then let me get back to work."

Penumbra watched the scene with some glee. "Take a break if you want."

Anna pinned her physical jabs with verbal ones. "You would kill Judgment because he damned you—because you were punished. You're not above this."

"I would kill him for his title. Knowing what I know now, I should have done that in life to get up the chain. Further my career. I cringe at how dumb I was."

She said something about his father that used to cut deep, but he let it roll right off his new exterior.

They continued like this for a couple minutes. The boy reached the steps back up to the casting floor. He lingered there, trying to stay out of sight.

Mrs. Bell's voice and speed grew with her frustration. "You owe me this, William. After every goddamn thing, you owe me."

"I owe you a fight?" She had his interest. With his left hand, he snatched the end of HABRE CIR before it was pushed against him again.

"A rematch, sure," Mrs. Bell said, struggling with him for her weapon back. "I'll have you be the one bleeding out on the rug this time."

Mr. Bell enjoyed challenges. The Bells enjoyed challenges.

They grinned at each other as they had on their wedding night, only in a more skeletal and porcelain way. William agreed. He released HABRE CIR and pointed his revolver at Mrs. Bell, who gripped her weapon tight and surveyed her immediate environment with that ceramic skeleton range of vision.

And they clashed.

The boy was with Mrs. Bell when he wasn't. Halfway up the stairs to the casting floor, he felt her beside him. He smiled—pleased that she listened to his reason—then turned to find no one. *The murdered live on in the minds of their killers,* he thought—he reminded himself. *Side effects of the Oughtside and all that.* He could see through her eyes if he wanted. If he focused. No, not through her eyes, exactly, more like a picture in his head—a faint line drawing formed from her running thoughts.

One bullet grazed Anna's right shoulder blade and another one her left leg by the time she landed her first true blow on William. He could fire two bullets for each second and never had to reload. The bullets cut black through the air—they were composed of shadow. His shadow. He had the advantage.

One of Anna's swings met William's neck, shattering it. Space was tight on the stairs, with little room to maneuver around each other or dodge, but Anna managed this blow. She hoped it would knock him off the side of the staircase and down into the basements, where she imagined there was more room to have it out. Less distraction, less chance of interruption. Less of the boy in her head running away. William, however, had very sure feet—surer feet than he had in life. He danced on the edge of the wooden step when he took the hit like a tight rope walker, pivoting with one foot and finishing it with the other. He faced Anna again when he was done, his gun right in her stomach.

Still in the recovery phase of her attack, Anna had to swing HABRE CIR up before she was even sure of where her momentum would take her. She knocked his hand away, and then tried, but failed, to grab him before she tumbled down a handful of stairs. They stood in each other's starting positions now.

"You always lost, Anna," William said, in a sympathetic tone. His eyes narrowed. He fired and took out one of her ribs. "But you always escalated things to this point." He fired again. It whizzed through where her spleen would have been.

Anna rushed him. She had those ceramic skeletal voids in her body. Few of William's cracking blasts found their targets, but Anna found hers. William blocked the first furious swing, backing up the stairs. The second one hit him across the chest. The third he blocked with his revolver hand; he fired it by her faux skin ear. He took the fourth to his chin, which didn't shatter. He always had a strong chin. The fifth swing was a thrust to his stomach. It landed. William fell backward, taking him and Anna the rest of the way up to the workshop and putting him on his back.

Anna did that thing from the movies and stepped on his gun hand. It actually worked well.

Penumbra, said, still watching. "Welcome back. That was amazing."

Antumbra shook her head, less enthused. She sent up another new casting to Umbra, told William he was fired, and then went back to work.

"You lost me my job!" William said, in a playful way. His eyes gleamed as they had on their honeymoon. He always had nice eyes—the porcelain version of them only enhanced their diamond sheen.

"I'll do more," Mrs. Bell said. She put Habre Cir to his throat.

"What are you going to do," he said, not quite as a question.

"Beat you, strip you of your porcelain."

"Then I'll be all shadow. What next?"

"I'll do it again until you're like me. Tear through your dark mass until you're ceramic bone."

Penumbra knocked on the railing. "Doesn't work like that." She leaned on the rail like a bored summer child. "He's too young—the 'molasses' is too thick."

It did kind of look like black molasses, but Mrs. Bell gave Penumbra a quick, foul look. She knew it was too thick; she sat in William's viewing room for a great amount of time—awfully bored—testing that very thickness of her own shadow before it drifted from her bones.

"So I'll wait right here," Mrs. Bell said. "And then do it again. We have time."

"It'll be just like we're married again." William winked. "How long could you stomach that for?"

"An eternity for that reward." She raised HABRE CIR. She aimed it at his porcelain face.

William turned his head left and right, craned his neck up. "There was someone else here before."

"Just a clay girl," Mrs. Bell said when she should have said nothing. She slammed her weapon down on her husband's skull. Strong material. It only cracked down the middle.

"I know clay and shadow and porcelain voices," William said. "I know the Umbras' voices. Yours. There was someone else. Someone with a velvet and perfect kind of voice I used to hear trickling from my own throat." He shut his eyes. "Human."

William could work backward like that. He used to watch detective shows after work. On nights when he was feeling vulnerable, he would tell Anna that the 1940s—the hardboiled 40s present in Dashiell Hammett and Raymond Chandler novels—was where he belonged as a P.I. or an assistant to one. No, definitely as a private investigator. The main character. The Marlowe.

William squirmed underneath his wife. "Judgment." He moved his head side to side. He fired his revolver two dozen times. He flailed like a fish.

"No," Mrs. Bell said. "This is you and I, William." She hit him again. Her weapon only glanced his skull, scarring his forehead. "You owe me, William."

"You brought him here, Anna. You would have been a terrible mother." He laughed. "Or you were both drawn here, huh? To me. My imposing influence, everlasting even in death." He loved this.

Penumbra and Antumbra just watched.

Mrs. Bell stabbed down again. She shattered half of William's face this time, the HABRE CIR sticking into the molasses underneath, and William took advantage. He whipped his head to the left with enough force to shift Anna's weight so he could free his non-revolver hand. From there, it was only a matter of keeping the momentum up with bullets crossing the room in chaos. In a beat, Mrs. Bell was on the ground with HABRE CIR through her chest cavity, Penumbra had been shot and was bitter about it, and William climbed the ascending stairs towards Judgment.

Bolting up, Mrs. Bell followed, cursing her husband.

О   О   О

The boy picked up his pace. He wanted to stop at the casting floor, to have a moment and watch Cameron's choice to be cast, then follow her up to Umbra and the neighborhood kids. *Like a car wash*, he thought. It was the least he could do for his sister.

But he could hear that William was coming—feel him up his spine—so he just ran. He made it through the molten casting floor on his own, and halfway up to the firing floor before Mrs. Bell's husband reached him, shoved him from behind, splitting the boy's forehead on the next step.

"Judgment," he said.

He could have shot me already, the boy mused. *From behind, when I wasn't looking.*

"I really should have shot you already." He was new to this. "I have a speech, though. All good men have speeches, don't they?"

Mrs. Bell arrived, in a flit of skeletal grace, and shoved William off the side of the steps and down into the casting pit filled with that sheer blue lava. None of it stuck to his molasses skin.

She helped the boy to his feet and urged him up the steps, his head bleeding over his brow and into his eyes.

"Do we run from the man with the gun *now*, Mrs. Bell?" he asked.

"For the moment," Mrs. Bell sighed. "Regrouping is what they call it." She picked him up and put him on her shoulders. He put his feet through her back like he was riding a shopping cart, using HABRE CIR as the handle.

On their way through the firing floor, they told Umbra and the neighborhood kids who it was that was coming after them. None of them cared, they had other important jobs to do. The boy and Mrs. Bell told every passing porcelain person the same and only received the standard question regarding the Oughtside in return. One of them might have been Cameron. The boy wasn't sure. He was woozy, his vision blurred, and all of the porcelain people looked and walked the same driven way.

"I'm sure Ryan and the figure will care," he said. "Don't worry, Anna. They'll help."

"I don't need help," Mrs. Bell said. "I need William to get over you."

William caught up with them just below the ground floor. He sprayed the level—the stairs, the beams, the front door— with shadow bullets. The front door had been left open. Mrs. Bell hurled the boy out of it. Outside, the figure caught him by the leg with one arm. The ceramic skeleton then shut the door, herself inside. She barred it, too.

"Anna Bell?" the figure asked.

Ryan Mont, who had hidden behind the figure, stared at the boy's crimson and slick skull. "You dying?"

"Just concussed." He slurred his words. "You could apply some pressure."

Ryan did. "Bet you want that red right now."

"Need," he said.

"I've been thinking that's how they keep people from leaving during judgment," Ryan said in a tapered way. "Immortality. It does feel good."

The mill's door exploded outward from Mrs. Bell having been kicked against it by William. The figure turned and shielded the boys, one more than the other. Mrs. Bell landed on one of her arms, separating it from her body with a brief snap in the breezy air.

William stepped out onto the beach. He fired at the boy. Again, the figure turned to protect him, the bullets scattering into gray dust as they hit its body.

"William Bell!" the figure said. It pushed the boy behind Ryan. When Ryan moved behind the boy—a better starting position to run away, no doubt—the figure lifted Ryan up and put him back in front.

"William Bell!" it said again, with an arc to its bored words. "Go back inside. You are a damned thing now. Work in the mill, earn some porcelain like a decent damned thing."

The husband talked to the boy alone. "I begged you, Judgment," he said. "I can't believe I begged you like that, on the floor of my own home. Worse, you turned me down. I never beg, and you turn me down."

The boy hid cross-legged on the sand behind his two mostly willing shields. He had regained his normal vision, though his head still pounded. "It *was* pretty embarrassing," he said.

"I wish I had seen it," Mrs. Bell said, one-armed now but standing with Habre Cir over her good shoulder, ready to scrap.

The husband winced, pointing his revolver at all of them except Ryan, in a rotation. "It would have been about my career and my marriage, Anna. If you had just held on—stuck it out, had the kid, been the dream. I would have been made a partner in months. We'd have been in a Victorian within a year."

Anna Bell nodded, her skeletal eyebrows up, wrinkling the dwindling skin on her forehead. "Wow, Bill, you're so over life. You're not holding onto anything, 'needless,' at all."

William chuckled. He picked at his teeth as he used to when he was nervous. "Fuck, you're right. That just came out of me." He sighed—a rough one that ended in an oblong sound. "Then I'll cut it out: you and Judgment. I'll cut the rot of Habre Circle from my spine."

"Tell yourself what you need to, Bill. Like always," Mrs. Bell said.

William fired in a wide arc—six shots a second. The boy counted. He felt drowsy, his eyelids heavy with more than blood. Fatigue had set in.

The figure seized William. It took William's empty hand from the side and broke it, tearing the molasses from it like a sleeve, leaving a thin and crumbling ceramic skeletal arm behind. William howled in pain.

The figure whipped around to the other side of William, preparing to savage the man's gun arm as well. It must have forgotten about its recent altercation with the damned wolf, for it held onto William's gun with its bare skeletal hand. When William squeezed a round off, the bullet blew the figure's hand apart—bone fragments everywhere. The figure stopped, though it still held William well in place with its one unbroken hand. Its eyes widened, the blue almost parting horizontally in the middle, revealing two distinct and wet pupils.

"Well, that's gone," the figure said with fear and panic in its throat. "I don't have another hand. The clay won't stick, Judgment! The clay won't stick."

William stepped out of the figure's hold. That's all he had to do—step out and a little to the side. Mrs. Bell took over. She threw HABRE CIR at William like a javelin, which he avoided, then straight on tackled him this time. They tussled on the beach like roughhousing kids. When they rolled to the very edge of the clay lake, Mrs. Bell got on top and held William's head under the liquid clay's surface. He struggled.

"I can't drown!" William said during intervals when he could speak. "You're doing nothing." He laughed globs of clay from his porcelain lungs.

Mrs. Bell had mischief on her lips as she continued to drown him for a few seconds more. At some point, the act satisfied her. She stood, and before William could recover, lifted him with her ceramic skeleton strength and overhanded him out into the middle of the lake. The hovering moon's reflection rippled away when he landed with a heavy swallowing sound. It soon lay still again. William didn't surface.

Anna Bell raised her arm in triumph before turning from the lake and giving a thumbs up to the figure. "That was amazing. I lost an arm, you lost a hand, but I'm proud."

"Your arm is right here," said the figure. "My hand is—" Its hand was everywhere, some of its pieces indistinguishable from the sand grains. The figure picked a few of its fingers up and was even able to reattach some of them, creating a vague, rough shape of a shattered hand that it could flex and move carefully. It sighed in actual relief.

The boy put his head in his dirty hands and shut his eyes. He massaged his temples. "Really solid teamwork," he said. "All around." He'd stopped bleeding.

"Judgment," Mrs. Bell said.

"Okay, mostly you, Anna."

"Judgment," the figure said. "Ryan Mont."

The boy looked up and then back down at his lap.

Ryan Mont had slumped over, two holes in his chest. Two gaping holes around the heart, steaming in the cool air. The boy had fresher blood on him than his own. It cooled his skin as it dried. The knees of his pants were saturated in the red of Ryan's pungent blood.

"Ryan," he said.

"I'm here—" Ryan gasped, but he didn't have much motor function. He twitched. "Death is all improvisation today. Still hurts, though."

"Ryan Mont," the figure said, hiding its damaged hand behind its back like no one had seen it explode. It moved closer to the boys. "You now have three options."

Mrs. Bell picked her arm up off the beach. She dusted it off by shaking it wildly. She retrieved HABRE CIR next, then joined the group crowding Ryan. A new porcelain person fell out of the mill's broken door. It played in the sand. The boy checked; it wasn't Cameron.

The figure continued. "We can throw you in the lake—put you in the queue for porcelain. You can stay on this beach like you are now, red holes in your body. Or, Ryan Mont—my preference." The figure stopped on an unresolved note.

Ryan choked out some words. "I won't die." *His lungs must be filling*, thought the boy.

"Absence of movement, inability to speak, pain, brain function diminished. But you won't die—not here, where you are between life and after. Maybe you could still guide some porcelain people." The figure encouraged the porcelain person over with the mention of the Oughtside. The person had built half of a rather sturdy and ornate sandcastle but demolished it to make his way over.

"Do you know the way to the Oughtside?" the porcelain person said.

The figure shook its head and gestured to Ryan. "We don't, but he does."

The porcelain person knelt in the sand next to the bleeding boy. "Do you? Please tell me."

Ryan's face twitched—it trembled, red pouring from his lips. His head drifted down. "That," he said. "Way."

"Which?" the figure said.

"Yes, which?" the porcelain person followed. "I need direction, please."

Ryan tried to move his arm—to point it in the right direction. He flopped over.

Mrs. Bell stared out into the clay water.

The porcelain person sat back. He pleaded with Ryan one more time, then gave up. Right where he sat, he started another sandcastle.

"Just come back, Ry," the boy said.

"Neither of us should, Judgment," Ryan said. His pronunciation was off and his words were elongating. "Even if this is natural."

"I have to."

The figure nodded.

"You want to," Ryan said.

The boy nodded. "Wouldn't you?"

"Corrupted." Ryan bore his red teeth.

"What?" The boy narrowed his eyes. He frowned.

"I think you're corrupted," Ryan said in a matter-of-fact way. "Do you remember my sister?"

"Sort of," the boy said. He would see her from his window most days.

"She was too. She let someone ill inside her for a while—it affected her head. Our very special episode. No laugh track, even." His crass words curled his lips into a slight snarl. Foggier, now. "From a pillbox or shadow lips—doesn't matter—"

"I'm not your teenage sister taking pills," the boy interrupted. "I know what I'm doing." He paused to decide if he should make the next claim. "If you come back, I'll prove it to you."

Ryan wheezed out an answer after half a minute. He shut one eye, the left. The other was stuck. "Well all roads lead to the Oughtside anyway."

The porcelain person jolted up to his feet, kicking another of his sandcastles to the ground. "All roads?" He grew excited as he grasped at something in his porcelain mind. "What a wisdom." Then he took off into the trees, entering them at a path far from the one the boy and company had taken from the Oughtside to the beach. He yelled a deified thanks to Ryan Mont. The damned wolves, those porcelain mosaics, rustled in the bushes beside him.

Mrs. Bell looked away from the clay water to say, "That was *my* wisdom, Ryan. From earlier."

"I didn't want credit," Ryan said. He grew colder on the boy's lap. Then warmer, then colder. His living fluctuated and would continue to do so out here. Mrs. Bell didn't seem to mind Ryan getting credit, her remark hitting as a thought she felt like vocalizing. She hadn't spoken in a while.

"That settles it," the figure said. "This wilderness is settled. Ryan Mont, we go back to the Oughtside." It drifted over and scooped Ryan into its arms, cradling him.

"I never had a choice, did I?" Ryan asked.

"No," Mrs. Bell said, a breeze whipping the strands of straw hairs on the side of her skull around. "That was cruel, figure. Pretending that he did."

The figure adjusted so that its shattered skeletal hand was still well-hidden, now mostly just a forearm, under Ryan's back. "Well, cruelty is necessary for these judged and laypeople, Anna Bell." It spoke like it was getting tired of her—and like it just wanted to go home. "Illusion, too. He came to his own conclusion to return to the Oughtside by way of cruelty and illusion. Much less of a chance for him to run off again now, don't you think?"

Anna Bell agreed but didn't want to. The boy could tell.

"Had you learned from me," the figure said, "maybe you would have gotten what you wanted from William Bell."

"I'm not sure what I even wanted." She paused. "But I don't want to be like you, figure."

"Maybe I'll be saying the same when I'm nothing but living bones like you."

Mrs. Bell held up her hand to the figure. "Your bones look so much like mine. Why are you so worried about it? I'm fine. Look at me."

"Yes, look at you," the figure said. It set off first, towards the forest. The boy followed it but stopped after a few steps once he realized Mrs. Bell wasn't moving.

"Are you coming?" he said.

"I shouldn't, Judgment," Mrs. Bell said. She was focused on the clay water. Like a predator, she latched onto every movement or ripple in the lake with her eyes. "He's in there."

"But you will, right?" he asked. "For me?"

It *was* a question of influence. The figure and Mrs. Bell. He felt better with both of them around.

"I'm afraid I'll be too preoccupied for you, Judgment. I have my own shit—William's in my thoughts and bones. And I am all thoughts and bones." She turned to the boy. "I'm not sure."

He mimicked her and crossed his arms. "Do you still think I'm like William?" he asked.

She'd forgotten she previously voiced that opinion of the boy. "Yes. I'm sorry."

"Then I have something to prove to you too, Anna." He smiled—he pushed it to look more genuine.

"You pushed that to look more genuine, Judgment."

"I pushed it from genuine to genuine plus," he said, taking it back down to what he called genuine.

Anna smirked. *She's in*, the boy thought. He knew how to read her smile.

"Let's see, then," Mrs. Bell said. William also knew how to read a smile.

She tapped him on the nose, like her mother used to tap hers—gently, but with the knuckles, her hand in a sort of faux fist. The boy's dad used to show him how to fight with a tap like that.

"Break the nose," he'd say, a lit cigarette dangling from his dried lips. "Like this."

The boy would then do a flashy uppercut and shout something. His dad would shake his head and tell him that flash and pomp takes too long.

"Just break the nose and go from there. They'll be staggered—improvise after."

Mrs. Bell wiggled her fingers and looked at them. "I don't know why I did that, Judgment."

"It's okay," he said, turning toward the forest.

Anna Bell noted bubbles out in the clay lake and told herself they weren't William's.

RETURN

The wilderness had fallen quiet. No wolves waylaid the group this time. The figure knew their path well. Tree trunks looked familiar to the boy within five minutes. The grass looked familiar within thirty. The group arrived at the remains of their tussle with the wolves earlier within forty-five. Footprints, porcelain dust, and shards of the boy's lost knife were scattered about. Everything was tired. Outside the Oughtside was tired. Old hat. The boy was ready to get back into the red—to continue with the main thrust of his story and responsibilities.

"If you happen to see a piece of my shadow body on the ground," the figure said. "Please grab it."

Mrs. Bell and the boy did a quick survey of the grass at their feet. They shrugged at each other.

"Wishful thinking," the figure said.

It dropped Ryan onto the ground. He made no sound. He was limp like a corpse, but his eyes flicked open. He licked his lips and winced.

"I need some lip balm when we get back," he said.

"The Oughtside's red moisturizes," the boy said, rubbing his hands together.

"Does it?" Ryan said.

"I feel dryer than I did before too. It must." The boy scratched at the right side of his chest, the skin over his ribs flaking. He could feel it. "Does it, figure?"

"I don't have skin," the figure said. It inspected the air in front of it. It ran its fingers across nothing and the nothing folded a bit—it moved like a curtain. He separated the nothing and a brief spike of red light shot out and through the woods. A porcelain wolf howled from a distance away.

"That sounded angry," Mrs. Bell said. She had her weapon, but not at the ready.

"We lied to the porcelain people," the boy said. "You knew the exact way."

"We lied to the damned *and* the saved to protect ourselves," the figure said. It bent over Ryan and lifted him with its one good arm, drops of blood falling from the holes in Ryan's chest. He smelled like meat. The figure went on. "We all know that the wolves will tear the porcelain from those peoples' shadows and take it—bastardize it—as their own. They all want the Oughtside. If I tell the porcelain people where it might be, the wolves would carve them for the answer and the porcelain would give it. Of course they would."

It paused. A lengthy pause. Then it shut its eyes and flexed its shadowy fingers on its good hand.

"They all want the Oughtside, but that changes as soon as you start taking their porcelain from them. Porcelain shells—those facsimiles of humanity—trump sanctuary and they'll confess the location, which means chaos. Which means paperwork."

"My dad," Ryan said. His head was half-covered by the dark of a tree from the boy's view. "He'll be torn apart, won't he? His porcelain, taken?"

"Paul is not your responsibility, Ryan," the boy said. Mrs. Bell agreed, then looked back down the path from which they'd come.

Ryan coughed, spitting on the grass. "Don't call him Paul."

The boy called Mr. Mont Paul again, then said, "I'm old enough to call him Paul." He thought for a beat. "We're all dead-ish enough to call him whatever we want."

"You're wrong. We're alive," Mrs. Bell said, not facing him. The wind carried her voice toward the group. "Don't say we're dead."

"It's a limbo, at least," the boy said.

The figure turned to the boy. "I like that. A limbo."

"You like things?" the boy grinned. "Besides Judgment, of course."

"Did you say 'Judgment,'" the figure said, "or 'judgment?'" It didn't give him a chance to answer. "Truth is, I'm not that fond of either."

The boy laughed.

The figure pulled the opening in the nothing aside with its good hand. Reality made its rounds from the ocean to crags, to a desert, and to the Oughtside. All their faces widened at the crimson light. Then, the figure hurled Ryan through the opening.

"Anna Bell," it said. "You can stay if you'd like. William will recover, I can tell you that."

"She isn't staying," the boy said.

"I'm not. No," Mrs. Bell said. "Judgment has something to prove." She tore herself from the direction of the mill and placed her hand on top of the boy's skull as she passed him. Reality rounded back to the red again and she stepped through, timing it well.

The boy was next. He fixed his hair and adjusted his pants. The figure beckoned him closer.

"I'll time it right the first time—this time," he said. "I don't want your help." He stepped up to the curtain and the figure stepped aside.

He watched reality behind the curtain round back to red. He didn't step through. He watched it round to a desert. In the sand—just ahead of him—he saw a porcelain man walking towards him. Reality rounded. The man stood inches from the boy's face the next time the desert showed, looking at him through the break in the curtain. They talked over several more rounds.

"Is that the Oughtside?" the man said. He had horn-rimmed glasses sculpted onto his face and half his porcelain had been stripped from him. Even some of his shadow had been torn from his torso, revealing ceramic rib bones. He was each stage at once. "It's not as glorious as I expected."

"No," the boy said. "That's a different one—it might be red?"

"Is that a question? I saw them all. None of them looked that glorious, to be honest."

Animated cacti roamed the sun-scorched view behind the man. They were porcelain, too. Their shells were like the wolves', from what the boy could tell. The sky had white stars, visible in the day.

"I'll step through one soon enough. Once I muster the courage." The man touched his ribs. "I was so certain of the Oughtside an hour ago." He spoke slowly now.

"I'm sorry," the boy said. A cactus in the distance stopped roaming and crept closer to the man.

"Judgment," the figure said, prodding him in the shoulder with a finger. "Come on, my time is even more valuable now."

The boy nodded, a flat expression on his face. He wondered how many mills were outside the Oughtside. He asked the figure, and it said infinite or close to it.

Reality rounded back to the red. He stepped through.

O   O   O

Ryan's wounds came alive. They squeezed out the two embedded slugs and tied themselves together. He remained on the ground even when he recovered.

The boy breathed in the red. He shut his eyes and let it fill his lungs. He released his breath in a slow, extended sigh.

Mrs. Bell stood as close to the wilderness as she could without stepping through. She put HABRE CIR down on the edge of the circle, perpendicular to the wilds. The boy asked her about this. Didn't she want her weapon?

"For William," she said. "If he steps through—over this line." She sat cross-legged on the ground, facing an ocean. The boy could tell she wasn't going to move from that spot. Still, he asked.

"You're not coming with me?"

She spun her head one hundred eighty degrees and chattered her teeth. "I'll know, Judgment. I just have to make sure he doesn't make it through."

Mrs. Bell tapped her cranium. He tapped his back.

"Okay." The boy said it low.

The figure emerged from the curtain, some minutes after the boy. It didn't stop moving forward, instead drifting down into the circle—down to the near dilapidated house of Davies Tuch—like they hadn't even taken the detour into the wilderness. As soon as it could get back onto its sidewalk rails, it did. But its hand had changed, and it laid at its side as bright as a beacon, its white-gray, ceramic covering cutting through the red murk. The figure noticed it and hid the thing. It stuffed it under its left arm. This gave his right arm the appearance of hanging in an invisible sling. The boy could see the tips of his skeletal bone peeking out the back.

Back to business, the boy thought.

Ryan still hadn't stood up. The boy walked over and poked him in the ribs with his foot.

"Come on," he said. "I want you with me on this one."

Ryan kept his eyes shut. He opened them on the second kick from the boy.

"So I don't run away?" Ryan asked. "All my roads lead to the Oughtside. We covered this at length."

"Maybe I just want a companion. And Mira will be there, I'm sure." He gave Ryan a thumbs up. "No lie."

Ryan sighed. He sat up. "I can barely remember why I even liked her. It's been so long."

It hadn't been that long.

"That'll all come rushing back when you see her again," the boy said. He helped Ryan to his feet.

Ryan started walking toward Davies Tuch's home. "What could Davies have possibly done?" he said. "I've known him since I was four."

"A man that old has to have a thousand secrets." The boy followed. "Do you want to get some better pants first? A shirt?"

Ryan shook his head and kept walking. Past William's home, past his own, and past the crumbled yellow house.

Mira stood in the doorway of Davies Tuch's home with an ax. She wore normal clothes. Her name tag had been polished. She was livid with the figure, who stood in the overgrown front lawn of the Tuch residence. The boy and Ryan joined them mid-conversation

"It might have been hours, it might have been days," Mira said. "I'm not sure." The ax was shined and sharpened. It was a classic fireman's tool, the one with the bright red back on the head.

"You can't tell," the figure said. "So what does it matter?" It drifted closer and spoke sternly. "We're back now, so we can continue."

Mira eyed the figure's bone hand. "What happened there?"

They spoke like they had a history—like they were old friends.

"Don't mind it, Mira Peretz."

"That can't be good." She smiled. The air around Ryan tensed.

"Don't mind it." The figure drifted up onto the porch and close to Mira. "And put the ax away. We are behind schedule."

Mira looked at the boy. "You were going to walk in, Judgment, and I was going to sink this into your chest." She swung the blade overhead as if her mind had broken. She made a savage face while doing it.

He put his hand in the middle of his chest. "Why?" It seemed like a lot of violence for nothing.

"Production," Mira said. "Surprise." She swung it again—harder—and didn't pull up before it hit the wood porch. The ax stayed there, embedded in the boards. "I'm bummed about it."

"Me too," the figure said. "Now Judgment will just have to listen to Davies Tuch's version of events and go from there." It looked back over its shoulder. "Because of Ryan Mont—running off, holding us up."

Ryan shrugged. "You're too punctual. Davies is an amazing storyteller." He shrugged again, then greeted Mira. She responded with a nod to his presence, but not much else.

The figure went inside. "Stay close, Mira. I'll have instructions for the next house shortly. I'd like to call it The Science House."

Following close behind, Mira sighed. "Your instructions are getting too unclear, shadow. Too improvised."

"I never promised clear instructions, Mira Peretz," came the figure's voice from inside the home. "Come along."

"What's a science house?" the boy asked. He looked over to the next home. Before the red, the house was white like his but so much more radiant. Cleaner, too. Now they all looked about equal. He had no connection to it beyond that. He never really saw the people who lived there. He had no connection to the house after the science one—the only one made of bricks—either. And the only connection to the one beside the brick house—Mira's—was through Ryan. The boy knew the Bells, the Monts, and his family. That's it. Davies Tuch was the creepy old man that every neighborhood has. The science house, the brick house, and Mira's, too. He never knew Habre Circle. He had detached himself from it even before his parents died. Maybe they never really knew Habre. Maybe it was unknowable.

He started forward—trudging through the grass at his knees—but Ryan put his hand on his shoulder.

"She didn't say anything to me," he said.

The boy mused, then patted Ryan's hand. "She's working. She's busy. Come inside and hang out with her. Listen to a story. Maybe we can find some popcorn to throw up."

"It's not a date," Ryan said.

"Who said it was?" the boy asked. He grabbed Ryan's arm and pulled him along into the house.

In the parlor, Davies Tuch sat in an upright recliner smoking a cigar. The air's smell reflected that of his lungs'. He had smoked many cigars today, as evidenced by the piles of ash and cigar butts surrounding the man. There was no lung cancer in the red. The house's interior peeled—ancient and yellowed. Picture frames clung to the walls, some of them empty, the rest filled with disintegrating photos. Many pictures were of people in the desert—of military men, military women, and an encampment. The boy stopped at one with a young, dirt-covered Davies holding a sizable rifle and grinning. Weary locals stood among the heatwaves in the background.

"Oh," the boy said. "This is going to be the heavy one."

"Not that heavy," Davies said, his voice dreadful with phlegm. "I had the rifle just for show." He adjusted his body and the chair. "That wealth of dirt was the real problem."

"Step carefully, Judgment," the figure called. Novelty plates—ones of major events in history available around two in the morning on home shopping networks—littered the floor. Most of them broken.

"Davies Tuch threw plates at me when I came in," Mira said. "What a dick."

"I'd do it again," the elder said. "This was my house in life. It's mine in death." He owned two acres, while the rest of them only had a third of of one. It was a problem for the developers, but he never sold. The second acre was something of a jungle that the boy, Ryan, and the neighborhood kids used to hang around in. They'd found a tortoise once and spent the day watching it roam under a fallen tree. It was a fond memory with those certain neighborhood kids that were not yet familiar with arson.

"We're only in limbo," the boy said. *Mrs. Bell would like that,* he thought. Then he thought of William, a heaviness growing in his heart as he did.

"Well," Davies said, "I'm much closer to death than I was before. And believe you me, children, I was on the very edge of life when this red encroached on us." His eyes were wet with age, not tears. He looked at Ryan, only now noticing the Mont boy standing in his home. "Little Mont."

"Davies," Ryan said. "I haven't been here since I was ten."

Davies put out his cigar in the fireplace just next to him, which had been his ashtray for years. "I used to give you chocolates. Can't do that anymore. The doctor lady had a kid next door for a while. She hollered at me when I tried to do that."

The science house was getting more interesting. The boy would have skipped right to that stage if he could.

Davies concluded, "Even Halloween is dead around here now."

The boy gave him his attention. "That *is* a most tragic thing," he said.

The figure directed the boy to an antique chair across from Davies's—floral printed, at one point—then stood behind him, lingering again.

Mira ushered Ryan to the floor. They sat cross-legged next to each other, Ryan inching closer to her.

"Let's get started," the figure said.

Davies settled in. He looked nervous.

He only had one lamp lit in the place—an ancient reading one with no lampshade on the tray table. It's one hundred twenty watts bulb flickered bright, then formed a strong yellow glow around the storyteller and his audience. The red lit the rest of the room.

Davies crossed and uncrossed his arms. "So, I just tell it now?"

The boy leaned forward. "Did you kill your wife?"

Davies smiled. He showed his teeth, and they were too white for a man his age. Fake. "A wife? No. In my time, they called me a lifelong bachelor." He and the boy had never talked before these words. The man studied him, then said, "I knew your dad, Judgment. What an asshole he was."

"Only sometimes," the boy said, offended. "*All* parents are assholes sometimes."

"Not Paul Mont," Davies said. "That was a good man. Your dad, though—what an asshole. He yelled at me for getting deliveries at my house for my damn business. And not just once." In the last decade, Davies owned and operated many different vending machines in the area. At the local middle schools, high schools, and community centers. It kept him busy and kept his house under his name.

Ryan looked back at the boy—who fidgeted—then to Davies. "You're hard to get along with, Davies. Even my dad says that."

The old man looked hopeful. "Did Paul survive? Is he around? I'd love to discuss this place with that idiot. Remember that doll you found? Clueless."

"Not yet," Ryan said. "He'll find us." Ryan looked out the dirt-crusted window behind Davies.

The boy turned in his seat and looked back out the front door. The figure turned him back hard.

"Davies Tuch," it said. "Get started. You're losing attention."

"Can't blame me for trying to get a short stay of execution, shadow."

The boy pitched his voice a little lower. "Are you so sure you'll be damned?" he asked.

"Judgment," Davies said. "I'm counting on it."

He picked up a cigar and gave it a considerate look, then set it down. The boy agreed with the decision since it would have been too standard of a way to start his story off, taking a long drag and puff some trenchant smoke out into his audience. Entirely standard.

Davies Tuch began the story with nerves shaking his low voice.

"I used to travel," he said, "with world militaries, but not as a part of them." He cleared his throat. "There's a place I went decades back called Arlit. In Niger. Do any of you know where that is?"

Ryan, Mira, and the figure raised their hands. The boy raised his last.

"West Africa," the first three said.

"Africa," the boy said a step after.

Davies pointed at the boy and clicked his tongue. Then he laughed. Then he coughed blood into a handkerchief.

"I was stuck there once," Davies said. "In that radioactive sandbox. On their way through Arlit, people sank into the sand. They sought Algeria."

ARLIT

On their way through Arlit, people sank into the sand. They sought Algeria.

Davies Tuch sat on a boulder—like a lizard—outside the city born from uranium mines. Davies appeared more vigorous, then. His hair gleamed blonde and his features were cut—almost chiseled around the cheek areas. Even with that vigor, he withered out there on his rock. A clogged rifle stuck in the ground beside him, reaching up out of the sand. A man's shadow cast over Davies.

"Frenchman," it said. Davies didn't open his eyes. The man said it again.

"I'm not exactly a Frenchman," Davies said. "They cut me loose here." Worries over any attack on the mines or cargo had subsided enough that they didn't need him along for the shipment south.

The man laughed—just one large sound. "And me, I'm not exactly African. I was cut loose here, too."

Davies opened his eyes and gave the man a needless once-over. "And what's your name?"

The man picked up Davies's rifle. He checked it over like he knew what he was doing, pulling springs and removing bullets.

"Ayedole," the man said with a wide smile. His skull glistened. He nodded his head for a moment and said, "Okay, so I am African. I was hoping to bond with you over our mutual expatriatism. You understand."

Davies understood. Next Ayedole might make an offer to him. A job. Something dangerous enough to be off the Arlit books if they had books. He hadn't done much sightseeing around the place just yet. He aided in the loading of a shipment, a job he took from the true French people before they left him there to burn. He wasn't great at making lasting connections.

Ayedole stuck Davies's rifle back into the ground. "Sir, do you just want to cook to death out here, or would you like some work?"

Davies was just guessing about the offer, to be honest. That is how his life usually went, though. Lose something, get something in return. An equal exchange of fortune. Lose a hat, find a better one. If he broke something in the house when he was a boy, his younger sister would take the blame for him. Free of charge. If he got blood on his hands—in Venezuela, Chicago, or Haiti—he could wipe it off on someone else's pants or leave it behind in the dirt or as a stain on the walls. The past could not haunt Davies Tuch. His past wasn't on him. Sure, it was related to him by some fleeting extension, but it was not on him.

Davies sat up. He shook Ayedole's calloused hand, their fingers grinding against each other like scraping stone when they pulled away. Davies stood, and the Saharan wind kicked up a cloud in between them.

"Don't you want specifics?" Ayedole said. "I don't want you to make a mistake—we aren't doing right work here."

Davies kept his mouth closed. His lips, jagged with dying skin, didn't open.

Ayedole crossed his arms and chuckled. "You don't care. Look at you, you steely Frenchman mercenary."

"I didn't say I didn't care," Davies said.

"And you won't say that you do either, will you?" Ayedole turned away. He put his hand above his eyes as if peering out into the grand unknown. "It's hard to spot in the sand sometimes, isn't it?" he said. Ayedole pointed west. "Aha."

The city of Arlit didn't loom over them. It couldn't. It was too short. The sound of mining processes echoed from the uranium pit, which mixed into the heated wind. Ayedole found something more to say. "Where do you sit, then? On the moral divide?"

"It's a quandary," Davies said in a light husk, following the man and leaving the rifle in the sand.

Ayedole turned back around and continued walking toward the city. He said it wasn't a quandary—that Davies sat inside the divide with him and the rest of the world.

Ayedole told him to keep the dying people hidden. And to mark them, too. These people were stuck like Davies. They were cut loose or ran out of money before reaching Algeria. The mines took the stuck in, down into their depths. Arlit took them into its furnace, forty kilometers away from the city's center. They extracted uranium, not knowing what it was—never knowing what it was. Not exactly, at least.

Yellow, cake-like when refined. It had to be torn from the earth with explosions, like the earth didn't want to give that power up to them.

Davies kept them in the dark. He had mastery of the language but pretended he was an amateur. Just an ignorant European man, sent by France to make sure the processes went smoothly. He was there to listen, but Ayedole's pesky phantom bosses always tied his poor helping hands.

He had an office—the first and only time in his life that he ever did or would. It lay bare, but it was an office. Every day, the stuck rolled in and complained to him. He shook their hands, covered in cancerous dirt and smelling of chemicals.

"The Dr. says my liver can't function proper."

"My friend dropped today because of you."

"Where are the higher wages, Tuch?"

"Where are they?"

Davies Tuch listened with knitted eyebrows and wet eyes. The sympathetic European man.

He said to one woman many times or many women one time, "Your husband's liver is withered from the smoking and the drinking. Our onsite doctors have examined him and there is no evidence to suggest that the work here caused his illness." He had her empty her pockets onto his desk. He confiscated her cigarettes.

"We should quit," she said. They all said.

"We really should." His tone was light when he spoke to them; sometimes he touched their stone skin with his. "Fucking Phillip Morris."

Everyone smoked. It was that decade and that kind of place. Most of the stuck people removed their cartons and put them on Tuch's desk. A week later they had another carton and another complaint. The European man filled his empty file cabinet with the cigarettes.

Ayedole visited often, for a smoke and a chat. He worked on his American English with Tuch. He said it wasn't that far off from the British English, just crasser and more in line with the "reprobate republic" rather than the "impotent imperialists." His words, not Tuch's.

"Co-worker!" he said once, entering the room two months after Tuch started. "Employee evaluations!" He always gave that reason for their interactions, then chuckled. He reared his head back when he laughed like a howling wolf. Tuch called him out on that quirk, so Ayedole did it more often.

Tuch's office was newer than most—nice. Freshly painted. It had fluorescent lights that hummed like angels above his chair.

"You need to put some pictures up," Ayedole said.

"Of whom, exactly?" Tuch asked. "I don't have a family." He did have a family, just not one that wanted anything to do with him. He picked up a pen and held it as if he had an urgent thought fit to pour out of him. The company—the city—didn't give him any paper when he started. It was best not to document the work if it could be helped.

Ayedole removed a picture of himself from his pocket; it was a profile, taken professionally by all appearances. "I'm glad you asked." He pinned it to the empty bulletin board over Tuch's head with a yellow tack. "We're family here. All of us." He put his hand on Tuch's left shoulder. Tuch sweat from the man's touch. "You, me—the men and the women. The stuck. All of us."

"We're letting people die, Ayedole. I wouldn't let my family die." He looked up at Ayedole, backlit by fluorescent lighting. The smoke from their cigarettes mingled.

"Your family could be dead right now, Tuch," Ayedole laughed. "Back where? Back in Chicago?"

Tuch gave him that. "But traditionally, people don't let their family members die."

"I suppose Arlit bucks tradition." Ayedole stood back from the bulletin board. He smiled. "I'll bring you more pictures. This will be quite the collage."

Davies checked his schedule, which was a thin scrap of trash in his pocket. "I have another appointment in an hour."

Many days went on like this. The collection of photos grew to include candids of the stuck entering the offices— Tuch's co-workers, the dying miners, and officials. Together they could pass for a loosely defined family. An eclectic group of commiserates.

Tuch and Ayedole lived in the building next door to their offices, on a modern business campus just to the east of Arlit's center. They didn't leave the campus, only hopping back and forth between living quarters and work. Food and water were flown in and they had their pick of groceries. Tuch was partial to caramel pops. Free caramel pops.

Tuch didn't see or explore the mines until six months after he started work. He should have been bored by then—bored enough to head through Arlit and out towards the mines to see them. This job was cushy—the first of this kind he'd ever taken. He knew Ayedole kept doors closed to him since that was the nature of this kind of work. Davies didn't mind that, but he liked to know the certain breadth of a job before ever even starting it.

He'd become complacent for once.

"I've never been complacent," he said to his empty office on the morning of his expedition to the mines, a caramel pop dangling out of his mouth. He lounged back in his cushioned chair, listening to the low hum of the lights and the breeze of the air conditioning from the vents.

Ayedole popped his head in through the always-open door. "What was that?"

The office had thin walls and Ayedole tended to linger. Davies wasn't even sure what he did there besides recruit him. They had the same title.

"Nothing," Tuch said. He had no more meetings that day. The only thing left to do until quitting was to sit and watch the clock with Ayedole and a glass of whiskey.

"You look ill, Davies Tuch," Ayedole said. "Very pale. European pale. Actual European pale, almost." He said it like a joke but didn't lean back in laughter.

"Yeah, I think I'll head home." Tuch ran with Ayedole's observation and hung his head a little lower. He breathed a little deeper and played like his eyes felt heavier than they did.

"Wise. I'll drink alone tonight." He took Tuch's chair—spun around in it a few times before pulling the bottle of whiskey from the European's desk. He sat back, putting his loafers up on the metal. He pulled a cigarette out of the file cabinet next. "Do what you need to do, Tuch. We want you healthy and of an eased mind."

Davies coughed as he went out the office door and then the building's front door, pressing his fist to his mouth both times. Ayedole saw it. The receptionist at the front desk did too.

○　　○　　○

A map and a flashlight. Davies Tuch needed both. A woman ran a tin shack general store just off the business campus. She'd come in one Thursday—was it Monday? —telling Tuch of her plight. Her husband, like all those other husbands, was dying, and her store served no purpose without traffic. Without people with the means to pay for wares. He made his way out to her first.

The night hadn't grown cold yet. Earlier evenings in Arlit were like a crisp fall midnight back in Chicago. Every street was a straight shot to the mines. Even in the case of ones that went in the opposite direction, Arlit's buildings would force a traveler toward the mines. Tuch could have just walked in no direction in particular and he would have wound up in a winding way at the mines regardless.

"The European?" the shopkeeper said. She sat at the counter, her hands folded on top of it. "Gracing me with his presence." She fanned her face.

The shelves stood bare. What little she was able to get from suppliers and farmers had been sold for the day.

Tuch took a second to look around. No map, no flashlight anywhere. He walked up to the counter and said, "I need some supplies." He moved in close to her sardonic face and lowered his eyebrows like what he was saying was a secret meant for no ears. "I'm going into the mines."

The shopkeeper feigned surprise, then settled back into her spot. "I have a flashlight." She did and she grabbed it from the back.

"I have euros," Tuch said, flicking the flashlight on and off towards the ceiling to check its power. It flickered if left on for more than a minute.

"I'll need francs," the shopkeeper said. She lit a cigarette and took a drag.

Tuch didn't have any francs. The vending machines at work only took euros.

An idea. "I can get you cigarettes. I have at least a thousand." She was interested, he could tell. *They must be her bestseller*, he thought.

"You told me my husband was dying of these sticks." She took another drag.

"And I'll say it again," Tuch said. "He is. You all are."

"And that alone?"

"What else could there be, Miss—?" He tried to remember her name and failed. The faces of the stuck sometimes lingered, but names never did.

"Ayedole," she said with a slash of a smile. She let Tuch's fear wash across his face before continuing. "You're afraid of him—the 'villain.'"

He was. Ayedole tended to linger, after all. He could pop in the door at any moment at work or home. Tuch looked back to the front door, to the backdoor, and back to the shopkeeper.

"He's not a villain," he said, his voice lower. "He's no more of one than I am."

The shopkeeper nodded. "A slight more, but not much." She put a beige and stained jacket over her muted blue dress. She adjusted the turquoise headband holding her hair back.

Tuch put the flashlight in his pocket, handle down. "Closing up? I still need a map." He whispered, "Of the mines."

"I am your map, your guide, your 'Sherpa,' Mr. European." She walked to the front door, with her own flashlight in hand. "For as many cigarettes as you have."

"For as many as I have."

"Eniola."

"Davies Tuch."

○   ○   ○

The uranium pit, entwined in the desert wind, howled up at the two of them. It was vast and open; it smelled like the core of an engine. Even this early into the evening, with the work lights all shut off and the stuck people all in their homes the pit looked deeper than it was—like it would pull them down by the ankles into its maw if they got too close. Davies expected Eniola to lead him into a trap of some kind—a group of the stuck fit to kill him with bats and other blunt instruments. He wouldn't have blamed her, and he wouldn't have fought back. But they arrived at the pit with no incident other than some ferocious looks seeping out of lit apartment windows and alleyways with no vacancies. They drove there in the shopkeeper's truck, shattering the city's evening silence with its plucky emissions.

"Don't mind the looks," Eniola said, speaking over the automotive beast under them. "You villains have struck plenty of fear into them—or is it disease you have struck into them?"

"Both, I'd imagine."

Eniola might have been seeking remorse in Davies Tuch, but she wouldn't find it. He spoke with a level voice and a steady tongue. She grumbled at him, but Davies heard it as nothing but a kick of the engine.

The truck quieted down when they reached the open desert, as if it prowled out in its natural habitat Eniola cracked a grin. The tires kicked sand into the cabin that pelted them.

The night grew icy, and the wind chilled Tuch. He hadn't been outside Arlit's main city since he met Ayedole. The Saharan stars were always a treat—even for the stuck, he figured. It was the most of the universe that they or he would ever see.

He first imagined Ayedole back at the office sipping whiskey, then imagined him jamming a knife through his spine from the backseat and laughing as he did. Both seemed like equally plausible events at the time.

When the truck died just in front of the pit, Tuch shivered. He looked around in a full circle twice. Eniola patted the dashboard, a leather one that had torn with age and had sand embedded in its frayed stitching.

"Just the radiator. She'll recover by the time we're done," Eniola said, unbuckling her seat belt. She unbuckled Tuch, too. "I like this unease around you, Mr. Tuch. Your air isn't so sickly when you're like this. I bet you could have been a good man, once."

"Is this where I die?" Tuch said. "Here, at the edge of this pit?"

"Shouldn't it be?"

Security made their rounds of the pit like they always did: slow and without much care for what was or wasn't happening.

Tuch might technically have been their boss. He wasn't all that certain of the chain of command but knew that security was a part of the company's portfolio. Ayedole had said something about it.

"Eniola, do you want the cigarettes or not?"

"Shouldn't you just end your tawdry life here, Mister Tuch—?"

"Eniola." Tuch gripped the back of his neck, annoyed. He enunciated plenty. "Do you want the cigarettes or not?"

She fell quiet, then. Her lower lip twitched. She bit the flesh to stop it. Then she pointed down into the pit,

"It is not a matter of want, Tuch, but need."

"I need to live, just like you do," Tuch said.

"You need to live like you do, Tuch."

Davies laughed and nudged the woman with his elbow, in part as a genuine gesture of amusement, but mostly as a way to force her to exit the truck first—to make sure she was his guide and wouldn't push him down into a suffocating tunnel from which he could never escape.

"I'm going," she said. "I'm going." She flicked on her flashlight and stood on the edge of the pit. A breeze whipped the ends of her dress around. "There's a path here." She shone her light on Tuch. "To my right."

Eniola stepped to her side and descended a winding path littered with blasted rocks. From Davies's point of view, she looked to be miming stairs behind a couch. He moved forward a shuffle and took in the path. It ended at the opening of a tunnel from which some light emanated. The rail was wood and twine. The air held a bouquet of burst metal and stone.

Tuch scratched at his chin. He had a scraggly sand-blonde beard now. There was no policy against it, as the office was business casual on its best day.

Tuch flicked on his flashlight. He cast the beam out into the pit, where the dark swallowed it up. He turned it to Eniola, down a ways to his right. Her body shifted to the sides with each step. She stopped and turned around—a sizable rock tumbled past her. It startled her.

"Did you drop that stone towards me, Mister Tuch?" She joked, and it was obvious. "Getting a little proactive with your murders now, aren't you—?"

Tuch stayed silent. *Do you want the cigarettes or not, Eniola. Do you want the cigarettes or not.*

The path narrowed as they moved closer to the tunnel. Then the rail fell away and the walls encroached on the two. A patchwork of lanterns hung along the rock walls, some lit, some not. Tuch coughed out a breath, then couldn't get it back. He gasped for it, but it wouldn't come. He thought about the stuck people, and it felt like his throat closed. He collapsed to his knees and Eniola had to bring him out of it.

"Tuch," she said, hitting him in the chest. "The air gets thin—I know it well. My lungs have adapted. I am like a fish down here in this dark ocean, whereas you are still human." She thought about that for a moment. "Then again, fish won't die from all the water they take in, will they? Unless it's poison."

Tuch slouched forward through the tunnel. Men and women worked in the shadows around him where it began to expand again. He knew it without even having to point his light or look in their direction. They were digging, setting charges—mining in the dark with only a few lamps strung against the walls to shine some light on their work. The scraping filled the tunnel. Every several minutes someone would wheeze a warning about a charge set to go off and the scraping would stop. The tunnel would erupt in sound and shake a beat later. Eniola didn't mind it. Neither did the workers. They stood in the exploding dust washing over them. Then they would get back to work.

Tuch took cover. He scrambled each time, and everyone around him laughed.

"You're afraid of these," Eniola said. "The stuck live in this atmosphere—these explosions are their music, the fumes their whiskey."

"You're a dramatic," Tuch said. "They don't live here, Eniola. They have homes to go back to at night."

"We might as well, Tuch. Arlit is the pit and the pit is Arlit—one and the same. Dead without the other."

Eniola's voice echoed. The tunnel expanded into a cavern. Freestanding lamps erected in the center of it made the flashlights unnecessary, so the two clicked them off. The air turned wet. The stuck dwindled; they shuffled past Tuch and Eniola in a line, out through the tunnel. They worked as they went. Tuch grabbed one by the arm, a young man around nineteen or twenty.

"You're going home, aren't you?" Tuch said.

Eniola translated. She flicked her flashlight back on and directed it the man's way. His skin was sandpaper. Now visible, the man looked nervous and swallowed hard. "We'll work on the way out, though. Get more pay—maybe get to Algeria in only a few years."

Tuch let him go, and the man set another charge in another tunnel out to the far right, one smaller and snake-like. The young man contorted his body in a trickster way and slid inside. Tuch wondered how they calculate all this time spent working with such a bizarre and haphazard schedule. He wondered about payroll. There was a man named Mark—Ayedole called him "Mark," at least—in payroll. No one knew what he did all day, but it didn't look like payroll.

The cavern was the size of a ballroom, the kind one might see in a genuine Victorian setting. Eniola urged him to come out into the center, among the construction lamps. The walls of the place separated as they neared the ceiling, forming tall and rectangular structures. They looked like skyscrapers from a certain distance. When Tuch reached Eniola, he felt like he was in a city square—a bustling metropolis of uranium and blasted stone surrounding him. Divots in the stone looked like windows, almost inverted.

"We're in Arlit now," Eniola said.

"That doesn't quite follow," Davies said. "We haven't walked nearly enough to be under it." He picked up a stone from the ground and put it in his right pocket.

"Not under it—in it. What did I just say about the pit?"

"I wasn't listening," Davies said. He stood in some awe of the view from the center. He spotted another rock—this one seemed to shine. He knelt for it.

Eniola removed a knife from her dress next. She stood beneath a humming lamp, casting light over her frame when Tuch turned, and she plunged it into his arm. He wasn't surprised by the blade piercing his bicep, but his body reacted. It made snarls and guttural sounds and shoved the woman away. It knocked her to the ground, then backed away and sweat against a wall, stabilizing the blade in its skin by the hilt. A thin line of blood trickled down from the wound.

Eniola scraped her elbows on the ground, but that's all. She stood.

"I should have checked you for knives," Tuch said, regaining some composure.

"I don't think you wanted to," Eniola said. She sat in a chair-shaped rock to her left. "I watched my husband's best friend die here once. He just collapsed, his lungs overgrown with unruly cells."

"And?" He took the seat beside her. The formation looked like a park bench or a bus stop.

"And you killed him. And you'll kill my husband."

"Is he a good man?" Tuch asked. He thought about pulling the knife from his flesh, and how much that might hurt. He winced at the idea.

"Since I have been stuck here, I have learned there is no such thing as good men—or good people," Eniola said. "Whether you die today or not, Mr. Tuch, I will take your cigarettes and I will market them as a kindness and salve to my friends and my family. I will let them come here into this pit and earn their wages to pay mine." She looked at him with her wet eyes, aglow from the construction lights. She put her hand on the handle of the knife, then let it go.

Tuch pulled a cigarette and lighter from his left pocket, fumbling with them until they were in the right position, then sparked the cig alight. Taking a drag, he said, "You're no better than me."

Eniola's eyes turned sharp. "I should die today, too, but I am much better than you, Davies Tuch."

"Then do it—"

"Is that what you want? You won't fight me?"

"It isn't what I *want*."

Eniola mused for a few seconds, her face tensing. "I think you should do it yourself."

That was an intriguing prospect, and Tuch snuffed out his smoke to ponder on it. "Stab myself to death?"

Eniola nodded. "Yes, please. The world would be much better off without you."

"And you?" Tuch said, grinning a bit, a bead of sweat dripping off his nose onto the ground.

"I would follow you." Eniola crossed her legs and sat back. She rested her head and patted Tuch's shoulder before sighing. "I think you want to. I think that's why you're here."

Davies Tuch did come out here when he could have stayed inside. He went out looking for something when he could have stayed with what he had—four walls, a friend, security, sanctuary, air conditioning, and caramel pops. He couldn't be sure if he was looking for death out here.

"Maybe a part of me would like to," he said, standing. A charge went off out in a tunnel somewhere. Another, and another after. "I'm not going to do it, Eniola."

Eniola's face widened. She was surprised. She gripped his bloody wrist.

"The world," Tuch said, "would be a much better place without people like us or places like this, but that's an impossible task for me."

He found his way out from the tunnel. Eniola followed him. She drove him back, a little dour now, but there was a relief in her breathing, too. Like him, she was at work the next day, with a stack of full cigarette boxes that reached the ceiling of her tiny shop.

Tuch and Ayedole bought a couple of packs after work. Tuch came by alone sometimes—once or twice a week—and he and Eniola shared some drags of a cigarette. As they smoked, they sat in lawn chairs outside the shop and watched the stuck returning home.

ELDER

Everyone stayed quiet, giving the ending time to settle in their brains.

The figure said, "The question is the same, Judgment: damnation or salvation?"

"I have some questions," the boy said. He easily ignored the figure.

"How many?" Davies Tuch asked. "I'm only going to answer one. I'll let the story stand for itself."

The boy counted in his head. He had more than one. "I have seventeen, though."

Davies sat unsympathetically. With the scratch and clink of an old lighter, he lit the cigar he had set down before his judgment began. He took a few puffs, then grimaced. "I miss cigarettes now. Isn't that interesting? I haven't touched them since back then."

"Not really." The boy rubbed the back of his neck. It was stiff after listening for that long. He—Ryan and Mira, too—had sat like well-behaved kindergarteners during the story, listening with wide eyes.

Davies had spoken with some disbelief. He had shifted in his seat—there was a lot of shifting during the length of his story. Somewhere between him and Ayedole sipping whiskey and making a collage of their victims, Davies commented that, at his age, his bones didn't quite work right anymore. Now, he said, "No? My nostalgia for a time when I facilitated the deaths of over two hundred people isn't interesting to you, Judgment?" He said it without much inflection.

"If you put it that way," the boy said, "I guess it's pretty interesting." He gave a thumbs up. "But you didn't put it that way at first, Davies."

"I shouldn't have to."

The boy sifted through his questions, trying to pare them down to just one. He did this with his head in his hands, like he was in pain—his palms over his eyes. It helped him to block everything else out when he had to condense his thoughts.

From middle school onto high school, teachers said he wasn't inattentive or hyperactive enough to have an actual disorder, but his parents begged to differ.

He settled on the simplest question he had for Davies, who had leaned back in his chair, his head half in the crimson, half in the lamp's light. The man let out a cloud of smoke, covering his dry eyes—eyes that watched the boy, even when he couldn't see them.

"Why?" the boy said. "Why didn't you care then, and would you care now?"

He looked at the figure, expecting it to stop him from asking any questions at all. It stood idle.

"That's two," Davies said.

"Two-parter."

Damnation or salvation. The figure spoke these words again, but they didn't register much in the boy's ears. He stared at Davies, the smoke having cleared.

"Alright," the man said. He leaned forward out of the sparse crimson light, his spine cracking twice along the way, putting his elbows on his legs. He bared his false teeth in a grin. The boy could tell it wasn't supposed to be menacing, but it was anyway. He always found the elderly to be menacing.

Davies continued, "Do I regret it now—today, at this moment? After my life experiences molded me into this man you see before you? The old kook down the street that the Monts liked to pity."

Ryan snorted. "We didn't pity you, Mr. Tuch. We never pitied you once. You were the lovable old kook. Lovable!"

The old kook disagreed, then moved on, not giving Ryan much attention after. Ryan didn't push the issue. Mr. and Mrs. Mont *were* the pitying types. The Mont boy must have realized that they and, by extension, he and his sister pitied Davies Tuch quite a bit. He was a sad man—alone in his crumbling house, with his morose face and sagging skin. He had no one. Ryan pitied him right then. He couldn't help it.

Davies said, in a bright way, "No, Judgment. I don't regret a stitch of my life." He fidgeted.

"Everyone has regrets, Davies," the boy said, glaring at the man. "Even at my age I have crushing regrets."

"Regardless, that's my answer, Judgment. You don't believe me?"

"No, I don't believe you."

Davies didn't shrug or anything. He looked ahead, hard-faced and straight into the boy, who smirked. Davies coughed. The boy waited for him to stop, then spoke again.

"I think you want to." He stood up out of his chair. The springs in the cushion creaked as he did. Its burlap fabric armrest had been scratching at his wrists. "I think that's why you're here."

Davies winced. "You steal the words of a dead woman, Judgment."

"Are they false, Mr. Tuch?"

"No."

"Were they false?"

"I don't remember."

The figure drifted next to the boy. "Judgment, damnation or salvation?"

Starting at the front door, a rush of red wind galloped through the house. The antique chandelier rattled. The boy itched his ear. "I need to think." He sat back down, sliding into the cushion and putting on a contemplative face.

Mira, Ryan, and the figure sat and stood in a semi-pensive silence. They watched the boy.

"So, what did you think of the story?" Ryan said, gazing at Mira with the look of a someone who had just watched his favorite film, wanting to share it with his date. He smiled. "I thought this one was pretty good."

"I heard it earlier," Mira said. She stretched, her back cracking as she let out a soft breath. "He practiced it on me."

"And you were a terrible editor," Davies said. He bit his knuckles. The boy's father used to do that. "She tried to make me scale it back." He dismissed the criticism with a wave of his hand.

"I was studying to be an English teacher," Mira said. "I know what I'm talking about. You can't just detach from reality like that suddenly. It's jarring."

Davies grumbled. "I'm almost ninety, I think I can detach from reality whenever I please." He looked away and cracked his knuckles again.

"You're an English major?" Ryan asked. He grasped at things to talk about with her. His mouth dried, judging from the way he kept licking his lips. The boy realized that the red did not heal chapped lips. An inconvenience. He still needed lip balm. They all—minus the figure—needed lip balm.

"Yes." She didn't continue with an explanation. She looked tired in this low light—like she had been doing this job in the Oughtside for years, not days or weeks—hours?

Ryan appeared angry—confused, too, just as he did before running from the Oughtside. Davies doused him in smoke. It billowed around in the room, into everyone's clothes and eyes. The boy, although trying to appear deep in thought, was ready to block Ryan from running out the door again if he had to.

"No more detours, Ryan Mont," the figure said. It watched too, ready to stop the Mont boy.

Mira looked ready as well, watching his feet. He wasn't leaving again.

Ryan stood up. "You're not interested in me anymore, are you?"

"I liked you before."

"Before—I haven't changed."

Mira played with the old area rug under her, looking down as she did. The rough fibers needed to be vacuumed with something other than the machine over in the far corner of the room—the one covered with rust. How old must a vacuum be to get covered in rust?

"Yes, you have, Ryan," Mira said. "You all have."

But not you, the boy thought. He didn't say it. He went back to thinking.

Ryan said it. "But not you?"

"Not me, no. I am unchanging."

"What does that mean?"

"It means I'm unchanging, Ryan." She looked at him like he was a fool; he hated that. "You're different than you were before the red. Judgment is different. I'm the same."

"No, you're not," Ryan smiled. "Listen to you, you're lifeless. I met a different Mira. She burst with energy."

"That wasn't me," Mira said. "This is me, Ryan. We're stepping closer to my house; I want you to understand that this is me before I'm judged. Before—was an act for you."

Ryan began to take a step toward the door.

The boy snatched his wrist. "I need your help, Ryan. I want your input. Damnation or salvation?"

"Salvation, obviously. Let me go."

"Don't let him go, Judgment," the figure said, reaching out with its bone forearm. "Please don't let him go."

"I won't, figure." The boy huffed. "You don't need to tell me that." He turned his attention back to Ryan. "Salvation? Why?"

Davies chucked his cigar into the fireplace and clenched his fists. He looked like he wanted an explanation too. All eyes but Mira's were on Ryan now.

"Why?" Ryan asked, incredulous. He didn't struggle to break from the boy's grip. "Because he's an old—"

"Don't you dare pity me, Ryan Mont," Davies said, his voice raising. "You little shit."

Ryan shouted back. His voice cracked in the middle. "I'm not pitying you, you old skeleton! Forget the old then, Judgment. Who he was is not who he is now. I know him and he is not a killer."

Davies launched from his chair and tackled Ryan to the floor. The boy let Ryan fall. Tuch was spry in the red. Strong, too. Still, he coughed while holding Ryan to the ground.

"Stop it," Davies said. "Let him damn me, Ryan. Do you think I deserve life—salvation?"

"You deserve reason, Davies," Ryan said, not resisting the elder for fear of hurting the man. "Everyone deserves reason."

"Stop it, Ryan," Davies said again. He wept, his voice growing empowered and throaty. "I have documents upstairs in a filing cabinet twice your age that I know would convince you. Don't make me get them."

"You'll have to," the boy said, gazing at Ryan.

The figure leaped through the living room's ceiling, coating everyone in asbestos snow falling from the hole's edges. It returned by way of the stairs, holding a stack of papers in its shadowy hand. It pored over them by the fireplace.

"There are children here," it said.

"Ryan," the boy said, kneeling next to him. "He wants it."

"Don't say it, Judgment," Ryan spit. "Save him. Let him leave."

Mira spoke. "With you?"

"With me. With us," Ryan said.

The figure spoke next, still by the fireplace. "You're trying to keep your life intact, aren't you? Your parents are dead and porcelain—sister and dog, too. No matter what is best for Davies Tuch, you want him in your life after the red because he was in your life before."

"Is that true, Ryan?" the boy asked.

It was. Ryan's eyes looked to the boy and then away and back.

"No," Ryan lied. "I'm not selfish like you, Judgment. Like any of you. He deserves salvation—mercy."

Davies let up off Ryan like he knew the impending outcome. He leaned back on the floor, so he sat next to Mira. "I deserve what I want. What I *need.*"

"Maybe I do, too," Ryan said, hiding his eyes.

"Judgment?" the figure said. It had thrown the documents into the ash at its feet. They lay, stained gray, in a collated heap. They were scanned death reports and pictures from Davies and Ayedole's collage. Yes, there were children in there. But only a few that the boy could see. More adults. People. The stuck.

"Damnation."

Ryan pounded his fist on the floor. The floor took Davies, slower than the other floors had taken William, Francis, and Malcolm. The boards curled around him like snakes and swallowed him up. Mira watched him go; she watched him more intently than anyone else.

"I made that happen," she said. "The boards doing that." She mimicked them with her hands and arms. "It's all technology, you know."

"Mira," the figure said, looking at her but approaching the hole in the floor. Its eyes were large circles, unlike the boy had ever seen them. "Be quiet."

The girl apologized. In a half-hearted way.

"Davies Tuch: damned," the figure rasped.

$$\text{O} \quad \text{O} \quad \text{O}$$

Everyone slouched out of the Tuch house. Once fully in the red again, the house whined and teetered over. It didn't look much different than it did when it stood. The wood even appeared at rest now—where it was meant to be.

Ryan exited first. Mrs. Bell was still at the edge of the circle.

"Don't run, Ryan," Mira—the second out—said. She touched his shoulder, and he breathed out, relaxing.

"I won't," he said

The boy followed Mira. The light hit his eyes hard. "You helped a lot, Ryan. Good job." He knew that sounded sarcastic, but that wasn't the intention. He gave Ryan a thumbs up, then realized that might only add to the sarcastic feel. "I'm not being sarcastic."

"But are you pitying me?"

A little.

"No."

Disbelief spread across Ryan's face. He licked his lips, then eyed Mrs. Bell at the edge of the circle. She looked over and waved at everyone. Everyone waved back. No movement on the Mrs. Bell front—no William. She sat alone at the edge.

"I think I'll just hang out with my decoration for this one." Ryan smirked. "She won't let me run."

The boy gasped, "But it's science house!"

"That doesn't mean anything to me," Ryan said.

"Me neither," the boy said, "but with a name like that it must mean something. Science house!" He nodded once for each syllable. "A house of science."

"It sounds boring, to be honest," Ryan looked to Mira. "Would you like me along?"

She watched the figure move past her—the last one out. "It's supposed to be pretty cool," she said. "Big ideas and all that, but we should have come up with a better name."

The way she said it was genial but less than excited.

"I'll sit it out," he said. "Maybe the next one."

"What's that one going to be like?" the boy asked, half to Mira and half to the figure.

The figure stopped, facing the brick home across the circle. In a somber way, it said: "Distant."

Mira agreed. "There you have it. Distant."

They wouldn't give them any more than that.

"Sounds as fun as any of the rest," Ryan sighed, rubbing his bare shoulder like he had a sore muscle. "Honestly I think I'm over this part."

"You're being a downer," the boy snapped back.

"You damned my surrogate grandfather, Judgment. I can be a downer if I want.

He's being dramatic, the boy thought—*unwilling to accept that he was being selfish before. Davies Tuch did not have that much of a presence in Ryan's life to be called a surrogate grandpa.*

"Okay," the boy said, throwing his hands out in too uncaring a way to actually be uncaring. "Say hello to Mrs. Bell for me."

A traveling party has to separate sometimes. There's no way around it.

Mrs. Bell shouted hello from down the street.

"Never mind," the boy said. "Ask her how I'm doing."

"If you're too much of a William Bell-type?"

"Yes."

"Right now? I think so."

The boy scoffed. "Well, it's not you that I need to prove anything to."

"Why would Judgment need to prove anything to anyone?"

They parted. The boy with the figure and Mira. Ryan, alone.

The sky darkened to an even deeper red. The figure noted that it looked like rain.

SCIENCE HOUSE

Up close, the science house's modern aesthetic set itself apart from the rest of Habre Circle. Compared to everything else in the circle, the boy would call it chic. Even with its new Oughtside scars, which were scant, it stood out from the other homes on Habre and even on Mill. Its skeleton was that of a colonial, but the rest of it had been flipped in such a way that it glimmered, especially after being inside Davies's musty dwelling for any length of time. Solar panels on the roof, a greenhouse in the back—an all-electric car in the driveway that was only slightly damaged beyond any hope of repair like the rest of the automobiles in Habre Circle.

The boy jogged up to the front door, ahead of the figure and Mira. The steel door stood strong in its frame, with only scratches on its finish.

The boy knocked. No answer.

He knocked again. No answer.

A voice—a woman's, light but substantial—answered after the third knock.

"Figure," the voice called. "It's open. This isn't how we discussed."

The figure pushed the boy out of the way, then shoved him back to the correct position.

It said, "Don't be so eager, Judgment."

"*You've* seemed 'eager' since the arson house," the boy said.

"Still," it said, "there is a set way to do things." It paused. It was learning how best to cover its damaged skeletal hand, but the boy still caught a glimpse of it. Not only were the shattered hand and ceramic bones uncovered, but the wrist, too, and most of the radius bone as well. "We can't deviate, nor can we doddle. It's not difficult, from what I've seen. I know what I'm doing. I know what I'm doing!"

"From what you've seen? Are you okay?" the boy said, trying to get a better look at its bones. "This hand thing is getting to you."

"I'm fine." It spoke in a terse way.

"What will happen if we don't do this the 'right' way?"

"Nothing important, if we're just expedient." It settled in its spot and breathed out—almost tantrically.

"Shadow," Mira said. "We never talked about my role in this house."

The figure stared Mira in the face, its eyes half-open. They had dimmed, making the human pupils more palpable. It missed a step somewhere along the way. The boy could tell it wasn't prepared, but it corrected itself. It breathed twice more. "Mira Peretz, you're on break."

Mira chuckled. "I don't get breaks," she said. "You said that to me: 'No breaks.' Did you forget?"

The boy was reminded how much he liked her chuckle. Or how much Ryan did. Or both. Did he ever like that chuckle?

"I recall," the figure said. "I said it, so I must recall. That should make this break all the better for you—a surprise from employer to employee. A bonus for an adequate job so far."

"I guess," Mira said. She surveyed the circle, from the next house to hers, to the boy's, to Ryan and Mrs. Bell sitting and chatting by the entrance to the wilderness, and so on. "Can I still come in?"

"Science house is too enticing," the boy said. "You're going to love the science house."

The figure nodded. "If you'd like. But remove your name tag."

"You told me never to remove my name tag."

"Another wonderful surprise for you, then." It whispered next—its voice almost inaudible. "And I would honestly rather the scientist not know my employees."

"It says 'Girl,'" the boy said.

"Still," the figure said. "The scientist thinks she knows me—the Oughtside, too. She'll think she knows you. She's a trickster. More cunning than the common folk."

Unsure, and with shaky fingers, Mira removed her tag and put it in her jean pocket.

The scientist, the boy thought. Science always eluded the boy as a school subject. He said he'd rather be kept in the dark to keep his sense of wonder intact about the world, but he said that to disguise the fact that he couldn't handle the math portion of the subject at school.

"Ready," Mira said. She tied her brown hair back in a ponytail.

"Was that style against its rules?" the boy asked.

"Too utilitarian, it said," Mira said. "I think it's my best hairstyle."

He agreed. She made it work—it showed off her cheekbones. He raked his hands through his own hair.

Settled, the group was ready. The figure opened the door in its usual way and they all stepped inside.

The boy remembered when the figure would preface these things with a verbalization of some kind—a message. Husband, child, fire: judgment comes for thee.

The boy said something under his breath. "Scientist, judgment approaches."

"What was that?" Mira asked.

"Something I'm working on. What did you think?"

"Perfect, I guess, if you're into that kind of thing."

It seemed that the figure wasn't into that kind of thing, anymore—not since it lost the shadow skin from its hand and some of the bone from it soon after. *Maybe I shouldn't be either*, the boy thought.

"The shadow is slipping," Mira said, just behind him, her breath on his neck. She said it in a coy tone—sneakily. She must have known the figure would hear her. She wouldn't have said it if she wasn't on break.

O   O   O

Technology and experiments—the science in the science house—lay up against the crown molding and walls. Piles of computer monitors, tangled cables, beakers, and instruments had been purposefully cracked and shattered—left for dead in the halls. The foyer narrowed because of it, so the group walked forward in a tight line, glass cracking beneath their feet. In the middle of the living room, a woman sat at a small desk. She was writing something out by hand. Basic art supplies— pencils, a child's watercolor set—rested on top of the desk. One tubular fluorescent light dangling from the ceiling lit the room.

The woman wore a lab coat, wireframe glasses, and her hair in a short bob cut. She looked well put-together—more put-together than anyone in Habre Circle at the moment, at least. She appeared ready for the Oughtside, not frightened of the place or unsure about it. Not just because of her clothes, her earrings, and her light makeup, but because of her calm expression, as if she had found an immediate complacency in the new world. She sipped a freshly brewed cup of tea that steamed into the air.

"I expected more," the boy said, down about the sight.

"More what?" the scientist said.

"Science in the science house."

"Oh, that," the scientist said. "I've just moved on to better things. There are plenty of scientific accomplishments that I've made just today." She swiveled forward in her chair towards the group, who stepped in from the hall. She gestured towards a chalkboard on the far wall covered in equations. "Take today, for instance. It's not a day here. Time doesn't move. It hasn't moved." Cables dangled from the ceiling, some of them so large and heavy that they pulled the ceiling toward the floor.

The figure, the boy, and Mira milled cautiously around the room. Some tables had been flipped against the wall. Beakers and test tubes stood in ordered rows on those that hadn't. The place looked like a messy college chemistry lab.

"We knew that," the boy said.

The scientist raised her voice. "But I knew that without a doubt. And the red—that all-numbing, all-healing red—have any of you cut off limbs in the interest of seeing its power full-on? I have."

The boy pondered. "My friend was shot, and he healed. I was lit on fire, and I healed."

The scientist shook her head and growled. "That doesn't compare, you see." She spoke in that intelligent, guest lecturer way. She stood and went to the board. "It doesn't take much to heal a gunshot wound—but to reconstruct two legs and an arm in a minute five, well, you're looking at energy more substantial than anything on our side of matter. It's the sun, but it isn't—it's filtered at an incredible wavelength. My favorite wavelength. It's your favorite too. Everyone with actual skin takes to it as if it were a healthy heroin seeping into their veins."

Mira picked a contraption up off the floor. It appeared to be an apparatus for the hand—a mesh glove with wires wrapping all around it. She put it on and tightened the strap at the wrist. When she stretched her fingers out, the glove glowed as red as the Oughtside sky. It stopped when she made a fist. Then, it burst into flames. Mira removed it and stamped it out at a measured pace. Her hand healed.

"Ah, a prototype," the scientist said. "I have one that works around here somewhere. On our side of matter, that would heal all illnesses. On our side of matter, it would be the secret to eternal life!"

Vials labeled *Cyanide, Arsenic, Old Lace,* and *Belladonna*—all shattered—lay at Mira's feet. Her shoes were wet with poison. A bucket labeled *Ammonia* sat in one corner, precariously close to twelve-gallon bottles of bleach, some overturned. The air hung thick with chemicals, now that the boy paid attention to it. It stung his nostrils like the neighborhood kids' kerosene. Someone had tied a noose to the bar in the walk-in closet beneath the stairs.

A miniature Tesla Coil encased in thick glass drew the figure's attention. It touched the glass with its shadowed hand and the machine didn't react. It touched the machine with its damaged skeletal hand and the scrambling electricity beamed to its touch. The figure sighed—one as gruff as usual but aching and human toward the end. Withered.

"Dr. Hodges," it said. "You've been too busy."

"I've been just busy enough, shadow. I told you what I could do with minutes on this side of matter. You gave me days that feel like years."

The boy set out to find a neat contraption himself. He kicked things around and shoved monitors out of the way. Dr. Hodges proceeded to explain all the equations in-depth. She showed how to solve for y in the most complicated assortment of numbers and letters the boy had ever seen. She held Mira's attention.

As he pulled a child's blanket covered in modern pop characters out of the pile by the front windows, a ball rolled from its folds onto the floor and across the room. Mira stopped it with her foot, picked it up, and tossed it to the boy, who caught it. He looked the thing over; he demonstrated the heft of it to the room. It was made of metal and had a purple button in a thumb hole bored into the middle. Whatever made it work had been encased in the metal. It had the texture of a cannonball.

"Should I press it?" he asked.

Mira nodded, smiling at him. "I will if you won't. I'd like my time off to be memorable. It might be the only vacation I ever get."

"Go for it," Dr. Hodges said. She sat back down at her desk.

"I'd rather you not, Judgment," the figure said. "The scientist is trying to distract. As I said, as I said: a trickster."

"A trickster," Dr. Hodges said. "I like that. I'll deny it to my last breath, shadow, but I like that. But you're the only deviant here, shadow."

"A deviant," the figure said, aglow in the light of the Tesla coil.

The boy pressed the button. The ball pulsed and his body went weightless. Gravity escaped the room. Everything in it drifted up. Dr. Hodges in her chair and desk, Mira surrounded by liquid poison. The figure's bare skeletal arm lifted, but the rest of it stayed down. It watched as its hand rose with an angry wonder welling in its blue eyes.

"Look at that," Dr. Hodges said, a soft, knowing smile on her face. "Anti-gravity! The rules on this side of matter are exquisite." She emphasized the "this side of matter" every time she said it.

The boy spun and tumbled in place as if underwater. He let go of the ball as he did, and the contraption pulsed in the air. Gravity returned, sending them all crashing back down to the floor. He had a piece of beaker glass in his chest when he stood. He felt sick—like he had just taken a trip deep into the gray Oughtside levels below. The void of his stomach churned.

Mira had several computers on top of her that she had to worm her way out from under. The figure stood, simply fine.

"It needs to be held to work," Dr. Hodges said. "Perhaps not my finest creation on this side of matter."

She wanted someone to ask about this side of matter, the boy could tell. What did she mean by that? Something scientific, no doubt. But he knew where that would lead—to a story, to judgment. He went back to picking through the piles of science against the walls for another device. *Give me a laser*, he thought. *Give me a jetpack or teleportation or interstellar space travel. Or*—

"Dr. Hodges," he said, with a sharp gasp. "What about time travel?" This should have been first on his mind.

"Call me Hodges, please," the scientist said. She leaned on her elbow over some artwork she was working on—a darker piece. A swirl of black on a page from what he could see. She grinned like she had the boy in some snare. "You can't really travel in time without time, but I did build something that would travel through it on our side." She pointed at the boy; she winked at him. "So, about time travel? That's upstairs in my son's old room. I'll tell you, Judgment, it's my finest accomplishment. Better than any healing hands or anti-gravity device."

"And you'll show me?" the boy asked.

More science tech blocked the way upstairs—an old computer, mostly, maybe the oldest ever invented. The 70s kind that was the size of an armoire.

The figure circled the scientist. In a snide tone, it said, "The trickster will show you if you ask what she is practically begging you to ask."

This side of matter.

Hodges followed the figure with her steely gaze and a grin.

"You know you're not asking questions, Judgment," Mira said. She sat on an old TV, ready to listen to another story. "Where's your curiosity? Your wonder? Nothing about her son, even. Nothing about the shadow and Hodges's rapport. You're doing it wrong."

It was uncharacteristic, she told him.

He knew where that lead, too—the wondering and curiosity. "Maybe I want a break too, Mira." He rubbed his temples. It helped.

"*You* don't get a break, Judgment!" the figure said. "I think I told you that."

Did it?

"*She* didn't either until she suddenly did," he said, pointing at Mira with his thumb.

"She isn't Judgment. At this point, she's expendable. Her time is expendable."

"Don't say that," he said.

Mira, though, seemed alright with being called expendable. It didn't faze her at all. She brushed aside the air and made a "pah" noise with her lips. Rolled her eyes like she was making excuses for a wacky or embarrassing relative—a little brother or a politically incorrect father.

"Or do," he said. "If you don't care."

"I will," the figure said.

A pause.

All trained on the boy, now. He looked longingly at the stairs.

"Dr. Hodges," he said.

"Yes?" Hodges said, sitting straight up in her chair like a private school pupil. She ripped open a drawer and pulled a book from it. It was square like a children's storybook but had wires and light-emitting diodes on the back of it. The cover was as thick as a steel plate.

Reluctant and gritting his teeth, he said, "What do you mean, 'on this side of matter'?"

"Well, Judgment, I'm *so* glad you asked." Hodges flipped a switch somewhere on the book and it started clicking and whirring like an older desktop computer. The diodes flashed twice, then stayed on. They emitted a soft purple. Hodges tore the tubular fluorescent light from the ceiling and let it smash into shards of glass and mercuric dust on the ground. A cloud of the dust lingered in the purple light.

She continued, "In preparation for my judgment, I've been placing my focus on the more artistic side of science." After kicking some coaxial cables and what looked like a space fax machine out of the way, she placed the book down on the floor, unopened. The title read: *Shadow(s)*, and a halfway decent drawing of the figure appeared on the cover. It was minimalist and done in acrylic and haste, but the eyes were perfect. Striking, even.

"I always felt I could be a children's author," Hodges said. "That was my fallback while I pursued my doctorate. I played like it was a joke when I said it to my peers." She was serious, her green eyes hued purple from the diodes. "I think it was a veritable dream of mine, though. There is something pure in that work."

"Isn't there purity in science?" the boy asked. "Pursuit of the unknown—of knowledge?"

"There is," Hodges said. "There was—" She knelt and opened the book. The few pages it had weren't pages, but circuit boards as flexible as paper. The device clicked when she opened it fully to the first page; a mechanism in its thick spine kept it open. Going back to the drawer and rummaging in it for a few seconds, she found a small remote. She pressed a button and a beam of gray-blue light shot up to the ceiling then flowered over the room. Then another did the same, but faster. And at least twelve more, in rapid succession. The pages turned on their own.

The light built and overlaid three-dimensional images on everything in the room. Two lab tables in the center, curtains on the windows, computers thriving, beakers and such unbroken. The lights crafted this living room, only younger. A de-aged Hodges walked in from the kitchen. A child walked in after her.

All of it rendered in a slight gray-blue tone. The boy's eyes had to adjust.

"Holograms," he said. He swiped at the air once, distorting the image of it surrounding him with his movement. It corrected itself in short order.

"Until I met a shadow," Hodges said.

"Until she met a shadow," the figure said.

The image darkened for a flicker—red.

What else, the boy thought.

SHADOW(S)

The holograms worked around the boy, the figure, Mira, and Hodges. They covered the rest of the room with convincing approximations of the space as it was before the Oughtside. The chalkboards scrawled with other equations, the upstairs accessible. Most of the contraptions ceased to exist and the lab equipment—tables, stools, beakers—all nestled back in its rightful place, ordered in cabinets and on the tables beside the Bunsen burners.

Where in reality there lay a mess of cables, in the hologram only a slight divot or bulge in the image covered the imperfection. If the boy strained his eyes, he could work against the book's technology and peer beyond the gray-blue curtain. He could see the frayed cables dangling from the ceilings, the current, far more complex equations on the boards. He touched the floor, cutting his ring finger on a shard of glass. It hurt. It didn't heal. The hologram blocked the red.

Holo-Hodges worked on something—a minor creation that would work on the right side of matter. A metal device with three intravenous tubes extending from the tops and bottom. She had vials filled with blood in the centrifuge, whirring around. Even as a hologram, her son—playing with a beaker

237

in the corner now—looked pale. Sickly. *Her kid's going to die*, the boy thought. *That was going to be her story.*

"Her kid's going to die," Mira said, whispering to him.

"I know."

"So what?" Hodges said, standing next to her hologram self, mimicking her movements with a look that said she was trying to remember the moment. "You know where it's going, but you don't know how it will get there."

"It is predictable," the figure said.

"It wasn't then," Hodges said. "It was a reality. It was my reality."

Despite his pale and spindly body, Wes had some energy. He set the vials up like a city, then knocked all of them down, making monster noises as he attacked. A couple of them rolled across the floor. Both versions of Hodges—holo and flesh—flinched at the sound of the glass on the tile floor.

"I hated him a little bit," Hodges said. The hologram of her yelled at Wes, telling him to keep it down. She called him annoying—ungrateful. "More than a little bit, at this point."

"Yep," Mira said. "Certain things will be said that she won't have the chance to unsay. We nailed it, Judgment."

The boy's face fixed in a dour expression. He looked at the figure; he knew when it watched him—he felt it. They made eye contact. The figure didn't have a mouth, but he could tell it was grinning.

Mira caught the two staring at each other. She tapped him with her foot. "I said we nailed it, Judgment. What is wrong with you?"

"It's personal," he said.

"Oh Judgment," the figure said. "Nothing's personal anymore."

"Then *you* tell her." *The figure knew me*, he thought. *From before all this. Of course it did.* Knowing this didn't ease his nerves. "Not my job."

Even in the hologram scene, the figure had found its way back to the Tesla coil. Electricity's cracked purple glow punctured the technology. The figure chuckled. "But if I must, I certainly will broadcast the sordid side of your personal history."

It would, now that its shadow had started falling away from his arms. It showed hints and inklings of emotion. Of sarcasm—of a vindictive side.

At the end of her life, the boy's mother had hated him. He had to dig for the memory, and when he found it, it parched his throat. "Maybe my mother died hating me. It happens."

Mira sent him a daring smile. "Why?"

Hodges paused her book with the remote. The holograms stood motionless.

Something wriggled in the boy's back pocket. The gifted eye of a porcelain person blinked against him. He'd forgotten about it until just now when he retrieved it. He held the piece close to his own eye and blinked with it. "Who can say?"

Mira's smile grew wider and went crooked. "You were supposed to give that back, you thief. Mama Bell will be disappointed."

"It was a gift," he said, holding the eye against his own like a monocle.

"Not one you should have taken," Mira said. "I know a thief when I see one."

The boy slipped the eye back into his pocket, and his heart rate accelerated. He spoke at a clip. "I'm not the one being judged here, Hodges. You tell me why."

Hodges resumed the book. The holograms moved again. Wes cried over in his play corner and Holo-Hodges put her head down, straddling a stretch of the table with her arms. She leaned forward, her face above an unlit Bunsen burner. Her eyes didn't tear.

"Because he was never what I envisioned," Hodges said. She sat down—cross-legged—next to Holo-Wes. "You have a child, and you say that you'll love them no matter what—but you won't. Because you are human. They will do something that rubs you the wrong way and you'll hold a grudge against them for it. Some part of you will treat your kid objectively— you'll hide it, but you will come to hate them for it. And *objectively*, Wes was a burden I was obligated to shoulder. A burden I was tired of shouldering"

The boy stepped closer to Hodges. "You're saying this like it's an absolute outcome—for all parents, for all children."

"It is," Hodges said. "I've done my research on this, you know. I've done my studies." She took a full breath. "I was removed from tenure for my outlandish studies."

Mira leaned off her makeshift seat. "The studies. Were they 'mad' studies?"

"Maybe a little," Hodges said. "Here." She hit a play button on her remote. A hologram television, over in the corner across from Wes, started playing Hodges's recorded lab notes. The Holo-Hodges and her son didn't react to the television. They paused again. Hodges nodded, looking proud. "For background, I embedded clips within the story—little notes, here or there." She smiled in proud excitement.

"Fun," the boy said.

The on-screen Hodges spoke in a matter of fact and terse way. The screen enlarged, filling the room. This Hodges was a disheveled mess.

"There is a darker side of matter," she said, sallow. "We all know that, but the truth of it eludes us." The hologram blackened, as dark as the figure. "Most of this—this universe—*is* that dark matter and energy." This Hodges laughed. "It's wild, how little of an idea we have." The video hitched there, then scrambled into white noise. And then, the entire hologram scrambled into white noise—into the ants that danced all over old television sets tuned to a channel with no signal. The group stood in a world of white noise, loud white noise. The boy and Mira covered their ears until they could adjust to the hissing of the world.

The boy couldn't open his eyes fully for long, so he squinted in the din. He and Ryan used to play a game where they would get up close to channel eight—their parents' cable package's dead channel—and see who could keep their eyes open there longest. The boy's nose tingled now, as if kissed again by the old static from his CRT television set.

Ryan always won.

The holograms still stood with them in the room, as slight shadows in and of the noise.

Hodges watched the figure. The figure watched Hodges.

"Bugs," Hodges said, relenting her gaze. She tossed the remote away and retrieved a screwdriver from her scrambling desk. She went to the book on the floor and opened a thin panel on the cover. "It is wild, shadow," she said, fiddling with components in her text. "How little of an idea we had of your side of matter."

"We knew all about yours, Dr. Hodges," the figure said. The static covered the Tesla coil. It seemed distraught at that.

The boy made sure to listen—to get every word that came from either of them right. His hand still bled.

"Because you had to," Hodges said. "Where would your side be without ours?"

"And where would yours be without the Oughtside?"

"We don't need you as much as you think we do," Hodges said. "We don't need to be remade—as clay, as skeletons, as shadows, as porcelain. We don't need your version of an afterlife."

"Perhaps," the figure said. "But that's the system. You just don't want this version. Shadows in my position hear this all the time."

"Bureaucracy," Hodges said. She muttered it, then spit it at the figure a second time. "Is that you, shadow?" She said that as if she knew the answer. "The Bureaucrat?"

"No," the figure said. Its eyes softened. "As you know, Doctor Hodges, death and judgment are all improvisations today." Its shadow had rotted past its shoulder now. The boy could see the side of a torso, with some skin—faux skin like the patches on Mrs. Bell—showing.

The figure laughed. Once. A small "hah" sound. It startled the boy. Mira, too, though she tried to hide that when he turned to her. Hodges didn't seem surprised by a laugh lurching from such a thing.

She loosened a screw in the book. The hologram's sound cut out. It went black after that. Still, the holograms stood there, as shapes in the long black. Figures among figures.

Hodges closed the panel, and the book scanned the environment again. It reset the scene to where the group left off and played from there.

Holo-Hodges apologized to Wes. She was still too stern, and she didn't move closer to comfort him.

The boy looked to Mira with cocked eyebrows. She shrugged and mouthed that she was on break. He looked to Hodges next, who winked at him. She backed away from the scene.

"You laughed," he said.

"I did," the figure said.

"Why?"

The figure returned to poring over the Tesla coil, touching it with its bones. "Because I'm happy, and I haven't been for the longest time. Things are moving along smooth enough—not hindered by other shadows, by the Oughtside, by top brass." It stared at him for the next remark. "And you're doing well as Judgment. So far, I'm proud."

"Wow," Mira said. "Not once have I ever received that kind of praise."

"Why would top brass interfere?" the boy asked, as more of an open question for the room.

The figure responded. "I had an idea."

"What kind?"

"A better one, Judgment—about this process. Less structured—simpler. Ah, improv, like I already said. Let Judgment do the heavy lifting. Let Judgment prove their worth."

It's a rebel figure, the boy thought. *How bold.* "So many people," he said, "want me to prove my worth."

"It's only two," Mira said. "Relax."

"I'd listen to me over Mrs. Bell," the figure said.

Now Hodges chuckled. "Success," she said.

The hologram scene set in the lab ended with Holo-Hodges getting back to work and Wes getting back to play.

○   ○   ○

The lab scene dispersed, letting some of the red back in to heal the boy's bleeding hand, then the scene reformed into a hospital room. Wes lay in the hospital bed, unconscious—dying, as predicted. He had the device with IV tubing attached to him, running through his chest and nose. Holo-Hodges sat in the corner chair, watching her son. Her hands clasped together and her eyes sunk. The boy recognized the room as one from the university hospital ten miles away from Habre Circle. His dad went there once—died there once, too.

"I cried here," Hodges said. "It wasn't working. My equations—" as several equations, with complicated variables, cosines, and coefficients, floated across the scene and through the boy, "were off."

The trapezoidal device glowed a solemn pink when Wes breathed in and a deep purple when he breathed out. It looked much more polished than it did earlier in her lab. The door to the hospital room was shut and the lights turned low. A doctor slinked in, like he was sneaking, with a chart and an indignant expression on his bearded face.

Hodges said, "I worked here. Research."

Holo-Hodges said, "I work here. This is an authorized experiment, nurse." She didn't look up from Wes.

"Hodges," the doctor said, "it's Doctor Baum. I'm here on behalf of—"

"The university funding committee," Holo-Hodges said.

"That's right, doctor. We all feel—"

Holo-Hodges mocked Dr. Baum. "This experiment has been too costly, too risky, too ethically unsound to continue." Holo-Hodges leaned back in her stained, hospital-level comfort chair and glared at the man. "I've heard it before. I'll hear it again."

Dr. Baum adjusted his glasses. "But you won't," he said. "Not from us, at least. There's an addendum, and it pertains to your employment."

Holo-Hodges stood up. "I'm tenured."

"And you won't fight us on this."

Wes breathed heavier.

Dr. Baum shook his hologram head. He removed his glasses and said, "You won't, because—because of what the hell you have done to your son." He pored over the chart in his hand. "You take him and other children with his condition on five trips to—what is this?—a Hadron collider. For what?"

"To save them, I'd argue." She said it weakly, sitting back down. "I can argue my research, Baum."

Dr. Baum had this ready: "Yours is the research of an astrophysicist reaching out into the universe, not a medical professional trying to save her patient, much less her son."

"It's the same," Holo-Hodges said.

"It looks like mad science," Dr. Baum said. "Objectively, your peers see mad science."

Mira—beaming—said to the boy, "I fucking love this drama." She was up from her television seat, watching the scene two steps from him. She danced in the hologram light. He smiled back at her, then to himself. Warmth settled in his stomach.

The device on Wes blinked red—that red. That certain other red. The world darkened outside the window.

Holo-Hodges leaned forward, then out of her chair. She shot to Wes's bedside, putting her hand over the device as if checking the temperature of cooling meat.

"Did you see that, Baum?" she said. "It was red again. It's supposed to be red."

She checked monitor after monitor in the room.

"Is he saved?" Baum asked, stepping to the other side of Wes.

"Does he look saved?" Holo-Hodges asked. She grew angry at the monitors for telling her nothing.

Dr. Baum's bushy brows showed some genuine concern as he stood over Wes. *He had a son, too,* the boy thought. *Malcolm Baum. He lived on Mill Lane—in the Victorian homes. He enjoyed setting fires. Now, he has no skin, no shadow, no porcelain. He's working with the craftsmen of the afterlife. Quite a trajectory.*

Holo-Hodges hit the wall behind Wes with her fist. She held her head.

"Do you feel that, Dr. Baum?" she asked. "Do you have a headache?"

"A small one," Baum said. He touched his temple. "It's just stress, Hodges. We're all stressed this time of year."

"It's a small one, Baum, but it's pressing, isn't it? Getting worse, too. It doesn't feel like it'll go away."

Dr. Baum sighed in pity for his colleague. Still, though, he rubbed his temple. He swallowed. "Effective immediately,

Dr. Hodges, your funding is cut. If you try to fight this, we will expose you, feigning ignorance until it was too late. You are a rogue element in our community, and they want you uprooted."

"Callous bureaucracy," the boy said, nodding.

Baum put his hand on Wes's arm, squeezed for a couple of seconds, then left the room.

"Something like that," Hodges said.

O   O   O

Holo-Hodges slept for a few hours. The hologram displayed this in time-lapse with digital clock numbers floating across the screen. Hodges enjoyed using that effect—the floating numbers. The boy thought about calling her out on it. *Twice in as many scenes. That's too much.*

Hodges stood at Wes's bedside now, watching him sleep. Her hologram—sitting in her chair, behind Hodges—woke up. She yawned.

"I needed more coffee," Hodges said. "So, I left him."

And Holo-Hodges did just that. She walked out of the room. The hologram moved with her. It focused on her.

Hodges watched Wes until the room shifted to a hallway.

Holo-Hodges moved down the hall, towards the elevator. The hospital slumbered in that half-dark state for the night. The nurses' station remained alight, with a group of them mingling around it, drinking tea. They gave Holo-Hodges a synchronized, cordial nod as she passed.

"They knew me there," Hodges said. "They let me stay."

"Machine's broken up here," one of them said.

"Head down to two," said another.

Holo-Hodges waved in thanks without looking.

The elevator arrived onto Wes's floor—ICU—without Holo-Hodges even having to press a button. She didn't stop walking, either. She moved straight into the elevator. The world seemed to move on her time. Someone else was already inside, back in the corner under a broken light.

"What floor?" asked someone, dark and sinewy. Barely as a question. The words came out garbled.

"Figure?" the boy asked.

"What floor?" the figure said, mimicking itself.

"Third," Holo-Hodges said. Again, garbles.

"Third," Hodges said. She knelt and fiddled with the book again. The holograms shifted and flickered. She huffed. "I think I can fix it."

"Stop that," the boy said. He didn't need the confusion. The hologram was beginning to look like reality.

"The experience is paramount, Judgment," Hodges said. Then the book sparked in her face.

He blinked at the flash of light, and she was gone. The figure, too. He stood in the hospital, now, on the tiled floor outside the elevator. Hodges held the door open for him.

He hated the smell in the hospital air: sick and ammonia.

"You look ill," Mira said from behind him. She hit him on the back. He pretended to enjoy her antics in the moment, then took her hand. She was with him.

"Are we in the hologram, Mira?" he said.

"I'd say yes, we are," Mira said, showing no concern. "Relax, Judgment, these things happen in the Oughtside— wild technology, wild results. You should know by now to just roll with it." She clicked her tongue. "It's like I told you, the apocalypse is the apocalypse is the apocalypse."

He continued it for her. "And we should just go along with the right deities."

Mira turned him toward her by his shoulders. She drew her eyebrows up and her lips into a lovely half-smile. "Did I say that to you?"

He nodded. He licked his dry bottom lip.

Mira chuckled a little. "It sounds naïve hearing it back."

He agreed and said, "I don't think this is an apocalypse either."

"It's *our* apocalypse, anyway," Mira shrugged. "We're dead, and that's the end of that world for us."

"But we're saved, Mira," he said. "We get to go anywhere after this—to the moon, even."

"Speak for yourself, Judgment."

It was too soon after Mira finished speaking for the boy to say this, but he did anyway, "I'm going to save you, Mira. Of course, I am. I pro—"

Her face dropped, and he didn't finish his word.

"Speak for and about yourself, Judgment. Please." She didn't want promises.

He shook his head. "No."

Hodges still stood in the elevator. Neither she nor the figure moved from their spots. They were paused.

"She's waiting for us," Mira said, looking at Hodges and then the figure. "So is the figure."

"I guess it's interactive," the boy said.

He reached out and touched the doctor's hand. His fingers went clear through everything—her, the door, the walls. Hodges wasn't bothered by it at all.

Mira urged him inside the elevator, and off to the side, where they'd be out of the way of the scene.

The figure, back in full, rich, and dark shadow—in its hey-day—hit a button: *B1*. The door shut and they started down.

"I said third," Hodges said.

"I was not listening," the figure said. "That was more of a greeting, Dr. Hodges. For effect, you understand."

She hadn't taken a full look at the figure yet—not until it said her name. When she turned to see who it was that knew her, she took one blade of breath in as if to scream, and then didn't. Instead, she pondered it. She touched where its chin would be located if it had one.

"You are interested," the figure said, "in another side of matter." It encroached on her, growing a bit larger as it did. The vibrancy and vigor of its eyes—the boy had forgotten what they looked like before the trip outside the red, before its open wound.

"On the other side of matter," Hodges said. "I have theories."

"I am aware of the theories," the figure said. "Parallel matter—parallel, shadow universe—just out of reach of yours. Surrounding yours. Of a certain light on a certain unreachable wavelength."

"That's right," Hodges said. She checked for a pulse on the figure's neck and was surprised by her finding—she didn't say whether it had one when the boy asked. She didn't answer him at all.

"She's a hologram," Mira said.

"I'm aware," he said. He'd forgotten. This Hodges was real. She was there. Her hair caught the light the same way Mira's did.

The elevator reached B1, and the door opened to the hospital's boiler room, made of brick, steam, and cast iron—industrial. The figure glided out of the elevator.

"I have," the figure said, "a question for you, doctor." It wheezed.

Hodges stood in the elevator door so it wouldn't close. "Ask it, shadow."

The figure hesitated. "And information, too."

"Then tell it, shadow," Hodges said. "In exchange—"

"Your son has died. Just now."

Hodges swallowed hard. Her pager, affixed to her belt, buzzed. She put her hand over her mouth and bit down on the tips of her fingers. She could only breathe in small gasps at first but recovered after a few seconds.

The boy checked the pager by peering around her waist: *911*, backlit by digital green.

The figure, out in the middle of the boiler room, said, "Please tell me, Dr. Hodges. Would you rather run to be with your son? To grieve over him? Or would you rather have insight?"

"Into?" Hodges said.

"Me," the figure said, swirling in the room. "your device, your failure, and another side of matter—into getting him back. Pick your motivation."

The figure held up a small piece of scrap paper in its hand and tossed it out to her.

She didn't move for it but she watched where it landed.

The boy and Mira stood behind her, still in the elevator.

Hodges spoke, "Is this a bargain, devil?"

The figure asked, "Are you religious?"

"Are you a religion?"

The figure held up its hands. "It is an equation, Kellyn Hodges. Pick it up, and you will understand the language and its purpose. I wrote it for you."

Hodges's pager went off again. She canceled it after a few beeps.

The elevator door chimed. It shut against Hodges, then opened.

Her brow glistened with sweat. She wiped her palms on her pants. Then she lunged for the paper, out in between her and the figure. A valve hissed. The figure loomed over her.

"It's a distortion—time and space," Hodges said, lying on the floor and consuming the information on the paper with her tearing eyes. "A way over."

The elevator shut with Mira and the boy still inside. The hologram curdled and a firework of sparks burst from the center of the elevator's door. The rest of the scene fell away and they were back in the science house.

Hodges—flesh, and blood Hodges—stood in front of them with the book closed in her arms. The figure lingered behind her.

"Sorry," Hodges said. "I was stuck in there once. It's not the best experience."

The boy went straight to a window in the kitchen—the red pouring in. He sucked it up.

"Motivation," he said, shutting his eyes. "Dr. Hodges. What was yours?"

Mira didn't need the red from the window. She just brushed the dirt off her knees and took her seat, back on the old television.

"Scientist," the figure said, laughing again. "Judgment comes for you."

"Motivation," Hodges said. She pointed at the figure with an accusatory finger. "What was yours?"

Dr. Hodges sat down at her desk. She sat back in her chair with ease, like she had something on the figure now—like she had positioned a chess piece just right to gain the best advantage. She picked some dirt from the nail of her index finger. Then she flexed all her digits. She had the fingers of a pianist—lengthy, bony. The boy looked at his own and they were similar. His dad used to tell him that with fingers like that he should play an instrument. He never did.

The figure took another seat in a chair across the room. It mimicked the doctor's demure demeanor. The boy moved away from the window in the kitchen. As he did, his eye caught a glint of light from a cracked glass beside the sink filled to the brim with water. He hadn't been thirsty since the Oughtside arrived. Not in the red, nor outside of it either. And he wasn't thirsty now, but he did think that a cool gulp of water might feel nice going down his throat. He was warm in this house. He was working hard in this science house. Some sweat poked out from his pores as he stood by the window. He grabbed the glass and brought it to his lips. He took three mouthfuls of the water. He couldn't keep it down and spewed it across the floor. Violently.

"Judgment," Mira said. "You are empty inside."

The boy didn't turn to see her but he did get up off the floor. He found his way back out into the main room—through the shattered sciences—and stood between the figure and Hodges, the two of them looking through him at each other. He felt as if he had just wedged himself between two steel plates welded together. Wiping a drip of the rejected water from his bottom lip, he cleared his throat.

Mira spoke. "You're going to stay empty, Judgment."

"I get it," he said, snapping at her—just a bit. He told himself it was just a bit, but she looked surprised by where he took the level of his voice. *It might have been more*, he thought.

The figure turned in its chair toward him because Hodges had turned in hers.

He took a breath, then focused on the figure. "Your motivation, figure. I'm interested too."

"I'll say again that I had an idea, Judgment," the figure dismissed. "Nothing more to it."

"On how to do this," the boy said. "Right."

"Better, Judgment. How to do this better." The figure was still more interested in Hodges, looking at her and only her.

"Than?" he asked.

"Than before." It anticipated his next questions. "Let me tell you, it was rigid before—all of this. So set. So composed in its process." It snapped its bony fingers with a touch of flourish in the twisting of its wrist. "I kept the basic, antiquated concept and livened it up a good deal." The figure clenched his good fist. It spoke with an impassioned voice—short and punctuated. "Believe me, Judgment, it was boring before. Watch his life. Saved. Watch her life. Damned. Watch their life. Damned. Sorted. Monotony after monotony, cassette after cassette. No room for deviation. Except here in my little slice of the Oughtside—my little slice of judgment."

The figure sighed, calming itself. It let its head fall forward then rolled it around as if trying to crack its neck.

"Judgment, my idea was my motivation. Death and judgment."

"Is all improvisation today," the boy said, the words rolling out of him.

Hodges shook her head. "Not good enough," she said. "Judgment, that can't be good enough for you. What do employees have?"

Mira answered with some excitement. "A boss, naturally."

Hodges put her elbows on the desk. "The figure employs the girl, but who employs the figure?"

The boy pointed to Hodges and nodded. "Yes, figure, I don't think it's enough."

The figure collapsed back into its seat, tired of this conversation. "The universe is my employer, Judgment. I am a cog in the natural machine. Nothing—no shadow, no porcelain person or arrangement of bones—employed me to be your guide. I found an opening, I had an idea. I seized it."

Hodges snickered under her breath, still at her desk. She pulled the front drawer out and removed a scrap of paper—the scrap of paper the figure had handed her in the distant hologram. Same writing, though its edges had torn and aged. She held it up to the room.

"This equation," she said, looking at the boy now. "It killed you, Judgment. It killed all of us. At once. Like that—like it was nothing."

The figure chuckled, this one more jovial than the last. "You killed them, Doctor Hodges. I offered you an opportunity and you let it slip away."

Hodges made a fist, crumpling the paper in her hands. Then, she slammed it on the top of her desk. She rose out of her chair, pushing the seat away with her legs. She grabbed a device next—one from another drawer, maybe the same one—and chucked it at the figure. It was round and covered in wires like many of the things in the science house. The device landed in the figure's chest and stuck there, even when the shadow pulled at it in a playful way like a cat smacking a grenade. The figure stood out of its chair, rising to meet Hodges's stare.

"I seized *your* 'opportunity,' shadow," Hodges said, almost in a whisper. "My device was sound. Your scrap numbers were faulty."

"Hodges?" The boy asked. "You killed us?"

The figure spoke over him. "Not all your devices can be successes, Doctor Hodges. There's no fault in that. It's just a fundamental part of the field you've entered. You tried to bridge a divide."

"Between?" Hodges said.

Between the Oughtside, the boy thought, *and this side.*

"Between who you are," the figure said, "and who you wanted to be."

"Judgment," Hodges said. "Turn to the end of my book."

He did as she asked. He kneeled on the floor and turned towards what would be the end of a traditional, non-metal, non-hologram producing book. The pages grew warmer to the touch—hot, even. Hodges stopped him when he was about three pages from the back cover.

The doctor brought Holo-Hodges to life again. She stood there, in her house, beside one of her devices: a console that appeared much more complicated than any of the others he had seen. A screen just above it projected numbers and readings across the room—holograms within holograms within holograms. Holo-Hodges looked perfectly *mad*, right around the eyes. She hit buttons in a controlled rage.

"Last night—last week, last year, whenever it was," Hodges said. "Did you feel it? In your skull. A pressure, building? Did your nose feel like it needed to gush blood, but could only spare a drop?"

Silently, the boy turned to Mira. She nodded.

"I felt it," she said. "Behind the eyes." She pinched the bridge on her nose.

"Same," he said, looking at Mira to let her know he could commiserate. "In the days before." He had headaches all the time, though. A migraine every other morning. Cameron had told him they would go away if he just slept normal hours.

"And Ryan, too," Mira said. She interlocked her fingers in front of herself, forming the shape of an egg with her hands. "Things, Judgment. Coming together."

The figure, still fooling with the device embedded in its chest, said, "That was the dear Doctor Hodges, inviting the Oughtside over."

"It was only supposed to be an entryway for me," Hodges said.

"It was," the figure agreed. "You went above. Too many numbers, not enough restraint, Doctor Hodges."

Holo-Hodges stepped back from the console. A small light blinked red—that red. It grew brighter. Panic contorted her face. The entire hologram leeched red now.

"Shadow?" Holo-Hodges said. But no shadow answered.

"Shadow?" Hodges said.

"For days," the figure said, "she chiseled at the bonds on your 'side of matter,' tucked away in this house. Failing to seize any opportunity I gave her."

"Until," Hodges said.

Holo-Hodges sat down in front of her console. Her eyes glossed over and her skin lost its color.

Hodges watched herself with intensity. "I felt myself die right here—only for a brief second, then I felt more alive than I ever had."

She watched the blinking red light until it shattered in her face. The windows did the same—bursting inward from the outside, a grand shard of glass flying into her shoulder, her skin pushing it back out. The new red world drew it from her.

Outside the hologram's front door, Habre Circle changed. The boy turned and watched it happen through his own eyes this time. Bathed in digital red, he watched leaves stripped from tree branches, houses removed of their siding, and cars whine as they rusted over.

"Is this exactly how it happened, figure?" he said, his mouth drying.

"Yes, Judgment," the figure said, coming up behind the boy. "By this point, I had already met with William Bell. Those children, too. Ryan Mont was next." A pause. "And Mira Peretz, of course."

Mira snorted, trying to contain a laugh. "Yeah."

The boy found something in the figure's voice: a fondness, a nostalgia.

The figure moved toward the faux front door.

"It would be interesting to see myself again—before this wound."

"Shadow," Holo-Hodges said, angry now, her face flickering.

"*You* killed us," the boy said. Not with any contempt for the doctor, just a mere statement of fact.

"Shadow," Hodges said. "My device acted as intended. It just wasn't my intention it acted on."

The book reached its end and closed on its own, shutting off the hologram. The boy recognized pieces of the console all around them now – a button here, a sprocket there. He noticed the glass shard spotted with the doctor's blood by his feet.

"Your device," the figure said, "was your device. All intention was your own. All failings were your own—with this, with your son. You would hold a stone responsible for tripping you."

Now they are repeating themselves, the boy thought, so he raised his hand and neither of them continued speaking. He savored this odd second of control.

"I have a judgment," he said. Then he paused to act like he was thinking. Then, he started thinking about it. Hodges and her son. The figure and Hodges. Motivation. It consumed him.

"I thought you had one," Mira said. "You wouldn't have to think if you did."

He shook his head and sent Mira a gentle glare.

"Salvation," he said.

Hodges showed no relief, only silent contemplation at her desk. He wasn't sure if she heard him. So, he said it again. She responded after the third time.

"My creation in your chest, shadow," she said. "Should have gone off by now."

"You see, Judgment," the figure said. "She admits her faults. This device—," it tried to pull it out again, struggling. "Another failure."

"What will it do?" Mira asked.

The figure answered. "Something to damage me, no doubt."

Hodges pointed at the figure and smiled like the shadow had answered some trivia correctly.

"Aren't you worried?" the boy said, touching the black and red wires. They hummed in his fingers. The thing had power.

"No—I can't say I have any faith in Doctor Hodges's abilities anymore. She wants to end me, but she is incapable of it."

Hodges removed her glasses and tossed them to the floor. She rubbed her eyes, then stood and walked across the room to the stairs in the foyer. She gestured up towards the second floor. "Now, who was it that wanted to see a time machine?"

The boy cheered and they all filed upstairs with Hodges leading them.

FAILURE

One side of the upstairs hallway had collapsed in on itself, narrowing the path. It was all askew—tilted to the right. The group had to stay in a single-file formation: Hodges, the boy, Mira, and then the figure. Wes's door hung to hinges at the end of the hall. Science didn't litter the floorboards up here, fallen picture frames did. Smiling faces—of Hodges, of a tiny Wes—looked up from the ground, glass crunching underneath their feet.

This is more like Davies Tuch's house, the boy thought, *at least this section of it*. Shattered pictures on the floor—a concealed, aching life in images looking out at the passersby. This was not a science house standing so far above and beyond the rest of them in Habre Circle.

"The door with all the giraffes on it," Hodges said, leading them towards Wes's room over the broken boards.

"Did he like giraffes?" Mira asked.

"I do," Hodges said. "I wanted him to. Isn't it curious, how we try to influence our children—force ourselves on them."

No one said anything for a step or two.

Then the boy let out an awkward laugh. "I don't have kids."

"Me neither," Mira said.

Hodges looked back at them, her eyes catching the figure's. "And you, shadow? I bet you had children."

The figure winced like it tried to remember faces and names, coming up short. It spoke with genuine interest. "What gives you that idea, Doctor Hodges?"

Hodges only answered with a shrug. "Intuition. Behavior."

The figure hummed as if mulling the idea over. Then, it stopped. It started looking around.

"Doctor Hodges," it said. "Why would you put this machine in your son's room?"

From what the boy could tell through the half-open or splintered doors, the second floor had at least two usable rooms besides Wes's: the master bedroom and an empty guest room. Neither of them had been damaged much by the caved-in wall or the Oughtside's arrival.

"I don't spend time in those rooms," Hodges said.

"Why?" Mira asked.

Hodges stopped at Wes's door. She tried the handle, but it was locked.

Seven cartoon giraffes—each with distinct personalities—watched them. They were characters from a new series on a kids' cable network. It was on when the boy woke up after falling asleep in front of the TV. It was on one morning back in May, a dozen minutes or so before he found his mom half on her bed, half not. A pit grew in his stomach. He cleared his throat.

"Locked?" he said. He had to clear his throat again.

Hodges knocked on the door next—in a light way, like she didn't want to disturb the other side.

"Doctor Hodges," the figure said, forcing Mira and the boy aside. "Who is in there?"

"Wes?" Hodges said. "Could you unlock the door?"

The door clicked and Hodges pushed it open. A shadow ran from the door to the back corner of the room. It was small with one shining green eye and another still with its porcelain covering. Hodges coaxed it out into the light of a dim overhead bulb. Cautious at first, it moved towards them.

"Wes," she said. "Remember me?" She turned back to the boy and the others. "He forgets after too long. It's the porcelain—then that muddy shadow."

"Mom?" Wes said. He grabbed his head. "Can I go out now? Back downstairs, please."

The figure stepped next to Hodges. "You found him?"

"Downstairs, in a video store," Hodges said. "I bet he would have been the kind of kid to hang around video stores."

"What do you think you can do with him? Raise him?" the figure said.

"It's a possibility," Hodges said, kneeling on the beige carpet next to Wes.

The boy looked around for a time machine. He couldn't see anything that resembled his idea of one—just a bunch of kid furniture, from the reading lamp to the bed. He let out a little sigh. Mira moved closer to him and whispered. "I know, I don't see it either."

The boy didn't bring it up to Hodges. It felt like she and the figure had moved into a separate room—into a separate reality, even. They paid no mind to either him or Mira, acting again like their hologram selves in lock step conversation. He found a giraffe figure on Wes's dresser—one with an extending neck activated by a button on its tail. He played with that. Mira laid down in Wes's bed.

Hodges went on. "I've been working on removing his porcelain."

This remark received everyone's attention. The figure's most of all, who turned to Hodges, its one eye wider than the other.

Hodges continued speaking. "It obstructs their humanity, shadow," she said. "The one thing I can do for him is try to unearth his humanity."

"It is their humanity, Hodges," the figure said, low and breathy.

"It's a facsimile," Hodges said, entirely sure about the assertion. "A shell to be shed."

"That's not how he sees it, Hodges," Mira said, her eyes shut.

"That isn't how any of them see it," the figure said, growing incensed—almost emotional, its eyes moving wildly. "Beyond it being a currency. Beyond its materiality. The first thing they know is that shell is their body—their very body. You can't tear it away."

"What a company line," Hodges said. "Judgment, do you agree?"

The boy stopped playing with the toy. He did another quick look around the room for a time machine. Then he tipped the giraffe over. "I guess they should shed it naturally, right? Conclude it by themselves." That sounded good to him—like the objective thing to say.

"Wrong," Hodges said. She leaned in closer to Wes, putting her forehead against his. She clutched the remaining porcelain and pulled it from his face. Shadow stuck to the piece for as long as it could, like chewing gum on the bottom of a boot. Hodges tossed the piece away when it was free. The figure tracked the porcelain to the floor, watching it land in the carpet. The boy picked it up off the floor and pocketed it right away. He felt Mira's heavy eyes on him. The device in the figure's chest beeped twice and glowed a dull orange.

"Finally," Hodges breathed out. "I've been working on removing this substance, too." She pulled at Wes's skin. "I can feel the bones underneath—now that, Judgment, is his actual body."

"Okay, Hodges, resort to fanaticism," the figure said. "Because you can't wait. Because impatience is the nature of your entire self."

Tensions are compounding, the boy thought. *He should ask now—quietly*.

"So, uhm, there was mention," he said, "of a time machine?"

The figure's torso took on the glow of the device, which beeped again—three times, in quick succession. The figure couldn't move. It winced, its skin rippling in dark waves.

The boy watched the figure shake in obvious pain.

"Figure?" he said.

Hodges leaped up from beside her son and body-checked the boy into the dresser. The drawers rattled. Then, she bundled the hair on the back of his head in a fist and slammed his face against the wall. She let him fall to the ground.

That was sudden, he thought, a little rattled.

"There was, Judgment," she said, grabbing the lit, diminutive lamp atop the dresser. She tore its blue shade off while walking back over to Wes and making sure the attached extension cord stayed together. She had filled the bulb with more than filament—a bundle of odd metal and frayed wires wound tight.

The boy tried to stand, but Hodges kicked him to the ground again.

Mira sat on the edge of the bed. In one fluid motion, Hodges picked up a small child's chair from the floor, hit the girl in the face with it, then placed the chair back upright on the ground.

"The hell?" Mira said, falling back onto the bed. "Stop hitting people."

Mira's nose dripped red. The boy's, too. The bones around his eyes had split. His vision blurred.

The figure's chest beeped four times.

"It's a one-time use," Hodges said. She sat back down on the floor—cross-legged—next to Wes. She made him cling to her. "I think I'll need it—well, depending on how this next bit goes." She watched the figure as she might the subject of a study.

"You won't travel," the figure said, gritting unseen teeth. "Not in your concept of time."

"Maybe not time, but space." Hodges held the lamp bulb-side down with both hands as if to stab the floor. "You're going to want to hurt me in the immediate aftermath of this, shadow. I just need to be away from you."

Orange filled the room. It covered most of the figure—from the inside.

The device beeped five times, then it clicked. Starting from the figure's torso, the skin began to lift from its bones and dissipate in the air. The figure shuddered, taking the device in its hands and trying to crush it. The shadow screamed.

Hodges watched with intent, her eyebrows up. Wes shut his shadow eyes and mumbled something.

The boy pulled a drawer from the dresser with some trouble and stumbled over to the figure. He started bludgeoning the device. The thing gave. It cracked, then burst into a flash of orange, throwing the boy and the figure back. The figure tumbled against the door and landed half out into the hallway.

"Hodges," it said, rising clumsily. It growled. "You were right."

"I was," Doctor Hodges said, smiling and telling Wes to hold her tighter. "See, Wesley. Those bones, that old clinging flesh under all that gunk. That is humanity, exposed and bare."

The figure lunged forward. Hodges plunged the lamp down, smashing the bulb and spreading sparks across the floor. The air changed—it expanded in the boy's lungs, then heated, then chilled. Hodges seemed to take it—hoard it all. It smelled like burnt hair.

Laying against the bed frame, he watched Hodges and her son—the lamp, too—vanish from the room. They left a campfire-sized blaze crackling in the middle of the carpet. The figure landed in it, then rolled out to the side, so that it was now lying next to the boy. Mira sat above them on the bed. She looked down over the side. Blood stained her face and the neck of her blouse.

The figure grumbled.

"Kellyn Hodges: saved," it said, drained. It lay there, most of its body exposed. The only thing left covered in shadow was its head down to the beginning of its shoulders, and even that was peeling away.

"Escaped," the boy said, inspecting the figure's body. Covered in ceramic dust, like Mrs. Bell's. He reached out to hold one of its ribs.

Then the floor gave, and the science house collapsed into itself.

MIGHT

The boy, Mira, and the figure clawed their way out from the rubble easily enough, with only a few snags—tears in their clothing and the like—to speak of. Doing things like this had become a common occurrence in the Oughtside. The three of them, at a workman's pace with workmen's' expressions, pushed through the fallen science house and out into the red.

"Judgment?" the figure said. When it saw him atop the grounded roof closer to Davies Tuch's house, it nodded and wheezed. It meandered and stumbled over to the brick house and sat in the driveway. It grew weak.

Mrs. Bell and Ryan stood in the middle of the circle, both holding one hand out. It started to drizzle, so they collected the water in their palms. They walked over to Hodges's mailbox.

"We saw the house crush you," Mrs. Bell said. She didn't have the street sign with her—that was back at the edge of the circle, stuck in the ground. "How was it?"

Mira helped the boy remove a piece of metal from his leg. He helped take a jagged piece of wood out of her stomach.

"Well, she killed us all," the boy said. He took a second to think. "Unintentionally, I'd say."

Mrs. Bell raised her bone hand. "Hey."

He corrected, after a beat. "She killed all of us who weren't murdered."

"It's her fault?" Ryan asked, his brow knitted. He looked past the boy at the rubble. "All of this?"

Mira walked up to Ryan and put her hand on his shoulder. "Doesn't matter—she traveled through time."

"Or space," the boy said.

"One of those," Mira laughed.

"Not before she wrecked the figure."

"No, not before that. That was intense."

They bounced off each other well. Ryan eyed them for it.

Mrs. Bell stared at the boy. "Was it her fault, Judgment?" She looked at the figure, lying down on the driveway now. It had curled into a ball like it had a stomachache, moaning.

"The figure," the boy said. "Couldn't you see? Aren't you convinced, Anna?" He tapped his head.

"I'm convinced, Judgment." She smiled with her skeletal, faux-skin face, and he smiled back. "We missed out." She was convinced again.

"Good," the boy said, forcing it a bit, "I'm glad we're together on the same page."

"We missed out, Ryan," Mrs. Bell said.

Mira hit Ryan on the shoulder as hard as she could. "Ready?"

"For what?" Ryan said.

"The next house. You're coming along, right?" She fake pummeled him in the stomach.

"Sure," Mrs. Bell said, her attention directed at the figure.

Ryan scratched the back of his head.

"You're coming, Ryan," the boy said. "It's pretty much the final house."

"But it's not."

"Oh, but it is," the boy said. "Look at us—look at this rag-tag group, Ryan. We're tight-knit. This is *Goonies*. This is *Final Fantasy VII*. Or *IX*. I love it!" He moved towards the figure, waving Ryan along with him and Mira.

Mrs. Bell followed until she stepped on a small glass orb that had rolled out of the science house and into the middle of the circle. It wasn't much bigger than a child's marble. It caught the red in such a brilliant way, warping it within itself and creating swirls of every permutation of the color. She picked the thing up, peering into it. The glass was warm to the touch—much too warm for an apparently lifeless thing like the orb. Like her. At its deepest and dark center, she thought she caught a glimpse of a universe, expanding to the reaches of the orb. When she blinked, it escaped her vision like the edge of Habre Circle until she found it again.

"What about William?" Ryan asked her, looking over her shoulder at the orb.

"Forget William!" the boy shouted back to them. The figure struggled to its knees. He and Mira stood over it. Mira undid and redid her ponytail tighter. She dusted her-self off.

"I believe I attained a clarity just now, Ryan," Mrs. Bell said, rattling away from him with the orb. "I don't want to be Anna Bell anymore. She is inextricable from William. She has let years of her time be stolen."

"Years?" Ryan said. He scoffed at the word like it had no meaning. "Aren't you immortal now?"

Mrs. Bell shrugged. "If I let myself be her, I will let him take my immortal years too. We should focus on judgment. Righteous judgment."

The boy wondered if she meant him or the concept—the process. He chose to believe she meant him, though deep down he knew that she meant the process.

Ryan stayed out in the circle. He stood on the manhole that he and the neighborhood kids used as the center in their street hockey games. The red rain picked up, beading down his bare torso. He stretched his body, then started towards the rest of the group.

Mrs. Bell helped the figure to its boney feet. Its shadow receded farther, leaving its shoulders and the beginnings of its neck bare. The boy could see through it now—get a clear view of the brick home through its open ribs. He wondered who it was—what it looked like with human skin, muscle, and fat covering its crusty bones.

It could stand on its own, so Mrs. Bell let it be.

"You look well, shadow," she said. "He was a man, Judgment. You can see it in the structure."

"Figure," the figure bit. "Please."

It *wanted* to be called a "figure," not a shadow like everyone else thought. The boy waited for credit from everyone. It didn't come.

The figure led them to the brick home's front door as it spoke. It had to force the voice—the cadence. "Mira Peretz, your break is over. Go home. Prepare."

Everyone looked at Mira. The boy raised his hand and gave her a small wave.

"Sorry," he said. "I'll see you in a bit."

"Damn," she said, trudging across the grass next door.

Ryan tried to say something to her, but Mira just moved along. He clenched his jaw. He met the boy's eyes. The boy gave him a thumbs up and said it wouldn't be a big deal, then changed the subject.

"Were you a man, figure?" he said. "That's interesting." He tried not to look at Ryan.

"Is it?" the figure said. "I feel that was obvious."

It probably was, now that the boy considered it.

"I guess," he said.

The boy blinked. When he opened his eyes, everyone stared up into the sky as if their lives' purpose was to stare upwards. Even the figure. Even Mira had stopped on the steps to her porch to gaze into the red.

"Was that lightning?" Mrs. Bell asked.

"Gorgeous," Ryan said. And he never used the word gorgeous, as far as the boy could remember from both his and Ryan's memories bouncing around in his head.

The figure relaxed with a slight smile on its face. The boy watched its bone chin moving underneath the shadow. "The lightning on this side of matter expresses the root system between our realities."

"The what?" the boy said. "I missed it."

"I can't explain it more than that, Judgment," the figure sighed. "It's above me."

Mrs. Bell gave the boy a comforting look—sympathetic, pitying. "It's really something you have to see with your own eyes."

Ryan had his hand on his forehead. His eyes widened like this world had just opened up to him and winked before sharing its divine secrets.

"Will it happen again?" the boy asked.

The figure chuckled. "That's the first time I have ever seen it, and I've been here for years." It spoke casually, now, like a veritable human. It liked to cross its arms and pick at its ribs— take pieces of the flexible ceramic hanging off him and chuck them away.

The figure fidgeted—it lost its place in sentences for a beat where it would place an "um" or an "uh." When it coughed, as it so often would, the reflex sounded less hollow, less otherworldly, but still terrible. The blue in the figure's eyes had faded enough to pronounce the human pupils underneath, peeking out as if behind a convincing Halloween mask.

"This house," the figure said, stretching its neck out, "is just your basic judgment. Nothing to note, really."

Ryan and Mrs. Bell, who sought something of substance after missing out on the house of science, couldn't conceal their disappointment. They looked at the boy like he had let them down. Mrs. Bell delicately placed her orb containing a universe in the front garden, beside a flowerpot and an old stone rabbit that had been tipped over for ages, before shuffling in with most of the group. The boy lingered outside. He stayed there looking up in the sky for more lightning until he felt some futility in his chest. The glean of Mrs. Bell's marble universe caught his eye, so he snatched it off the cradling ground and pocketed it with Wes and the porcelain stranger's discarded eyes. *Souvenirs*, he thought, *for whenever this was over. No harm or foul.*

He entered the brick home. A flash of lightning behind him cast his shadow into the foyer as he did, but at least no one else even saw it that time. Expresses roots between realities and all that. He could tell all the others that he saw them, and he would at his earliest convenience.

Mira watched him from her porch.

O   O   O

Despite its red and refined exterior, the brick home was just another colonial like the rest. The inside remained mostly untouched by the Oughtside, only because there wasn't much to touch. It had never been abandoned like the yellow house, because it did appear to be relatively well-kept and clean, but it lacked furniture. What furnishings it did have—a couch, an entertainment center, a dining table—were covered in ghostly white sheets.

The figure led them through the dining room with a table holding a full spread of a wax turkey dinner. The room smelled like Thanksgiving, wafting from the wood floor.

"Who lives here?" the boy asked.

"The Ferrars, I think," Mrs. Bell said. "I don't know that for sure as they're kind of nestled back here, out of the way—kept to themselves, mostly." She took a seat in one of the dining room chairs. Ryan took the one next to her.

"This," Mrs. Bell said, picking up a wax drumstick and dropping it on her plate, "looks pretty boring." She slammed her skull forward into her faux hunk of mashed potatoes. "There was anti-gravity in that science house, Ryan. Tiny universes in marbles. And we missed it." She bullied her voice. "Because of that fucking William."

Ryan put his head forward into his mashed potatoes too. Not quite as hard. "I think I'm just depressed."

"Who am I judging?" the boy asked, crossing his arms and surveying the room.

The figure moved through the house, looking around. It was difficult for the boy to see him walk on ceramic skeletal feet. He used to have an elegance—a presence as he glided through the red. Now, he moved with a half-jaunty rattle.

"Where did I put him?" the figure asked, stumbling into the kitchen to open the pantry.

A full box of cereal spilled over his head, each piece of it— O-shaped, grain-based—clicking on the tile floor after tumbling off his shoulders.

"I'll admit I'm having trouble remembering where I put your next case," the figure said. "This process—my skin." It trailed off.

Mrs. Bell popped her head off her deflated taters. She spoke with frowning lips. "It is a difficult process"

The figure pulled a box of granola bars—all-natural— from the pantry and chucked it at Mrs. Bell, hitting Ryan instead. His aim was poor.

"You were nibbled on by wolves," he said. "And sat in a room where your skin trickled away. Mine was torn from my bones. You had time, Anna—time to come to terms with this." He looked across his bone hands. "This humanity—this bare, transparent humanity."

"I have never felt human since waking, figure," Mrs. Bell said. She slammed her head back down. In a somber tone, she said, "We are not humans."

Something stirred in the pantry. At the bottom, behind the condensed soup cans. The figure didn't notice, but the boy did.

"Someone's there," he said.

"These memories," the figure said, looking at the boy. "Am I a person or still an 'it' to you, Judgment? Man, woman, child, entity, being, binary, non?" he asked the boy and only the boy, like the two of them were the only things in the room.

The boy stood there with an unsure look shaping his face.

"I don't know," he said, knowing he would still call the figure "it" if he spoke of it to anyone. It didn't strike him as a person, yet. Not really. Not like Mrs. Bell.

While trying to decide how to tell the figure this, the boy watched a child tumble out of the pantry and latch onto the figure's legs. The child looked a year or so older than Wes—a teenager for sure, but not quite. He had braces, but no greasy skin just yet and red hair turning brown. He wore a blank gray t-shirt and a pair of tattered black jeans.

The figure lost its balance and fell back onto the linoleum floor.

The child screamed; his voice had a light squeak to it. "Got you, shadow."

"That's right," the figure said as if just remembering something. "I put you in there."

"You didn't," the child said, tearing the figure's arm off and beating him with it. "I hid from you. Successfully avoided the shadow. Level complete."

The figure didn't move during the beating—it just took the hits. Mrs. Bell looked on. She shook her head. Even she would have pushed the child off by now with her ceramic skeletal strength. A house or two ago, the figure would have put him through a wall.

"But not Judgment," Mrs. Bell said, melancholic. "You avoided the wrong one!"

The boy huffed. "I was going to say something like that. He can't even see you sitting there."

"Nope," the child said, stepping off the figure and turning to the boy. "There is no escaping judgment."

He had to turn his head up to meet the boy's eyes.

The boy imagined what he looked like from the kid's point of view. How tall and imposing he must be.

"Smart kid," the boy said. He bent down to meet him at eye-level. "What's your name?"

"I haven't decided yet." The child looked back at the figure. "This shadow said I could have a new one here if I wanted."

The figure—upright again, though not standing—nodded. Its eyes grew distant, then focused. "I did say that. I remember, now." It took its arm back from the child, who had lost interest in using it, and popped it back into place.

The boy scrunched his face up in a sour look for a tick. "I didn't realize that was an option."

The kid shrugged. "Now you do, huh?"

It's too late to change my own name, the boy thought. He was Judgment, now, who knelt there smirking at the kid. "So, what did you do?"

"Something neat, I hope."

He threw a punch at the boy, aiming right for between the legs. The boy blocked him, then shoved him back. As a child, the boy had thrown the same punches at his older brother. He laughed heartily in the face of this nameless kid.

The figure crawled across the kitchen floor into the dining room. Everyone watched it use a chair to pull itself up into a seat next to Mrs. Bell and Ryan. It composed itself and relaxed. It gestured for everyone to take seats around the dining room table with the boy at the head. The still-nameless kid sat across from the boy at the other head of the long table.

"I can't see you that well," Ryan said to the boy, weaving left, right and craning his neck to see past Mrs. Bell. He was always a little shorter than the boy.

Mrs. Bell contorted herself in odd skeletal ways to let Ryan see. She plucked some dirt from her back. "You should find a shirt for this gathering, Ryan."

"Yes," the figure said. "It's a refined dinner."

Ryan looked around the room. He stretched. "I'm good."

The boy leaned forward, putting his hands over the wax turkey in front of him. The figure handed him a real knife, which he used to slice into the poultry. The hollow bird collapsed immediately.

"I think," the figure said. It paused like an actor trying to remember lines. It put its hands on either side of its head and squeezed until he knew what he was going to say. "I think we should all go around the table and express what we're most regretful for." It said this like it wasn't sure if it was supposed to say this.

The room fell further into silence as they all traded glances. Mrs. Bell toyed with her faux potatoes, Ryan made pictures with his corn, the figure stared into a never-ending void with a dim look on its face, and the nameless kid slumped back in his chair. The boy poked at the wax turkey remains with his knife.

"Mrs. Bell?" he said.

Mrs. Bell chattered. "We've seen my regrets made manifest several times since we found ourselves dead." With her hand, she played with a beam of red coming in through the front windows. "I regret most of my decisions in my life, but— nothing in my death so far."

"Ryan," the boy said.

Using his spoon, Ryan flicked some corn across the table at the boy. "This is sad, Biter. Twenty years old and we're both still in Habre Circle. We'll never leave, either. We died on this ground where we might as well have been born." He flung corn at the figure, next.

"Figure," the boy said.

"I regret," the figure said. "I regret, I regretted, I've regret since I was born anew with clarity in an endless mill. I regress into a man, now. Open. Weak. Exposed." It brushed away the shadow over its chest cavity, saying it had no use for it now. Not this far around the bend.

"Me," the boy said. "I regret—" He thought for truly long seconds, tapping the wax food around him with his knife, to a changing beat. "I guess I actually regret never getting to know my parents as people."

He figured they would be here in the Oughtside. It seemed obvious that they would—that he would meet them somewhere along the way like did Cameron.

Mrs. Bell and Ryan leaned into the table and looked at the boy with concern, with actual feeling welling in each of their eyes. The figure looked farther into the void.

"Screw this," the nameless kid said. He shoved himself away from the table and stomped into the living room, hard enough to make a statement and rattle the floorboards, which sounded hollow beneath his feet. A tarp caked with dust was draped over the room's entertainment center; he pulled it with the grunt of a selfish little creature to reveal a television and a gaming console, both of them clearly built in the Oughtside. He sat as close to the screen as he could and clutched the sole controller. The CRT television and the console blipped alive at the kid's touch. A game's title embedded itself from the screen into the kid's eyes: MIGHT.

The boy followed the nameless kid out into the living room. He took a seat next to him on the floor, the way his older brother used to when he needed help with a game.

"Nothing," the kid said to the television. "I don't regret anything. I never will."

The screen urged the nameless kid to PRESS START with flashing colors and a soundtrack of dated computer tones and chiptunes rising in a slow crescendo.

White, pixelated text rolled onto the screen.

WELCOME TO MIGHT.

PLEASE CHOOSE A NAME OF ANY LENGTH.

A menu popped up over the black background for the nameless kid to input letters.

"Oh," he said, melancholy about it. "I guess I need a name already." He moved around the menu. He tried typing a few names, then deleted them. "I don't know."

Ryan came into the room from the kitchen and sat behind the kid.

"Christopher?" Ryan said. "It's the name I'd have chosen for myself."

Mrs. Bell shuffled in from the kitchen and sat behind the boy.

"Rufus?" Mrs. Bell said. She caught sour looks from the others. "It's an underrated name."

"Robert," the boy said. He looked like a Robert to him— not a Bob, but a Robert.

The figure—stumbling over the chairs in the dining room out into the living room—didn't share a suggestion. It gave up its turn with a cough and a dismissive wiggle of its jaw. It sat centered and behind Ryan and Mrs. Bell.

"Robert," the kid said. "It's kind of tame."

"It works," Ryan said.

"It does," Mrs. Bell nodded.

The figure even agreed, saying, "It is tame, but you are a blank slate."

In the dim living room, the figure looked like it still had some shadow covering its body. The boy knew its bones were bare. They took on the dominant color of the TV screen and the room. He paid more attention to it than anything else. Its faux fleshed face was mere minutes from being revealed, and he could generate faces from the figure's in the dark. He could force it to be anyone he wanted.

The nameless kid said, "I guess I am a blank slate. Robert, it is." He started inputting it onto the screen too quickly and it came out wrong.

WELCOME, ROBORT.

"Damn," Robort said.

KILLSCREEN

A couple of seconds after Robort chose his name and all hope of correcting it was lost, rings of chronic neon enveloped the room. The floor beneath the group disengaged and the living room descended into the ground at a slow, controlled speed, leaving its walls behind. Grease and gears burnt and sparked as they all sunk beneath Habre Circle. A bit of Earth fell away during the process, dirt raining down around them. It smelled of worms.

Below, back in the vast twilight floors of the Oughtside, the boy surveyed the neighborhood kids' production still ablaze. He pointed to the abandoned video store like it was a house where he used to live, eager to show everyone. The room stopped, suspended in the sunset sky. It moved forward, building to a steady speed. Mrs. Bell leaned out one side, using the figure's shoulder as a grip to keep her balance.

"We're on a track," she said. "Moving across the sky."

Closer to the under-sky than ever before, it appeared to the boy as genuine and infinite. The Oughtside reached and climbed and dug farther beyond the limits of the boy's role in it, beyond the production of some arson children, beyond a sparsely stocked video store. In the distance and even just below him, dazzling buildings shifted—skylines, too. Cities of the porcelain dead churned from his mill or another, each of them living spent lives.

"It's big," the boy said. He felt like a third grader learning geography for the first time, failing to comprehend a globe.

Ryan laughed. "No shit."

"That's me," Robort said, pointing everyone to the ten-inch television screen. They all gathered right around it. Onscreen, an eight-bit fetus grew in a womb from a zygote, pixels compounding with each passing second. The group settled down into their seats on the floor to watch. No music backed the process. The whirr of the track filled the stale air. A metal wind flowed through the open room.

"Yes," the figure said. It rubbed its temples. The boy could see its chin now—a prominent one with a strong jaw.

Two flashing arrows appeared on the screen, one labeled BIRTH and the other GESTATE.

Robort tilted the joystick on the controller toward the decision to gestate and he watched himself with wet eyes. The arrows appeared onscreen again: GESTATE or BIRTH. He chose the former. The living room slowed to a crawl on its track.

"Robort," the boy said. "You'll have to leave eventually."

Light hit Rob's prenatal face and hands pulled him out from the dark. He cried eight-bit cries.

"See?" the boy said. "It's not so bad."

Another decision popped up, with only one arrow: LIVE.

The game moved ahead through levels and lives, with static and jagged pixels around the monitor, as if every frame was a new killscreen for a decades-old arcade game. Sometimes the killscreens stopped long enough for the boy to see an image—a brief, innocuous moment in Robort's time. A birthday party, a day at elementary school, and so on. The boring stuff. The filler. The game's graphics evolved and grew with Rob. The world centered around him, the camera focused on his back, mainly—a tight, third-person perspective.

Rob had a mother, a father, and a hamster as a pet, running along on its little wheel. As revealed in a lengthy loading screen, he'd moved from a townhouse to the brick one in Habre Circle. The console was old and it needed to load for a while between actual gameplay and killscreens. This frustrated all but the figure and Mrs. Bell.

"I just picked whatever was laying around," the figure said. "These widgets are all the same."

"It's not taking that long," Mrs. Bell said. "Be patient."

Rob's hamster died. He found her lying in its bedding, curled up like she was sleeping. Off-screen, the voices of his parents tried to console him, telling him that animals that live shorter lives than us still live full ones. Four arrows appeared on the screen this time, with a clock counting down from thirty in the middle of them. Decisions: FEEL, DON'T FEEL, LAUGH, RUN. Rob clutched the controller and nudged the joystick towards DON'T FEEL. Ryan grabbed the controller, stopping him. The clock ticked to twenty.

"What are you doing?" Ryan asked. "That's not right."

"It's what happened," Rob complained.

"If it's what happened," the boy said. "We should know."

Ryan—in a slight huff—let the kid go to make his choice. They killscreened through another handful of levels. Polygonal edges softened, and the living room accelerated. The boy felt gravity pushing against him now.

Robort's parents separated for a while. His dad left for six months and lived in an apartment for a reason Rob couldn't discern with his little pixel head. The day he came back, he and Rob's mom visited the kid in his room while he played with his new hamster. His father did most of the talking, while his mother leaned on the wall closest to his bedroom door, her arms crossed.

"So just pretend," his dad said. "Pretend that this never happened, that I never left."

"It was a mistake," his mom said.

When the decision to agree with his parents covered the screen, in one singular arrow, the joystick moved on its own.

"Sometimes we're automated," Mrs. Bell said.

The figure curled up on the floor like Rob's hamster. "We're unmoored now," it said. "From absolute truth, but not from absolute possibility."

The boy found enjoyment in the figure's words, if not in the way it was currently sitting. It talked like it still had shadow and mystique. *Gravitas.*

Onscreen, the decisions grew more frequent. The screen flashed and the soundtrack performed a perilous descent into hard and aggressive music. Rob engaged in an altercation at school, the camera moved to an active angle with him on one side and another kid on the other. This other kid looked like the kind that would start something like this fight. He was heavy with muscle and issues with his dad. In the background, their schoolmates, their audience, pumped their fists and nodded like this was *Street Fighter II.*

Decisions: FIGHT, DIFFUSE, ITEM, RUN, TATTLE. The timer began at twenty seconds.

"Fight him," the boy said.

Mrs. Bell gave him a stern look, her dark eyes narrowed. "Diffuse the situation."

"Run," Ryan said. Of course.

"Fight," the figure offered. It played with the word.

The boy spoke again after considering. "Maybe diffuse." He had never been in a real fight when he was Rob's age—never had that rite of passage.

Rob breathed heavy and licked his lips. "Fight, then." It was obvious that was the one he wanted, anyway. He moved the joystick and the Rob onscreen threw a punch. It connected, but the other boy didn't go down. More decisions—a multitude of physical actions—presented next. Robort continued attacking. He had to dodge a few times—had to block twice. Rage burned on his small face.

FIGHT.

Orchestral music swelled.

FIGHT.

RUN remained an option.

FIGHT.

He busted the other boy's jaw—permanently. A principal took the other kid's place on the battlefield. She held up a phone, and the text CALL PARENTS overlaid on the screen. Killscreen to a courtroom, pitting Rob against a judge towering over him. DETENTION CENTER. Killscreen to juvie, pitting Rob against a whole room of other kids.

"Shit," the boy said. "That escalated."

"See," Ryan said, pleased with himself. "You should have run."

"That wouldn't have taught him anything," Mrs. Bell said. "He's got a bloodlust in him. What are you so angry at, kid?" She put her hands on his shoulders and shook him.

"I don't know," Rob said "It felt right in the moment. Did I lose?"

The game killscreened ahead. The boy caught images of bars and cages. The room slowed. A well-rendered, photoreal-istic adult Rob worked on a dock, loading shipping containers. He was up against two approaching men who had pale faces and sunken eyes. They were deep into abusing a substance.

Decisions: START A CRIME SYNDICATE, FIGHT, RUN. The timer started at fifteen.

"Which one?" Robort said, looking around the room.

"Well let's not fight," the boy said. "You seem battle-hard-ened enough already."

He did. Dockworker Robort had broad shoulders and a rigid, scarred face.

"Run," Ryan said. "Keep your head down. You're prob-ably on parole. I think I saw that you were on parole."

The boy nodded. "Definitely on parole." It had been somewhere in the killscreens.

Mrs. Bell patted Rob's head and sat back. "Listen to them."

The figure suggested he start a crime syndicate, but no one could be sure if it was serious. It didn't sound all that present.

"I don't want to be this," Rob said. "I don't want this life." He leaned back, away from the console. The timer fell to five.

Everyone let it fall to zero, at which point the decisions faded from the screen. Dockworker Rob turned from the approaching criminals and walked into a shipping container, shutting the doors behind him. He curled up in the back corner and died like a sick animal. They watched his body decompose and the shipping container rust away. The world around Dockworker Rob's bleaching bones thrived without him. Then society collapsed and nature overtook everything. The world recovered from humanity. In a millennium or ten, the sun went supernova and decimated what was left of the earth. Dockworker Rob hung on in space as cosmic dust. Eventually, the ultimate fate of the universe was to collapse in one instant. Even that was unsustainable. With its collapse, the last of Dockworker Rob truly died, and the words TRY AGAIN faded in onscreen.

Silently, the boy, Ryan, Mrs. Bell, and Robort agreed not to discuss the dread on each of their faces after watching their universe perish. They all wondered if the Oughtside was subject to the death of the universe. The knowing look on the figure's face—a creeping smirk palpable beneath its dwindling shadow—got them thinking that, yes, it probably was. But the figure wasn't of sound mind, surely, so they could all convince themselves that the figure had no true idea. Then, the living room stalled.

"I'll do it myself this time," Rob said, gripping the controller tight and furrowing his brow.

Decisions: BIRTH, GESTATE

BIRTH.

This time, Robort avoided the pitfalls of the detention center. He chose to tattle at the onset of the fight and the other boy received an in-school suspension for his repeat offense of being—as the principal put it—a little shit nuisance. They applauded him.

After that, he was never popular during this playthrough, and that consumed him whole.

"Were any of you ever popular?" he said to the group, who had remained silent despite itching to speak.

"I was," Ryan said. "I don't know how, but I was."

"Me, too," Mrs. Bell said. "I like to trace it back to my personality, but I know—at that age—it was my beauty. And my skin." She sighed. "I miss my skin."

A low grunt emerged from the figure's mouth. "Me too."

"Real skin, not shadow," Mrs. Bell said. "True skin."

"I'm aware."

The boy could see the form of a nose on the figure's face. It was on the larger side, like his.

"You don't need it, Robort," he said. "Popularity. You're falling into these traps that we can totally steer you away from."

Killscreen to high school and Rob was infatuated with an individual. They were the head of some clubs, with long raven hair. He approached them in the hall with designs on asking them out.

Decisions: JOKE, BLUNT, BEG, GRAND GESTURE, FIGHT, RUN.

Rob chose to perform a grand gesture, though the group tried to convince him not to.

"Something like that," Ryan had said, "needs to be done at the right time by the right person. I don't think this is the right time and I don't believe this you is the right person. Just be cool about it."

High School Rob had dark hair and a scrawny body. He was short, too, with a few strands of a mustache on his upper lip. His dad hadn't gotten around to teaching him to shave yet.

Rob pursued the grand gesture anyway. High School Rob walked up to his crush—in the hall, at their lockers in the morning—and pulled a sign cut into a heart from his backpack. *It was a solid sign*, the boy thought. It had been crafted well in art class. He also wrote a poem for them. They laughed at it because it dripped with sentiment and was poorly constructed; they felt bad about that. They didn't mean to.

Decisions: WEEP, WAIT TO WEEP, GO TO THE BATHROOM AND WEEP, FIGHT, RUN, EAT, WORK OUT, CUT, PLAY IT OFF, BLAME THEM, BLAME POETRY, BLAME PARENTS, RAGE, RAGE, RAGE. The timer was at five seconds.

Ryan punched Rob in the arm lightly. "As I said," he said. You need to lay low, you idiot." He took these games seriously.

Rob let the clock drop to zero, and High School Rob, with every eye in the hallway on him, entered the custodian's closet and pulled it shut. It had no windows and he didn't turn on the light. He died in there like a sick animal. The universe eventually died after him. A pixel blinked into existence in the middle of the screen, and Robort put his head in his hands.

"I don't want that life either," he said.

"It might have been okay," Mrs. Bell said. "You might have been a late bloomer."

"I don't want to be a late bloomer, skeleton woman."

"Well, now you're just being picky, honey."

The living room stayed stalled above the Oughtside, moving forward in only the slightest of increments. Shadows and porcelain people milled about below them. Their lives echoed up. The place sounded like any other city street. Above them, faux stars twinkled.

Mrs. Bell patted Robort on the head.

"Let me try," she said. She spoke with confidence next. "I'm a woman of two worlds, kid. Follow my lead."

○   ○   ○

Mrs. Bell had the idea that choosing to gestate once would create a healthier mind and body, so she had Rob do that. But the kid still insisted on not feeling for his hamster's death. Even when pressed and told that he must have felt something for it—told that he just couldn't articulate it at that age or put it into words—he moved the joystick towards that decision. No one put up too much of a fight on the matter. It was accurate, after all, and they all agreed that Judgment should work off accurate evidence.

"Well," Mrs. Bell said, "that's only one forked road in a life of the millions you'll have." She did look a bit worried, though.

She diffused the situation with the boy in middle school, and they became friends in high school. When he went to ask his crush out, Rob was confident—bolstered by a modicum of popularity. The crush wanted to know him. Killscreen to college and the time came for Rob and the crush to separate. They brought it up first.

Decisions: WEEP, AGREE, DISAGREE, RAGE, RUN

Mrs. Bell answered every decision quickly, with utmost confidence like she knew the path through the maze of this kid's life. She scoffed at this one.

"Easy," she said, telling Rob to choose AGREE.

And he did, with a smile. He was moving forward in a life he could see himself having—enjoying.

Mrs. Bell decided Rob should major in a STEM field. Rob found a match there and they were married two years after their post-grad work. Three years later and they were looking to adopt a child. Success! Rob found a cushy job with a pharmaceutical company—a place with many ladders and built-in plans to climb them. Mrs. Bell could craft a life like an expert—like a god. A skeletal, Halloween décor god.

The room moved again at a fine clip, and the graphics of the game polished, evolving beyond anything the boy had ever seen—beyond photorealism, too far beyond reality.

The game loaded a few years into Robort's job and a few days into a work week there. Rob had some girth to him now. A belly that wouldn't stop growing and anxiety that wouldn't stop mounting. He had two kids, a mortgage, and a corner office, too. It was late at night. His family was expecting him. Confusion sank Mrs. Bell. Her jaw dislocated, but she fixed it.

"What the hell happened?" she asked. "What the hell did I do wrong? Fucking thing's rigged."

Ryan laughed a bit. "He's just a little pudgy, Anna." He moved his arms to pantomime running. "A little exercise is all he needs."

Anna Bell stared at the screen, trying to solve the puzzle.

Success Rob pulled some documents from his desk and pored over them. They held equations and data on their pages—graphs and pie charts. He bit his nails as he scoured the information. Along with smoking, nailbiting was a habit he had developed in college.

He then removed a large envelope from the desk, made out to the city's largest newspaper, written in the game's pixelated font. It included a note, which read:

I HAVE KILLED AND WILL KILL AGAIN. THERE IS BLOOD ON MY HANDS AND I HAVE ENJOYED THE REWARDS OF ITS RED STAINS, BESTOWED ON ME BY THE MEN AND WOMEN ABOVE.

"Did I create a Zodiac killer?" Mrs. Bell lamented.

Decisions: MAIL, CONFRONT, SHRED, RUN, LOSE JOB, LOSE FAMILY, LOSE EVERYTHING. The timer counted down from five seconds.

Mrs. Bell swallowed hard, which interested the boy because she didn't have a throat anymore. So, the decision flustered her enough that she had to mimic swallowing.

"Shred it," she said, and Rob listened. The living room squealed as its brakes engaged. The couch slid across the floor, so the figure stopped it by laying on it. It appeared to fall asleep. It faced away from the television and into the cushions.

Success Rob, in his broad tie and sky blue short-sleeved dress shirt, walked over to his shredder. He knelt down and held the document over the machine, then fed it through, followed by the envelope.

The figure snickered into the couch. "Of course, Anna Bell. That will solve it. Absolutely."

"We have a family to consider, shadow," Mrs. Bell said.

Success Rob went to the window and hit his head against it lightly. He shut his eyes.

Decisions: JUMP, NOT TODAY. The timer set to five.

"Oh," the skeleton woman said, her head cocked to the side. "I thought it would get better." She sat back.

"Because it always has for you," the figure said. "Sometimes I think you are an exercise in futility."

When the timer hit zero, Success Rob opened the window and stepped out onto the concrete ledge of the company building. It towered over a city. Below, protesters camped out at the entrance. Taking a half step forward, he exhaled, and the wind helped him drift off into the night air above the city. He rose into the stars instead of falling. He curled into a ball up there and died like a sick animal in space—like Laika, the Russian cosmonaut dog. In time, the universe did too. It condensed into one pixel, then spread into more.

Rob gripped the controller tight, then tried to tear it from the console.

"RAGE, huh?" the boy said. There was so much of it in the room, now.

Ryan stopped the kid from destroying anything, with a casual and smug look on his face.

"I got this, little guy," he said. "Just do as I tell you."

O   O   O

Ryan had RUN on the mind. He ran from the schoolyard fight, he ran from asking out Rob's crush, and he ran away from home after high school. He worked odd jobs to buy himself a little sailboat to live in, then took it out to the middle of the sea and stayed there for as long as he could without returning, becoming as grizzled and scraggly as a leftover pirate.

"You see, Judgment," Ryan said, "Escape is always an option. It might not always work, but when it does, you're golden. It's an easy life."

"He's not doing anything," the boy said. "He's not growing. He's barely living. We're barely moving."

Ryan nodded. "But he's not a criminal. He didn't help start the opiate epidemic."

They loaded and killscreened through most of Pirate Rob's years on the sea, and from what the boy could gather they were uneventful. He just sailed and took the salted air into his skin and bones. The man kept to himself, did some work when he needed money, and lived away from typical life. He had no pictures on the walls of his lower decks. He existed, but not much more.

Decisions: RUN, RAGE. The timer set at ∞.

Ryan told Rob to run and the screen killscreened forward about two days to the same scenario.

Decisions: RUN, RAGE. The timer set at ∞.

And again, to the same scenario.

Decisions: RUN, RAGE. The timer set at ∞.

"You broke him, Ryan," the boy said, grinning. "Is this the life you wanted? Everything's missing." Pirate Rob sat alone in a small room with a bed. The boy chewed on the inside of his cheek.

Ryan hunched. "No," he said. "I really thought that would work out better."

"I don't want this either," Robort said, crying.

"At this pace," Mrs. Bell said, looking back out over the Oughtside below the living room, "we'll never get back to the circle. Did you ever consider that, figure?"

The figure spoke, still laying on the couch, in a calm and open tone. "I considered every, and anticipated most, things."

It sat up—rattling—and took the controller from Rob, shoving him over. In a flash of speed, the mostly skeletal figure started inputting a code: start, up, down, down, left, diagonal left, start, full rotation left, full rotation right, start. If the boy closed his eyes, the clacking of the buttons made the living room sound like the old local arcade where he and Ryan used to go when they could scrounge up enough quarters.

Ryan shut his eyes too and they listened together.

The arrow blipped off the screen. Pirate Rob stood up out of his bunk. He climbed out of his home, into the open sea air. It was night—overcast—and the ocean only seemed to exist in sound. He dove into the black and sunk to the pixel deep, fish picking at him as he did. His picked bones settled into a forgotten trench with prehistoric life. Together, they were the last to collapse when the universe eventually died.

"Just needed a soft reset," the figure said, laying back down on the couch.

Decisions: Birth, Gestate.

○   ○   ○

The boy knew. He knew the best way to judge Robort and how to win the game—the point of the challenge. It was an obvious notion, but one he didn't think any of them wanted to consider or entertain to the extent that they needed to.

"My turn," he said, moving closer to Rob. "Listen only to me."

Birth.

Killscreens. Loading times.

Little Rob found his dead hamster. The boy watched with intent.

"Here," he said.

Decisions: Feel, Don't feel, Laugh. No timer here. They could sit in this space until the universe imploded or collapsed or flitted away into nothing.

Robort shook his head. "I didn't feel anything. Honest, Judgment. Neither sadness nor the need to laugh."

"You didn't," the boy said. "I believe you." He scratched his nose. "What does it matter, though, huh? We'll just see everything we know collapse and die again if I'm wrong. No big."

The boy could tell Rob didn't want to tilt the joystick towards FEEL. The kid's hands shook, and he breathed heavier.

"I'll do it if you won't," the boy said.

"No." Rob stared at the dead hamster exactly like his counterpart onscreen.

He chose to feel, and the living room rocketed forward, taking loops and turns in the track above the Oughtside city with ease. The group had to hold on to each other, to the television, to the floor. The ones with stomachs had butterflies in them when they took the drops.

The screen killscreened through Rob's years—all of them—and they worked. Rob worked—he functioned and never hit a wall that would lead him back to the womb. The universe went on to die, but not before Rob passed away quietly surrounded by loved ones and consumed with satisfaction in his memory.

Robort looked down at the floor and whispered, "That's it. That is the life I want."

CONGRATULATIONS.

"But," the boy said. "Not the one you'll have. Not the one you'll ever have."

The screen killscreened to now, showing them all in the living room watching the screen watching the living room in an infinite mirror.

Decisions: SALVATION, DAMNATION, RUN.

"Am I an exercise in futility, too?" the nameless kid said, looking at the floor.

"Yes," the boy said. "I would say that you are. Any decision made will lead you down the same path—a path you don't want—because you are broken. You are fundamentally broken."

Ryan grabbed the boy with one hand. "You, Judgment, are fundamentally broken. He's just a kid. There is a thing called therapy." He was surprised, but he knew he shouldn't have been. "So, he didn't care about one hamster. He didn't understand. Kids can be cruel little dicks. You know that."

The living room spun forward.

"I understood," Rob said. "Truly, I understand." He latched onto the controller's shoddy plastic joystick with both hands and snapped it off. He then lunged at Ryan and stabbed him in the neck with the broken piece. A steady stream of blood gushed from the wound, down Ryan's chest.

RAGE.

"Fuck," Ryan said, drifting out of consciousness, down here where the red couldn't fully reach.

Mrs. Bell wrapped her bone arms around Rob and lifted him off Ryan, bleeding in the corner of the room. The kid swiped at the figure on the couch, who sat up delighted in the attack.

The boy put pressure on Ryan's gashed neck, looking him in the eyes.

"You keep dying," he said.

"Because you keep getting me killed."

The boy ticked and gritted his teeth. "You're not adapting, Ryan. You're not becoming anything more than what you were before."

Ryan raised an eyebrow. "Oh fuck off, I don't need to." He paused to gurgle in some air. "Do you want to know why?"

The boy did, but he wouldn't say that. He put on a stoic look.

"Because at my core, Biter, I actually like who I am." He laughed like an entire studio audience, then dissolved into a soft singular cry. "I know what you're going to do to Mira—I could see it in the shadow's face when he stepped inside my home. I could always see the strings, but I convinced myself I couldn't. I hoped you might see them too. I hoped you might hear the laugh track underneath all of this." His eyes glossed over as he passed out, the noises he made as blood filled him indistinguishable from an obvious laugh track on a bad sitcom.

"There are no strings," the boy whispered into Ryan's ear. "You haven't known me for a long time. I *know* what I'm doing."

The living room grinded to a stop. It had gone the full length of its circuitous track and arrived back at the platform it brought them down on. A hiss of hydraulics followed its arrival, and the platform rose slowly.

The boy stood and shook his hands free of Ryan's blood. There was a good deal more this time. It pooled on the shag rug.

"Damnation," he said, turning to the console, "is not an absolute ending, Rob."

He felt like that was a solid line but couldn't tell based on any of the reactions in the room which were either manic, in Rob's case, or stern.

Mrs. Bell spoke in a soft timbre. "Judgment," she said, "You know this is a kid, right?" The kid frothed at the mouth.

A chewy granola bar, like one his mom would pack in his lunch every day, fell out of his pocket. "An innocent, regardless of what he may or may not do in the future."

He could still become a serial killer, a librarian, a fire-fighter, or a doctor.

"He did jam a piece of plastic into Ryan's neck just now," the boy said.

"I'll give you that, but regardless—"

He held up his hand. "Regardless, Anna, I get it."

He picked up the warm controller from the floor. He looked down at the broken, bloodied joystick, then back.

"Would you liken me to William right now, Anna?" He stood taller, his chest out.

Mrs. Bell shook her head. "No, and that was faulty thinking on my part. I don't see any William in you. You are your own entity—your own unique beast."

Decisions: SALVATION, DAMNATION, RUN.

"Judgment," the figure yawned.

The boy tilted toward damnation.

The figure tore Rob from Mrs. Bell's arms.

"This nameless kid, this blank slate—this futility," he said, holding Rob by the collar. "Damned." He then dropped him off the side, down into the Oughtside below just before the platform finished its ascent and the group, sans that nameless kid, breathed in the red air of Habre Circle.

This surprised Mrs. Bell and the boy, who shared an expression.

"That wasn't damnation," the boy said. "You just dropped him. He was supposed to—" he stopped. What was supposed to happen? He recalled the process. It had changed so much, house to house, but the result was pretty much the same: the damned are sent outside Habre—outside the Oughtside—where they roam and where they work in the clay mill or scavenge for porcelain from the newly minted people. "He was just supposed to leave the Oughtside, figure." An exile from a pseudo-paradise.

"Well, I decided," the figure said, sitting back down, "to throw him down into it instead. A slight deviation from the norm, I know, but I think whether that kid is down there, out there, or in here, the pattern of his existence won't change."

"You're making the decisions now?" Mrs. Bell said, grabbing the figure by the jaw and inspecting its face, side to side. It didn't struggle.

"Yes, Anna," its voice rattling through her bone fingers, grinning like it had a secret she already should have known. "I decided to do that again." Taking Mrs. Bell's arm in its hand like it held the barrel of a gun to its hardboiled head, it focused on the boy and continued, "We humans seem to cling to grand designs, Judgment, no matter how many times we're shown they don't exist."

The boy shook his head. "Isn't a pattern a design?"

The figure nodded as best it could. "Of course."

It was just a hamster.

Killscreen.

Mrs. Bell chattered her teeth. "I need air."

But she doesn't breathe, the boy thought. Though he did notice that the air in the room—in the whole brick house—had turned stale and metallic from Ryan's blood.

Anna let go of the figure and it of her. The boy stepped out of the home first. The TV screen back in the living room blinked with a message and played a victory fanfare in the minor key.

Winners Don't Do Drugs!

○　　○　　○

All features but the figure's eyes were bare and free from the shadow. Faux skin covered the ceramic skeleton frame from the cheeks up in abundance, giving it a pudgy, tanned look. It had curls of salt and pepper hair. As the figure limped out of the brick home, the boy caught its face in the light, and his brain decided that he knew it. It was familiar with a sudden snap of internal fingers. The face was just short of obvious.

"I know you, figure," the boy said.

"Yes," the figure said, sounding more like a simple man with throat issues. "We've been through a lot together, Judgment. Perhaps it is my lack of this shadow skin speaking, but I feel like I know you too." It fooled with him in a comic tone. "As much as you've learned from me, I have learned—"

"No," the boy said, his mouth open. "I know you. I knew you." His eyes narrowed, his stare sharpening.

"Ryan Mont lost almost all of his blood,' the figure said. "Look at it, all over my bone feet—your clothes."

Ryan's blood did decorate them both. And a large part of the floor.

Mrs. Bell tended to Ryan. She carried the Mont boy piggyback style. Past the boy. Past the figure. She laid him out on the lawn where he could bathe in the red. She shook him, then looked at the boy and shrugged.

"Sure. He'll wake up," he said. To the figure, he said, "You might as well tell me who you are, or who you were. As soon as I can see your eyes, I'll know."

"Then as soon as that, Judgment, but no sooner." He grinned. "Come along, now. We've almost finished. You have a girl waiting for you for once, don't you?"

It coughed—a familiar one with a tickled wheeze at the tail end. And again. It had a bit of a fit. More chunks of the faux, plaster skin fell from its face.

"You're right!" the boy said, slicking back his tangled, matted hair.

The boy walked with the figure to the mauve colonial, purpose in his steps. The figure sat on the porch. It pointed its thumb back towards Mira's doorbell, one of those light-up buttons so visitors could see it in the dark.

"I'll be in before showtime," the figure said, almost inaudibly.

The boy rang the bell, then fixed his hair. He called over to Mrs. Bell for a quick confidence boost.

"You're covered in blood," Mrs. Bell called back in a rude tone. "What do you think?"

But she's just sore, he thought. *After Robort. After Ryan.*

The brick homes never collapsed. The masonry stood too strong, he guessed. They should have built the rest of Habre like that.

He rang Mira's bell again in excitement. Habre Circle was dead silent otherwise like it was another mid-afternoon day, with everyone at work or school.

MIRA

Mira wore a white cocktail dress and black tights, her hair in a loose bun save for a wisp hanging down in front of her left eye. A light dusting of makeup pronounced her features. She wasn't wearing shoes and she hadn't removed her name tag.

"I like your hair," the boy said, stepping by her and inside the home. He shut the door behind him and asked how she felt. Then he rescinded the question, knowing she probably felt the same as the last time they saw each other. Eons or hours ago. His nerves shook his fingers.

"You're covered in blood," she said, "but you look okay."

Mira pulled him by the arm into the kitchen, which was in the midst of collapsing into a sinkhole moving slowly in a swirling centrifugal pattern. The hole crushed and enveloped the sofa Mira and Ryan kissed on as the boy watched. The whole house cried, the walls splitting.

"I guess the house is going to collapse already?" the boy asked.

"I guess," Mira said, stopping at the basement doorway sans door. She didn't care. This hadn't been her house for long. "Do you like going to the movies?"

The continuous flapping sound of a projector running after the end of the film reel climbed up from downstairs, as did the smell of freshly popped and buttered popcorn.

"Really, Mira," he said, "The house is going to bury us."

"Judgment," she said. "I want you to ask me."

"If you like movies?" he said, realizing he never answered her. Everyone likes movies.

"No, not that. Everyone likes movies. The other thing."

"Oh," he said. She wanted the usual phrase. He put on a pleasant tone. "There's no need, Mira."

"Just ask it."

He took her hand and spoke with minimal inflection. "What did you do?"

"You should try and sound genuine." Mira wore a cold expression that the boy had never seen before on her face. She took this more seriously than any of the other judged. This aroused some anger in him. To him, this meant she wasn't taking him seriously when he told her she would be saved. Squeezing her hand now, tight enough to hurt anywhere but the Oughtside, the boy said, "What did you do, Mira?"

The girl smiled. "There we go. Please, Judgment, this is an important one." She pulled her hand away and ran down the wood basement steps, skipping the last few by jumping just like he would have. She landed on her feet. The basement had been finished with drywall and a blue carpet.

The boy followed her and jumped the last steps too, plus one more. He landed wrong, snapping his right ankle and collapsing forward into the wall headfirst. His brother could always jump from one step higher than him. They made a game of it. One that Ray Jr. would always win.

Some red had found its way down there through cracks in the top of the foundation walls; it healed the ankle sprain, snapping it back into place. He played it off, hoping Mira hadn't seen, but knowing she had.

"You're a terrible judge," she said, forcing a hard breath out her nose.

The basement had led to a small Oughtside movie theater—one with stadium seating and cup holders on every arm. A popcorn machine, the kind found at carnivals and fairs, hummed in the back. Two porcelain people sat in the last row, one's arm around the other.

The boy's eyes widened. "Did the figure do all this?"

No one had home theatres in Habre Circle. That was a feature for the Victorian houses on Mill. He was in one once before and he recalled the experience.

His dad—stable in his career, then—once toyed with the idea of moving the family a couple of streets over. He took him to an open house. The place was serpentine compared to his house on Habre. It creaked with age and history.

"It has character," his dad had said, peering into the home theater with a lit cigarette in his mouth. "Space, too. We could bring Grandmom here. Wouldn't that be nice?"

The boy fought to stay in Habre at dinner that night. He wasn't sure why. It was only a street or two over, but it felt farther. Farther from home, from Ryan. Even from the neighborhood kids. Cameron had joined his cause. His brother played like he didn't care, but the boy liked to think he might have.

It was better that they didn't move, because of all the parental death in the kids' near future, but the boy saw the disappointment on his dad's face, then, and the image stuck with him—a slight frown surrounded by his salt-and-pepper five o'clock shadow. The boy only realized then that the man had dreams.

Mira sat in the middle row of the theater. The seat squeaked, reclining with her body.

"Help yourself to the popcorn," she said, settling into a comfortable position to watch the screen, bright and dancing white. The Oughtside style projector stood at the back wall, sputtering along and clicking at certain intervals. Buttery, salty goodness saturated the air. It delighted his nostrils, tugging him towards the back of the room. The popcorn machine's warming element lit the small space like a cozy beacon in the dim light. He pulled open the greasy door and let the warmth of the exploded corn kernels wash over his face. Large tubs condensed in a stack towered to his right. He slid one off the top and filled it, using the provided scoop that was slick with buttered salt. After which he licked a patch of the sodium from his thumb, enjoying the spark of it. His favorite food. A girl with his favorite hairstyle. He had butterflies.

Nausea crept up from his stomach to his throat as soon as he swallowed. He stepped away from the machine.

"Oh, that's right," he said, his dead stomach churning. He spit.

The two porcelain people, seated only a few chairs away from the popcorn station, had been watching. They both had tubs filled with popcorn. A couple of sodas, too, from somewhere. They were elderly, judging from the painted-on dress sense.

"It's just for the look," one said haughtily. The man missing his whole porcelain chest. "To pretend to be human, like we were before."

The boy glared. "I am—"

"At least you can pretend to eat," the other said in a more furious way. He was a man with only porcelain legs and a head. "It's your flesh and your muscle." He threw popcorn at his mouth, none of it able to enter his porcelain lips. "Either that or I can't remember how to eat. How long has it been?" His companion shrugged.

In that dark corner of the theatre, their porcelain parts appeared to float in the space. No connective shadow holding them together.

They didn't seem keen on the boy's flesh. Still, he spoke. "But I am hu—"

Mira interrupted him with a whistle, her silhouette a few rows ahead. "Judgment, It's about to start."

The porcelain couple settled into their seats, making grinding sounds as they did. He hurried back to Mira and took the seat next to her, their elbows touching. This was no time for idle chat with the dead.

"What are we watching?" he asked, offering her heated, greasy corn.

"Me," Mira said.

He sighed. "I've done this before. Watch the screen. Judge. Can't we just skip to the last bit?"

"No," Mira said, curt and sure. "This is the cinematic experience."

Something shambled down the stairs. The figure. The boy didn't need to look and see.

"Because of the figure?" he asked. "Salvation, figure, I choose salvation for Mira Peretz."

The figure, taking a seat a couple rows back, wheezed. "Too early, boy. Wait for your cue."

"No," Mira said, more forceful this time. "You're going to damn me, Judgment. Not because I want it. Not because I even deserve it. You're going to damn me because of who you are, who you were, and who you will always be."

The projector clanged, setting its film reel.

Countdown, film grain, showtime.

Something coughed in the dark.

The boy watched Mira, then the show.

In silence, a porcelain woman appeared on the screen. She sneezed and part of her porcelain veneer fell away. Standing there, she looked out at the audience as a shadow now. Then a strong wind blew that skin away and she was just a ceramic skeleton. She took an unseen seat and, with marked intensity, watched the audience watching her. Her lips moved. Text dribbled out from her mouth like blood, landing to form some words around the audience's eye level.

Oughtside Films.

"That was elaborate," the boy said. "That's how you know it's going to be a good movie."

Piano music—the kind played live in old theaters—opened the title credits, as they faded in from black. The title held the aesthetic and font of a golden age film: sweeping cursive and lots of swoops. No color. The cast appeared: *Un ombre, Femme, Jugement.*

"Ah, Francais," he whispered to Mira using the hard "C". "I took a class in high school."

"And failed," the figure said, low but loud enough for everyone to hear.

The boy shushed it. Not that it was wrong.

The film had subtitles: *A shadow, Girl, Judgment*

Final billing. Second only to first. He turned to look over his shoulder at the figure. Mira brought his attention back to the film with a swift nudge of her elbow.

"Watch," she said.

Starring in: Le Voyage à Habre.

○   ○   ○

Exterior, the boy thought.

Busy street outside a shopping mall, the camera pushes in through the sliding doors and weaves through the throngs of people, their conversations a tableau of sound, the audience forbidden from hearing any one person. The camera continues until it reaches the storefront of a high-end boutique, replete with upscale shoes and accessories for both men and women. A girl steps in front of the camera and hogs its attention. It tries to get away—looking left, looking right—but can't. She winks at the camera with a smirk, then waves goodbye back toward the direction she came.

The camera is the girl's now, and it stays with her as she enters the boutique. The lighting and simultaneously broad and intimate angles scream New Wave movement student film.

"My parents would drop me off," Mira said. The movie said it after, in the girl's French voiceover and subtitles.

Femme: Mes parents me déposeraient. Travailler là où je n'ai pas travaillé.

GIRL: My parents would drop me off. To work where I didn't work.

The boy had his eyes on the Mira next to him.

"No," she said, her attention on the film. "Watch the real one, Judgment."

"Are you," the boy asked, pausing here, "a fake Mira or something?" He had seen more outlandish things in Habre Circle lately.

"Close," the figure said, like a dry heckler.

Mira tried to take the popcorn tub from his hands, but he pulled it closer to his chest—a force of habit.

"Oh," he said, smiling. "Sorry. Do you want some popcorn?" He held the tub out to Mira, who tore it from him and nailed the figure in the skull with it. Kernels showered down through its bones like heavy rain. It crossed its legs and sat back, looking comfortable with itself.

"Leave it, figure," Mira said, turning. Her eyes had a vicious look. "Everyone, just pay attention to my fucking movie. Be a damn audience." She said it like it was her movie—something she had written and directed. Her award-worthy brainchild. Her Oscar bait.

The two porcelain people in the back of the theatre noted that they had been trying to do just that, as they murmured to each other. They must have traded some of their shells to get in.

Antsy without his popcorn, the boy fidgeted while he watched the film. Mira cut the rest of the world out, staring straight ahead. The images on the screen danced in her eyes and spoke in her voice. Her accent was impeccable. The boy listened; he watched and let the movie envelop him.

"I have always had shadows following me," Mira said, "I see them in waking dreams, early in the morning, or late at night when I can't move under the weight on my chest."

"Wait," the boy said. *The Mira next to him wouldn't say that.*

He closed his eyes and shifted in his seat so that when he opened them only the film filled his vision. He breathed out.

Interior, he thought.

A boutique. Its décor is typical of these kinds of places. Deep grayscale walls with white accents. The molding looks like ancient Grecian pillars—not quite fancy enough to be tacky, though. Workers arrange the merchandise here in strict patterns; everything is just so. Stick-thin or chiseled mannequins wear the most expensive items, pushing the right designers and setting trends. There is no such thing as "on-sale" here. Girl *moves through the racks like she's hiding, though she looks like she belongs. With her clothes she fits in well with the store.*

Subtitled.

GIRL (v.o.): Sometimes I see one when I'm fully awake. In high school, I noticed this figure hanging around in my actual shadow, making it a little longer—a little more warped—than the other kids'. He's there most days now. He tells me he has attached himself to me from an outside place.

Cut to the figure, its bones covered in shadow again and standing beside a mannequin behind GIRL. *He holds a tennis racket with a ball glued onto the plastic netting, creating the country club illusion of connection. He has a lit cigarette in his mouth, its smoke curling up and caressing the head of a sprinkler. Judging from her shifting eyes, the audience should be aware that* GIRL *sees him but doesn't want to look over.*

FIGURE: *with intensity.* Mira Peretz, I think today will be my day.

GIRL (v.o.): He tells me that he needs help—my help. He needs an employee, and that he's bored of looking around so I will do.

FIGURE *drops the racket. The other people milling in the shop don't notice; it's not even picked up on audio.* GIRL *pulls a piece of plastic the size of an eating utensil from her pocket: a magnetic tool for removing security tags. She eyes the cashier ringing a customer up, then crouches next to a rack of blouses and chic skirts, popping the security tags off four of each. She brought a plastic bag with her, filled with five-dollar department store clothes. She mixes these clothes in.* GIRL *is a thief.*

FIGURE: *Picks up the racket.* I think I've made you enough offers.

Cut to: offers made, in GIRL's *bedroom while she lays on the bed in a bout of sleep paralysis, her eyes open but her body asleep. Wealth, intelligence, perks of life to make it less uneventful. If she were smarter, it said, it would offer her an equation to solve the mysteries of the universe.*

GIRL (v.o.): He likes to degrade people. Push them down to meet the reality of their existence.

Cut back to the store.

The camera moves enough to capture FIGURE's *presence. And a* faceless security guard's, *too, standing behind* GIRL. *The* GUARD *has a lit cigarette in her mouth. Most of the characters do, the audience realizes. In some frames—flashes of the film—even* GIRL *does.*

Interior: an interrogation room, still at the mall. The room is much like a prototypical police interrogation room, straining the audience's suspension of disbelief. One small lamp sits in the center of the table with a low-wattage bulb casting soft shadows on the shadows. GIRL *sits in a steel chair. The camera centers on her face. The* FIGURE *stands behind her, in her shadow. Attached to it, breathing and moving with her. The people questioning her have stepped out already to call her parents.*

FIGURE: It was only a matter of time.

GIRL: *Whispering, head down on the desk.* I suppose so. Do you have an offer for me? To get me out of trouble?

FIGURE: *Shakes his head.* You wouldn't take it.

GIRL: That's right, shadow.

FIGURE: I've realized you aren't one for offers.

GIRL: What am I one for?

It puts its hands on her shoulders. GIRL *plays with a pen the guard left on the table, rolling it forward and back. The audience should note that the pauses between lines are long. This is an attempt by the director to add suspense and weight to the dialogue.*

FIGURE: Guidance. Nudges in the direction in which I want you to go.

GIRL: *Incredulous.* And which direction is that?

Both of them put on such serious tones that the camera pulls away towards the door as if backing out of the room. It pulls back to position itself over the shoulder of someone watching. The audience is supposed to feel more of that suspense—a welling of it in their stomachs.

FIGURE: Forty miles or so east to start. *Glances up at the camera briefly. The fourth wall cracks.* Your father is at the door. He looks furious.

The audience doesn't see her father's face. The camera hovers from that tight over-the-shoulder perspective. Both the figure and Mira stare at Mr. Peretz. To the audience, the two appear to be looking straight at them through the screen. Straight into them. It's a bit much.

GIRL: My father. *She is ashamed by his stare.*

FIGURE: *Nods.* He's made deals with you. 'Pull this kind of shit again' type deals.

GIRL: He won't make good. My father has allowed me to take full advantage of him. He is a louse.

FIGURE: Look at his face now, though.

It leans closer to her. Its lips are not even an inch from her ear. The audience is unsure about the girl's use of "louse"—there may be a vague, different energy between the figure and Mira. The audience doesn't see her father's face, even as he walks deeper into the room and takes the seat across from Mira. She will not look at him.

MR. PERETZ: We told you what would happen, Mira. Your mother wants to throw you to the wolves—let the police have you. They now have footage of every time, at every store on the street.

She is an adult now. The film reminds the audience of that. The figure carries his conversation over the man's voice.

FIGURE: As my first attempt at guidance, I have whispered dreams of a nothing street to your mother and father while they sleep.

GIRL: You're making offers again.

MR. PERETZ: *Unaware of the figure in his daughter's shadow.* I'm making one more offer, Mira. One more and that's it.

FIGURE: Oh, hardly. This is guidance. I will leave you alone if you choose not to take it. *It sighs.* I will find someone else to suit my purposes. However, Mira Peretz, if you stay in your world—in your life—I see jail time, but also boredom. I see a person who will never have a footing. She'll steal, she'll hurt—she'll take advantage of those any normal person would love.

Mira expresses a range of emotions to find the right one for the scene: conflicted. Her body is tense.

GIRL: Dad.

The man stops talking. He is the kind of father who will give his children chance after chance.

FIGURE: Glorious. Vous avez pleinement profité de lui.

GIRL: *She makes her voice soft—daughterly.* Can't we just move? Get out of here. Go somewhere and just exist?

She accepts her father's one more chance, whatever it may be, knowing it is the figure's design.

MR. PERETZ: Your last chance. A fresh, boring start for all of us on a street in the suburbs—a place I found on Zillow, in a dream I can't always remember. *He laughs.* But I know we'll be okay there, love. I really do. Don't ask me how, Mira, because I couldn't say and I don't know if I would even if I did. *He holds his daughter's hand.* I want us to capture this feeling. Each dream of mine begins in a different way, but I always end up trudging through a wilderness I can barely fathom. And when I reach the edge of it, after years of approach, my daughter is standing there. Waiting for me. She is happy and carefree, clearly living a life of harmony and joy. We embrace, a warm and loving embrace, nothing withheld. I awake with a feeling of optimism and confidence about you and your future, Mira. I say dream, but as I speak to you now, my heart demands I say vision. That was my vision of you, Mira.

The camera pushes in on Mira, the figure beyond her, her eye's wet and distant.

Long fade to black in the company of a maudlin piano.

Credits. Produced by a shadow. Directed, written, and catered by Mira Peretz. Special thanks: Judgment.

A montage of storyboards appear during the final credits, showing Mira and the figure together in Habre building trap doors, looking at blueprints, sitting together on top of Judgment's house as the Oughtside rolls in like a sunset.

The last image lingers longer than the others.

The screen burned white and the porcelain couple discussed the short film as they shambled toward the exit. They enjoyed it for what it was but wouldn't see it again. They would not purchase it at the video store if it became available.

"I have better things to spend my self on," one said.

A wide-angle of burnt orange light cut into the basement theatre when they pushed open the exit door opposite the basement stairs. It didn't swing completely closed.

"What did you think?" Mira asked, in a quiet, almost sheepish way. "It was originally seven hours long."

The boy's face fell. He swallowed, knowing what she wanted or expected him to say, knowing what he was supposed to take from the film. Instead of sharing that, he smiled and let a laugh slip out.

"You stole, Mira. That's it?"

That was a development he didn't see coming, but he welcomed it. He fished a piece of porcelain—the shell eye of a person—from his pants pocket and showed it to her along with the warm glass marble that contained a universe and Wes's porcelain eye. "I've stolen, too."

Sympatico, he thought. Then he remembered that it was an admirer down here that had given him the eye—it wasn't exactly stolen. Wes's eye was left behind. *And who really had claim to a marble with a universe inside? Mrs. Bell? Kellyn Hodges?* He had stolen before, though. Money from his father's wallet or his mother's purse. That would be a fine conversation topic for another date. Letting a couple of weighty skeletons loose from his closet as they grew closer.

She cut him off before he could say anything else.

"I know, Judgment, but what of the film as a whole? Critically. Personally. I'm a film student, you know. Any feedback is greatly appreciated."

The figure had an answer. "I thought it turned out pretty well, considering the time constraints. I'd cut the monologue."

She wasn't a film student earlier, the boy thought. "You're going from business management to literary criticism to film," he said, stretching, his spine cracking.

"So? What, I can't do that? People change their minds all the time about their majors."

Her stern face was hued twilight orange from the cracked door. The white screen danced on her.

He made his way back on topic. "I get the point, Mira. You're a fake. A fraud. A pretender. A classic zero-hour moment. You've known more than any of us, and so on. You think that's worth damnation?"

"That wasn't the point," Mira said. She watched the figure stand and start towards the stairs. "Not the main one, anyway."

The figure leaned against the wall by the first step, its bones scratching against the concrete blocks. It had its hand over its eyes as if it blocking the sun. It spoke. "You missed it, Judgment. I had an inkling you would."

The boy looked at both of them, one after the other, growing flustered. "Then just tell me."

Mira's voice rose in annoyance. "I told you, figure. The conceit should have been storybook. That would have been more feasible."

"Feasible?" the boy said. "Fuck you, feasible. Maybe I just interpreted your garbage differently than you do. That's allowed." He breathed. He tried to think of something snarky to say next but left it there instead.

"Hey, it has potential," Mira said. She stood and walked to the projector, stepping whimsically on the backs of the seats to do so when the aisle would have sufficed. She played the part of a quirky film student well. Instead of flipping the switch to kill the projector, she kicked the thing over. A small fire spawned from the projector's searing bulb, melting the reel, its images casting on half of the screen, warping and separating. "With some rigorous editing, sure." Mira grinned.

The smell of burning chemicals overtook the smell of popcorn.

She tried to take herself farther from the boy's first impressions of her, back when she was in this whole thing with him, not doing this *to* him.

"The point," Mira said, sounding calm and altogether sane, "was us, Judgment. You and I were a perfect match."

His heart jumped. No one had ever called him a perfect match for anything, let alone themselves. "I—I think so too, Mira."

He would have had the same reply to anyone who had said that, smiling just as wide.

The figure chuckled. "Still not there, Judgment."

"Stay out of this figure," the boy said. "You heard her. We're a perfect match."

"He's in this, though," Mira said. She knocked over the popcorn machine next, which the boy felt was uncalled for. She pointed at the figure. "Inextricably tied to all of us."

"It's trying to ruin this, Mira. Don't listen." It likes to degrade. As you said.

"I don't love you," Mira said. "I never could."

The boy cleared his closing throat.

"He picked me because of you, Judgment," Mira explained. "Because of who you were: a thief, a liar, a pretender, a depressive stagnant *kid*. A shit-heel of a person who the world would be better off without."

He turned to the figure with wide eyes, but the figure had already started up the stairs, the wood creaking under its bones.

"I'm not a shit-heel." His voice wavered. Cracked. He didn't need to put on anger. He found rage like Robort's. "I am the only one in this whole circle worthy of judging!"

"Nope," Mira said in a crafted, inducing matter-of-fact way. "The figure knows you. I know you. Shit-heel, through and through. Every bit like me. I brought my parents to their deaths, Judgment. Walked them right into this damned circle because of you."

"And now you want me to damn you, too. A suicidal girl with a hard-on for misery. You're just another one of those sadist neighborhood kids trying to trick me into it."

Mira sat down in the handicap section of the theatre. There was nothing else in the room left for her to topple.

"Do you want to be damned, Judgment?" Mira asked.

Of course not. He didn't need to say it. He didn't deserve it.

"Then neither do I." Mira put her arm straight out to him. She shut one of her eyes like she was creating an angled line to him. "We are straight sympatico, man."

He shook his head. "I'm your better. I am innocent."

"If we polled your family—mother Maureen to your brother Ray Jr. to your sister Cameron—would they say the same?" She acted as if she knew and spoke all truths.

Cameron had forgiven him, outside of the Oughtside. She had been clay, mud, and an unfinished person, but she forgave him for everything. And, she had sheer clarity when she did it. Certainty in what she was saying.

He took a hard stance and tone. "Yes, they'd understand. Even my mother."

"Even your father?"

Especially.

"Especially, my father," he said.

At the time Raymond Sr. died, the strongest relationship he had was with his youngest boy. The kid that had helped him with the lawn on Sundays and other errands and chores that needed doing. The boy was always around to help—always upstairs or just across the street at Ryan's while Ray Jr. or Cameron worked their high school jobs or took the car to meet friends somewhere for an unchaperoned party.

Suddenly, a memory cut in. Of his father in that hospital bed with tubes penetrating the man's weathered skin. He was out of it, hopped up on pain pills and half-asleep. Maureen, Ray Jr., and Cameron stood around him. The boy was there, too. Maureen, with a quiet voice, told the kids they should go home and get some sleep. The three looked at each other. They wanted to leave—get as far away from their dying father as they could. Put it out of their minds until tomorrow or Wednesday when he would finally pass. So, they did. Raymond Sr. said something as they walked away. It was clear, it was lucid. The boy shoved it out of his mind. It had no right to come creeping back now—here, of all places.

"You delude yourself," Mira said. "Just like I would have."

He winced and nodded. "I'm done with you, Mira."

"Same here, Judgment." She scooped some floor popcorn up with her hand and started munching on it. She wretched.

"Do you want me to tell Ryan anything?" he asked.

Mira smirked. "He's a rube, isn't he? Give him something sweet, like 'If I could never like you as my equal, I could never love him as my better' or something." A pause. "But 'you' meaning him and 'him' meaning you, of course. I'm not talk-ing about you, Judgment. I could never."

Her words lit the boy's eyes. "I get it." He held out his hand.

"Oh, theatrics now?" Mira said. "That's fun."

She appeared honored.

"Damnation," he said.

Then, he clicked his fingers with a bit of flourish, pretend-ing like that would actually make something happen. And it did. Wind poured into the space, blowing his hair around like that of the anime villains that he always admired.

The sinkhole swirling in her home grew into the space and pulled the screen down first, its rumble and metal whines drawing his and Mira's attention. Then, it took the first row of seats into its spinning maw of dirt and debris, followed by the second. Mira sat in the third row. The boy rushed up the stairs, dirt particles stinging the back of his legs as he took them two at a time.

And Mira fell. Consumed by the dirt. She forced her hand out of the hole before she was fully taken so that her final moments could appear appropriately cinematic as her tight palm and clawed fingers sunk into the earth. She gave the boy a thumbs up. Then, she flipped him off.

DAMNATION

The boy met the figure on the front porch of the mauve colonial, most of the house in the ground behind them. His bone back faced the kid. 'It' was forever a 'he' to the boy now. Through the figure's ribs, the boy spotted Mrs. Bell on the front lawn. She held HABRE CIR in her hands again. Ryan sat on the curb a few meters behind her, facing away from all of them.

"Your skin's all gone, figure, isn't it?" the boy asked.

"Halfway through the movie, the last of it lifted from my eyes."

"How does it feel?"

The figure hunched forward. "It hurts, Judgment. Like I woke up in the pitch black and had to turn a light on."

The boy wondered how bones could hurt but realized it was the eyes instead that pained—the glass eyes that, if the boy could only see them, he knew he would understand something critical.

"I know you, figure," he said. "Look at me. Let me see you." He put a hand on the figure's shoulder. The figure shrugged him off.

"I remember that sort of pain," the figure said. "Human pain. Bumps and bruises. Diseases. Desires. The porcelain

324

conceals all of it. The obsidian skin, the shadows, is porous enough to make you plan and act on it. Deliver on your emotions." He sobbed. A dry, dusty one—empty. "Now it's all there."

"But we're done, right?" the boy asked. "I've judged the circle. It's time to move on, the four of us." The yellow house smoked in the corner of his eye. "Five, if we fish that neighborhood girl out of that rubble." Reactions from the group suggested at least the figure and Mrs. Bell had forgotten about Lynn Mears, saved and buried. He found some pride in the fact that he did not forget his sinners.

"I am at a crossroads, Judgment," the figure said. "A crisis. A decision."

The red wind blew along the street, taking some dust from the figure and Mrs. Bell's bones with it.

The boy shrugged. "Look at me, figure, and I'll help you decide."

The figure turned, peeking through the cracks between his fingers over his eyes, and surveyed him. The kid did the same right back.

"You damned Mira Peretz, Judgment."

The boy looked down and away, then at Ryan who watched them now over his shoulder.

"I did," he said. "Did you hope I wouldn't?"

"I knew you would," the figure said like it was unsure. "I did."

"She thought she knew me—how to judge me. How to judge Judgment." The boy had a distasteful look on his face

The figure nodded. He cracked a smile on his faux-skin face.

The boy shook his head. "Then what's the crisis?"

Mrs. Bell moved closer to the porch and the figure turned to meet her stern gaze.

Just by looking at her, he could tell that she had a fight on the mind. It hovered around in his head, too. A deep uncertainty clung to it.

The figure walked out to her. He followed him close.

"Figure," Mrs. Bell said, holding the wieldy street sign over her shoulder. "I've been thinking about influence out here."

"Oh, Anna?" the figure said. He let her see his eyes, but she didn't react. Ryan turned and saw them, then turned back, breathing heavier.

"Your influence on Judgment. And mine. William's on me. And mine on him. Your influence on Mira. This place on me and you and all of us. Yes—influence."

"And?" the boy asked, eyeing Ryan instead.

Anna readied HABRE CIR. "Ryan and I have decided that we should pull you two apart. Separation."

Ryan mumbled something over on the curb. Mrs. Bell—exasperated—shook her head like she was dealing with an obstinate child and chattered her jaw.

"What did he say?" the boy asked.

The figure shrugged. "Must not have been important."

Ryan spoke louder the second time, in a correcting tone to start. "Mrs. Bell has decided to pull you two apart." His voice grew. "I have told her eight times now that it's pointless, but she won't listen."

"Ryan," Mrs. Bell said like he was ruining this for her, "has lost his nerve."

He never had one, the boy thought. *Not since the Oughtside came calling.*

Ryan sighed and growled at the same time. "They are inexorably tied together, Anna. Inexorably? No," he clicked his fingers, "Inextricably."

The boy wanted to correct him, but he got there.

Mrs. Bell snapped back at Ryan, throwing him a skewed face. "So are we, Ryan. Would you *fucking* listen, please? You and me and Judgment—"

"Have nothing," Ryan said, "compared to what he has with the figure. We're too late, Anna. We would always have been too late."

The boy had something to say. They talked like he wasn't there. Like he was a matter to be dealt with remotely—like anything that was going to happen was a foregone conclusion and he wasn't a variable in their equation.

"Anna," he said.

Mrs. Bell chattered her next word. "Still." She tensed and gripped Habre Cir with that ceramic skeletal strength one more time. And one more after that.

Ryan sighed. "What a shitty reason."

"Just sit there, then, Ryan," Mrs. Bell said with an annoyed tinge. "Sit there and let this play out. Watch. Wait. Do nothing and be your stagnant self."

That was harsh, the boy thought.

At least he wasn't running off again. She knew it was harsh. She wanted it to sting him.

For an instant—and a flash of a glare at the boy and the two skeletons—it looked like Ryan Mont might do something. Then, he shrunk over on his curb, curling into a sitting ball.

"Of course," Mrs. Bell said. She locked glass eyes with the figure.

The air between them didn't move until Anna swung.

SALVATION

The figure lost a few of his ribs to Mrs. Bell's first swing. They shattered on contact with the pole of HABRE CIR. Either the figure didn't anticipate Mrs. Bell's sudden attack or couldn't get out of the way quick enough without his skin. He had been fast before. Regardless, Mrs. Bell struck and bone fragments flew into the air, some of them bouncing off the boy's face. A few found their way into his parted lips and he spit them out in disgust. They tasted like chalk and sawdust.

He could have warned the figure. The attack—the idea of it, anyway—was right there with him. This connection with Mrs. Bell nagged at him when he thought about it, like it tried to push him in one direction when he wanted to go another.

Influence, he thought. *She's right.*

Doubled over in the dried grass, on his knees with pieces of his rib cage littering the ground, the figure coughed. A typical cough of his—not one that indicated he was anything but slightly fazed and made structurally unsound by his missing ribs.

Ryan Mont stayed seated on the curb, now facing his fallen house.

Mrs. Bell nodded, looking pleased with her ability to inflict damage; a fire shone beneath her scratched, weathered glass

328

eyes. The way she looked as she drowned William in the clay. She swung her sign down this time—down on the back of the figure's skull. When it connected, it sounded like a shovelhead hitting sidewalk concrete, the sound travelling up through the pole. The figure's skull weathered the hit, but he was full on the ground now, sprawled.

"Oh, that ceramic skeletal strength, Anna," the figure said. "You have me at a disadvantage." He rose to his knees.

Anna had been bone longer than the figure. The wolves had stripped her of her shadow before she was ever brought into the Oughtside proper.

"Someone does, finally." Mrs. Bell added with just the right amount of smug satisfaction to her words.

The boy had a touch of satisfaction whirling in him, too. *Mrs. Bell deserved this*, he thought. *Some happiness—vengeance.* He wondered if that might be her effect on him. A pressure darted through the back of his head. It throbbed there. Pulsed. He held the back of his skull.

"Anna," the figure said, looking up at her. "I feel like there have been many opportunities for someone to put me at a disadvantage." A cough. "But no one seized them in their fleshy little fingers."

He lunged forward next, looking to throw a punch or tackle Mrs. Bell. The boy couldn't tell exactly what he was trying to do, but he tried to do *something*. After the attempt, the figure lay sprawled on the ground again.

"Shadow," Mrs. Bell said, her words sharp and quick. "Figure. Creature."

"Creature," the figure said, laughing into the dead grass. "No one has ever called me that. How about savior, Anna? We found you in the wilderness, the damned wolves tearing the shadow from your body."

Mrs. Bell pinned him by sticking the pole between two of his intact rib bones and into the parched earth. "You needed me," she said.

"That does not diminish what I did for you," the figure wheezed. "You were bone when my employee and I met you. You would have been dust by the time the wolves finished." In a quick movement, he broke two of his ribs with his own hand and freed himself from the ground. He and Mrs. Bell stood in front of each other. HABRE CIR stood with them, positioned between the two, with Mrs. Bell clutching it tight.

After catching his balance, the figure spoke again. Missing ribs affected equilibrium, the boy guessed. And aesthetics. Some symmetry had been lost. The figure listed to one side.

"Do you know what happens to us when these bones become dust, Anna?"

The boy remembered this question. Outside the Ought-side, both of them claimed they didn't know.

"No," Mrs. Bell said. "And I don't care, shadow." She pulled her sign from the ground and took a stance that she must have seen in some movie because it took a few light adjustments for her to get it right.

"Guys," the boy said, as he considered stepping between them. He decided against it.

"No one here speaks of it," the figure said. He had no weapon, but he actively looked for one. Cable boxes, rusted cars, basketball hoops—he had a large selection to consider while keeping his focus on Mrs. Bell. "They shun it as a phantom possibility, the way we evaded the deaths that lead us to the Oughtside. They fight it—fear it. After bone, we are nothing—we are particles in the red wind, and that is true death, Anna."

Mrs. Bell took a brief moment where she looked unnerved by this information. A second of contemplation over this issue. She was stubborn, though. She had been stalwart in her actions since dying and she wouldn't stop now. Even in the face of that possibility.

A true death. An actual departure.

The boy looked over the skin on his dirty palms and wondered where that left him in the grand scheme of things. He had flesh. He had blood and bone and humanity covering him. In a sweeping swell of his stomach, he felt as if he had never belonged in the Oughtside. He was an immortal outlier that just needs a little red light to patch him right up. *A god*, he thought. *What a cliché.*

"Guys," he said again, holding his hands out like he was about to do an accentuated shrug. "We're done. There's no point to this."

Mrs. Bell nodded. "Of course you would say that, Judgment. From the start, he has saturated you with *his* influence. You are not you. You have shifted."

The figure took a brief look back over his shoulder at the boy, but the boy—unpacking Mrs. Bell's assertion—didn't catch it in time to see the man's eyes. He berated himself for that.

"She's grasping at straws, Judgment," the figure said. "Have you shifted?"

"You never knew me before, Anna," the boy said. "You were just my babysitter every so often." She never came over to express condolences for either of his parents. And why would she? She was busy.

"I did," Ryan said, raising his hand like this was fifth period. "And you weren't this way." He didn't move from his curb. "You never had to be a Biter or Judgment."

The figure took several awkward steps back, which tensed Mrs. Bell. He stood in front of the boy, his back turned to him.

"He was always this way, Ryan Mont," the figure said. "Am I right, Judgment? Do you know yourself enough to speak the truth?"

Was he right?

"No," Mrs. Bell said, her voice rising as if trying to get a dog off a nice couch. "The murdered live on—"

"You're projecting," the figure laughed.

He grabbed a fistful of the boy's shirt. The figure wasn't as quick as he was when he had shadow on his bones, but still the boy couldn't match his agility. He lifted and hurled the boy at Mrs. Bell, who batted the flying Judgment right back with HABRE CIR, Judgment flailing through the air like a ragdoll. The figure caught him by the ankles—the hilt of him—and swung him at Mrs. Bell like he was a metal folding chair, in a wrestling match, advancing on her.

Anna didn't hesitate to clash HABRE CIR with Judgment— to engage with her enemy using all the force she could muster. She didn't look at the boy any differently than she would look at an inanimate—if an unwieldy—weapon. The boy's bones broke, his skin snapping open. Air rushed over and through him until the red shone down and sowed him shut.

When he was young, he—

The figure blocked a horizontal swing with the boy's skull, which muddled the memory he was about to have. Something about his dad, would play out in the yard—this yard connecting his house and the next. Something about connections and youth.

Mrs. Bell—smelling of the boy's blood—parried a counter from the figure and shoved him into the dirt. Holding a muffled Judgment to the ground with HABRE CIR, she closed the short distance between herself and her opponent and dislocated one of the figure's shoulders along with its arm. It made a popping sound.

The figure kicked her away, bellowing as he did. With the remaining arm, he spun the boy around with incredible skeletal force and used him to sweep Mrs. Bell's legs out from under her. Her legs separated at the knees.

Momentum separated the boy and the figure's good arm away from the battle, over toward Ryan Mont.

"Ryan," he called, trying to warn him before they collided. But he hadn't spoken out loud enough. And Ryan didn't care to listen.

The boys collided; they tumbled out into the middle of the street. Ryan shifted under the boy, getting his arm out from under the weight of him. He hit the boy in the ribs over and over again. After some time, the boy rolled off Ryan and onto cool asphalt. He shut his eyes and sighed.

It was all supposed to done, dammit.

"Ryan," he said between the blows to his stomach, his voice ragged. "Mira wanted me to tell you something." He coughed. "Some lie about the two of you. I'll need a moment to get my thoughts together and remember." He spat a tooth out and in its place a new one grew back—a baby one. Then that one fell out, too, and an adult one sprouted from the hole in his gum.

The noise of the ceramic skeletal battle—sounding like one of those wooden wind chimes—raged. The boy just lay there staring up at the crimson sky.

Ryan hit the boy in the face, pounding on it with his fists. Ryan growled as he did.

"I get it," the boy said, dodging the fists that he could. "You're angry." Contact. "It's an old emotion for you, Ry-Guy." Ryan's mother had always called him that. It felt endearing to the boy, who never had a nickname. His name doesn't lend itself to the concept.

"I didn't want to be surprised when I saw you come out without her," Ryan said, relenting to speak. "Though, I was, Biter. It knocked the wind right out of me." He winced. "And I wanted to care more. I should care more. But I didn't."

One of the figure's arms still clutched the boy's leg. His hands found it and he was able to pry it off to remove it. He rapped Ryan on the back with it. The skeletal digits flailed. As a weapon, it wasn't very effective.

"You won't," the boy said. "And I can tell you why." Mira was a fraud—a falsehood. The kind of person Ryan thought the boy was. The boy gritted his teeth, relishing the idea of telling Ryan how misplaced his affections were. Instead, he said something else. "But it's not important, Ryan. We're here, and we're done."

They'd been in this position before, in the red, fighting on the floor. It was an empty endeavor. Yet still, they found themselves here again. *There's a statement to be made about humanity somewhere in that*, the boy thought. But not one that should be spoken out loud. That would be too blatant.

Ryan stopped mid-pummel, and the boy released the smooth ceramic arm from his grip, letting it fall to the ground. It scraped on the asphalt.

"Please don't tell me you think that, Biter." Ryan's eyes narrowed, and a pained expression dropped his face. "Haven't you seen the figure's face?"

"He hides his eyes from me."

Ryan nodded. "I know him, Judgment."

"You do?" his face flashed with some surprise.

Ryan took a glance at the skirmish between the figure and Mrs. Bell. "You know him better. Look now, and you'll see him."

"I will."

But he didn't take that opportunity. He remained on his back, convinced that his body didn't want to move.

"Have some guts, Biter," Ryan sighed. "Mrs. Bell and I decided that this is the figure's narrative and that you are the resolution. Because who—honestly—would pick you to judge the dead, Biter?"

The boy arched an eyebrow. "So, Mira told me to tell you that—"

Ryan interrupted. "We might disagree on what to do about it, but Mrs. Bell and I think you have one more house, Biter." He forced the boy to sit up and tried to make him take notice of the figure and Mrs. Bell. "Because *of course* you have one more house."

The white home—his home—untouched by the Ought-side's arrival. The boy looked at it instead of the figure's face. The cat Antigone sat in his bedroom window. She seemed fine.

"I knew that, Ryan" he said. "I just hadn't put any thought into it yet."

He didn't know that. He hid from the idea.

"Right," Ryan said. He let go of the boy. More like shoved him lightly back to the ground. "Once he's crushed Anna, Biter, he'll turn back to you." He walked farther out into the street and over to the porch of his house. Wading into the rubble beyond it, he whistled. A dog call he used for Missile.

The boy watched him pull something from the pile: a green ball. He squeezed it in his hand, and it squeaked. Then, he took a wide gander from the end of Habre up to the circle.

"You could run," Ryan said. "She wants you to run. She's giving you that opportunity. There is a wide other world out there for you in the wilderness."

There *was* a wide other world, too. The boy viewed the shifting end of Habre's road—that break in reality. A desert, an ocean, the woods. Cameron was in the woods, inside the mill. Ray Jr. might be in there, too. They might be walking this way right now, searching for the Oughtside below, where their parents might be.

But no one *runs* from the last boss, even when it's an option. That only delays the fight.

"Missile!" Ryan called, moving unevenly on the remains of his house. He fell on a piece of glass, slicing open his bare stomach. A minor inconvenience for half a second. He'd been shirtless this whole time and the boy hadn't paid it much mind. This was just what Ryan wore—his uniform, his costume, his key character art. The red sewed Ryan's stomach shut, the light glistening off the blood on his perfectly curved chest.

"What are you going to do?" the boy asked, knowing that he presently watched what Ryan was going to do.

"Missile!" Ryan called louder. "I'll start by finding my dog, Biter." He wouldn't look at him. He wore a matter-of-fact and plain expression, like this was just another day in his life. "I'll search up here, then I'll search downstairs, and then in the wilderness if I have to because you won't listen to me. *Anna* won't listen to me. So, I'll start by just finding my dog, then I'll go from there." He moved out into the street with the boy, hovering over him.

"You should stay close to me, Ryan," the boy nodded, giving a warm smile. He sat cross-legged and breathed out. "You've been saved. You can go anywhere once we're done, you know."

"Derek," Ryan said, in a choked and sad voice. The Mont boy moved up the street a little, the houses encompassing him. "There is no such thing as salvation today."

Ryan would have seen Missile by now if she was around— she always listened—but he kept calling anyway. The boy's eyes lingered on Ryan for a moment. Ryan caught his stare and brushed it off. He called for his dog, instead. He continued to call.

The boy knew who the figure was. Judgment knew him. Biter knew him. Derek knew him.

ANNA

The figure scrounged for his other missing arm—he had already found one—while Mrs. Bell re-attached her legs at the knees. They'd taken a short break to reassemble themselves.

"The murdered live on in the minds of their killers, Anna," the figure said. He said it a few times while milling around for his other arm. After picking up a couple of his rib bones, he tried to attach them, but they crumbled.

"You keep telling me," Mrs. Bell said. She stood, back on her skeletal feet, waiting for the figure. She leaned on HABRE CIR in her lackadaisical way.

"It seemed," the figure said, "like the right thing to say. When I found you out there. When I brought you to William's viewing room."

Assuming an aggressive stance, he looked like he could and would make do with one arm. He must have known that the boy had the other arm with him. The kid stood in the street, inspecting it. It couldn't function away from the body— that's how they worked. That's how the Oughtside worked. Mechanically. Explainable enough.

"It's the lie you needed to hear," the figure continued. "The influence you wanted."

And they clashed again, circling each other. The figure knew his body better than earlier. He carried himself well. He was quick and moved around like a fleet-footed boxer, dodging before attempting an attack.

Mrs. Bell chuckled. "The lie? You've seen it yourself, shadow. You've seen the connection." She spun her head around and the boy caught her stare at him on each rotation.

He wanted raisins, suddenly. A swell of nostalgia rose in him. He recalled the national ad that made all the kids crave raisins for a couple months. The rhythm of the phrase "the candy fruit that kids crave" that once wormed its way into the heads of every adolescent in the school district. As did the delightful major-key jingle. Mrs. Bell hummed it. The boy hummed it.

"Influence," the figure said, pivoting out of danger then back into it. "Simple influence, Anna. Yours and his. Intermingled. Feeding one another. You made my claim real in this place."

This threw Mrs. Bell into a light rage. The word "simple" affected her more than any of the others. She swung wildly at the figure, decimating the rest of his rib cage, throwing bone fragments across the dividing line between the boy's and Mira's lawns. Without ribs to give him a stable structure, he hunched over as he continued to fight.

Anna held tight to that connection, the boy thought. The figure didn't hide his eyes from him. He could see them, but he convinced himself he needed a better look.

The figure went on, coughing, "I have been in his influence, Anna. I have felt obligated to protect him—to care for him." He barreled into her, tackling her to the ground then rolling off.

Rising to her knees, Anna left a hand in the grass. It was crushed—dust. She glanced at the boy, who took a few steps toward her.

They weren't far from the edge of Habre. The figure leaned towards it, narrowing his glass eyes. "I think I see William out there in the wilderness, heading this way."

"I don't care, shadow," Mrs. Bell said, focusing on the figure. HABRE CIR weighed on her one side. She was slower without the one hand.

Standing, the figure disagreed with enough fervor and a mild annoyance in his voice. "You do. Of course, you do. Get out there, Anna, and seek your revenge. Look at how your focus is split. William. Judgment. William. Judgment."

"That's done, shadow. This is my decision—to wedge myself between you."

The shadow shook his head like he didn't hear. "And your bones are brittle. I mean come on, Anna, I forced the very processes of death to behave according to my parameters. My focus has been narrowed to these next moments. Never split. Never faltering." He knew himself with unequivocal certainty. No confusion. No masking. No hiding anymore.

"Mrs. Bell," the boy said. He was sorry he ever convinced her to come back with them from the wilderness. He thought he should say that. Most of this was his fault.

Echoing herself, Mrs. Bell did not care. "This is a sham, not a process. Death is a cruel sham," she said, taking up

HABRE CIR. She sounded muted and resigned to this fate—to this connection with the boy.

"Ryan Mont and Anna Bell," the figure said. He sighed into the open universe. "Trouble."

They fought for what was at once a moment and, to the boy, a crucible longer. The figure, as squirrely and quick as he had ever been, took the advantage. He tore HABRE CIR from her grip and planted it in the ground by the sizeable tree that had been there since the boy had gained object permanence. She, in turn, focused on his spine, that had a deep black mark in the center of it.

The two pummeled each other with a ceramic skeletal pugilism. From there, they took advantages away from one another, back and forth. To and from. One would be on the ground one second, then the next, the other was there.

Mrs. Bell would lose. She knew the outcome. It felt to the boy like that was the intended outcome. Her intended outcome. An image of William Bell, young and naked and standing in the doorway to their bedroom, crossed her mind. This was a moment of happiness and ease, early in their relationship before they had started bickering, then outright fighting.

The boy thought he should act when she urged him to run away. He took a few steps into the fray. A single fragment of bone—a jagged piece of a scapula—shot out toward and through the boy's heart. He collapsed, dead for the next few seconds.

When he recovered, Mrs. Bell was in ceramic pieces and idle dust on the boy's front lawn. A dart of pressure cut across his skull and he couldn't see straight after it passed. He had spots in his vision that he kept trying to catch. He screamed.

The figure sat in the grass, in the midst of a violent cough-ing fit. He crawled on his hands and knees, hacking up his and Mrs. Bell's dust. Fragments of him fell away by the second. The damage Mrs. Bell inflicted would be his end, eventually. That much was clear. He collected what he could of himself and turned his attention toward the boy.

"For—for the record, Judgment, I would have truly liked to save the innocent," he said. He watched the boy trying to navigate his clumsy way to him and scoffed. "There was no deep connection, Judgment. The murdered do not live on in the minds of their killers. You both took the simple effects of Oughtside products and machinery and made a whole big deal out of them."

The boy's vision cleared in a moment, his head still feel-ing lighter, almost severed from his neck. He rubbed his hand across his intact throat.

"Even so," the boy said, brushing the dust off his shirt. "You killed one. You could have thrown her off the edge of Habre, but you crushed her."

"Part of the job," the figure said. "Hands tied." Then he shook those words away, like he didn't mean to say them. "No, actually. That's another lie. In a typical adjudication, a shadow won't—can't—interfere." A pause.

"Why, figure?" the boy asked with an unintentional sincer-ity easing its way out of him.

"But hey," the figure said, ignoring him. "Ryan Mont is alright."

Yes, he was. Ryan Mont was altogether fine—saved—down near Davies Tuch's fallen house calling for Missile with futile repetition. An arc of maddened lightning burst up from the Science House's rubble and into the sky, startling the Mont boy. But still, he was fine.

"Now come on, Judgment," the figure said, bumbling to his feet.

They had another house.

○   ○   ○

Listing and limping all the way, his bones scraping and parts of them falling apart, the figure made his way to the front door of the boy's home. As if this was any other of the houses, the boy followed him to the porch. The cement porch. The boy knew the pattern of it—the swirls of how its molded form and the growing cracks moving their way across. The figure faced him. Hunched over like he was, he and the boy stood eye to eye. Mellow brown iris to mellow brown glass. The boy studied the curves of the man's brow, crafted from fake flesh. Some of it hung down, so he pressed it to the skull.

"Raymond," the boy said, almost as a question. His breaths became short.

The figure wheezed like Raymond used to wheeze. "Senior or Junior? That distinction is important." He sat down on the porch chair beside the door and acted like he had returned home from a hard day at the office. Just the way he used to.

"Senior," the boy said, his mouth dry and his voice quiet. "Dad."

His dad tried to smile, but his jaw was barely attached, so it came out skewed.

"Good, but I wanted there to be more of a reveal," the figure said. "A shroud lifting. Gasping from the crowds, applause from the seats. A show."

"Impossible," the boy said. "It's been done too much."

Raymond Sr. was never one for theatrics and showmanship, but he did sit in the family room and watch his youngest grow up consuming television, films, and games.

"I thought it would be fitting for you, Judgment."

The boy breathed sharply. "Don't call me that. Please."

"What do you want to be called?"

"Derek," the boy said. "It's Derek, Dad."

"No," Raymond Sr. said. "Judgment, yes. Biter, maybe. Kid. Boy. You are not the baby I named Derek. Judgment is your title—it's your identity." Any affectations to his voice had fallen away. Raymond Sr. spoke, clear and vivid in the boy's ears.

He sucked back tears and cleared his throat. "Fine, Raymond."

An awkward moment hung between them. The boy broke it.

"So who am I judging here?" he said, even if he had an idea already. He had other questions, but this one felt safest.

Raymond Sr. fell forward out of the porch chair and the boy helped him to his feet.

"Help me upstairs," Raymond said, speaking with a timid weakness. "I had plans for this part, too. Flourishes for you." A pause as the boy adjusted him against his shoulders. "Maureen and I bought this house the year our youngest Derek was born. Enter and observe, Judgment."

They shuffled through the screen door, and then the main one.

A sharp whistle echoed in the circle, followed by Ryan's call for his dog.

RAYMOND SR.

The boy couldn't remember the last actual, genuine exchange he had with Raymond Sr., but as he moved into the foyer of his house and unloaded Raymond's skeleton self onto the landing of the hall stairs, he pictured the fleshed version of the man in a hospital bed. The position of Raymond's bones, laying there half sitting, half flat on their back, sparked the image. It spread over the boy, cutting through. It overtook the foyer—all the rooms of his house and head.

Raymond was out of it, hopped up on pain pills and half-asleep. Maureen, Ray Jr, and Cameron stood around him. Derek, too, but he stood farther away. Maureen, with a quiet voice, told the kids they should go home and get some sleep because it was past midnight by this point. The three looked at each other. They wanted to leave—get as far away from their dying father as they could. Put it out of their minds until tomorrow or Wednesday when he would finally pass. So, they did. Raymond Sr. said something as they tried to leave the room. It was clear, it was lucid, and it was said in the most pitiful voice anyone had ever heard trickle out of their father's mouth.

"Wait," he said. "I didn't get to see the kids."

The words stopped each of them cold. He saw them for a whole hour before, asking them about school today and if they had tests coming up. Ensuring them that he would be okay—that he would beat this sudden onslaught on his bones and organs.

And it was sudden. Hospitalized on Sunday, dead on Wednesday. Raymond Sr. was a proud man. A smoker, too. He hated doctors. He feared them.

Maureen swallowed hard and just waved the kids off. She would stay there for the night. She would live there for the next two nights while the kids did their best to pretend this wasn't happening. Cameron threw herself into school and work. Ray Jr. disappeared for a day. The boy lay in front of the television set and let Rod Serling tell him sweet platitudes. No one talked to each other.

Ray Sr. slept again, and they would keep him under, unconscious while machines pumped him with air and worked his heart, dialysis rotating in the corner. The boy had touched his hand when he was allowed to go in and say goodbye. It was warm like it was when the man could move—when he used to hold it as a child. But it felt thinner, like bone.

"Those were my last words, weren't they?" Raymond Sr. said, his bone hand in the boy's fleshed one. "You were mouthing them, Judgment. You do that in your sleep sometimes." The boy's surprised expression didn't change. "While I can't interact much with this side, I have kept an eye on it."

The boy sat next to him on the hall stairs' landing. "Do you want to walk around the house for a bit? See some pictures? Experience what you once knew?"

The cat Antigone bounded down the carpeted steps and rubbed herself against the bones of the man who had brought her home ten years ago.

"Antigone," Raymond Sr. said. "How I've missed you." He stroked the feline with one finger, leaving a line of dust down her back. The cat shook it off. Raymond looked over his hand and clenched the fingers, frowning as far as the boy could tell.

Antigone leaped onto the boy's lap, and then to the linoleum hallway floor. She walked into the crimson kitchen and laid belly-up in a beam of red light coming through the glass.

Raymond Sr. leaned back on the landing.

"No," he said. "There's nothing I want to see."

The boy knew where his father wanted to go in the house: the master bedroom. He dragged Raymond up the stairs by the shoulders. The smell of fresh paint wove into his nostrils as he progressed. No sounds other than their own movement seemed to exist in the house, so he made idle conversation.

"Ryan once dared me to ride down these stairs in one of the computer paper boxes in the basement."

"And did you?"

He did, and there was a general worry between the two that he might break his neck on the way down. But he was the only one that could curl up into such a small box at the time and the folly opportunity needed to be seized. He didn't break his neck, but he did do an incredible flip while curled up in the box.

"Of course I did."

The figure grumbled.

When they reached the top of the steps, the boy had to stop and retrieve a piece of Raymond's face that had tumbled halfway down and re-attach it. The man was adamant about this. He said that he needed to be as whole as he could be for this next part. To get it as close to what he envisioned as possible.

"Do you know," Raymond Sr. asked, "what your mother's last words were?"

Standing over his father, the boy shook his head. "To me? Something about a sundae." The extent of it was that she was going to make herself a sundae out of the ice cream and strawberries in the fridge. After Raymond's death, she worked two or three jobs each day to keep the house from the banks and would nearly break down when anyone suggested selling it and moving out.

"It was a breathy and whimpering, 'help,' Judgment," the figure said. "She said it as she died on the floor upstairs." He turned his head around to look at the boy. "What were you doing again? You were downstairs, weren't you?" He knew the answers and made that much clear in his voice.

Sleeping, the boy thought. "I was just sleeping."

He dragged Raymond Sr. towards the master bedroom, its door shut, at the end of the hallway. He never went in there much—not since May. None of them did. Storage had quickly overtaken Maureen's long vanity. It piled in her closet, covering the sight of her clothes and the ones she wanted to keep of her husband's.

As the boy walked past Cameron's open room and then Ray Jr.'s, he looked inside, hoping to see them standing by their beds as newly minted porcelain people. Hoping they would be there to defend him in some way. He knew where this was going.

Oil paintings on canvases lined the floor of the master bedroom, leaned up against the walls. They were freshly done—well done, too. They had a Renaissance composition, style, and quality to them. Some were unfinished.

"Here we are," Raymond Sr. wheezed. "These cost me the last of my porcelain." He shook his head, sounding disappointed. "I'm sorry they're not hung on the walls. Mira was supposed to do that earlier. This would have been a gallery, in an ideal construction of this scene."

The boy leaned him up against the wall and Raymond Sr. patted the kid on the shoulder. "Take your time."

The boy crossed his arms like as if visiting a museum of fine art. Red lit the room from the open blinds.

By the bed, either the figure or Mira had spilled a bucket of red paint. It had been done with care to mimic the pattern of blood on the carpet the boy had first seen when popping the door open with a screwdriver back in May. Maureen hit her head on the floor after falling out of bed during a cardiac event and blood had pooled in the area from the cut. There hadn't been a bucket of it then, but the exaggeration felt appropriate, considering the effect Raymond wanted to achieve.

"It was dark for a while," Raymond said. "Then I was clay."

The paintings depicted Raymond's cancerous death through to the beginning of this adjudication process. There he lay in the hospital bed, with his family all around him, Derek being the only one with his eyes open and looking out at the audience. There he stood in a sea of black, becoming clay as the viewer's eye moved down the painting. There he sprawled inside the mill, on a slab in the surgical theatre section with

Penumbra, Umbra, and Antumbra crafting his new body—his mold.

"I had my idea as Cameron had hers," Ray Sr. said, nostalgic. He had always been proud of his daughter. "A clay clarity and epiphany about where you were headed. Your knack for taking things that weren't yours to take. Money from when I left my wallet out. From where your brother hid his. Using our credit card numbers." He grew ragged and loud. "But more than money, right? Lives, too."

A memory: The boy's dad, downstairs in the living room telling his son that he hadn't raised him to steal. That much was true enough.

The next painting—a large collage or tableau—showed Raymond Sr., now porcelain, wandering through the wilderness and finding his way through to the Oughtside. There he spent bits of his porcelain on experiencing touches of humanity: plays, theatre, watching the seasons of his sons and daughter. His wife. He binged on Derek's series, then re-watched it twice at a more measured pace. The artist captured well the intensity of Raymond's porcelain eyes as they took in Derek's life. As he gained a clearer picture of his son.

He worked too much.

The boy wondered what kind of series it was. "What genre would you put my series in?"

"Dramedy," Raymond said curtly.

"Sure," the boy muttered. He hoped for something with more weight. Film Noir Tragedy, but done well, with reverence to the genre.

The only piece hanging in the master bedroom gallery, albeit lopsided, depicted Raymond, still in the video store but without most of his porcelain. He held the last few pieces in his shadowed hand. The stark blue the artist had used for the eyes—a perfect representation—drew the boy deeply into the art.

In the four-painting series laying on the bed, the artist nurtured and expressed their talents in the chiaroscuro technique. Each of them focused on Raymond's limited interactions with his family, standing in their shadows—grazing their reality at night and watching them all sleep. The artist then contrasted the family with the shadow, who appeared to be wailing in most of the depictions.

"I couldn't quite get the full scope of my visits in these pieces," Raymond said, pulling a pack of cigarettes from under the carpet, in a hole he once cut into the floorboards to hide them from the family. They were Davies Tuch's brand. He lit up a cigarette with a match from the pack and took an impossible drag. "Without a porcelain shell, I lost my taste for just watching my family on video screens or pretending to still be a human. I needed purpose—a goal to strive for. For most others, that means scrounging for porcelain in the Oughtside, maybe the wilds around it if you're brave. Or selling a service that will give a porcelain person that twinge of humanity."

"And for you?" the boy asked. "What purpose did you find?" A drop of paint fell onto the back of his hand. Another work looked down on them from the ceiling. The edges of it dripped red down the walls.

"Don't look up yet, Derek," Raymond said. "There's an order to these things. Always an order." Once satisfied that the boy wasn't going to look, he continued. "I didn't know. Not with this figure's skin suppressing my clarity. I just had you in my head. You, pilfering and making a mockery of my skills as a father. Something had to be done."

So, according to a few small sketches at the foot of his bed-post, Raymond wandered. Through the Oughtside and the surrounding wildernesses. To the mill out there, in the woods at night, in parched living deserts, and in plains of tidal snow.

The boy nodded. "Did you know after these—these pilgrimages? What had to be done about me? Revenge? Rehabilitation?"

Raymond pulled his legs to his chest and held his head between them. "This doesn't show everything. I tore porcelain from wolves out there. I tore it from newly minted people, too. I felt that should stay out of the artworks."

"You're not listening to me," The boy said. He used to do that—the whole family did. "And you just said you didn't want porcelain."

"Need, not want, Judgment. Machines like Kellyn Hodges's miserable failure—machines that let shadows visit the living side of reality—cost me exorbitant amounts of porcelain. Even a forbidden service like that run by the porcelain dregs down in the bowels of the Oughtside is ruled by a system of strict bureaucracy."

Kellyn Hodges. The figure must have duped her into killing the circle's residents. *Someone already said that*, he thought. *Was it Ryan?* It might have been the boy himself. *Or maybe it was just Dr. Hodges. She was the only one to make it out of all this unscathed—out there time traveling with Wes and her lamp-based time machine.* A pang of jealousy hit the boy.

Raymond hadn't stopped speaking—jumping through his words with a touch of mania. "The more they wanted, the more I gave. Until——" He tried to remember here; he looked up at the ceiling, then back down at the boy

"Until?" the boy asked. He moved over to Raymond and crouched in front of the man. "Are you losing it? You look like you're losing it."

"I'd forgotten," Raymond said, his eyes moving around, erratic in their sockets. "I tore into the dregs—shattered them and ground their bones into dust. Took their machines and made them my own."

"For what purpose?" He knew the answer. He stood and turned to the next painting already.

"You, Judgment."

Of course.

"Any repercussions, dad?" the boy asked. "Consequences?"

Raymond Sr. chuckled like he hadn't felt the need to consider those. "Not yet, and they've all run out of time."

The next painting showed Raymond back in the Oughtside, standing in a crowd outside a skyscraper towering beneath the red sky. He had a paper in his hand. The artist made sure the viewer could read most of it: *Oughtside Employment Presents: Genocides! Battlefields! Tragedies! Paid in Porcelain. Shadows Only. Skeletal and Porcelain Citizens Need Not Apply.*

"Genocides, battlefields, tragedies," Raymond Sr. said, looking at the painting from across the room. "Death tolls above twenty or so in any given place spark Adjudications like this one. Consider just how many genocides, battlefields, school shootings, and tragedies we have each decade, year, month, day, Judgment." He sounded proud of himself.

Next, in a spot lit garden, Raymond Sr. and Mira held their hands out to a skeletal woman. Several bastardized

porcelain wolves, conflated and drawn larger and more menacing than the actual wolves the boy and company had seen
in the wilderness, lay wounded or destroyed outside the light.
This one struck him as propaganda for a savior figure helping
Mrs. Bell out of her predicament. And the final framed image,
unfinished and over by the bathroom, was a sketch of Raymond Sr. standing at the bottom of this home's foyer stairs,
in full shadow waiting for his son to wake up. They had come
right back around.

Another drip of paint fell from the ceiling, this one onto
Derek's cheek. Out of habit, he wiped the tickling moisture
with his hand, smearing blue across his face. He looked to
Raymond for some sort of permission to look up; the man's
head was already tilted towards the artwork above them, taking in the latest work.

"Now, that's a masterpiece," Raymond Sr. said in awe.

The boy followed Raymond's gaze. The artist had considered the low light in the room by using colors that both contrasted with and complemented the red. Painted above, across
the whole of the ceiling, was a map, spanning around and
below Habre Circle. Deep into the core of this world. Oughtside Cities stood beneath them and the wilderness—all of it,
depicted here—went on for longer than he ever imagined.
Habre Circle—Mrs. Bell, et al—was a far off-center speck in
the expansive, incredible Oughtside.

"In this insignificant universe that will die with a killscreen,"
mumbled the boy.

"Consider," Raymond said. "Yes, consider just how many
genocides, battlefields, and tragedies occur in our old world."

"I don't think there are as many genocides a day as you think."

The exquisite Sistine-esque representation on the ceiling seemed to stare back into the boy when he stared at it. The boy obsessed over it, catching new details at every inch—strange bazaars full of porcelain people, packs of wolves and beasts in the wilderness. He found other ruined streets, fields, fractured cities from his side of matter. He tried to guess where exactly in the world those cities were from and what happened to their people. The wet oil paint drizzled down on him as he did.

"Not here," Raymond said. "Not yesterday or today. But there are Adjudications still going on from a decade ago. Two decades, two centuries in the past. The process for some is slow. It is careful and considerate. But this—this circle in a suburb in a township in a city and so on—is nothing. A flash in life and the afterlife. You asked about repercussions, Judgment. Punishment for a guide forcing an Adjudication. Bending one to their will?" Raymond Sr. tried to stand, but couldn't. A shame, because it really would have made his argument pop at this moment. "The higher-ups are not all-seeing. There are no gods. They are porcelain and shadow and bone like me—like you will be. I have affected some change in this antiquated system and all it took was you as a purpose, Judgment. I have molded death to my specifications—improvisations."

Ray Sr. took another impossible drag from his cigarette. He missed the nicotine and the stench of the act.

"Purpose?" the boy asked, paint lining his features and splotching his clothes. It streamed down his face. "Rehab or revenge?"

Raymond Sr. didn't answer, looking at the boy like he should know this. Paint trickled down the wall and through his bones. In this light, it appeared to be blood.

O   O   O

The boy tightened his face, sticking it in a scowl. He took a lap around the room and sat on the bed, having moved some of the frames out of the way. The mattress, saturated with paint, squelched when he sat, and the old inner springs whined like a creaking door. His parents encouraged jumping on this bed when he was younger. Nostalgia seeped into him with the paint.

"What do you think of the gallery, Judgment?" Ray Sr. perked up. "As a whole?"

Ill-conceived as a medium to judge anything other than the art, the boy wanted to say.

"Keep in mind that I was running out of ideas."

Ray Sr. entered a foggy state of mind, in part because of his crumbling bones.

"Oh it's great," he said. "Don't worry about that."

Raymond Sr., relieved, said, "Fantastic. I didn't want to tell you before, but the artist?" Was him. "Was me."

The boy's father never did have any artistic talent. He should have been impressed that he gained some out here, and a distant part of him was.

"Where is mom?" he asked, as if expecting her to pop out of her closet—the closed one across from the bedroom door.

Raymond Sr. stretched forward, dropping flat onto the floor. The cigarette couldn't hold on in his lips, so it fell to the carpet, singeing a button-sized area of it. He pressed his one fist to the floor, stamping it out.

"I couldn't find her," he said. "Not many survive the trip from the mill to the Oughtside without being picked apart by the damned wolves. You know that. She may well be a damned creature out there, hungry for porcelain. I can't say."

The boy kept his eyes on the closet, holding out hope for a handful of seconds longer. He then imagined Mrs. Bell popping out of it. The thought squeezed his heart.

"But that's not why we're up here," the boy said, laying on the bed and closing his eyes.

"No. Had I found her, I think you would all still be alive." Raymond held for a beat. "Save for Anna who probably would have been shot regardless because that was just a bad situation."

The conversation moved at a rhythm that the boy had missed in his life. Father and son, awkwardly trading thoughts.

"And then you killed Mrs. Bell again," he said, digging. "A true death."

"I expect to be damned right alongside you, Derek."

He sat up. Raymond didn't let him respond.

"Damnation, then," the boy said, knowing it wouldn't work. He chipped at the paint on his arms. It dried smooth like a shell. "What the hell did I even do?"

Raymond smiled, the last of his faux skin falling to the carpet. "There was a noise back in the mid-May morning of Maureen's death."

It woke the boy.

THIEF

A noise back in that mid-May morning: a hearty thump upstairs, against the floor of the master bedroom. It woke the boy who had fallen asleep on the downstairs couch watching reruns of *Cheers*. Infomercials had taken the place of worthy programming and the sun was just finding its way through the trees.

The boy shot up and started pacing around the dripping room. "What's the rub, then?"

"The rub?" Raymond said.

"The conceit." he shuddered. That noise, it had flooded his senses before he went to sleep on recent nights. Exacerbating his migraines, just like the smell of all the paint in this room. An infinite supply seemed to coat the walls, running and drying in equal measure, building layers and closing the wall in on the scene.

Raymond fell to his knees and picked a small black device up sitting next to one of the paintings. Brilliant blue paint poured from its metal seams. "I think," he said, tossing the wet device into the boy's hands, now dry with myriad of colors, "this was my best idea for you." A resentful tone slipped into his voice. "But like the gallery, it is unfinished."

The boy rolled the device around in his hand. It was meant to be held like one of those squeeze grips for hand strength training. A red button blinked on the top, meant to be pressed by a thumb. From the overall look of it, it appeared to be another creation of Dr. Kellyn Hodges.

"A bomb?" he asked. He pressed the button anyway.

A studio audience laughed as if they sat right in a sound-stage with them, watching the two perform.

"Imagine," Raymond Sr. said with panache. "A whole stage for you, with phony set décor and a loft-style New York apartment no one your age could ever hope to afford even with roommates."

Again, studio audience laughter. He could hold the button longer to make them start whooping. He could tap it twice to make them boo and hiss. It had lost most of its novelty already.

"There was a noise," the boy said. "I can't be expected to assume every noise is Mom dying."

"I heard it too," Raymond Sr. said. "I watched you hear it. All the possibilities cross through your skull. After all your bullshit—your fights, your troubles at school. What did you do before you found her? Before you even cared to check?"

The studio audience murmured as the boy teased the button.

The boy heard them now without the device.

All this domestic drama bullshit, left behind at the Bells so long ago.

Maureen kept her purse by the kitchen table. The boy went there and pulled a twenty-dollar bill from it first. An innocuous moment, not out of the ordinary. He didn't need the money for anything in particular, but the opportunity presented itself and he took it. The boy removed the porcelain person's eye and the marble with the universe inside it from his pocket and looked them over.

"She needed *help* after I died, Derek," Raymond said. He stood and clacked towards his son. "And you devastated her instead. You took from her—took advantage of her. She went to bed crying four nights out of the week. She slept through the afternoons."

Derek shoved Raymond Sr. back. It wasn't difficult; he could crush his brittle bones if he wanted, and he started to. He checked Raymond against the wall, one of his paintings—the garden one—breaking underfoot. Derek crushed the old man's leg. Up close, Raymond smelled of cigarettes, a sickly gorgeous scent of remembrance for Derek. The man's shoulder was giving to the boy's sweaty grip. Raymond wore a blank expression, his glass eyes staring straight into Derek's.

"What about you, Ray." Derek spoke like he had the highest of moral grounds. He made his voice low and gravely like the shadow's original one. "I was just a teenager, and you were dead in three days. *You* let your body fill with tar-black soot and renegade cells. *You* killed yourself and left your wife—your kids—to fall apart." Tears cut slight lines through the paint on his face.

The studio audience laughed. They rolled on the phantom floor, broken.

"I know," Ray said. His shoulder crumbled. His head leaned to that side.

Derek shouted. "And please tell me what the *fuck* Junior and Cameron did for mom, huh? Where were they? Off. Away. Dicking around the city thinking that just because they're not at home, their problems were out of sight.

"I know," Ray said, putting one arm around him. "And we're here now, right? Dead, the whole family. But you and me, kid. You, me, Mira, and William. We deserve to be damned. The negligence of your siblings doesn't compare to our willful acts." Raymond pulled Derek closer, putting his forehead against his son's. "This is the only way to absolve us, Derek. I have killed, and so have you, Judgment. Damnation or salvation?"

"You first," he said. "Was this revenge or rehab for me?"

"Neither," Raymond said in a low and raging voice. "Both. It could have been one, but it turned into the other. I don't know. At one point, I wanted to save you. At the next, I wanted you removed from existence."

"I'm your kid," Derek snapped.

"And I can't forgive you."

"Salvation," he screamed with a paint-crusted smile. "I can go back. Anywhere I want. To the moon, if I so choose!"

"False," Raymond said, leaning back while his skull disintegrated around the eyes. The eyes fell out of his sockets, the glass so degraded that they shattered when they landed on the carpet. "I don't have those means."

Derek took a few haggard breaths. His home trembled and split.

"Salvation," he begged. His mother's face, pale and open and sucking for air on the floor of this room crawled across his vision. He knew she died, back in that mid-May morning. He almost hoped. The noise of her fall resounded in his skull. Her voice called for help, long before he ever cared to check on her. While he pilfered her purse in the early light.

Did she call for me?

He stared into the empty sockets of his father's dwindling bones slacked against the wall, unable to tell if Raymond Sr. was still present in the room. The house shook. Pressure built behind Derek's eyes. He stood on the cusp of a migraine, a long-forgotten feeling in the gracious red.

"Damn—"

And Derek fell.

Ryan Mont whistled outside the room's window that faced Habre Circle's edge. The sound grew distant, swallowed whole by the wilderness.

THE END